"Having an already exceptional series exceed your expectations is a rare and wonderful thing, but Andrews unquestionably pulls it off with this astonishing read. For fans invested in this series, the emotional payoff is huge, opening up exciting plotline possibilities. Balancing petrifying danger with biting humor is an Andrews specialty, leaving readers both grinning and gasping. Put [*Magic Bleeds*] on your autobuy list immediately!"

—*Romantic Times*

PRAISE FOR THE KATE DANIELS NOVELS

MAGIC STRIKES

"Andrews blends action-packed fantasy with myth and legend, keeping readers enthralled. *Magic Strikes* introduces fascinating characters, provides a plethora of paranormal skirmishes, and teases fans with romantic chemistry."   —*Darque Reviews*

"Ilona Andrews's best novel to date, cranking up the action, danger, and magic . . . Gritty sword-clashing action and flawless characterizations will bewitch fans, old and new alike."

—*Sacramento Book Review*

"Doses of humor serve to lighten the suspense and taut action of this vividly drawn, kick-butt series."   —*Monsters and Critics*

"From the first page to the last, *Magic Strikes* was a riveting, heart-pounding ride. Story lines advance, truths are admitted, intriguing characters are introduced, and the romance between Kate and Curran develops a sweetness that is simply delightful."

—*Dear Author*

"An engrossing, superbly written urban fantasy series."

—*Lurv a la Mode*

"Write faster . . . I absolutely love the relationship between Curran and Kate—I laugh out loud with the witty sarcasm and one-liners, and the sexual tension building between the couples drives me to my knees, knowing I'll have to wait for another book."

—*SFRevu*

continued . . .

Ace Books by Ilona Andrews

The Kate Daniels Novels

MAGIC BITES
MAGIC BURNS
MAGIC STRIKES
MAGIC BLEEDS

The Edge Novels

ON THE EDGE

MAGIC BLEEDS

—◆—

ILONA ANDREWS

ACE BOOKS, NEW YORK

THE BERKLEY PUBLISHING GROUP
Published by the Penguin Group
Penguin Group (USA) Inc.
375 Hudson Street, New York, New York 10014, USA
Penguin Group (Canada), 90 Eglinton Avenue East, Suite 700, Toronto, Ontario M4P 2Y3, Canada
(a division of Pearson Penguin Canada Inc.)
Penguin Books Ltd., 80 Strand, London WC2R 0RL, England
Penguin Group Ireland, 25 St. Stephen's Green, Dublin 2, Ireland (a division of Penguin Books Ltd.)
Penguin Group (Australia), 250 Camberwell Road, Camberwell, Victoria 3124, Australia
(a division of Pearson Australia Group Pty. Ltd.)
Penguin Books India Pvt. Ltd., 11 Community Centre, Panchsheel Park, New Delhi—110 017, India
Penguin Group (NZ), 67 Apollo Drive, Rosedale, North Shore 0632, New Zealand
(a division of Pearson New Zealand Ltd.)
Penguin Books (South Africa) (Pty.) Ltd., 24 Sturdee Avenue, Rosebank, Johannesburg 2196,
South Africa

Penguin Books Ltd., Registered Offices: 80 Strand, London WC2R 0RL, England

MAGIC BLEEDS

An Ace Book / published by arrangement with the authors

PRINTING HISTORY
Ace mass-market edition / June 2010

Copyright © 2010 by Andrew Gordon and Ilona Gordon.
Excerpt from *Bayou Moon* copyright © by Andrew Gordon and Ilona Gordon.
Cover art by Chad Michael Ward.
Cover design by Annette Fiore DeFex.
Interior text design by Kristin del Rosario.

ISBN: 978-0-441-01852-9

ACE
Ace Books are published by The Berkley Publishing Group,
a division of Penguin Group (USA) Inc.,
375 Hudson Street, New York, New York 10014.
ACE and the "A" design are trademarks of Penguin Group (USA) Inc.

PRINTED IN THE UNITED STATES OF AMERICA

10 9 8 7 6 5 4 3 2 1

To our children,
Anastasia and Helen

ACKNOWLEDGMENTS

Magic Bleeds turned out to be a very difficult book to write. It needed multiple drafts and a lot of patience from everyone involved.

I would like to thank my agent, Nancy Yost, for holding my hand through it, and my editor, Anne Sowards, who worked on the manuscript as hard as I did.

Thank you very much to Michelle Kasper, the production editor, and Andromeda Macri, the assistant production editor, both of whom I've probably made prematurely gray by this point. Thank you to Judith Lagerman, the art director, Annette Fiore DeFex, the cover designer, and Chad Michael Ward, the artist, for creating a stunning book. Thank you very much to Kat Sherbo, Anne's editorial assistant, for dealing with my unreasonable requests, and thank you to Rosanne Romanello, the publicist, for tirelessly promoting the book.

When I was writing the book, the dog had no name, so I ran a contest on my website, asking the readers for suggestions, and the following people offered entries that made it into the book: B. Carleton, Annika Bergstrand, Vina Patel, Zach Hughes, Nneka Waddell, Vanessa Yardley, and Andrea Jackson, who came up with the name we finally used.

As always, thank you to the beta readers who suffered through many reincarnations of the book: Beatrix Kaser, Ying Chumnongsaksarp, Reece Notley, Hasna Saadani, Elizabeth Hull, Brooke Nelissen, Ericka Brooks, Melissa Sawmiller,

Susan Zhang, Becky Kyle, and Megan Tebbutt, and special thanks to Chrissy Peterson.

Finally, thank you very much to Jeaniene Frost and Jill Myles. This book does have sex in it. Please don't hit me anymore.

MAGIC
BLEEDS

PROLOGUE

———◆———

NO MATTER HOW CAREFULLY I PATTED THE chopped apples into place, the top crust of my apple pie always looked like I'd tried to bury a dismembered body under it. My pies turned out ugly, but they tasted good. This particular pie was rapidly losing the last of its heat.

I surveyed the spread in my kitchen. Venison steaks, marinated in beer, lightly seasoned, sitting in a pan ready to be popped into the oven. I'd saved them for last—they wouldn't take but ten minutes under the broiler. Homemade rolls, now cold. Corn on the cob, also cold. Baked potatoes, yep, very cold. I'd added some sautéed mushrooms and a salad just in case what I had wasn't enough. The butter on the mushrooms was doing its best to congeal into a solid state. At least the salad was supposed to be cold.

I plucked a creased note from the table. Eight weeks ago, Curran, the Beast Lord of Atlanta, the lord and master of fifteen hundred shapeshifters, and my own personal psycho, had sat in the kitchen of my apartment in Atlanta and written out a menu on this piece of paper. I'd lost a bet to him, and according to the terms of our wager, I owed him one naked dinner. He'd added a disclaimer explaining that he'd settle for my wearing a bra and panties, since he wasn't a complete beast—an assertion very open to debate.

He'd set a date, November 15, which was today. I knew this because I had checked the calendar three times already. I had called him at the Keep three weeks ago and set the place, my house near Savannah, and the time, 5 p.m. It was eight thirty now.

He'd said he couldn't wait.

Food—check. My most flattering set of bra and panties—check. Makeup—check. Curran—blank. I drew my finger along the pale blade of my saber, feeling the cold metal under my skin. Where exactly was His Majesty?

Did he get cold feet? Mr. "You'll sleep with me and say please before and thank you after"?

He'd chased a flying palace through an enchanted jungle and carved his way through dozens of rakshasa demons to save me. Dinner was a huge deal to shapeshifters. They never took food for granted, but making a dinner for someone you were romantically interested in took a simple meal to a whole new level. When a shapeshifter made you dinner, he was either pledging to take care of you or he was trying to get into your pants. Most of the time, both. Curran had fed me soup once, when I was half-dead, and the fact that I had eaten it, even without knowing what that meant, amused him to no end. He wouldn't miss this dinner.

Something must've held him up.

I picked up the phone. Then again, he enjoyed screwing with me. I wouldn't put it past him to hide outside in the bushes, watching me squirm. Curran treated women like wonderful toys: he wined them, dined them, took care of their problems, and once they grew completely dependent on him, he became bored. Maybe whatever I perceived to be between us was only in my head. He'd realized he won and had lost interest. Calling him would just give him an opportunity to gloat.

I hung up the phone and looked at my pie some more.

If you opened a dictionary and looked up "control freak," you'd find Curran's picture. He ruled with steel claws, and when he said, "Jump," there was hell to pay if you didn't start hopping. He infuriated me and I drove him out of his skin.

Even if he wasn't truly interested, he wouldn't miss a chance to see me present this dinner in my underwear. His ego was too big. Something must have happened.

Eight forty-four. Curran served as the Pack's first and last line of defense. Any hint of a significant threat, and he'd be out there, roaring and ripping bodies in half. He could be hurt.

The thought stopped me cold. It would take a bloody army to bring down Curran. Of the fifteen hundred homicidal maniacs under his command, he was the toughest and most dangerous sonovabitch. If something did happen, it had to be bad. He would've called if he'd been delayed by something minor.

Eight forty-nine.

I took the phone, cleared my throat, and dialed the Keep, the Pack's stronghold on the outskirts of Atlanta. Just keep it professional. Less pathetic that way.

"You've reached the Pack. What do you want?" a female voice said into the phone.

Friendly people, the shapeshifters. "This is Agent Daniels. Can I speak to Curran, please?"

"He isn't taking calls right now. Do you want to leave a message?"

"Is he in the Keep?"

"Yes, he is."

A heavy rock materialized in my chest and made it hard to breathe.

"Message?" the female shapeshifter prompted.

"Just tell him I called, please. As soon as possible."

"Is this urgent?"

Fuck it. "Yes. Yes, it is."

"Hold on."

Silence reigned. Moments dripped by, slowly, stretching thinner and thinner . . .

"He says he's too busy to talk to you right now. In the future, please go through proper channels and direct all your concerns to Jim, our security chief. His number is—"

I heard my voice, oddly flat. "I have the number. Thanks."

"Anytime."

I lowered the phone into the cradle very carefully. A tiny sound popped in my ears, and I had the absurd idea that it was my heart forming hairline cracks.

He stood me up.

He stood me up. I cooked a huge meal. I sat by the phone for the last four hours. I put on makeup, my second time in the past year. I bought a box of condoms. Just in case.

I love you, Kate. I'll always come for you, Kate.

You sonovabitch. Didn't even have the balls to speak to me.

I surged off the chair. If he was going to dump me after all that shit, I'd force him to do it in person.

It took me less than a minute to get dressed and load my wrist guards with silver needles. My saber, Slayer, had enough silver in it to hurt even Curran, and right now I very much wanted to hurt him. I stalked through the house looking for my boots in a fury-steeped daze, found them in the bathroom of all places, and sat down on the floor to put them on. I pulled the left boot on, tapped my heel into place, and stopped.

Suppose I did get to the Keep. And then what? If he decided he didn't want to see me, I'd have to cut my way through his people to get to him. No matter how much it hurt, I couldn't do that. Curran knew me well enough to recognize that and use it against me. A vision of me sitting in the lobby of the Keep for hours popped into my head. Hell no.

If the asshole did condescend to make an appearance, what would I say? How dare you dump me before the relationship even started? I've traveled six hours to tell you how much I hate you because you meant that much to me? He'd laugh in my face, then I'd slice him to ribbons and then he'd break my neck.

I forced myself to grope for reason in the fog of my rage. I worked for the Order of Knights of Merciful Aid, which together with the Paranormal Activity Division, or PAD, and the Military Supernatural Defense Unit, or MSDU, formed the law enforcement defense against magical hazmat of all kinds. I wasn't a knight, but I was a representative of the Order. Worse, I was the only representative of the Order with Friend of the Pack status, meaning that when I attempted to muscle my way into Pack-related problems, the shapeshifters didn't tear me apart right away. Any issues the Pack had with the law usually found their way to me.

The shapeshifters came in two flavors: Free People of the

Code, who maintained strict control over Lyc-V, the virus raging in their bodies; and loups, who surrendered to it. Loups murdered indiscriminately, bouncing from atrocity to atrocity until someone did the world a favor and murdered their cannibalistic asses. The Atlanta PAD viewed each shapeshifter as a loup-in-waiting, and the Pack responded by ratcheting up their paranoia and mistrust of outsiders to new and dizzying heights. Their position with the authorities was precarious at best, saved from open hostility by their record of cooperation with the Order. If Curran and I got into it, our fight wouldn't be seen as a conflict between two individuals, but as the Beast Lord's assault on an Order representative. Nobody would believe that I was dumb enough to start it.

The shapeshifters' standing would plummet. I had only a few friends, but most of them grew fur and claws. I'd make their lives hell to soothe my hurt.

For once in my life, I had to do the responsible thing.

I pulled the boot off and threw it across the room. It thudded into the wood panel in the hallway.

For years, first my father and then my guardian, Greg, had warned me to stay away from human relationships. Friends and lovers only brought you trouble. My existence had a purpose, and that purpose—and my blood—left no room for anything else. I had ignored the warnings of the two dead men and dropped my shields. It was time to suck it up and pay for it.

I'd believed him. He was supposed to be different, to be more. He'd made me hope for things I didn't think I'd ever get. When hope broke, it hurt. Mine was a very big, very desperate hope, and it hurt like a sonovabitch.

Magic flooded the world in a silent wave. The electric lamps blinked and died a quiet death, giving way to the blue radiance of the feylanterns on my walls. The enchanted air in the twisted glass tubes luminesced brighter and brighter until an eerie blue light filled the entire house. It was called post-Shift resonance: magic came in waves, negating technology, and then vanished as abruptly and unpredictably as it had appeared. Somewhere, gasoline engines failed and guns choked midbullet. The defensive spells around my house surged up, forming a dome over my roof and hammering home the point: I'd needed protection. I'd dropped my shields and let the lion in. It was time to pay the piper.

I got up off the floor. Sooner or later my job would bring me into contact with the Beast Lord. It was inevitable. I needed to get the hurt out of my system now, so when we met again, all he would get from me would be cold courtesy.

I marched into the kitchen, trashed the dinner, and strode out. I had a date with a heavy punching bag, and I had no trouble imagining Curran's face on it.

An hour later, when I left for my apartment in Atlanta, I was so tired I fell asleep in my car moments after I steered my vehicle into the ley line and the magic current dragged it off toward the city.

CHAPTER 1

———

I RODE THROUGH THE STREETS OF ATLANTA, ROCK-ing with the hoofbeats of my favorite mule, Marigold, who didn't care for the birdcage attached to her saddle and really didn't care for the globs of lizard spit dripping from my jeans. The birdcage contained a fist-sized clump of gray fuzz, which I'd had a devil of a time catching and which might or might not have been a living dust bunny. The jeans contained about a half-gallon of saliva deposited on me by a pair of Trimble County lizards, which I'd managed to chase back into their enclosure at the Atlanta Center for Mythological Research. I was eleven hours and thirteen minutes into my shift, I hadn't eaten since that morning, and I wanted a doughnut.

Three weeks had passed since Curran had stood me up. For the first week, I was so angry I couldn't see straight. The anger had subsided now, but the dense heavy stone remained in my chest, weighing me down. Strangely, doughnuts helped. Especially ones drizzled with chocolate. As expensive as chocolate was in our day and age, I couldn't afford a whole chocolate bar, but the drizzle of chocolate syrup on the doughnuts did the job just well enough.

"Hello, dear."

After almost a year of working for the Order, hearing Maxine's voice in my head no longer made me jump. "Hello, Maxine."

The Order's telepathic secretary called everyone "dear," including Richter, a new addition to the Atlanta chapter who was as psychotic as a knight of the Order could get without being stripped of his knighthood. Her "dears" fooled no one. I'd rather run ten miles with a rucksack full of rocks than face a chewing-out from Maxine. Perhaps it was the way she looked: tall, thin, ramrod straight, with a halo of tightly curled silver hair and the mannerisms of a veteran middle school teacher who had seen it all before and would not suffer fools gladly . . .

"Richter is quite sane, dear. And is there any particular reason you keep picturing a dragon with my hair on its head and a chocolate doughnut in its mouth?"

Maxine never read thoughts on purpose, but if you concentrated hard enough while "on call," she couldn't help picking up simple mental images.

I cleared my throat. "Sorry."

"No problem. I always thought of myself as a Chinese dragon, actually. We're out of doughnuts, but I have cookies."

Mmm, cookies. "What do I have to do for a cookie?"

"I know your shift is over, but I have an emergency petition and nobody to handle it."

Argh. "What's the petition?"

"Someone attacked the Steel Horse."

"The Steel Horse? The border bar?"

"Yes."

Post-Shift Atlanta was ruled by factions, each with its own territory. Of all the factions in Atlanta, the People and the Pack were the largest and the two I most wanted to avoid. The Steel Horse sat right on the invisible border between their territories. A neutral spot, it catered to both the People and the shapeshifters, as long as they could keep it civil. For the most part, they did.

"Kate?" Maxine prompted.

"Do you have any details?"

"Someone started a fight and departed. They have some-

thing cornered in the cellar, and they're afraid to let it out. They're hysterical. At least one fatality."

A bar full of hysterical necromancers and werebeasts. Why me?

"Will you take it?"

"What kind of cookies?"

"Chocolate chip with bits of walnuts in them. I'll even give you two."

I sighed and turned Marigold to the west. "I'll be there in twenty."

Marigold sighed heavily and started down the night-drenched street. The Pack members drank little. Staying human required iron discipline, and the shapeshifters avoided substances that altered their grip on reality. A glass of wine with dinner or a single beer after work was pretty much their limit.

The People also drank little, primarily because of the presence of shapeshifters. A bizarre hybrid of a cult, a corporation, and a research institute, they concerned themselves with the study of the undead, primarily vampires. *Vampirus immortuus*, the pathogen responsible for vampirism, eradicated all traces of ego from its victims, turning them into bloodlust-crazed monsters and leaving their minds nice and blank. Masters of the Dead, the People's premier necromancers, took advantage of this occurrence—they navigated vampires by riding their minds and controlling their every move.

Masters of the Dead weren't brawlers. Well-educated, lavishly compensated intellectuals, they were ruthless and opportunistic. Masters of the Dead wouldn't be visiting a bar like the Steel Horse either. Too lowbrow. The Steel Horse catered to the journeymen, navigators-in-training, and since the Red Stalker murders, the People had tightened their grip on their personnel. A couple of drunk and disorderlies, and your study of the undead would come to an untimely end. The journeymen still got roaring drunk—most were too young and made too much money for their own good—but they didn't do it where they'd get caught and they definitely didn't do it with the shapeshifters watching.

A shadow scuttled across the street, small, furry, and with too many legs. Marigold snorted and kept on, unfazed.

The People were led by a mysterious figure known as Roland. To most, he was a myth. To me, he was a target. He was also my biological father. Roland had sworn off children—they kept trying to kill him—but my mother really wanted me and he decided that, for her sake, he could suffer to try one more time. Except he changed his mind and tried to kill me in the womb. My mother ran and Roland's Warlord, Voron, ran with her. Voron made it, my mother didn't. I never knew her, but I knew that if my natural father ever found me, he'd move heaven and earth to finish what he started.

Roland was legend. He'd survived for thousands of years. Some thought he was Gilgamesh, some thought he was Merlin. He wielded incredible power and I wasn't ready to fight him. Not yet. Contact with the People meant the risk of discovery by Roland and so I avoided them like a plague.

Contact with the Pack meant the risk of contact with Curran, and right now that was worse.

Who the hell would attack the Steel Horse anyway? What was the thinking behind that? "Here is a bar full of psychotic killers who grow giant claws and people who pilot the undead for a living. I think I'll go wreck the place." Sound reasoning there. Not.

I couldn't avoid the Pack forever, just because their lord and master made my sword arm ache. Get in. Do my job. Get out. Simple enough.

The Steel Horse occupied an ugly bunker of a building: squat, brick, and reinforced with steel bars over the windows and a metal door about two and a quarter inches thick. I knew how thick the door was because Marigold had just trotted past it. Someone had ripped the door off its hinges and tossed it across the street.

Between the door and the entrance stretched potholed asphalt covered with random patches of blood, liquor, and broken glass, and a few moaning bodies in various stages of inebriation and battle damage.

Damn, I'd missed all the fun.

A clump of tough guys stood by the tavern's doorway. They didn't exactly look hysterical, since the term was conveniently absent from their vocabulary, but the way they gripped makeshift weapons of broken furniture made one want to approach them slowly, speaking in soothing tones. Judging by the battle scene, they had just gotten beat up in their own bar. You can never lose a fight in your own bar, because if you do, it's not your bar anymore.

I slowed my mule to a walk. The temperature had plummeted in the past week, and the night was bitterly, unseasonably cold. The wind cut at my face. Faint clouds of breath fluttered from the guys at the bar. A couple of the larger thuggy-looking citizens sported some hardware: a big, rough-hewn man on the right carried a mace, and his pal on the left wielded a machete. Bouncers. Only bouncers would be allowed to have real weapons in a border bar.

I scanned the crowd, looking for telltale glowing eyes. Nothing. Just the normal human irises. If there had been shapeshifters in the bar tonight, they'd either cleared off or kept their human skins securely on. I didn't sense any vampires nearby either. No familiar faces in the crowd. The journeymen must've taken off, too. Something bad went down and nobody wanted to be tarred by it. And now it was all mine. Oh, goodie.

Marigold carried me past the human wreckage and to the doorway. I pulled out the clear plastic wallet I carried on a cord around my neck, and held it up so they could see the small rectangle of the Order ID.

"Kate Daniels. I work for the Order. Where is the owner?"

A tall man stepped from the inside of the bar and leveled a crossbow at me. It was a decent modern recurve crossbow, with close to two hundred pounds of draw weight. It came equipped with a fiber-optic sight and a scope. I doubted he'd need either to hit me at ten feet. At this distance the bolt wouldn't just penetrate; it would go through me, taking my guts for a ride on its fletch.

Of course, at this distance I might kill him before he got off a shot. Hard to miss with a throwing knife at ten feet.

The man fixed me with grim eyes. Middle-aged and thin, he looked as if he'd spent too much time outdoors doing hard labor. Life had melted all the flesh off his bones, leaving only leathery skin, gunpowder, and gristle. A short dark beard hugged his jaw. He nodded to the smaller bouncer. "Vik, check the ID."

Vik sauntered over and looked at my wallet. "It says what she said it did."

I was too tired for this. "You're looking at the wrong thing." I took the card out of the wallet and offered it to him. "See the square in the bottom left corner?"

His gaze flicked to the square of enchanted silver.

"Put your thumb over it and say, 'ID.' "

Vik hesitated, glanced at his boss, and touched the square. "ID."

A burst of light punched his thumb, and the square turned black.

"The card knows you're not its owner. No matter how many of you mess with it, it will stay black until I touch it." I placed my finger over the silver. "ID."

The black vanished, revealing the pale surface.

"That's how you tell a real Order agent from a fake one." I dismounted and tied Marigold to the rail. "Now, where is the corpse?"

The bar owner introduced himself as Cash. Cash didn't strike me as the trusting kind, but at least he kept his crossbow pointed at the ground as he led me behind the building and to the left. Since his choice of Order representatives was limited to me and Marigold, he decided to take his chances with me. Always nice to be judged more competent than a mule.

The crowd of onlookers tagged along as we circled the building. I could've done without an audience, but I didn't feel like arguing. I'd wasted enough time playing magic tricks with my ID.

"We run a tight ship here," Cash said. "Quiet. Our regulars don't want trouble."

The night wind flung the sour stench of decomposing vomit in my face, and a touch of an entirely different scent, syrupy thick, harsh, and cloying. Not good. There was no reason for the body to smell yet. "Tell me what happened."

"A man started trouble with Joshua. Joshua lost," Cash said.

He'd missed his calling. He should've been a saga poet.

We reached the back of the building and stopped. A huge, ragged hole gaped in the side of the bar where someone had busted out through the wall. Bricks lay scattered across the asphalt. Whoever the creature was, he could punch through solid walls like a wrecking ball. Too heavy-duty for a shapeshifter, but you never know.

"Did one of your shapeshifter regulars do that?"

"No. They all cleared off once the fight started."

"What about the People's journeymen?"

"Didn't have any tonight." Cash shook his head. "They usually come on Thursdays. We're here."

Cash pointed to the left, where the ground sloped down to a parking lot punctuated by a utility pole in its center. On the pole, pinned by a crowbar thrust through his open mouth, hung Joshua.

Parts of him were covered by shreds of tanned leather and jeans. Everything uncovered no longer looked human. Hard bumps clustered on every inch of his exposed skin, dark red and interrupted by lesions and wet, gaping ulcers, as if the man had become a human barnacle. The crust of sores was so thick on his face I couldn't even distinguish his features, except for the milky eyes, opened wide and staring at the sky.

My stomach sank. All traces of fatigue fled, burned in a flood of adrenaline.

"Did he look like that before the fight started?" Please say yes.

"No," Cash said. "It happened after."

A cluster of bumps over what might have been Joshua's nose shifted, bulged outward, and fell, giving space to a new ulcer. The fallen piece of Joshua rolled on the asphalt and stopped. The pavement around it sprouted a narrow ring of flesh-colored fuzz. The same fuzz coated the pole below and slightly above the body. I concentrated on the lower edge of the fuzz line and saw it creep very slowly down the wood.

Fuck.

I kept my voice low. "Did anybody touch the body?"

Cash shook his head. "No."

"Anybody go near it?"

"No."

I looked into his eyes. "I need you to get everyone back into the bar and keep them there. Nobody leaves."

"Why?" he asked.

I had to level with him. "Joshua's diseased."

"He's dead."

"His body's dead, but the disease is alive and magic. It's growing. It's possible that everyone's infected."

Cash swallowed. His eyes widened and he glanced through the hole and into the bar. A dark-haired woman, slight and bird-boned, wiped up the spills on the counter, sliding broken glass into a wastebasket with her rag. I looked back at Cash and saw fear.

If he panicked, the crowd would scatter and infect half the city.

I kept my voice quiet. "If you want her to live, you have to herd everyone back into the bar and keep them from leaving. Tie them up if you have to, because if they take off, we'll have an epidemic. Once the people are secure, call Biohazard. Tell them Kate Daniels says we have a Mary. Give them the address. I know it's hard, but you have to be calm. Don't panic."

"What will you do?"

"I'll try to contain it. I'll need salt, as much as you've got. Wood, kerosene, alcohol, whatever you have that might burn. I have to build a flame barrier. You've got pool tables?"

He stared at me, uncomprehending.

"Do you have pool tables?"

"Yes."

I dropped my cloak on the slope. "Please bring me your pool chalk. All of it."

Cash walked away from me and spoke to the bouncers. "Alright," the bigger bouncer bellowed. "Everybody back into the bar. One round on the house."

The crowd headed into the bar through the hole in the wall. One man hesitated. The bouncers moved in on him. "Into the bar," Vik said.

The guy thrust his chin into the air. "Fuck off."

Vik sank a quick, hard punch into his gut. The man folded in half, and the bigger bouncer slung him over his shoulder and headed back into the Steel Horse.

Two minutes later one of the bouncers trotted out with a large sack of salt and fled back into the bar. I cut the corner of the bag and began drawing a three-inch-wide circle around the pole. Cash emerged from the hole in the tavern carrying some broken crates, followed by the dark-haired woman with a large box. The woman set the box down by the lumber. Filled with blue squares of pool chalk. Good. "Thank you."

She caught a glimpse of Joshua on the pole. The blood drained from her face.

"Did you call Biohazard?" I asked.

"Phone's out," Cash said softly.

Can something go right for me today?

"Does that change things?" Cash asked.

It changed a short-term fix into a long-term defense. "I'll just have to work harder to keep it put."

I finished the salt circle, dumped the bag, and began laying the wood into another circle around the pole. The fire wouldn't hold it indefinitely, but it would buy me some time.

The flesh-colored fuzz tested the salt and found it delicious. Figured. I didn't feel any different, and I was closest to the body, so I'd be the first one to go. A comforting thought.

Cash had brought down some bottles, and I dumped their contents onto the crates, soaking the wood in hard liquor and kerosene. One flick of a match, and the wooden ring flared into flames.

"Is that it?" Cash asked.

"No. The fire will delay it, but not for long."

The two of them looked as though they were at their own funeral.

"It will be okay." Kate Daniels, agent of the Order. We take care of your magic problems, and when we can't, we lie through our teeth. "It will all turn out. You two go inside now. Keep the peace and keep trying the phone."

The woman brushed Cash's sleeve with her fingers. He pivoted to her, patted her hand, and together they went back into the tavern.

The fuzz crawled halfway across the salt. I began to chant, going through the roster of purifying incantations. Magic built around me slowly, like cotton candy winding on the spire of my body and flowing outward, around the flame circle.

The fuzz reached the fire. The first flesh-colored tendrils licked the boards and melted into black goo with a weak hiss. The flames popped with the sickening stench of burning fat.

That's right, you bastard. Stay the hell behind my fire. Now I just had to keep it still until I finished the first ward circle.

Chanting, I grabbed the pool chalk and drew the first glyph.

CHAPTER 2

———◆———

"HOLY MOTHER OF GOD." THE TALL, THIN SPIRE OF a woman that was Patrice Lane, Biohazard's in-house med-mage, crossed her arms on her chest. She seemed even taller from where I sat, huddled on the slope under my cloak. The cold seeped through the fabric of my jeans and my butt had turned into a chunk of ice.

The telephone pole had become a mass of flesh-colored fur. Around it the entire parking lot was covered in my glyphs. I had used up all of Cash's chalk.

The pole slowly rained skin-colored fuzz. The same crap spread in a circle around its base. The fire had died down to mere coals, and the fuzz had spilled over it in several places, pooling against the first ring of glyphs. I'd chopped off the wires going from the pole after completing the second circle of glyphs and threw them into the ward. The fuzz had swallowed them so completely, you'd never know they were there.

Medmages and medtechs swarmed the scene. Biohazard was technically part of PAD, but practically speaking, it had its own separate quarters and its own chain of command, and Patrice was pretty far up that chain.

Patrice raised her arm and I felt a faint pulse of magic. "I can't feel a thing past the chalk," she said, her breath escaping in a cloud of pale vapor.

"That's the idea."

"Smart-ass." Patrice surveyed my handiwork and shook her head. "Look at it crawl. Persistent blight, isn't he?"

That was why I'd made the second circle in case the first failed, and then it occurred to me that the telephone pole could take a dive. The wards of the first two circles extended only about eight feet up, and if the pole fell, the disease would land outside the barrier, so I drew the third ward circle. It had been a very wide circle, too, because the pole was painfully tall, about thirty feet. Four medtechs now walked along the outer circle's perimeter, waving censers which trailed purifying smoke. I'd sunk everything I had into those wards. Right now a kitten could touch me with her paw and score a total knockout.

A young male medtech crouched by me and raised a small white flower in a pot to my lips. Five white petals streaked with thin green veins leading to a ring of fuzzy stalks, each tipped with a small yellow dot. A bog star. The tech whispered an incantation and said in a practiced cadence, "Take a deep breath and exhale."

I blew on the flower. The petals remained snow-white. If I had been infected, the bog star would've turned brown and withered.

The tech checked the color of the petals against a paper card and chanted low under his breath. "One more time—deep breath and exhale."

I obediently exhaled.

He took away the bog star. "Look into my eyes."

I did. He peered deeply into my irises.

"Clear. You have beautiful eyes."

"And she has a big, sharp sword." Patrice snorted. "Be gone, creature."

The medtech rose. "She's clean," he called in the direction of the tavern. "You can speak with her now."

The dark-haired woman, who'd brought the chalk to me hours earlier, stepped out of the bar and carried a glass of whiskey. "I'm Maggie. Here." She offered the glass to me. "Seagram's Seven Crown."

"Thank you, I don't drink."

"Since when?" Patrice raised her eyebrows.

Maggie held the whiskey to me. "You need it. We watched you crawl around on your hands and knees for hours. It must hurt and you've got to be frozen solid."

The parking lot proved a bit rougher than anticipated. Crawling back and forth drawing glyphs had shredded my already worn-out jeans into nothing. I could see my skin through the holes in the fabric and it was bloody. Normally leaving traces of my blood at the scene would've sent me into panic. Once separated from the body, blood couldn't be masked, and in my case, advertising the magic of my bloodline meant a death sentence. But I knew how tonight would end, and so I didn't worry. What little blood I left on the asphalt would be obliterated very soon.

I took the whiskey and smiled at Maggie, which took some effort since my lips were frozen. "Did you finally get the phone working?"

She shook her head. "It's still out."

"How did you contact Biohazard?"

Maggie pursed her narrow lips. "We didn't."

I turned to Patrice. The medmage frowned at the circle.

"Pat, how did you know to come here?"

"An anonymous tipster called it in," she murmured, her eyes fixed on the pole. "Something is happening . . ."

With a loud crack, the utility pole snapped. The dark-haired woman gasped. The techs dashed back, waving their censers.

The pole spun in place, fuzz swirling around its top, tee-tered, and plunged. It smashed against the invisible wall of the first two ward circles, toppled over it, and slid down, dumping the flesh-colored shit onto the asphalt. The pole top rammed the third line of glyphs. Magic boomed through my skull. A cloud of fuzz exploded against the ward in an ugly burst and fluttered down harmlessly to settle at the chalk line as the pole rolled to a stop.

Patrice let out a breath.

"I made the third circle twelve feet high," I told her. "It isn't going anywhere, even if it really wants to."

"That does it." Patrice rolled up her sleeves. "Did you put anything into those wards that might fry me if I cross them?"

"Nope. It's just a simple containment ward. Feel free to waltz right in."

"Good." She strode down the slope to the glyphs, waving her hand at the tech team fussing with some equipment on the side. "Never mind. It's too aggressive. We'll do a live probe, it's faster."

She tossed back her blond hair and stepped into the circle. The chalk glyphs ignited with a faint blue glow. The ward masked her magic, and I could feel nothing past it, but whatever Patrice was working up had to be heavy-duty.

The fuzz shivered. Thin tendrils stretched toward Patrice.

I wondered who'd called Biohazard. Somebody called. Maybe it was just a good Samaritan passing by.

And maybe I would sprout wings and fly.

Maggie leaned over to me. "How can she enter but the disease can't leave?"

"Because of the way I made the ward. Wards both keep things in and keep them out. It's basically a barrier and you can rig it several ways. This one has a high magic threshold. The disease that killed Joshua is very potent. It's heavily saturated with magic, so it can't cross. Patrice is a human, which makes her less magical by definition, and so she can go back and forth as she pleases."

"So couldn't we just wait it out until the magic wave falls and the disease dies?"

"Nobody knows what will happen to the disease once the magic falls. It might die or it might mutate and turn into a plague. Don't worry. Patrice will nuke it."

In the circle, Patrice raised her hands. "It is I, Patrice, who commands you, it is I who demands obedience. Show yourself to me!"

A dark shadow rolled over the fleshy fur, spreading into a mottled patina over the pole and the remnants of the body. Patrice stepped back out of the circle. The techs swarmed her with smoke and flowers.

"Syphilis," I heard her say. "Lots and lots of magically delicious syphilis. It's alive and hungry. We're going to need napalm."

Maggie glanced at the still untouched whiskey in my glass. I raised it to my lips and took a sip to make her happy. Fire rolled down my throat. A few seconds later, I could feel my fingertips again. Woo, back in business.

"Did they clear all of you?" I asked.

She nodded. "Nobody was infected. A few guys had broken bones, but that's all. They let everyone go."

Thank the Universe for small favors.

Maggie shuddered. "I don't understand. Why us? What did we ever do to anybody?"

She was looking for comfort in the wrong place. I was numb and exhausted, and the stone in my chest hurt.

Maggie shook her head. Her shoulders hunched.

"Sometimes there is no reason," I said. "Just a bad roll of the dice."

Her face was drained of all expression. I knew what she was thinking: broken furniture, busted wall, and a bad reputation. The Steel Horse would forever be known as the joint where the plague almost started.

"Look over there."

She glanced in the direction of my nod. Inside the bar, Cash pulled apart a broken table.

"You're alive. He's alive. You're together. Everything else can be fixed. It can always be worse. Much, much worse." *Trust me on this.*

"You're right."

For a while we sat in silence and then Maggie took a deep breath as if she was going to say something and clamped her mouth shut.

"What is it?"

"The thing in the cellar," she said.

"Ah." I pushed upright. I'd rested enough. "Let's go take care of that."

We went in through the hole in the wall. The techs had evaluated and released most of the patrons, who were only too happy to clear off. The tavern lay virtually empty. Most of the furniture hadn't survived the brawl. An icy draft swept through the open doors and windows to blow out of the ruined wall. Despite the unplanned but vigorous ventilation, the place stank of vomit.

Cash leaned against the bar. Long shadows lined his haggard face. He looked worn out, like he'd aged a year overnight.

Maggie paused by him. He took her hand into his. It must've twisted them into knots to sit there for hours, watching each other's faces for the first signs of infection.

They were killing me. If I could've gotten a hold of Curran right now, I would have punched him in the face for making me think I could have that and then taking it away from me.

At the door, two Biohazard techs packed away an m-scanner. The m-scanner registered residual magic at the scene and spat it out in various colors: purple for vampire, blue for human, green for shapeshifter. It was imprecise and finicky, but it was the best tool for magic analysis we had. I stopped by the team and flashed my Order ID. "Anything?"

The female tech offered me a stack of printouts. "Patrice said for you to have a copy."

"Thanks." I flipped through them. Every single one showed a bright blue slice streaking across the paper like a lightning bolt, cutting across pale traces of green. The green were the shapeshifters, and judging by the watered-down color of the signatures, they had taken off at the beginning of the fight, leaving behind only weak residual magic. Not surprising. The Pack had a strict policy regarding unlawful behavior, and nothing good ever came from a drunken brawl in a border bar.

I studied the blue. *Human mundane*, basic human magic. Mages registered blue, healers, empaths . . . I registered blue. Unless you had a really good scanner.

"Maggie, how many people would you say were here when this happened?"

She shrugged at the bar. "About fifty."

Fifty. But only one human magic signature.

I glanced at Cash. "I need to talk to your people."

He headed behind the bar to a narrow stairway leading down. I followed. At the bottom of the stairway Vik and the bigger bouncer guarded the door secured by a large deadbolt.

I sat at the top of the stairs. "My name's Kate."

"Vik."

"Toby."

"Thank you," I said. "I know it had to be hell to keep everyone put for this long and I appreciate how you've handled it."

"We had a good crowd tonight," Cash said. "Most of them were regulars."

"Yeah," Vik said. "If we'd gotten a lot of out-of-towners, there would've been blood."

"Can you tell me how it started?"

"Someone hit me with a chair," Vik said. "That's when I got into it."

"A man came into the bar," Toby said.

"What did he look like?"

"Tall. Big guy."

Tall was a given. I'd gotten a good look at Joshua's body while I was crawling around the parking lot. Joshua had been five-ten and his feet were about six inches off the ground. Whoever nailed him to that pole probably held him at his own eye level, which made our guy close to six and a half feet tall.

Cash disappeared for a minute and returned with five glasses. More whiskey.

"What did the big guy wear?"

The three men and Maggie knocked back their glasses. There was collective grimacing and clearing of throats. I sipped mine a bit. Like drinking fire spiced with crushed glass.

"A cloak," Toby offered.

"Like this?" I fingered my own long plain dark gray affair. Most fighters wore cloaks. Used properly, the cloak could confuse the attacker by obscuring your movements. It could shield, smother, and kill. It doubled as a blanket in a pinch for the person or for the mule. Unfortunately it also made a dramatic fashion statement and was easy to make. Every two-bit bravo had one.

"His was one of those hooded cloaks, long and brown. And torn up at the bottom," Toby said.

"Did you get a look at his face?"

Toby shook his head. "He kept the hood on the whole time. Didn't see the face or the hair."

Great. I was looking for the proverbial "guy in a cloak." He was as elusive as the legendary "white truck" had been when cars still filled the roadways. All sorts of crazy driving accidents had been blamed on the mysterious white truck, just as all sorts of random crimes had been perpetrated by "some guy in a cloak" with his hood pulled over his face.

Toby cleared his throat again. "Like I said, I didn't see his face. I saw his hands, though—they were dark. About this color." He nodded at the whiskey in my glass. "He came in, stood at the bar, sized up the crowd for a while, and then came up next to Joshua. They said a few words."

"Did you hear what he said?"

"I did," Cash said. "He whispered. He said, 'Do you want to be a god? I have room for two more.'"

Oh boy. "What did Joshua say?"

Cash's eyes were mournful. "He said, 'Hell yeah.' And then the man punched him off his feet and the whole place went to hell."

Hell yeah. Famous last words. Some guy sidles up to you in a bar and offers you godhood. And you say yes. Dumb. Over thirty years had passed since the Shift. By now every moron should know to watch their mouth and not accept bargains with random strangers, because when you said yes to magic, your word was binding, whether you meant it or not. A life wasted. All I could do now was to find the killer and punish him. Just once I would've liked to be there before this sort of shit happened so I could nip it in the bud.

"That's when all the shapeshifters left," Maggie said.

"That's right." Cash nodded. "They ran out of here like their tails were on fire."

"These shapeshifters, do they come often?"

"Once a week for about a year now," Cash said.

"They drink a lot?"

"One beer each," Maggie said. "They don't drink much, but they don't cause any trouble either. They just sit by themselves in the corner and eat barrels of peanuts. We started charging them for it. They don't seem to care. I think they all work together, because they come in at the same time."

In times of trouble, shapeshifters snapped into an us-versus-them mentality. The world fractured into Pack and Not Pack. They would fight to the death for one of their own or to protect their territory. This was their hangout, their place. They should have waded into this fight, and in this case, the Pack

Law would be on their side. Instead they took off. Odd. Maybe Curran had come up with some new order forbidding fights. No, that didn't make sense either. They were shapeshifters, not nuns. If they didn't blow their steam off once in a while, they'd self-destruct. Curran knew that better than anyone.

I filed this tidbit to puzzle over in the future. Right now the guy in the cloak was my primary concern.

Joshua was killed for a specific purpose. The guy had gone through a lot of trouble, starting a fight, busting walls, arranging Joshua to impersonate a human butterfly, and infecting him. It was unlikely he'd done it just for kicks, which meant he had some sort of a plan and he wouldn't stop until he followed through with it. Nothing good could possibly come from a plan that involved turning a man into a syphilis incubator.

"We run a quiet tavern," Maggie said. "Usually guys don't want to fight here. They just want to get a drink, shoot some pool, and go home. If there is a fight brewing, they'll talk shit for a while and wait for Toby and Vik to break them up. But this . . . I've never seen anything like this. That man threw one punch, and the whole crowd exploded. People were screaming and fighting, and growling like wild animals."

I looked at Vik. "Did you fight?"

"I did."

"And you?" I turned to Toby.

"Yeah."

I glanced to Cash. He nodded. I could tell by their faces they weren't proud of it. The bouncers were paid to keep a cool head, and Cash was the owner.

"Why did you fight?"

They stared at me.

"I was mad," Vik offered. "Real mad."

"Angry," Toby said.

"Why?"

"Hell if I know." Vik shrugged.

Interesting. "How long did the fight last?"

"Forever," Toby said.

"About ten minutes," Maggie answered.

That's a long time for a fight. Most bar fights were over in a couple of minutes. "Did it get worse with time?"

She nodded.

"Did anybody see Joshua die?"

"It was all a blur," Toby said. "I remember hitting some-body's head against the wall and . . . I don't even know why I did it. It's like I couldn't stop."

"I saw it." Maggie hugged herself. "The fight broke out. Joshua was in the middle of it. He was a big man and he knew what he was doing. I was screaming for them to stop fighting. I was afraid they'd bust up the place. Nobody listened to me. Joshua was mowing people down with his fists and then that man grabbed him and they hit the wall. The man dragged Joshua to the pole, grabbed a crowbar, and stabbed. Joshua was wriggling on the crowbar like a fish. That bastard put his hand on Joshua's face. A red light flashed and then he walked away. I saw Joshua's eyes. He was gone."

This just got better and better.

Maggie hugged herself. Cash put his hand on her shoulder. Neither said anything but I watched the haunted expression ease from Maggie's face, as if she drew strength from him.

One day I'd find someone to lean on as well. It just wouldn't be Curran. And I really had to stop thinking about him, because it hurt.

"Did you see any part of the man during the fight? Any-thing at all?"

Maggie shook her head. "Just the cloak."

Biohazard's techs would've taken statements before they let the brawlers go. I'd bet a chocolate bar nobody had gotten a look at the John Doe in the cloak.

A ten-minute fight, fifty eyewitnesses, and no description. That had to be some kind of record.

"Okay." I sighed. "What about the critter in the cellar? What do we know about it?"

"Big," Vik said. "Hairy. Big teeth." He held his hands apart, demonstrating teeth with his fingers. "He was like the spawn of hell."

"How did this spawn get into the cellar?"

The smaller bouncer shrugged. "I was trying to make my way to the bar, where the shotgun was, and then some asswipe hits me with a pool cue and I take a tumble down this stair and hit my head a bit. Once the room stops spinning, I try to get up and I see this huge thing coming down. Wicked fangs, eyes glowing. I'm thinking I was done for. It jumps right over me and into the cellar. I slam the door shut and that's that."

"Did anybody see this beast come in with the man who killed Joshua?"

Nobody said anything. I took it as a no.

"Did it try to get out?"

Both bouncers shook their head.

I rose to my feet and pulled Slayer from my back sheath. The opaque saber caught the blue light of feylanterns. A light mother-of-pearl shimmer ran along the blade. Everybody took a step back.

"Lock the door behind me," I told them.

"What if you don't come out?" Maggie asked.

"I'll come out." I unlatched the heavy wooden door, opened it, and ducked inside.

Darkness mugged me. I waited, letting my eyes adjust to the gloom.

The cellar lay quiet, steeped in shadows and the thick odor of hops and liquor. Dark curves of large beer kegs defined a narrow path. I moved forward, ready to dodge at any second. My back and knees hurt. The last thing I wanted was something big with teeth the size of Vik's fingers jumping at me from above.

Nothing but moonlight, crawling through the narrow slit of a high window to my right.

A black shadow stirred against the far wall.

"Hi there." I shifted my stance.

A low throaty whine answered me. A very plaintive whine, followed by heavy wet panting.

I took another step and paused. No flash of teeth. No glowing eyes.

My nose caught a whiff of fur. Interesting.

I put a bit of excitement in my voice. "Here, boy!"

The dark shadow whined.

"Who's a good boy? Are you scared? I'm scared."

A faint sound of a tail sweeping the floor echoed the panting.

I slapped my leg with my palm. "Come here, boy! Let's be scared together. Come on!"

The shadow rose and trotted over to me. A wet tongue

licked my hand. Apparently he was a friendly kind of demonic beast.

I reached into my belt and clicked a lighter. A shaggy canine muzzle greeted me, complete with big black nose and infinitely sad dog eyes. I reached over and slowly patted the dark fur. The dog panted and flopped on the side, exposing his stomach. Wicked fangs and glowing eyes, right. I sighed, flicked the lighter off, and went to rap my knuckles on the door. "It's me, don't shoot."

"Okay," Cash called out.

A metallic sound announced the deadbolt being slid open. I cracked the door slowly to find myself staring at the business end of the machete. "I've got the spawn of hell cornered," I said. "Can you get me some rope?"

In ten seconds I had a length of chain in my hand thick enough to hold a bear in check. I felt the dog's neck—no collar. Big surprise. I looped the chain and slid it around his head, and opened the door. The beast docilely followed me into the light.

It stood about thirty inches at the shoulder. Its fur was a mess of dark brown and tan, in a classic Doberman pattern, except his coat wasn't sleek and shiny but rather a shaggy dense mass of rank curls. Some sort of mongrel, part Doberman, part sheepdog or something long-haired.

Vik turned the color of a ripe apple.

Cash stared at it. "It's a damn mutt."

I shrugged. "Probably got scared during the fight and just ran blindly through the bar. He seems friendly enough."

The dog pressed against my legs, rubbing a small army of fetid bacteria into my jeans.

"We should kill it," Vik said. "Who knows, it might turn into something nasty."

I gave him my best version of a deranged stare. "The dog's evidence. Don't touch the dog."

Vik decided he liked his teeth in his mouth and not on the floor and beat a strategic retreat. "Right."

I'd kill a dog in self-defense. I'd done it and I felt bad about it afterward, but at the time there was no way around it. Killing a mutt who just licked my hand was beyond me. Besides, the dog was evidence. Ten to one, he was a local mongrel who had a panicked reaction to whatever magic John Doe in the cloak had been throwing around. Of course, he could also sprout tentacles in the night and try to murder me. Only time would tell. Until I'd watched him for a few days, the spawn of hell and I were joined at the hip. Which wasn't necessarily a good thing, considering he tried his best to singe away the lining of my nose with his stink.

I took the dog to the medtechs to get cleared of the plague—he passed with flying colors. They drew some blood for further analysis and advised me that he had fleas and smelled bad, just in case I'd failed to notice. Then I took paper and pen from Marigold's saddlebag and sat down at one of the tables to write out my report.

In the parking lot the inside of my ward circle blazed with orange flames. Three guys in heat-retardant suits waved their arms, chanting the fire into a white-hot rage. I couldn't even see the pole or Joshua's body inside the inferno.

The magic crashed. It simply vanished from the world in a single blink. The inferno in the parking lot began to die down. The guys in flame-retardant suits switched to flamethrowers and went on burning.

Patrice came up. "Nice dog."

"He's evidence," I told her.

"What's his name?"

I looked at the mutt, who promptly licked my hand. "No clue."

"You should name him Watson," Patrice said. "Then you can tell him 'Elementary, Watson,' when you solve a case in a blaze of intellectual glory."

Intellectual glory. Yeah, right. I waved my write-up at her. "I'll show you mine if you show me yours."

"Deal."

I handed her my notes. "The perpetrator is male, olive complexion, approximately six feet six inches tall, wears a long, sweeping cloak with a tattered hem, and likes to keep his hood on."

She grimaced. "Don't tell me. A guy in a cloak did it."

I nodded. "Looks that way. Other fun characteristics are preternaturally hardy constitution and superhuman strength. There were roughly fifty people in the bar, but the m-scanner registered only one magic signature, probably our murderer. Fifty violent guys and nobody used magic."

"Sounds unlikely," Patrice said.

"It was a big brutal brawl. Nobody can explain to me why they started fighting, but apparently they went from zero to sixty in three seconds. I think our dude in a cloak emanates something that hits people on a very basic level. Makes them really aggressive. It's also possible that animals run away from him, but we only have one test subject." I petted the demon dog. "Your turn."

Patrice sighed. "He's a Mary."

I nodded. Marys, so named after Typhoid Mary, were disease vectors—individuals who either spread or induced disease.

"A very, very strong one," Patrice said. "Our guy didn't just infect—and we can't say for sure that he did, since the victim could have been syphilitic prior to the fight—but he actually gave the disease life, making it more potent and almost self-aware. The last time I saw this was during a flare. It takes a great deal of power to make a disease into an entity."

Godlike power, to be exact. Except that no gods were prowling Atlanta's streets. They only came out to play during a flare, which occurred roughly every seven years, and we had just gotten over the latest one. Besides, if he'd been a god, the m-scan would've registered silver, not blue.

"We have to find him now." Patrice's face was grim. "He has pandemic potential. The man's a catastrophe in progress."

We both knew that the trail had gone cold. I'd missed the chance to go after him, because I was busy crawling around and trying to keep his handiwork from infecting the city. He would strike again and he would kill. It wasn't a question of if, but a question of how many.

"I'll put an alert out," Patrice said.

Find a guy in a cloak without any eyewitness sketches and apprehend him before he contaminates the whole city. Piece of cake.

"Can you find out more about the Good Samaritan who called it in as well?" I asked.

"Why?"

"You're Joe Blow. You walk by and see me crawl around the fuzzy pole drawing shit on the pavement. Are you going to figure out immediately that I'm trying to contain a virulent plague?"

Patrice pursed her lips. "Not likely."

"Whoever called it in knew what I was doing and knew enough to call Biohazard, but didn't stick around. I'd like to know why."

Half an hour later, I dropped Marigold in the Order's stables and surrendered the dust bunny to the assistant stable master, who also was in charge of collecting all living "evidence." We had a slight disagreement as to the living status of the dust bunny, until I suggested that he let it out of the cage to settle the issue. They were still trying to catch it when I left.

I dragged the dog into my apartment and into my shower, where I waged chemical warfare on his fur. Unfortunately, he insisted on shaking himself every thirty seconds. I had to rinse him four times before the water ran clear, and by the end of it, a wet spray blanketed every inch of my bathroom walls, my drain was full of dog hair, and the beast smelled only marginally better. He'd managed to lick me in the face twice in gratitude. His tongue stank, too.

"I hate you," I told him before giving him leftover bologna from the fridge. "You stink, you slobber, and you think I'm a nice person."

The dog wolfed down the bologna and wagged his tail. He really was an odd-looking mutt. Once the diagnostics from Biohazard came back, if he was just a regular dog, I'd have to find him a nice home. Pets didn't do well with me. I wasn't even home enough to keep them from starving.

I checked my messages—nothing, as usual—took a shower, and crawled into bed. The dog flopped on the floor. The last thing I remembered before passing out was the sound of his tail sweeping the rug.

CHAPTER 3

———◆———

I MADE IT TO THE OFFICE BY TEN. I'D HAD ROUGHLY four hours of sleep, awoken in a foul mood, and my face must've shown it, because people took pains to move out of my way on the street. Of course, it could've been because a giant fetid mess of a dog trotted next to me, growling at anyone who came too close.

The office of the Order of Merciful Aid occupied a plain box of a building. When the magic was up, it was shielded by a military-grade ward, but now while the technology had the upper hand, nothing distinguished the bastion of knightly virtue from its fellow office buildings. I climbed to the second floor, entered a long drab hallway, and landed in my tiny office, painted plain gray. The faithful canine companion flopped on the carpet.

I pushed the button of the intercom. "Maxine?"

"Yes dear?"

"I believe I'm due two cookies."

"Come and get them."

I looked at the canine companion. "Me cookies. You stay."

Apparently "stay" in faithful canine companion language

meant "follow with enthusiastic glee." I could shut my office door in his face, but then he'd probably howl and be sad. I had enough sad in my life right now.

We trotted down the hallway and crashed to a halt before Maxine's desk. She surveyed the demon dog for a couple of stunned seconds, then reached under her desk and produced a box of cookies, each the size of my palm. The scent of vanilla hit me. I did my best not to drool. One must maintain the sleek and deadly image, after all.

I snagged two cookies, broke one down the middle, picked the chocolate chips out of one half, and gave it to the mutt. I chomped on the other half. Heaven did exist and it had walnuts in it. "Any messages for me?" Usually I got one or two, but mostly people who wanted my help preferred to talk in person.

"Yes. Hold on." She pulled out a handful of pink tickets and recited from memory, without checking the paper. "Seven forty-two a.m., Mr. Gasparian: *I curse you. I curse your arms so they will wither and die and fall off your body. I curse your eyeballs to explode. I curse your feet to swell until blue. I curse your spine to crack. I curse you. I curse you. I curse you.*"

I licked cookie crumbs off my lips. "Mr. Gasparian is under the impression that he has magic powers. He is fifty-six years old, terribly unhappy because his wife left him, and he keeps cursing his neighbors. Magically, he's a dud, but his ranting scares the neighborhood kids. I kicked his case to Atlanta's finest. I'm guessing they paid him a visit and he's a bit upset that I didn't take his magic mojo seriously."

"People do the strangest things. Seven fifty-six a.m., Patrice Lane, Biohazard: *Joshua was a shapeshifter. Call me now.*"

I choked on my cookie. Shapeshifters didn't get sick, at least not in the traditional sense. The only time I'd seen one of them sneeze was when they got a bit of dust in their nose or when they became inexplicably allergic to giant tortoises. Their bones knitted together in a couple of weeks. What the hell?

Maxine kept going.

"Eight oh one a.m., Derek Gaunt: *Can you ring me when you get in?*

"Eight oh five a.m., Jim, no last name given: *Call me.*

"Eight twelve a.m., Ghastek Stefanoff: *Please call me at your earliest convenience.*

"Eight thirty-seven a.m., Patrice Lane, Biohazard: *The dog's clean. The Good Samaritan was a woman with an accent of some sort. Why haven't you called me?*

"Eight forty-four a.m., Detective Williams, Atlanta PAD: *Agent Daniels, contact me about your statement in regard to the incident at Steel Horse ASAP.* And that's all of them." Maxine gave me a bright smile and handed me a stack of pink message slips.

Andrea emerged from the armory, carrying a manila envelope, and headed my way. Short and blond, she was armed with a pretty face, a charming smile, and a pair of 9mm SIG-Sauers. Which she used to shoot things with preternatural accuracy many times and very fast. She was also my best friend.

Andrea braked a couple of feet from me. I shook my giant stack of pink slips at her.

"I see—you have messages. That's nice." Andrea nodded at me and snagged a cookie from the box.

The canine companion growled under his breath. Just in case she was trouble.

"What is that?" Andrea's eyes widened.

"What is what?"

"The beast." She waved the cookie at the dog.

The beast trotted over to her side, sniffed her, and wagged his tail, indicating he had decided she was good people and she should give him a piece of her cookie.

"He's evidence."

"Don't get me wrong, I think a dog is a great idea. I just never pictured you with a mutant poodle."

"He isn't a poodle. He's a Doberman mix."

"Aha. Keep telling yourself that."

"Where have you seen a poodle colored like that?"

"Why don't we ask Mauro? His wife's a vet and he breeds Dobermans."

I growled. "Fine. Let's go ask him."

We padded down the hall to Mauro's office, canine enigma in tow. If I had to partner up for a job and Andrea wasn't available, I usually conned Mauro into joining forces. A huge, hulking Samoan, he was steady as the Rock of Gibraltar. Bringing him to a job was like having your own portable howitzer—people took one look at him and decided making trouble wasn't in their best interest.

Mauro's office was only marginally bigger than mine, and his body was substantially larger, so the examination of the faithful canine companion had to be taken to the hallway. Mauro knelt by the dog, felt his sides, stared at his mouth, and rose, shaking his hands.

"Standard poodle. Probably purebred, even. Aside from being freakishly large, he's actually a very nice-looking dog under all that fur. You won't get any breeders lining up at your door, because you can't show him. He's too huge. But otherwise, a very fine specimen."

You've got to be kidding me. "What about the color?"

"That's a recognized bicolor for the breed. They're called phantom poodles."

Andrea snickered.

The phantom poodle sat by me, looking at my face like it was the best thing he'd ever seen.

"They're very smart dogs," Mauro said. "Canine Einsteins. They're protective and they make good guards." He cleared his throat and slid into an atrocious Southern tinged with Samoan accent. "You know, a young wallflower such as yourself, Ms. Scarlett, shouldn't be on these vicious streets without a male escort. It's just not proper."

Andrea doubled over, croaking with laughter.

"Screw you guys."

Mauro shook his head, gazing mournfully at Andrea. "See? The streets have affected her: she's become coarse."

There were times in life when nothing short of spitting fire would do.

"Have you thought of what to name him?" Mauro asked. "How about Erik? After the Phantom of the Opera."

"No."

"You should name him Fezzik," Andrea said.

"Inconceivable," I told her and took the canine traitor back to my office.

"You might want to shave him," Mauro called after me. "His fur's all matted and it's uncomfortable for him."

In the office I pulled out my brown bag. I'd stopped by a food stall on the way to the office. It was a dingy stall marked with a big sign that said HUNGRY MAN and operated by a thin blond guy. You'd have to be a very, very hungry man to stop by that stall. On the brink of starvation. And even then, I think I would go for a raw rat instead. The smell alone was known to send people running for their lives. However, the dog had found the aroma emanating from Hungry Man curiously enticing, and so I bought a bag of small round fried things that were supposedly hush puppies.

I reached into the bag, pulled a round object out, and tossed it at the poodle. Big jaws opened for a blink, caught a hush puppy, and snapped shut. He must've spent some time being a stray, because he'd learned the two things all strays know: food is rare so eat it quick, and stick to the sap who feeds you.

I folded the bag over. Kate Daniels and her deadly attack poodle. Kill me, somebody. Julie, my adopted niece, would have a field day with this. It was a good thing she was away at a boarding school until Thanksgiving.

Maybe the corner store would have hair clippers.

I flopped behind my desk and spread my pink slips in a fan on its scarred surface. In a perfect world, Joshua's vertically gifted murderer would've had himself a monologue before rampaging, during which he loudly and clearly would've announced his full name, occupation, religious preference, preferably with his god's country and time period of origin, his goals, dreams, and aspirations, and the location of his lair. But nobody had ever accused post-Shift Atlanta of being perfect.

The killer was likely a devotee of some deity who enjoyed plagues as means to motivate and discipline his or her faithful. A very powerful devotee, able to overcome the regenerative powers of Lyc-V, which was pretty much impossible as far as common wisdom was concerned. Obviously common wisdom had once again proven itself wrong.

Of course, the killer could also be some psychopath who thought all disease was divine and just enjoyed infecting people in his spare time. I leaned toward the first theory. The man had specifically wanted Joshua, he killed him in a very odd way, and he strode off once the deed was accomplished. He didn't stay to soak in the reaction. All this pointed to some sort of method to his madness, some definite purpose.

Why start a fight? If he had wanted Joshua, he could've ambushed him on some lonely street instead of starting a brawl in a bar full of tough guys. Why take the risk that he or Joshua would get injured? Was this some sort of a message? Or did he think he was just that much of a badass?

The only hint I had was the link between disease and the divine. I pulled a piece of paper from the drawer and took a stack of books off my shelf. I wanted some background before I started returning calls.

TWO HOURS LATER MY LIST OF DEADLY DISEASE-related deities had grown to unwieldy proportions. In Greece both Apollo and his sister, Artemis, infected people with their arrows. Also from Greece hailed the nosoi, daimones of pestilence, disease, and heavy sickness, who escaped the confines of Pandora's jar. In the myths, nosoi were mute, and my guy definitely spoke, but I've learned not to take myth as gospel.

The list kept going. Every time an ancient man stumbled, there was a god ready to punish him with an array of agonizing maladies. Kali, the Hindu goddess of death, was known as the goddess of disease; Japan was riddled with plague demons; the Mayans had Ak K'ak, who was the god of both disease and war and looked to be a good candidate, considering Joshua's killer started a brawl; the Maori boasted a disease deity for each body part; the Winnebago Indians tried to secure blessings from some two-faced god they called Disease-Giver; the Irish had the plague-bringer Caillech; and in ancient Babylon, Nergal gave out diseases like they were candy. And that wasn't even counting deities who, while not specializing in illnesses, used an odd plague here and there when the occasion called for it.

I needed more data to narrow this down. My butt hurt from sitting still for too long. I'd fed the dog four hush puppies so far and curiously he seemed no worse for wear. I half expected him to blow up or upchuck on the carpet. Attack poodle with the stomach of steel.

When my eyes glazed over, I took a break and called Bio-hazard.

"A shapeshifter?"

"Werecoyote," Patrice said.

"How sure are you of this?"

"Without a shadow of a doubt. Several pissed-off Pack members showed up at my office demanding his remains."

"How is that possible? Shapeshifters don't get sick."

"I don't know." A note of worry vibrated in Patrice's voice. "Lyc-V is a jealous virus. It exterminates all other invaders with extreme prejudice."

If the plague did that to a shapeshifter, what would it do to a regular human?

The rest of the conversation went in a similar vein. The guy in a cloak now had an official code name—the Steel Mary. The attack poodle was all dog, the Good Samaritan was gone forever, and we were all out of clues as to the Steel Mary's identity. The statements of eyewitnesses proved useless. The medmages had crawled all over the scene and discovered diddly-squat. No names of forbidden gods written in blood on the wall. No accidentally discarded matchbooks from five-star hotels. No mud prints made with one-of-a-kind mud found only three feet to the left of some famous landmark. Nothing. I asked Patrice if she thought praying to Miss Marple would help. She told me to stuff it and hung up.

PAD was next in line. Williams mostly flexed his muscle and rattled his sabers, because PAD hadn't been called to the scene and Biohazard got all the glory, but after my vivid description of Joshua's nose falling off, the good detective decided that he had a very pressing and very full caseload, and while he would love to assist my investigation in any way possible, he was simply swamped. Regretful, that.

I checkmarked the three pink slips from Patrice and Wil-liams and called Jim, because I had to. One had to take pains to be polite when dealing with the Pack's security chief. Even if that chief was your buddy.

A male shapeshifter named Jack put me on hold. I flipped the pink slip over and doodled an ugly face on it.

Jim and I went way back. Before my job as a liaison

between the Order and the Mercenary Guild and his job as the Pack's head spook, we both earned our cash as mercs, contractors for the Mercenary Guild. The Guild assigned each merc a territory. Mine happened to be crap, and well-paying gigs came my way very rarely. Jim's territory, on other hand, often generated good gigs, but they frequently required more than one body. Usually he cut me in on it, mostly because he couldn't stomach working with anybody else. During that time I learned that, with Jim, the Pack always took precedence. He could have the guy we hunted by his throat, but one call from the Keep, and he'd walk away without a word.

He was probably going out of his mind. Shapeshifters spent all their life thinking they were free of disease. Last night had ripped their immunity away from them.

I colored the doodle's nose black and added a spiky mane of wild hair.

"Kate?" Jim said into the phone. Jim looked like he broke bones for a living, but his voice was heavenly. "What the hell took you so long?"

"You say the sweetest things to me, honey bear," I told him. "I was trying to track down the Mary who killed Joshua."

Jim growled a little, but didn't bite back. "He was only twenty-four years old. A werecoyote, good guy. He worked for me once in a while."

I gave the doodle two sharp horns. "I'm very sorry."

"Biohazard told me he was infected with syphilis and it ate him from inside out."

"That's . . . accurate."

"They won't release the remains to us."

I knew where he was coming from. "Doolittle wants a sample to analyze?"

"Yeah."

Doolittle was the Pack's medic and the best medmage I'd ever had the privilege of driving to the brink of near insanity. He was the reason why my friend Derek still had a face. He was also the reason why I was still around at all.

"Jim, Joshua was extremely contagious. Pieces of him fell off, grew pale fuzz, and crawled across the pavement. Biohazard torched him down to his skeleton, which they locked in a hermetically sealed coffin and then cremated. They would've dropped a nuke onto the parking lot if they thought they could get away with it."

"Is there anything left?"

I drew claws on the doodle's arms. "Unfortunately, no. Georgia Code, Title 38: under Georgia Supernatural Emergency Management Act of 2019, in the event of a clear threat of epidemic, Biohazard has broad emergency powers, which trump everything, including the Pack's claim on the remains. As far as I know, they didn't even keep a sample for themselves. It was extremely virulent, Jim. It slithered over salt and fire. If it got out, most of the city would be infected by now."

The poodle raised his head, a low warning rumble rolling deep in his throat.

I looked at him.

"Visitor," Maxine's voice whispered in my head.

"I'll have to hang up in a minute, so very quickly," I murmured into the phone. "There were other shapeshifters in the bar. Why did they leave?"

He hesitated.

"Jim. We went through this before: I can't help you if you don't level with me."

"They were driven out. Something that bastard did terrified them out of their minds."

"Where are they now? I need to interview them."

"You can't interview Maria. She's under sedation."

"What about the rest?"

There was a tiny pause. "We're looking for them."

Oh crap. "How many are missing?"

"Three."

There were three panicked shapeshifters lost in the city, each a spree killer in waiting. If they went loup, they'd paint the city red. Could this get any worse?

An emaciated shape scuttled into my office with preternatural quickness and perched in my client chair. It might have been a man at some point, but now it was a creature: gaunt, hairless, corded with dried muscle as if someone had stuck it into a dehydrator for a few days and all of the fat and softness had drained from it. The vampire stared at me with glowing eyes and in their red depths I sensed a terrible hunger.

The attack poodle exploded into wild barking.

Why did I even bother asking that question?

"Once again, I'm very sorry. Please pass my condolences to his family," I said. "If there is anything I can do to help, I'm here."

"I knew you would be." Jim hung up.

I hung up and looked at the vampire. Its mouth gaped open and it showed me its fangs: two long curved needles of ivory. Seeing bloodsuckers during daylight wasn't unheard of, but usually they appeared smeared with sunblock. Considering the dense gray blanket of clouds smothering the skies and weak, late fall sun, they probably didn't need to bother today.

The vampire spared a single glance for the attack poodle and looked back at me.

I would've liked to kill it. I could almost picture my saber slicing into undead flesh right between the sixth and seventh vertebrae of his neck.

I pointed a finger at the attack poodle. "You—quiet."

"An interesting animal." Ghastek's voice spilled from the bloodsucker's mouth, sounding slightly muffled, as if through a phone.

The vampire repositioned itself in my client chair and crouched like a cat, arms in front.

Of all the Masters of the Dead among the People in Atlanta, Ghastek was the most dangerous, with the exception of his boss, Nataraja. But where Nataraja was cruel and chaotic in his behavior, Ghastek was intelligent and calculating, a far worse combination.

I folded my arms on my chest. "A personal visit. Don't I feel special."

"You don't return your phone calls." The vampire leaned forward, tapping my doodle with a scimitar claw. "Is that a lion with horns and a pitchfork?"

"Yep."

"Is he carrying the moon on his pitchfork?"

"No, it's a pie. What can I do for Atlanta's premier Master of the Dead?"

The vampire's features twisted, trying to mirror the emotion on Ghastek's face. Judging by the result, Ghastek was struggling not to vomit. "Someone attacked the Casino this morning. The People wish to petition the Order to look into it."

The vampire and I stared at each other. "Can you run that by me again?" I asked.

"Some mentally challenged individual attacked the Casino this morning, causing roughly two hundred thousand dollars' worth of harm. The bulk of the cost came from four vampires he managed to fry. The damage to the building is mostly cosmetic."

"I meant the part where the People petition the Order."

"It was my understanding that the Order extends its protection to all citizens."

I leaned forward. "Correct me if I'm wrong, but aren't you the same guys who run the other way the moment a badge gets involved?"

The vampire looked insulted. "That's not true. We always cooperate with law enforcement."

And pigs gracefully glide through clear sky. "Two weeks ago, a woman robbed a vendor at gun point and fled into the Casino. It took the cops fourteen hours to get her out, because you claimed some sort of sanctuary privilege that was last invoked by the Catholic Church. As far as I know, the Casino doesn't stand on hallowed ground."

The vampire looked down on me with an air of haughty disdain. Whatever faults Ghastek had, his control over the undead was superb. "That is a matter of opinion."

"You don't cooperate with authorities unless forced, you lawyer up at the first hint of trouble, and you have a stable of undead capable of mass murder. You're the last group I expected to petition the Order for assistance."

"Life is full of surprises."

I chewed on that for a minute. "Does Nataraja know you're here?"

"I'm here on his direct orders."

Warning bells went off in my head.

Ghastek's superior, the People's head honcho in Atlanta, called himself Nataraja after one of Shiva's reincarnations. There was something odd about Nataraja. His power felt too old for a human and he packed a lot of magic, but I had never actually witnessed him pilot a vampire. About three months ago, I ended up getting involved in an underground martial arts tournament, which resulted in me fighting shapeshifting demons called rakshasas. It also resulted in my owing Curran a naked dinner.

If that furry bastard could stop intruding on my thoughts for five seconds, I might have to dance a jig in celebration.

The rakshasas had made a pact with Roland, the People's leader and my biological father. He provided them with weapons and in return they tried to destroy the shapeshifters. The Pack had grown too large and too powerful and Roland wanted it out of the way before it grew any larger. The rakshasas failed. If Nataraja turned out to be a rakshasa, I wouldn't be surprised. Roland still wanted the Pack out of the way and Nataraja answered to Roland.

Maybe Nataraja had hatched some sort of a plan in retaliation, and he sent Ghastek here to me to create an appearance of propriety.

Maybe I was just getting paranoid . . .

I looked into the vampire's eyes. "What's the catch?"

The bloodsucker shrugged, a revolting gesture that jerked his whole body. "I have no idea what you're talking about."

"I don't believe you."

"Should I take that as a refusal to accept the petition?"

Ghastek one, Kate zero.

"On the contrary, the Order would be delighted to accept your plea." I pulled the petition sheet from the stack of forms. The People accumulated money to fund their research. Their extreme wealth went hand in hand with severe frugality. They were notoriously tightfisted. "The Order charges on a sliding scale, according to one's means of income. For the impoverished, our services are free. For you, they will be shockingly expensive."

"Money is no object." The vampire waved his claws. "I've been authorized to meet your prices."

They really wanted the Order involved. "Tell me what happened."

"At six oh-eight a.m. two men wearing ragged trench coats approached the Casino. The shorter of the men burst into flames."

I paused with the pen in my hand. "He burst into flames?"

"He became engulfed in fire."

"Was his buddy made out of orange rocks and did he at any point yell, 'It's clobbering time'?"

The vampire heaved a sigh. It was an eerie process: it opened its mouth, bit the air, and released it in a single hissing whoosh. "I find your attempted levity inappropriate, Kate."

"Consider me properly chastised. So what happened next?"

"The pyromancer directed a jet of flame at our building. His companion aided it by creating a strong wind, which carried the fire toward the Casino's entrance."

Most likely a fire mage and a wind mage. A firebug and a whistler, working together.

"The fire swept the front of the Casino, scorching the outer wall and the parapet. A team of four vampires was dispatched to deal with the issue. Their appearance caused the two intruders to shift the flames from the Casino onto the approaching vampires. The intensity of the fire proved to be higher than anticipated."

"They took down four vampires?" That was unexpected.

The vampire nodded.

"And you let them walk away?" I couldn't believe this.

"We did give chase. Unfortunately, the two intruders disappeared."

I sat back. "So they appeared, sprayed some fire, and vanished. Did you receive any demands? Money, jewels, Rowena in lingerie?" Personally, I was betting on Rowena—she was the Master of the Dead who handled the Casino's PR, and half of the city's male population would kill to see her naked.

The vampire shook its head.

Was this a prank of some sort? If it was, it ranked right up there with dropping a toaster in your bath tub or trying to put a fire out with gasoline. "How badly did they burn the vampires?"

The vampire gagged. The muscles of its neck constricted, widened, constricted again, and it disgorged a six-inch-long metal cylinder onto my desk. The bloodsucker grasped it, twisted the cylinder's halves apart, and retrieved a roll of papers. "Photographs," Ghastek said, handing me a couple of sheets from the roll.

"That's disgusting."

"He is thirty years old," Ghastek said. "All his internal organs, with the exception of the heart, atrophied long ago. The throat makes for a very good storage cavity. People seem to prefer it to the anus."

Translation: be happy I didn't pull it out of my ass. Thank the gods for small favors.

The two photographs showed two charred blistered ruins that might have been bodies at some point and now were just burned meat. In random places the undead flesh had peeled away, revealing bone.

A mage who could deliver a blast of heat intense enough to cook a vampire was worth his weight in gold. This wasn't some two-bit firebug. This was a high-caliber pyromancer. You could count those guys on the fingers of one hand.

I held out my hand. "The m-scan, please."

The vampire became utterly still. Many miles away, Ghastek was deep in thought.

"You have enough diagnostic equipment in the Casino to make the entirety of the Mage College giddy with joy," I said. "If you tell me the scene wasn't m-scanned, I'll be very tempted to make a new storage cavity in your vampire with my saber."

The vampire peeled another page from the roll and handed it to me. An m-scan printout, streaked with purple. Red was the color of undeath, blue was the color of human magic. Together they made the purple of the vampire. The older the vamp, the redder the signature. These four were relatively young—their residual magic registered almost violet. Two bright magenta lines sliced through the vampiric traces like twin scars. No matter how old a vampire would grow, it would never register magenta. The tint was wrong. Bloodsuckers ran to the deeper tones of purple.

But magenta still had red in it, which meant . . .

"Undead mages." Holy shit!

"It seems so," Ghastek said.

"How is this possible?" I was beginning to sound like a broken record. "The use of human elemental magic is directly tied to cognitive ability, which ceases to exist after death."

The vampire shrugged again. "If I had answers, I wouldn't be here."

Just when I got comfortable with the rules of the game, the Universe decided it was time for a swift kick to my rear. Werecoyotes caught deadly plagues, the People asked the Order for assistance, and undead creatures used elemental magic.

"Do you have any idea who could be behind this? Any suspicions at all?"

"No." The vampire leaned forward. A long yellow claw traced the slice of magenta across the m-scan. "But I'm dying to find out."

CHAPTER 4

———◆———

WHEN YOU HAVE NO IDEA WHERE TO START, GO
back to basics. In my case, the basics involved gluing myself
to the phone and calling the Biohazard units of major cities
around Atlanta. Being with the Order had its disadvantages,
but it did open some doors and anything concerning an epidemic had a high profile among Biohazard staff.

In two hours I had a better picture and it wasn't pretty. So
far the Steel Mary had left his skid marks in five cities: Miami,
Fort Lauderdale, Jacksonville, Savannah—hit my home turf
and I didn't even know it—and finally Atlanta. He was moving
north, working his way up the coast, which probably meant he
came off the boat in Miami. Sea travel was a dicey affair; he
would've stayed away from the ocean if he could help it. Several sea routes ran out of Miami. I had a sick feeling he came
by the one curving down from West Africa. Africa churned
with old magic, ancient, powerful, and primal.

In Miami a man in a cloak had been sighted in the marketplace. A herd of cattle waited to be slaughtered. He walked
right into the enclosure, raised his arms, and the herd broke
through the wooden corral and stampeded through the market. His magic hit the shoppers as well, and in seconds people

fled the marketplace, trampling each other and causing a city-wide panic. Then he unleashed smallpox, which proved to be too strong to cause trouble. It killed its carrier in seconds and burned itself out.

The citizens of Fort Lauderdale had no idea the guy in the cloak existed but their Biohazard unit did report an outbreak of extremely virulent influenza, which affected everyone who visited an underground bare knuckles tournament. Fancy that.

The PAD in Jacksonville got his number pretty fast, but he dumped a hellish strain of dysentery on them, and by the time they cleaned up the bodies, he was long gone. They did mention that he had four flunkies with him. They also called ahead to just about every city in Georgia with a warning, which Savannah and Atlanta's Biohazard units promptly ignored.

Savannah paid for it with an outbreak of bubonic plague that started after a battle royale in one of their infamous Irish pubs on River Street. I knew the PAD detectives down there, and all three of them were very sore about the whole thing, so sore that they offered to box their case evidence and send it up to me. I jumped on the chance with both feet.

Every incident took place during a magic wave. Every incident involved a rough crowd and a brawl, and in every case the toughest fighter ended up pinned to the first available hard surface. Sometimes the Steel Mary used a spear. Sometimes a harpoon or a crowbar. Women seemed mostly unaffected. Either his magic didn't work on them as well or he wasn't interested in the more dangerous of the sexes.

Animals ran from him. Shapeshifters seemed to have issues as well. In Miami the three werewolves in the market went berserk. Of the berserkers, one was killed by the cow stampede, and the other two were apprehended and taken into police custody. The first survivor ripped out his own throat and bled to death in his cell. The other escaped and the upstanding members of the Miami PD blew the back of his head to pieces and collected the bounty. Some things even Lyc-V couldn't fix. A shotgun blast to the head was one of them. The Miami PD had issued a formal apology to the Pack, but it was clear the Pack had no leg to stand on. In the cops' place, I would've shot him down, too.

I tapped my notes with my fingernails. I had to warn Andrea about it. She was female, true, so she'd have some protection against the Steel Mary's magic, but she was also beastkin. Lyc-V, the shapeshifting virus, infected people and animals alike. Sometimes, the result was an animal-were, a creature that had started life as a beast and gained the ability to turn into a human. Most animal-weres were violent, mute, sterile idiots, unable to cope with the rules of human society. Murder and rape had no meaning to them, which was why some shapeshifters killed them on sight, no questions asked. Very occasionally the animal-weres developed the ability to reason and learned to communicate. Even more occasionally they could procreate.

Andrea's mother was a bouda, a werehyena, but her father was a hyenawere, which made her beastkin, the child of an animal. She hid this fact from everyone: from the Order, because they would jettison her from their ranks, and from the Pack, because some shapeshifters would kill her. Only a handful of people knew what she was and we all quietly decided to keep it to ourselves.

There was no telling what this guy's power would do to her. If she panicked and ran or went berserk, we'd all be in deep shit.

The growing number of the Steel Mary's flunkies worried me. According to Toby the bouncer, this guy told Joshua that he had an opening for two more gods. What did that mean? Was he gathering himself a posse and calling them gods?

I rubbed my face. His MO said he might move on to another city, but I had a feeling he would stick around. He was obviously building to some sort of goal, and if he got whatever it was he wanted from Joshua, that left the Steel Mary with only one would-be-god spot. Something big would happen when he filled his quota. Atlanta was the center of the South. The largest Pack was here, the largest Guild was here, the Southern MSDU was headquartered here. It made sense that Atlanta has been his goal all along. I didn't know where he would hit next, but at least I could thrust some sticks into his wheels.

I pulled up the phone and grabbed the phone book. My tenure in the Mercenary Guild was about to pay off.

I dialed the first number. A gruff male voice answered. "Black Dog Tavern."

"Hey, Keith, it's Kate Daniels."

"Hey, Order Kate, how are ya?"

I almost choked. Order Kate? Really? "I'm good. How about yourself?"

"Can't complain, can't complain. What're you hunting for today?"

"I've got a troublemaker who recently moved to town, a really tall guy in a tattered cloak. He likes to come into bars when the magic's up and throw around some heavy-duty spells to start fights."

"Sounds like a fun fella."

Depends on your definition of fun. "Do you still have that girl working for you, Emily?"

"Yep, she's here every night."

"Apparently, this guy's power bounces from ladies. Would you do me a huge favor and make sure you have Emily working during the magic waves? Give her my number and tell her to call me right away if any crazy fights break out. He's costing the bar owners an arm and a leg in broken furniture."

"Just so you know, he comes in here, it won't be my furniture that will get broken. I'll snap his legs."

Sure you will. "You do that. But make sure you give the girl my number anyway? I know your crew can handle him, but humor me. I'd really like to get my hands on this guy."

"Will do," Keith said.

"Thanks." I hung up. That was the best I was going to get. I slipped my fingers to the next number and dialed.

"Devil's Pit," a woman answered.

"Hey, Glenda, it's Kate Daniels. How are you?"

"Good, how about yourself?"

"Still trucking. Listen, I've got this moron who just cruised into town. He likes to start fights and I want to head him off at the pass . . ."

In an hour and a half, I'd hit every tough-guy watering hole I could remember. I'd called PAD and apprised them of the situation. I'd called the regular cops and given them the description of the guy. I'd called the local gossips and asked them to spread the word around. I'd called the Guild, where the Clerk picked up the phone. I'd known the Clerk for years. A trim, middle-aged man, he manned the counter and all mercs saw him twice per every gig, first, when they got the job, and second, when they turned in their capture tickets at the end. Somewhere along the way he'd lost his name and the multitude of us knew him simply as "the Clerk."

I gave him my spiel and he chuckled at me. "If he comes in here, I'll just tell the fellas there is a gig ticket on his head. They'll dismantle him to parts."

"He's a tough guy to deal with. Let Solomon know."

"Sure."

I could tell by his voice that he would blow me off. Just as well. I doubted the Guild's founder would pay me any mind. Solomon Red didn't even know my name. But I had to try. "I tell you what, put me through to him."

"Sorry, he's on DND."

Do Not Disturb. Fine. "Give me his voice mail, then."

"Suit yourself."

I left a long and detailed message, explaining all about the Steel Mary and his penchant for picking fights. Fat good it would do me.

Solomon Red was a legend, the king of the mole hill that was the Mercenary Guild. If mercs did have to elect a king, he probably would've gotten the job, too: huge, rust-haired, with a bulky jaw and different color eyes, one blue, one brown. He lived in the Guild, but was almost never seen, save at the obligatory Christmas celebration, when he personally gave out bonuses to the best mercs. In my six-year tenure with the Guild, I had seen him exactly twice and not because I stood in the bonus line. I seriously doubted he'd listen to my warnings of a mysterious ass kicker in a torn cloak.

I called a couple of local dojos and the Red Guard and Fist & Shield, the other premier security guard outfit. I called to Biohazard and spoke to Patrice to bring her up to speed. Patrice liked what I had to say so much, she cursed for a full three minutes. She especially enjoyed the part where I explained how her staff had failed to make use of Jacksonville's warning. I let her vent—it's not often you got to hear the head of the Biohazard Rapid Response unit promise to rip out someone's guts.

At two, I left to go home. I needed sleep and a new jaw, but if the guy in the cloak so much as showed his nose in one of Atlanta's bars, I'd know about it first.

THE DOG AND I STOPPED AT THE ORDER'S STABLES and I checked out Marigold again. I did have a beat-up old truck by the name of Karmelion which ran on enchanted water, but it took a good fifteen minutes of intense chanting to get it started, and if the guy in the cloak attacked somewhere, I didn't want to waste time begging my engine to start.

My apartment building came equipped with a set of garages, which the residents used for everything, from extra storage to makeshift stables. I used mine mostly to store wood for the winter and to put up an occasional mount I borrowed from the Order's stables. With Marigold safely installed in the garage, the faithful canine and I went down to the store.

The corner store didn't have clippers, so I generated a new plan, one that involved leaving the shaving of attack poodles to people who actually knew what they were doing. The dog and I jogged three miles to the groomer.

We stepped through the door, announced by a bell, and a smiling plump woman emerged from the depths of the place, glanced at the dog, and smiled wider. "What a lovely poodle."

We both growled a little bit, I because of the poodle comment and the dog out of a sense of duty.

The happy woman, whose name was Liz, secured my poodle to a long iron pole and turned on the electric clippers. The moment the clippers touched his skin, the dog whirled about and tried to clamp his teeth on Liz's arm. Instead I clamped my hand on his muzzle and turned him to face me.

"Pheew, you're fast," Liz said.

"I hold, you cut."

Twenty minutes later Liz had swept away a rank mass of matted poodle fur, while I received a new dog: an athletic-looking mutt with smooth ears, long legs, and a build similar to an abnormally large German pointer. The dog got a home-made dog biscuit for suffering through the indignity and I was relieved of the awful burden of thirty dollars.

"Have you picked out a name yet?" the woman asked.

"No."

She nodded at the pile of black matted fur. "How does Samson sound?"

WE JOGGED HOME. THE MAGIC WAVE CAUGHT US on the way and I gave silent thanks to whoever it was upstairs that we'd managed to get the poodle trimmed before the magic rendered the electric clippers completely useless.

I let the chain sag as an experiment, but the dog seemed content to stay by my side. In the parking lot, he proved that not only did he have a stomach of steel, but his bladder was also magically connected to one of the Great Lakes. We made a circle, as he enthusiastically marked his territory. The sleepless night was catching up with me. My head swam and my legs kept trying to fold, pitching me into a horizontal position. I'd put a lot of effort into the wards around Joshua's corpse and my body demanded a few hours of sleep.

The dog snarled.

I looked up. He stood with his feet planted wide, back humped, his body frozen stiff. Hackles rose on his spine. He stared left, where the parking lot narrowed between my apartment building and the crumbling wall of the ruins next door.

I pulled Slayer from the sheath on my back. The ruins had once been an apartment building as well. The magic had crushed it, chewing it down to rubble, and now crumbling brick walls served as purchase for ivy frosted with the cold. The greenery obscured my view.

The attack poodle bared his teeth, wrinkling his muzzle, and let loose a low, quiet growl.

I took a step toward the ruins. A figure dashed from behind the wall with preternatural speed, veered left, and jumped. It sailed through the air, clearing the six-foot-tall wall with a couple of feet to spare, and vanished from view.

Alrighty, then.

I jogged to the spot where the person had been hiding, comparing the memory to the wall. Whoever it was, he or she wasn't very tall, near five feet. Swaddled in some sort of drab garment. Not much to go on. Chasing the person through the ruins wasn't an option. I'd never catch up, not with that kind of speed.

Who would want to keep tabs on me? No way to know. I'd pissed off a lot of people. For all I knew, it could be one of the Steel Mary's flunkies. Assuming he had flunkies.

I headed back to my apartment, dog in tow. "If this person is following me, he or she will continue to do so. Sooner or later, I'll snag them," I told him. "If you're really good, I'll let you bite them first."

The attack poodle wagged his tail.

"What we need now is something to eat and a nice shower."

More adoring wagging. Well, at least one creature in this Universe thought my plans were genius.

I heard the phone ringing when I unlocked the door. Phones were funny things: sometimes magic took them out, and sometimes it didn't. When I desperately needed it, the damn thing failed, but when I didn't want to be bothered, it worked like a charm. I got inside and picked it up. "Kate Daniels."

"Kate!" The frantic note in the Clerk's voice knocked the sleep right out of me. "We've been hit!"

CHAPTER 5

————◆————

I DROPPED THE PHONE AND DASHED DOWN THE
stairs, slapping the door shut in the poodle's face. I cleared
six flights of stairs in seconds, sprinted across the parking
lot, unlocked my garage, got Marigold out, mounted, and we
thundered out of the parking lot.

We turned up the street, nearly plowing into a cart. Marigold thudded up the wooden ramp onto the highway. The
ruined city dashed by me, a long smudge of wrecked buildings and overcast sky.

The Mercenary Guild occupied a converted Sheraton
Hotel on the edge of Buckhead. I brought Marigold to a halt
before the thick iron gates, jumped down, grabbing a canteen
of kerosene I used to obliterate my blood, and took off, praying that whatever disease the magic hit man induced wouldn't
go active.

I dashed through the gates into the lobby and nearly col-
lided with the Clerk. A huge red welt marked his face and his
left eye was rapidly swelling shut. "Inner hall!" he yelled.

"Did you call Biohazard?"

"Yes!"

The inner door hung crooked on its hinges. I ran through the doorway and into the inner hall.

The Sheraton was built as a hollow tower. In its other life, the inner hall housed an on-the-premises restaurant, a coffee shop, and a happy hour area, raised on a platform above the main floor, and a gift shop. The old photographs showed a small stream winding through it all, flanked by carefully selected plants, its waters sheltering huge surly koi. At the far wall, an elevator shaft of transparent plastic rose up to the fourth floor.

The happy hour platform now held the job board, the gift shop contained one of the numerous armories, and the restaurant had been converted into a mess hall, where tired mercs filled their stomachs between jobs. The elevator no longer worked, the plants, stream, and koi had vanished years ago, and the main floor lay bare.

The first thing I saw was the body of Solomon Red, pinned to the elevator shaft by a spear through his throat.

Three mercs rapidly drew a chalk warding semicircle around the body. Another dozen hugged the walls. I grabbed the first warm body. "Where is he?"

"Gone," the merc woman told me. "About five minutes ago."

Damn. I was too late.

Solomon's body swelled, expanding.

"Back up!" I barked, in tune with two other voices.

The mercs scattered.

A flood of blood and feces drenched the clear plastic, gushing to the floor to form a wide puddle. The stench hit us. People gagged.

The body shriveled, drying up right before my eyes like some sort of mummy. I didn't need Patrice to diagnose that for me. I've seen that before. It had the same name in English, Spanish, and Russian—cholera. Only this one was on magic steroids.

The foul puddle turned black. A shiver ran along the surface. The liquid slithered, testing the chalk edge of the ward circle, and rolled right over it, heading right. I glanced in that direction and saw an old drain in the floor, a remnant of the koi brook. Cholera spread through water.

"It's going for the drain!" I sprinted before it, pouring kerosene across the tile. Behind me, Bob Carver struck a match, setting the fuel stream on fire.

The puddle reached the flame, recoiled, and rolled to the left.

Ivera, a tall, large woman, folded her hands together, let out a piercing screech, and jerked her hands apart, palms outward. Magic snapped. Twin jets of flame rolled from Ivera's hands and licked the puddle. It shrank back, to the half-moon of burning kerosene. I poured more, trying to corral it.

Ivera's arms shuddered. She gasped. The flame vanished and she stumbled back, her nose bleeding.

The puddle oozed out of the flaming trap.

I took a deep breath, bracing myself for the pain of a power word. I didn't know if a power word would stop it, but I was out of options.

A chant rose from behind the mercs, a low soft voice murmuring Chinese words in a practiced singsong melody. A long scaled ribbon slipped past the mercs—a snake. The snake tasted the air with her tongue and stopped, swaying slightly in tune with the chant. Ronnie Ma emerged into the open. His real name was Ma Rui Ning, but everyone called him Ronnie. Ancient, wizened, Ronnie was one of those rare and endangered mercs who'd managed to reach retirement. He'd done his twenty years and got his pension. His house was only a minute away and he spent most of his time hanging out in the Guild, sipping tea and nodding at the crowd with a small smile.

He circled the puddle, carrying several small sacks, the chant rolling from his lips.

The puddle made a beeline for the drain. Somehow Ronnie got there first, reached into his sack, and lowered something to the floor. A scorpion. The arachnid danced in place, curling its tail. The puddle shrank away.

Ronnie dropped the sack on the floor and moved on. A few more steps, and he reached into another sack, and deposited a large toad.

Flanked on three sides by animals, the puddle reversed its course and almost ran into the fourth creature, a long twisting millipede, just as Ronnie dropped her on the ground. A few more steps, and the old man emptied the last sack on the floor, revealing a large spider.

The creatures swayed in tandem with his voice. The puddle hovered in the center, caught. Ronnie took a small canister from his waist and walked up to the puddle. His fingers flickered, very fast, and he pulled a small yellow piece of paper from his sleeve. The paper fluttered onto the puddle, a small Chinese symbol written in red lying faceup. Ronnie uncorked the canister and poured its contents onto the paper in a vermillion stream.

A dark miasma surged up from the puddle and vanished, as if burned off. The nasty fluid lay placid.

Ronnie Ma smiled.

"IT'S AN ANCIENT CHINESE RITUAL," PATRICE SAID as two medtechs fumigated me with mugwort smoke while I stood behind the salt line drawn on the floor. "Five poisonous creatures to hold the disease at bay. We know it because it was part of the Fifth Moon Festival. The Festival fell over summer solstice and coincided with hot, humid weather and a spike in infections."

"What did he pour on the cholera?"

"If I had to take a guess, wine with cinnabar." Patrice glanced at Ronnie Ma, still smiling serenely as two techs unsuccessfully tried to get him to exhale at the diagnostic flower. "We've been looking forever for someone who knows how to perform it. Do you think he would come to work for me?"

"I'd say yes. Mr. Ma enjoys being useful. Can I go? I feel fine, no pain, no discomfort."

Patrice put her hand onto my forehead. Magic struck me. Circles swam in my eyes. My skin felt on fire. I sucked in a breath and shook my head, trying to clear it.

"Now you can go," Patrice told me.

"Was I infected?"

"No. Just a precautionary measure. Five poisonous creatures," she said, nodding at the five animals still sitting in their places. "They put all disease to sleep. But once away from them, it will wake up and I don't want to take chances."

Good to know.

I stepped over the chalk line. Around me a controlled chaos reigned as the Biohazard team swept the scene, examining two dozen mercs and taking samples of the puddle.

I leaned toward Patrice. "That puddle went straight for the drain. That implies intelligence or instinct. Either it knew the drain would lead to water or it sensed the moisture. How can a disease sense anything?"

Patrice shook her head. "I don't know. I'm not suggesting you're wrong. I just have no answers. I can tell you that it's instinct rather than intellect. The organisms that caused both diseases are simply too primitive to develop intelligence. There are limits even to magic. And in this case, my guess would be physics." She pointed to the floor. "It slopes toward the drain. The puddle may have simply tried to take the path of least resistance."

CHAPTER 6

———◆———

IT TOOK ME FIFTEEN MINUTES OF QUESTIONING TO ascertain that nobody in the hall had actually seen how the attack on Solomon started. Two men saw the Steel Mary enter. He kept his face hidden. In the hall full of street bravos, nobody paid him any mind. The man crossed the floor and took the stairs up to the fourth story, where Solomon Red made his quarters. The altercation ensued there; my present pool of witnesses became aware of it only when the stranger and Solomon stumbled out of his rooms into the hallway and took a dive over the railing into the inner hall. According to Bob Carver, the man landed on his feet, holding Solomon Red by his throat. That got everyone's attention in a hurry, given that Solomon Red was six feet two inches tall and weighed close to two hundred and forty pounds.

The fight itself was short and brutal.

"Did any of you wade into it?"

The four mercs at the table shook their heads, all except Ivera, who still had gauze up her nose. Bob Carver had twelve years in the Guild, Ivera and Ken both had seven, and Juke was coming up on her fifth. All four were trained, seasoned, tough, and worked well as a team. In the Guild they were known as the Four Horsemen. Most mercs were loners, occasionally working with a partner when they had no choice about it. The Horsemen worked the jobs that required more than two bodies and they were damn good at it.

"He's good," Bob said. "I stayed clear of him."

"He didn't do any fancy shit," Juke added, rubbing her hand through her spiked black hair. She was probably going for frightening, with black hair and smoky eyes, but her features were too sharp and delicate and she ended up looking like a pissed-off Goth Tinker Bell. "None of the spinning whirlwind or whip qiang stuff. He slammed Solomon against the elevator and stuck the spear into his throat. Wham, bam, thank you, ma'am. That was it for the fearless leader."

"It was a practiced thrust," Ivera added. "No hesitation, didn't aim, nothing."

"What happened after he added Solomon to his butterfly collection?"

"The magic hit," Ivera answered.

Did the Steel Mary sense the magic coming? That would be a hell of a trick. "And then?"

Bob looked to Ken. The tall, lean Hungarian was the group's magic expert. Ken had a habit of sitting very still, so quiet you forgot he was there. His motions were small, in direct contrast with his lanky body, and he rationed out words like they were made of gold. "Extraction."

"Could you explain that, please?"

Ken mulled it over, weighing the benefit to mankind against the terribly taxing effort of producing a few more words. "The man placed his hand over Solomon's mouth." He held his long fingers apart to show me. "He said a word and pulled his essence out of him."

What the hell did that mean? "Define essence."

Ken regarded me for a long minute. "The glow of his magic."

That made no sense. "Can you describe the glow?"

Ken halted, puzzled.

"It looked like a wad of bright red cotton candy," Juke supplied.

"Glowing with Solomon's magic. I felt it. Powerful." Ken nodded. "The man held his essence in his hand, and then he left."

"He just walked out of here?"

"Nobody was dumb enough to stop him," Juke said.

And that was the difference between the Guild and the Order in a nutshell. If the cloak-man walked into the Order's Chapter, every single knight would have to be dead before he came out.

"Her," Ivera said.

Bob looked at her. "Iv, it was a man."

She shook her head. "It was a woman."

Bob leaned forward. "I saw the hands. They were man-hands. The guy was six and a half feet tall."

"Nope, about six eight," Juke said.

"It was a woman," Ivera said.

I glanced at Juke. She raised her arms. "Don't look at me. I only saw him from the side. Looked like a man to me."

"Ken?"

The mage folded his long fingers in front of him, pondered them for a long moment, and met my gaze. "I don't know."

I rubbed my face. Eyewitness accounts were supposed to narrow the pool of suspects, not make it wider.

"Thanks," I said, snapping my notepad closed. I had taken to carrying it, because it was necessary. It made me feel stupid. I could duck in a room for half a second and tell you how many people were in it, which of them were a threat, and what weapons they carried. But when it came to interviewing witnesses, if I didn't write it down, it was gone in a couple of hours. Gene, a knight-inquisitor with the Order and a former Georgia Bureau of Investigations detective, whom I strove to emulate because he knew what he was doing and I didn't, could listen to a witness or a suspect once and recall what they said with perfect accuracy. But I had to write it down. It made me feel like I had a hole in my head.

It was time to wrap it up. "On behalf of the Order, I appreciate your cooperation and all that."

Juke gave me the evil eye. She was trying hard for an early version of me, but although Juke was good, by her age I had already dropped out of the Order's Academy. I'd eat Juke for breakfast, and she knew it, but kept at it anyway.

"So you're in the big leagues now. Investigating for the Order and all that. I feel like bowing or something."

I fixed her with my little deranged smile. "Bowing not necessary. Don't leave town."

Juke's eyes went wide. "Why? Are we under arrest and shit?"

I kept smiling. We stared at each other for a long moment and Juke glanced into her cup before tipping it down to her mouth. "Screw you!"

"Now come on, sugar, you know I don't swing that way."

"Whatever!"

Curran's alpha-staring habits must've rubbed off on me. Curran. Of all the people, why did I think of him? It's like I couldn't shrug him off.

"It comes," Ivera murmured.

Mark trotted through the crowd toward me, looking well put together in a navy business suit.

The Four Horsemen glowered in unison.

Mark had a last name, but nobody remembered it. When someone condescended to add some moniker to his first name, it was usually "corporate asshole" or "that bastard," and if the speaker was particularly displeased, "massa." At least he got to keep one name, unlike the Clerk.

Officially the Guild's secretary, Mark was more of an operations manager than an admin. Solomon Red had created the Guild and earned the lion's share of its profits, but it was Mark who solved day-to-day problems and the way he went about that didn't make him any friends. The universe created him with his "understanding" setting stuck permanently on zero. No emergency or tragedy, real or fabricated, made a dent in his armor as he raced to a better bottom line.

Part of it was his appearance, too. His skin was unstained by the sun and probably generously moisturized. His toned body marked him as a well-off man who paid attention to his appearance, rather than a fighter who used his body to make a living. His face was meticulously groomed. In a crowd of blue-collar thugs, he stood out like a prissy lily in a flower bed full of weeds, and he broadcasted "I'm better than you" loud and clear.

He came to an abrupt stop in front of me. "Kate, I need to talk to you."

"Is this regarding Solomon's death?"

He grimaced. "It's regarding its consequences."

"If it doesn't directly relate to the investigation, it will have to wait."

Bob narrowed his eyes. "Moving fast, are you, Mark? Wasting no time."

Mark ignored him. "Do I have to make an appointment?"

"Yes. Give the Order a call tomorrow and they'll make sure to coordinate something with you." I headed toward the stairs to examine Solomon's quarters.

Behind me, Bob said, "Tomorrow the front page of the *Atlanta Journal-Constitution* will be screaming all about how Solomon Red voided his bowels and then his mercs had to chase the puddle of his blood and shit across the floor. Shouldn't you get on that?"

"Mind your own business, and I'll mind mine," Mark said.

Solomon's death created a power vacuum. Something had to fill it and they were already drawing the battle lines. They could draw all they wanted. You couldn't pay me to get involved in it.

I walked up the stairs, past a desiccated Solomon. The Guild leader sagged on the spear shaft, reduced to a sack of dried-out skin over the skeletal frame. The man who'd built himself into a living legend had died with great indignity. The universe had a razor-sharp sense of humor.

The Biohazard team was filing out without Solomon. All of the disease had ended up in the puddle, which Biohazard took into custody. Solomon's corpse was now a mere inert shell. Mark must've convinced them to let the Guild have the body for burial.

I climbed up to the third floor and entered the internal stair leading to Solomon's quarters. A variety of weapons decorated the walls: bearded axes, slick Japanese blades, simple elegant European swords, modern tactical weapons . . . I came to an empty space between two bare iron hooks. Just large enough for a spear. My hope that the spear in Solomon's neck belonged to the Steel Mary just went up in flames.

He could have anything he wanted, but he chose the spear. Why a spear?

The stairs led me to a hallway bordered by a balcony. Four

floors below, in the main hallway, mercs mulled about, still shell-shocked. The front door of Solomon's quarters hung ajar, its left side splintered. The Steel Mary must have shattered the wood around the lock with a single kick.

I stepped inside. Barren walls greeted me. No paintings broke up the malachite green paint. The plain, almost crude furniture supported no knickknacks. No photographs on the mantel over the small fireplace. No magazines on the coffee table. No books. The place resembled a hotel room awaiting a guest, instead of lived-in quarters.

I stepped through to the left into the bedroom. A simple bed, a simple desk with a flurry of papers. Chair overturned on the floor. Solomon must've been sitting here when the Steel Mary broke in.

A tape recorder lay on the desk. I picked it up and pushed play.

"Seven lines down. Sign," Mark's voice said. "Count three pages. Page six. Count three lines from the bottom of the page. Sign."

What in the world . . . I rewound for a few seconds.

"It's just like the old contract," Mark said. "You should still have the tape of it in the box from last year. It's the one numbered thirty-four. The only thing we did was change the dates and two paragraphs involving the new city ordinances. The first is on page three. Count two paragraphs down. It now reads . . ."

Solomon Red couldn't read. And Mark had covered for him all these years. None of the mercs knew.

"Kate?" Mark's voice called.

What now?

I stepped out of the room and looked down. Mark stood on the floor below. Next to him waited two men. The first was muscular and dark. He didn't really need help in the menacing department, but he chose to amplify his badass status by wearing a long, sweeping black cloak edged with wolf fur. Hello, Jim.

The man next to him wore Pack sweats. For shapeshifters, sweats meant working clothes—they were easy to rip off before a fight. The man stood with the easy animal grace particular to the very strong. Even from this distance, his pose

telegraphed violence, tightly coiled and reigned in, but ready
to explode at the slightest provocation. The mercs sensed it
and gave him a wide berth, like scavengers recognizing a
predator in their midst.

The man looked up, tilting his head of short blond hair. His
face matched him—powerful and aggressive. A square jaw,
prominent cheekbones, nose with a misshapen bridge that had
been broken but never healed quite right. Gray eyes glanced
from under thick golden eyebrows and locked on me.

Curran.

CHAPTER 7

THE TRICK HERE WAS INDIFFERENCE, I DECIDED AS I took my sweet time coming down the stairs. Act cool. Detached.

Something potent and violent boiled inside me and I strained every nerve in my body to keep it on its chain. I could do this. I just had to stay cool. Zen. No punching in the face. Punching would not be Zen.

The stairs ended. I wished I knew the jackass who'd made the staircase so short. I'd throw him down the damn steps so he could count them with his head. I stepped onto the floor and walked over to the two shapeshifters, looking straight at Jim.

"Jim. What a lovely surprise." I smiled, aiming for cordial.

Mark winced and took off. I caught a glimpse of my smile in the wall mirror. Very little cordiality but lots of homicidal maniac. I dropped the smile before I caused an interagency incident.

Jim nodded at me.

Out of the corner of my eye I saw Curran's face. Like looking into a glacier.

"Please relay my greetings to the Beast Lord," I said. "I appreciate his willingness to alter his extremely busy schedule and make an appearance."

Curran showed no emotion. No gloating, no anger, nothing at all. Jim looked at me, looked at Curran, looked back at me again. "Kate says hi," he said finally.

"I'm ecstatic," Curran said.

My hand twitched to touch Slayer's hilt protruding over my shoulder.

Silence stretched.

"What can I do for you?" I asked finally.

Jim glanced at Curran again. The Beast Lord remained stoic.

You stood me up, you sonovabitch. If I made it through this in one piece, I'd need some sort of medal to commemorate it.

"The Pack would like to extend an offer of assistance to the Order in the matter of the Steel Mary," Jim said.

Knock me over with a feather. The Pack cooperated only when forced. The shapeshifters almost never volunteered. "Why?"

"Why is irrelevant," Curran said. "We're willing to put our considerable resources at the Order's disposal."

We stared at each other. Add some whistling and a rolling tumbleweed, and we'd be all set.

A green sheen rolled over Jim's eyes. Reacting to the tension.

A couple of mercs lingered some distance from us. A third one stopped. They were expecting a brawl and didn't want to miss it. We needed to get away from the audience.

I nodded at the small workout room, separated from the main floor by a wall of frosted glass. The hotel had used it for private dining. The mercs had emptied it, thrown some mats into a corner, and turned it into a makeshift dojo. "Let's go someplace more private."

We moved off the main floor. Curran stalked into the room as if he owned it, turned, and crossed his arms on his chest. Biceps bulged, stretching the sleeves of his sweatshirt. If there was any justice in the world, he should've gone bald, lost all his teeth, and developed a terrible skin rash. But no, the bastard looked good. In perfect health.

Just keep cool. That's all I had to do.

I shut the glass door and locked it.

"The Pack has a personal stake in the matter," Jim said.

"I see no basis for the Pack's involvement."

"Solomon Red was a closet shapeshifter," Jim said softly.

The world stood on its hands and kicked me in the face.

"The man was deeply religious. It was a difficult thing for him. He didn't shift but he had to live with the urge. The Pack gave him special permission to operate on his own in exchange for a cut of the Guild's profits. First Joshua, now Solomon. There is a pattern."

"How much of a cut?"

"Ten percent."

Ten percent of the Guild's take was a lot of money. Someone had killed two shapeshifters and just bit a large chunk out of the Pack's income.

Curran kept watching me and I couldn't shut him out enough to properly concentrate. "Who else knew about Solomon?"

"The Council."

Fourteen people, two alphas from each clan. "So either this was a coincidence, or you have a traitor among the alphas."

Jim's eyes flashed green. "There are no traitors on the Council."

I sighed. "Of course not—how dare the mighty shapeshifters have human vices."

Curran leaned half an inch forward. "We're not mercenaries, Kate. Don't measure us by your standard."

Thank you, Your Majesty. I looked at Jim. "The Order appreciates the offer of aid from the Pack, but given the sensitive nature of our investigation, we decline your assistance at this time."

Curran showed me the edge of his teeth. "Are you implying my people can't be circumspect?"

I looked at Jim. "Please relay my congratulations to His Majesty on learning such a big word all by himself."

If Jim had been in his feline form, his whiskers and his fur would've stood on end.

I kept going. "Also please explain to him that either he has a traitor in the ranks, which means that his people aren't circumspect, or Solomon's murder was a coincidence and the Pack has no reason to bully its way into the Order's investigation."

"Why aren't you talking to me?" Curran took a step from the mats.

"I'm following your orders to the letter. I was told to address all queries to your chief of security. But if you wish to speak to me directly, I'll be happy to oblige."

Curran's eyes narrowed. "When did I say that?"

"Don't be coy. It doesn't suit you." Stay cool, stay cool.

He shook his head. "It doesn't matter. You have a tiny bit of power and you used it. Run with it while you can. In the end, the Order will let us in. I'll go over your head."

Jim took a small step forward. His teeth were clenched and the muscles on his jaw stood out. I actually felt sorry for him.

Stay calm. Don't give him the satisfaction of seeing you lose it. I unclenched my teeth. "Right now you have nothing to justify your involvement. If I accept your offer of cooperation, I'll have to clear it with Ted, who'll block it, because he distrusts you on principle. It's in your best interests to wait, until you can give me irrefutable proof that the Pack is being targeted, forcing Ted into a corner. If you want direct access to the knight-protector, you're, of course, welcome to it. But please keep in mind that expecting understanding from Ted Moynohan is like waiting for wine from a stone. I, on other hand, am sympathetic to the Pack's needs as a whole, no matter how much I might dislike interacting with you personally." Because of Jim, and Derek, and Raphael, and Andrea, who wasn't yet part of the Pack but who might end up there one day.

"So now you dislike me? Ironic, considering you pulled the plug on us."

"I pulled the plug? You stood me up, you arrogant asshole!"

"You ran away!" He moved toward me. "I deserve an explanation."

Slayer left its sheath almost on its own. It was the fastest draw of my life. One moment empty space lay between us and the next my saber jumped into my hand. "You deserve nothing."

Gold rolled over Curran's eyes, so briefly that had I blinked, I would've missed it. His face gained a slightly bored expression. "Do you honestly think your toothpick can hurt me?"

"Let's find out."

"Let's not." Jim stepped between us.

Curran looked at him. His voice rasped with the beginning of a snarl. "What are you doing?"

"My job."

He had lost his mind. Curran was hovering on the verge of violence and Jim had just made himself into a target. "Jim, you want to step back."

Jim remained rooted to the floor.

Curran's gaze fastened on me, the gold burning scalding hot. Like looking into the eyes of a hungry lion and realizing I was food. My body locked, tiny hairs on the back of my neck rose on their ends, and inside me a tiny voice whispered in desperation, "Don't breathe and he might forget you're there."

I flicked my saber, warming up my wrist. "Your headlights don't scare me."

Jim squared his shoulders. "You can't do this. Not here and not now."

Curran's voice slid into icy calm. "Be very careful, or I might start thinking you're telling me what to do."

If Curran ordered him to move, and Jim refused, it would be a challenge. Curran would have to fight his own chief of security and his best friend. They both knew it. That was why I was on the receiving end of Curran's alpha stare. If he leveled it at Jim, there would be a fight.

I sidestepped. Jim moved with me. I stared at the ceiling and growled.

"Cute," Curran said.

Die. "Why don't you come over here and I'll show you cute."

"I'd love to, but he's in the way. Besides, you had your chance to show me anything you wanted to. You'd just run away again."

For the love of God. "I didn't run away. I made you your damn dinner, but you didn't have the decency to show."

Jim's eyebrows crept up. "Dinner?"

Curran's eyes blazed. "You took off. I smelled you. You were there and then you got cold feet and ran. If you didn't want to do this, all you had to do was pick up the phone and tell me not to show up. Did you actually think I'd make you serve me dinner naked? But you didn't even bother."

"Bullshit!"

"Hey!" Jim barked.

"What?" Curran and I said at almost the same time.

Jim looked at me. "Did you make him dinner?"

He'd find out sooner or later. "Yes."

Jim turned on his foot, went out of the room, and shut the door behind him.

Alrighty, then.

"He thinks we're mated." Curran moved forward, too light on his feet for a man of his size, his gaze locked on me—a predator stalking its prey. "In the Pack, one doesn't stand between mates. He's being polite. He doesn't realize you broke it off."

"Oh no. No, I didn't break it off. You had your chance and you blew it."

Curran's mask cracked. "The hell I did."

All of the pain and anger of the past month smashed into me. Having him near was like ripping the dressing off a raw wound. Words just came tumbling out and I couldn't stop them.

"So it's my fault? I made you your bloody dinner. You didn't show up. Just couldn't pass up a chance to humiliate me, could you?"

Curran bit the air as if he had fangs. "I was challenged by two bears. They broke two of my ribs and dislocated my hip. When Doolittle finally finished setting my bones, I was four hours late. I asked if you called and they said no."

He'd sunk enough gravity into that "no" to bring down a building.

"If you were late, I would've turned the town inside out looking for you. I called you. You didn't answer. I was so sure something happened to you I dropped everything and dragged myself to your house. I came to check on you with broken bones and you weren't there."

"You're lying."

Curran snarled. "I left a note on your door."

"More lies. I waited for you for three hours. I called the Keep, thinking that something happened to you, and your flunkies told me that the Beast Lord said he was too busy to speak to me." I was shaking with rage. "That in the future I should address all my concerns to Jim, because His Majesty declared that he didn't want to be bothered with talking to the likes of me anymore."

"That phone call happened in your head. You're delusional."

"You stood me up and then rubbed my nose in it."

Something hissed behind the frosted glass in the main hall.

Curran lunged toward me. I should've thrust straight through him. Instead I just stood there, like an idiot. He clamped me to him, spinning us so his back faced the glass.

The glass wall exploded.

Shards pelted the dining room behind us, breaking against Curran's back. A black and gold jaguar crashed against the opposite wall. Twin jets of water burst into the room from the main floor. The first thudded into the wall, pinning Jim. The second smashed against Curran's spine. He grunted and clenched me to him.

We were caught out in the open. No place to hide. Oh, the stupid, stupid idiot. He was shielding me.

Jim snarled, trying to get to his feet, but the water slapped him down and kept him there.

Gold flooded Curran's eyes. His big body shook.

I jerked left, trying to see past Curran's shoulder. A man stood in the middle of the main hall, his hands raised. Behind him a broken pipe jutted from the wall, spilling water under his feet. Two pressurized jets shot from the water, following the direction of his arms. A water mage. Shit.

I pressed closer to Curran to speak into his ear. "One-man fire brigade, dead center of the room. He's broken the main pipe and is emptying the Guild's water tower into the lobby. Let me go."

"No." Curran gripped me tighter. "Too risky."

"He's sanding the skin off your back."

"I'll heal, you won't."

Until he let go of me, he couldn't maneuver. If he did, the mage would cut me down.

The jet that pinned us was only a foot wide. I pulled out a throwing knife. Slayer was too long for close-up fighting. "Throw me."

Golden eyes looked into mine.

"Throw me at him."

He grinned, showing me his teeth. "Over or under?"

"Under."

"Say please."

Red spray hit my lips. Magic nipped at me—I tasted shapeshifter blood. The water was scraping the skin off his back, but he didn't give an inch.

When this was over, I would rip his head off. "Throw me, *please*!"

"I thought you'd never ask."

He spun, twisting, and hurled me like a bowling ball. I slid across wet floor and broken glass, the twin water jets shooting above my head, right at the mage standing in a ten-inch whirlpool. Water drenched my face. The mage's bare feet loomed before me. I grabbed his left ankle. The momentum jerked me behind him, and I sliced across the Achilles tendon of his right leg.

The mage dropped to his right knee, his back to me, his filthy cloak pooling about him. I knocked his left leg out from under him and sank a throwing knife deep between his ribs. He twisted to me. I saw the fist coming, but could do nothing to avoid it. The blow smashed into my jaw like the strike of a sledgehammer. I slid across the wet floor, through the whirlpool, and rolled to my feet on instinct. The world shuddered and swam sideways in a haze of pain. I stumbled back, shaking my head. Things snapped into focus.

The mage grinned at me from twelve feet away. Pale hair framed a narrow face. Mid-twenties, maybe a bit younger. His tattered cloak hung open, revealing a martial artist's body: hard, crisply defined, and completely nude. Too short. Five ten at most. I had a guy in a cloak, he was naked, and he wasn't the Steel Mary. Only I could be this lucky.

The jets behind the water mage kept spraying, changing direction. He was still tracking Curran and Jim. How the hell did he do that?

Water swirled around his feet, surging up. A needle-thin jet hit me, burning my left thigh. A narrow cut sliced through my jeans and skin, like a slash from a scalpel. Another jet singed my ribs. He was playing with me. If he hit me straight on with one of those, the water would punch right through me. As long as he didn't hit heart or eyes, I would survive. Everything else medmagic could fix.

The mage pulled my knife out of his side and looked at it. "Nice knife."

The voice was deep but female.

I threw my second knife. The blade bit into the mage's chest. Shit. Missed the neck. "Here, have another one."

The mage laughed. Definitely a female voice. The only way he could sound like a woman would be if he . . .

A demonic shape leapt above the man: a seven-and-a-half-foot tall muscled monster, sheathed in gray fur, half-human, half-beast, all nightmare. He came sailing above the water as if he had wings, huge arms opened wide, eyes burning with gold on a terrible face.

God damn it. "No!"

The mage spun about. Water shot from him in dozens of sharp narrow jets. Curran backhanded him. Bones crunched. The mage's head spun on his shoulders, turning completely around: hair, face, hair again.

The mage's body froze, rigid. He toppled back like a log, crashing on the wet floor with a splash. The whirlpool fell apart.

Broken neck, severed spinal column, instant death. There goes my chance at a chat. I swore. "Did you have to kill him?"

Gray eyes stared back at me. Prehistoric jaws opened, revealing enormous teeth. "Yes, I did." The words came out perfectly. Curran's control over his warrior form was absolute. "You're welcome."

You're welcome, my ass. I pulled Slayer from the back sheath and strode to the corpse. Why the hell was I so relieved that Curran was mostly unhurt? I wanted to strangle him, not celebrate the fact that he was in one piece. "Thank you for killing my suspect before I could talk to him."

"Don't mention it."

Jim trotted over and sniffed the mage's body.

I reached them and crouched by the corpse. Jim decided it was a good moment to shake. Wet spray hit me in the face.

"Thanks. That's just a cherry on my day." I wiped wet jaguar out of my eyes and stabbed Slayer into the mage's stomach.

"He's dead already," Curran told me.

"The Casino was attacked this morning." I leaned closer, watching the skin around Slayer's blade. "Two elemental mages fried some vampires and enhanced the Casino's walls with a lovely burn pattern."

Curran shrugged his monstrous shoulders. "Stupid, but not remarkable."

"They registered magenta on an m-scanner."

Jim snarled.

Curran wrinkled his muzzle. "Undead mages?"

It was my turn to shrug. "We'll see in a minute. Fire, air, water are all part of the same brand of magic."

The mage had spoken in a female voice. The room was noisy with the sounds of running water, but I had heard a woman laugh. The body before me was unmistakably male. The only way he could speak like a woman would be if he was undead, and a female navigator was riding his mind. But I'd never heard of any other types of undead being piloted. Vampires, yes. But nothing else.

Well, no, wait, I'd seen undead mermaids being piloted, too, but they weren't undead in the traditional sense of the word.

I leaned closer to examine the wound. My saber liquefied undead flesh and consumed it, building thickness onto the blade. If this was a vampire, the wound would've sagged by now.

A thin streak of white smoke curled from the blade. It could be something, or it could be just Slayer reacting to me being pissed off out of my mind.

"Clerk?" I yelled.

"Hey!" The Clerk's head appeared above the third-story balcony rail. A moment later more heads joined it. That's the Guild for you. Would it have killed one of them to shoot the damn bastard with a bow? I didn't say it out loud. They would've laughed. People inclined to help others ended up in PAD or the Order. These guys were exactly where they wanted to be. Unless money or their hide was involved, they didn't give a damn. They weren't getting paid, so why bother?

"You all okay up there?"

"We're fine," Juke called back. "Touched you care."

Slayer hissed. I tapped the saber with the tip of my index finger. It careened to the side. The edges of the wound drooped, as if the man's flesh were heated wax. I pinched the muscle near the wound and watched a telltale burgundy fluid seep from the cut.

Curran inhaled next to me, sampling the scent. A grimace troubled his nightmarish face. "Undead."

"Yep."

Just like the two undead mages who had attacked the Casino with elemental magic. It would be a miracle if they weren't connected.

There were things I could do with an undead body that I couldn't do with any other corpse. I had to hurry. I'd need magic and herbs for this. The herbs waited in my apartment and there was no telling how long the magic wave would last.

I looked up at the Clerk. "What happened?"

"He came in through the front," the Clerk shouted. "I saw he was naked and cleared out. He busted the pipe and went after you."

Except it wasn't me he was after. True, the People hired me to investigate the attack, but I hadn't had a chance to do anything warranting this sort of retaliation. No, he went right after Curran. He and Jim were the primary targets. I was a bystander.

"Get the firebugs to torch the floor and call PAD."

"Who'll pay for the torching?" Mark called out.

"The Guild will, Mark, unless you'd like us to keep walking around in undead blood."

If Mark had any other objections, he decided to keep them to himself. There were at least a few pyro-talented mercs, and once they were done with the floor, all traces of the undeath and of my blood would be gone.

I raised Slayer and sliced across the corpse's neck. It only took one cut—Curran had broken his neck and tore the muscle, leaving only skin for me to sever. I grasped the head by the hair and got up to my feet.

"The Order accepts the offer of aid from the Pack," I said quietly. We had an audience and this wasn't something I wanted them to hear. I was about to force Curran into a corner, and while he might come to terms with it in private, in public he would immediately refuse. "With the understanding that the Order is in the position of authority and our agreement can be terminated at will. This is mine." I showed the head to Curran. "The rest is yours. We compare results later."

"Changed your mind?" Gold rolled over Curran's eyes, but he kept his voice low. To the peanut gallery above, we appeared to be having a pleasant conversation.

"I can now take this to Ted. It's hard to refute eyewitnesses. If I fight hard enough, he'll let it stand. Let Jim know what Doolittle finds out about the body."

"I'll call you."

"Jim's better."

Curran leaned to me. Bones crawled under his skin. His jaws shrank, his muzzle shortened, his claws receded. Gray fur flowed, melting into human skin. In a blink, he stood nude in front of me. A month ago I would've needed a moment to cope. Today I just looked straight at his face.

"I'll call you," he repeated.

"If you call me, I won't pick up the phone."

"You will wait by the phone for my call, and when it rings, you will pick it up and you will speak to me in a civil manner. If you don't know how, ask someone."

That did it. I pivoted to him. My voice came out quiet and cold. "Do you need me to draw you a chart? You stood me up. You made me think there was something between us. You made me want things, things I thought I could never have, and then you crushed it. Don't come near me, Curran. Don't call. We're done."

I turned and walked away, heading to the Guild changing room, where I still kept clothes in a locker. I had to strip off my soggy rags, seal my cuts, and drag the head home. I needed to ask it some questions.

CHAPTER 8

———◆———

THE WEATHER DECIDED IT WASN'T UGLY ENOUGH. Usually our winters ran to rainy and dreary. Once in a while it would snow, but mostly it wouldn't stick. For some reason, for the last few years winter in Atlanta had decided to play Russian roulette: three times out of four we'd get the usual sludge, but about a quarter of the time it hit hard with snow and deep freeze. Some said it was because of magic; some said it was the side effect of global warming. Whatever caused it, I didn't like it. By the time I arrived at my apartment, every inch of me was frozen.

I dragged myself up the stairs and reached for the door. The ward spell licked my skin and drained down in a wave of blue, letting me in. I opened the door and saw a huge slimy pile of dog puke cooling in the middle of my hallway carpet. The attack poodle sat nearby, an expression of perfect innocence on his narrow mug.

I pointed at the puke. "That was a dick move."

The attack poodle wagged his tail.

I stepped over the vomit and headed to the kitchen. The magic still held but the wave could end at any moment. If the magic fell, I could as well play soccer with the head for all the good it would do me.

I pulled out a large silver platter from the cabinet, set it in the middle of the table, and collected the herbs. I'd premixed most of them, but some things had to be combined on the spot or their effect would have worn off with time.

Seeing Curran again hurt. The rock in my chest just got heavier and heavier. A bastard and a liar.

I came to you with broken bones . . .

In ten minutes I spread the herb mixture on the platter, retrieved the head, and set it onto the aromatic mix, stump down. Necromantic magic came naturally to me. It repulsed me, but still I gravitated toward it, as if it were an itch I had to scratch. My revulsion might have been nature, but most of it was nurture. Voron did his best to suppress this part of me, since I was a baby. Strange that I found myself needing to shrug off his training more and more often.

I slid a shallow baking pan under the platter and poured an inch of glycerin into it. The attack poodle watched me with a very focused expression. "Watch out," I told him. "It's about to get ugly."

I nicked my thumb with the point of a throwing knife and let a drop of my blood fall onto the herbs. Magic surged through the dried grasses, like fire along a detonation cord, and exploded into the head. The undead flesh shivered, revived by the burst of power. I touched my thumb to the undead forehead, driving a spike of magic into the brain. "Wake."

The head's eyes snapped open, focusing on me. Its mouth gaped, contorting. Foul magic flared about it in a swirling storm of malice, furious and hungry.

The poodle bolted like the road runner from an ancient cartoon. I waited for a second to see if the carpet would catch on fire in his wake. Fortunately, no ACME fire extinguishing equipment needed to be used.

I leaned to the head. "Show me your master."

The words weren't necessary. The old Arabic woman who taught me the ritual when I was eleven said they helped one concentrate, so I said them all the same.

The magic convulsed. A foul stench rose from the herbs.

The head shuddered. Thick burgundy blood slid from the tear ducts, dripping down the cheeks into the herbs, then into the pan, spreading on the glycerin in a thick dark stain.

"Show me your master."

The stain swirled. Faint glimpses of a face appeared in its depths.

"Show me!"

The magic raged and boiled. The image flared, fuzzy but clear enough to recognize. My own face stared back at me from the stain.

What in the world . . .

I scrutinized the ghostly image. It was distorted, but I saw the matching skin tone, long dark hair, and dark eyes. Me.

I let go. The magic collapsed on itself.

I leaned my elbow on the table, rested my chin on my fist, and looked at the head. I'd done the ritual six times in my life. Always with vampires. It never failed.

Why did it show me?

The head stared at me with unseeing eyes. The surge of magic during the ritual cooked the *Vampirus immortuus* pathogen, and once it vanished, the vampire heads decomposed in minutes. This one looked no worse for wear. I needed someone with more expertise. I got up and tried the phone. No dial tone. Argh.

Enthusiastic barking echoed from under my bed. A moment later someone knocked.

"Who is it?"

"Kate?" Andrea's voice called. "You're home?"

"Nope." I opened the door.

Andrea grinned at me while tapping a manila envelope against her palm. "I suppose I walked into that. What is that stench?"

"Something I have in the kitchen." I stepped aside, motioning her in. "Don't land in the dog vomit." Which I now had no excuse not to clean up.

She stepped over the attack poodle's offering to the digestive gods and saw the head and the herbs sitting on the platter in the kitchen. Her face stretched. "That's just not right. What is that stuff it's lying on?"

"Herbs. Rosemary, coriander—"

Andrea's blue eyes went wide as saucers. "If you're going to cook it, I'll barf next to the dog."

"Why would I cook it?"

"Well, it's lying like a turkey on a roaster and you have herbs under it."

I marched into the kitchen, grabbed the head, and stuffed it back into the plastic bag. The bag went into the fridge, the rest went into the garbage. "Better?"

"Yes."

I went to clean up puke, while she set the water for tea on the kerosene stove. Magic robbed us of electricity, but kerosene still burned and I kept a camper burner in my apartment for small jobs. It once saved my life and Julie's.

As soon as the offending evidence of his disgrace had been removed, the attack poodle deemed the area safe. He emerged from under the bed and licked Andrea's hand.

"He looks good with his hair off," she said.

"He thinks so."

The poodle licked her hand again. Andrea smiled. "You don't mind my scent, do you, dogface? Maybe he was raised around shapeshifters."

"You're not a regular shapeshifter."

She shrugged. "I still smell like my father."

Given that Andrea's father was a hyena, the poodle was showing remarkable restraint.

We went into the kitchen, where I poured us some tea. "Before we do anything else, let me tell you about my guy in a cloak."

Fifteen minutes later she frowned at me. "So male shapeshifters go berserk."

I nodded.

"What about the female shapeshifters?"

"I don't know."

She tapped the edge of the table with the envelope. "So there is a good chance that the other me will make an appearance. Clearly my life hasn't been complicated enough."

"My sentiments exactly."

Don't let Ted put you on this, if I fail. Her eyes told me that if I said that, she'd suggest I stick my opinion where the sun didn't shine.

Andrea suppressed the part of her that was beastkin. She'd made it through the Academy, earned knighthood, served with distinction for five years. She carried a handful of medals and the Iron Gauntlet, the fourth highest decoration the Order could award to its knights. A year ago she was well on her way to take the step up from knight-defender to master-at-arms, firearm. To earn the designation of a master in a weapon or magic use was a great achievement.

All of it came crashing down one night when Andrea and another knight had gone out to check the report of a loup sighting. The trip left several loups dead, including Andrea's partner, who caught Lyc-V and tried to turn Andrea's stomach into an "all you can eat" buffet. Standard procedure after an encounter with loups mandated comprehensive tests to confirm your humanity. Andrea passed the m-scan and tests. She did it by means of an amulet embedded in her skull and a silver ring under the skin of her shoulder, which had almost cost her her arm. She was pronounced free of the shapeshifter virus and fit for active duty, and then her Chapter shipped her off to Atlanta to ease the trauma.

In Atlanta, she ran into a brick wall called Ted Moynohan. Ted knew there was something wrong with her. He felt it in his gut but he lacked proof, so he assigned her to "support." She had no office, no active cases, and the only time she saw action was when nobody else could get there in time.

Despite it all, she was determined to serve. Pointing out that if the Steel Mary showed up, she should abandon her knighthood and run the other way would only get my head bitten off. So I clamped my mouth shut and said nothing.

I kept her secret and she kept mine. Only two people besides me knew my ancestry and Andrea was one of them. If I had a choice, I would've kept it from her, but she had figured it out on her own.

"Thank you for the warning." Andrea handed me the manila envelope. "My turn."

Unsealing the tape took a moment, and then a stack of papers slid into my hand. A photograph occupied half of the first sheet. It showed a tall, powerfully built man, standing next to a roan horse, one hand on the mane.

He had handsome, very masculine features, roughly cut,

with a heavy jaw and slightly dimpled chin. His nose was broad and straight; his mouth wide; his long hair almost blue black. His was an attractive face, honest and strong, the kind that would inspire confidence and convince you to follow him into the breach. The few times I'd seen him, he wore a pleasant, affable expression that made him appear approachable.

He must've sensed the photographer and turned toward him just as the shot was taken, because the camera caught him with his mask down. He stared directly into the lens. His eyes, shockingly blue under the straight slashes of black eyebrows, radiated arrogant power. It was a look that snarled a warning. The glare of a predator whose rest had been disturbed. Indignant, he demanded to know who dared and he looked as if he was committing your face to memory, so if you met again by chance, he would remember to kill you.

I sat into my chair. The blue eyes stared at me.

Hugh d'Ambray. Preceptor of the Order of the Iron Dogs, head of Roland's personal guard. Warlord of Roland's armies. My stepfather's greatest pupil.

The paper bore a copy of the Order's classified stamp—a mace crossed with the polearm on a shield. These papers were well above Andrea's clearance, let alone mine. I leafed through the rest of the sheets. They were filled with facts of Hugh's life. A condensed summary of everything the Order knew about Roland's Warlord. "How did you get this?"

Andrea gave me a smug smile.

If Ted found out she'd accessed the Order's database to get this information, he would boil her alive. "You shouldn't have done this on my account."

She crossed her arms. "Oh, thank you, Andrea! You're the best! What would I do without you? I know how much you worked to obtain these papers, vital to my survival."

"You're already on Ted's shit list. If he gets a whiff of this—"

"He won't," she said. "I was very careful. The administrators at the Midnight Games kept very detailed records. The name of every patron was recorded. I was doing my write-up and came across Hugh. Hugh's name was mentioned very frequently during my advanced security briefing. Things made total sense: the rakshasas had to have gotten Roland's sword from somewhere, and who better to give it to them than Roland's Warlord, Hugh? I put two and two together and started digging and I took the long way around, which is why it took me so long to get this stuff. Did you know who Hugh was before we went into that pit?"

The sandy arena of the Midnight Games flashed before me. Hugh had been in the audience during the final fight. "Yes. I knew."

"You shattered an unbreakable sword made of Roland's blood. Hugh is Roland's Warlord. He isn't just going to let it go, Kate."

"I realize that." I drank my tea. "I didn't have a choice."

"Of course you did. You could've taken off before the fight started. You didn't have to try to kill yourself to break the sword."

"I wasn't planning on killing myself," I growled.

Andrea waved at me. "Details. The point is, you sacrificed yourself to save us. For me, that's twice."

"You were in the pit, because of me. I asked you to come." And dragged around a load of guilt because of it.

Andrea shook her head. "I came, because for the Pack to survive, the rakshasas had to be killed and I'm good at killing. I may not be just like the rest of the shapeshifters, and some of them may despise me, but I still grow big teeth and go furry. I came for our common good. But you don't sprout fur, Kate. You came because you wanted to help your friends. You're my friend and now I'm going to help you. And I will keep helping you. You have no choice about it."

I hit her with the best version of a hard stare I could manage. "Stay out of this. I don't need your help."

She snorted. "Well, too bad. You don't always get to pick what your friends do for you."

I put my tea down and rubbed my face. In Savannah, Voron was rolling in his grave. What was I supposed to do with her?

Kill her, Voron's voice said from the depths of my memory. *Kill her now before she exposes you.*

I crushed the thought and threw away the pieces.

"If I were Hugh, I would be waiting for an opportunity to

subdue you and take you someplace where you can be quietly questioned," Andrea said.

"No. He won't do that. He'll gather as much information as he can about me and then, when he's confident he knows what he has, he'll approach me. Kidnapping isn't his style."

"How can you be sure?"

I got up, shutting down Voron's ghostly voice barking warnings at me, went into the spare bedroom Greg had turned into a library and storage room, and brought out an old photo album and a leather-bound notebook. If I could convince her to keep her distance, it would be worth it. "I can be sure, because I know how Hugh thinks."

I put the album on the table, opened to the right page, got a knife, and carefully split the invisible seam holding the two pages together. Two thin pages slid into the light. I handed Andrea the first one with a picture on it.

She stared at it. Her eyebrows crept together. "Is that Hugh d'Ambray as a teenager?"

I nodded.

She studied the photo. "Well, he grew up into a handsome bastard. Who's that next to him?"

"Voron."

"Voron the Raven? Roland's ex-Warlord?" Andrea's eyes widened. "I thought he died."

"He did, eventually." I looked at her. "He raised me. He was my stepfather."

"Holy shit!" She blinked at me. "Well, that explains all the . . ." She waved her teaspoon around in a wild fashion, as if trying to shake stuff off it.

I raised my eyebrow. "All the what?"

"Swordplay."

I slid the second picture to her. On it, Voron stood with his arm around a petite blond woman next to Greg and Anna, my guardian's ex-wife.

"Your mother?" Andrea pointed at the blond woman.

"This is the only picture I have of her. I found it among Greg's things after his death. Roland loved my mother very much. You'd think after six millennia he'd lose all capacity for human emotion, but from what Voron said, Roland's just as volatile as the rest of us. He fell in love with my mother. He wanted to make her happy, and she wanted a child, so despite swearing off siring any more monstrosities, he decided to try one more time."

"What does he have against kids?" Andrea gently turned the photograph of my mother to the light.

"We all turn out like him." My laugh dripped with bitterness. "Stubborn and violent. Picture a brood of people just like me, loaded with unimaginable power and a willingness to use it."

Andrea's face turned a shade paler.

"Sooner or later we all go to war with him," I said. "And he has to kill us or we'll tear the world apart. Some of the worst wars this planet has seen were started by my family. Roland gave up on his progeny. We're too much trouble. That's why, even though he made an exception in my mother's case, he changed his mind before I was even born. She realized which way the wind was blowing and ran away with Voron. Very few people know about this and none of them are dumb enough to risk Roland's attention by opening their mouths."

Andrea looked at my mother. "She was beautiful."

"Thank you."

"Do you think she loved Voron?"

"I don't know. I don't remember her. I used to hope I'd recall some details—a scent, a sound, anything—but no. I have nothing. No memories of her, no recollections of them being together. I think she must've cared for him, because the two of them had some time on the run, before Roland caught up with them, and it must've been bliss because when Voron spoke of it, everything about him changed. His voice, his face, the look in his eyes. It's like he became a different person when he remembered her. He didn't talk about her often."

Maybe I was getting through to her.

"You have no idea how cool this is," Andrea said. "It's like having tea with Wyatt Earp and listening to him tell you about Dodge City and Doc. This stuff is legend."

Nope, not even a little bit. "My mother let Roland find her to buy Voron time to escape with me. I don't know what happened between my parents, but my mother stuck a dagger into Roland's eye and he killed her. He murdered the only person he loved just so he could wring my neck. Killing me was more important. Eventually Roland will find me. This won't be one of those 'cry tears of joy' moments. He will kill me, Andrea. He'll rip the entire city down just so he can lock his hands on my throat and watch the light fade in my eyes. He'll destroy all my friends, he'll obliterate my allies, and he'll kill anyone who dares to show a shred of kindness to me. Hell, he'll probably salt the ground, so nothing would ever grow here. I'm not joking. This isn't an exaggeration. It may be the stuff of legends, but these legends come to life in a really painful way."

She gave me her own version of a hard stare. The funny blonde vanished and in her place sat a knight of the Order: hard, dangerous, and controlled. "That's why you need me. You can't do it alone."

"Did you hear a word of what I said?"

"I heard you loud and clear. You don't get to make my choices for me, Kate. Last time I checked, I was still in charge of my life."

Fuck me. I raised my hands. "I give up."

"Good," she said. "Does this mean we can go back to Hugh?"

I sighed. "Fine. Tie your own noose."

"What do you know about him?" Andrea pulled Hugh's file toward her.

I passed her the notebook. "Everything there is to know up until the last twenty years. He was found by Voron when he was six. Roland saw potential in him. Voron was a genius swordsman, one in a million, and he was a decent commander, but Roland wanted a true Warlord."

I tapped a piece of paper. "My father put me through a variety of trials. I fought in gladiator rings, I survived in the wilderness, I received training in a dozen martial arts. He did the same thing with Hugh. In a way, Hugh was a practice run for me."

I refilled my cup.

"Voron trained me to be a lone wolf. I'm a self-reliant killer. I'm designed to cut through the ranks and kill my target. Hugh was groomed to lead armies. He fought in dozens of regiments in hundreds of conflicts, all across the world. Roland's magic keeps him young. It makes him stronger than an ordinary human and harder to kill. Hugh is the ultimate warrior-general. He's patient, cunning, and ruthless."

"If you're trying to scare me, it's not working," Andrea said.

"I'm trying to explain to you the kind of enemy Hugh is. Hugh won't permit himself to be embarrassed. He'll gather as much information as he can, so when he presents my existence to Roland, he'll have a wall of facts to back it up. He won't move until he has absolute proof of my ancestry. I'm guessing that right now he's making circles around me, piecing my life together. He has patience and time. He can't be bought off, intimidated, or convinced to let me alone. And I'm not sure I'm strong enough to kill him."

Andrea's face turned sour. "You don't want to kill him. If you do that, Roland will flood the area with his people trying to figure out who nuked his Warlord."

"Exactly." I drank my now lukewarm tea. "My only option is to lay low and try not to draw any attention to myself. Voron has been dead for over a decade. Not that many people remember him. My track record is mediocre—I worked very hard to keep it that way. I shouldn't be viewed as anything out of the ordinary."

"That's nice, but there is the matter of the sword," Andrea said.

"Yeah." There was the shattered sword. No matter what I told myself, I couldn't dodge that bullet. There was a price for everything. The price for keeping my friends alive was being found and I paid it. At the time, I was sure I would die and risking discovery didn't seem like a big deal.

"If the shit hits the fan, I can always disappear," I said.

"What about Curran?" Andrea asked.

"What about him?"

"Fifteen hundred shapeshifters in a freaking castle will make anyone think twice about breaking in. Could you go to Curran? You guys are—"

"There is no me and Curran." Saying it hurt. No bag to punch to relieve it. I smiled instead and poured us another cup of tea.

Andrea stirred hers with a spoon. "Did something happen?"

I told her everything, including what happened in the Guild. The more I talked, the more pained her face became.

"That was very asshole of him," she said when I was done.

"No argument there."

"But it doesn't make sense. When he brought you back from the rakshasas, he almost killed Doolittle because he couldn't fix you fast enough. I think he might actually be in love with you. Maybe he did come to your house looking for you."

"It doesn't matter."

"You guys should talk."

"I'm done talking."

"Kate, don't take this the wrong way, but you haven't been yourself since you came back from leave. You're . . ."

I gave her my look of doom. It bounced right off her.

". . . grim. Really grim. It's almost painful. You don't joke, you don't laugh, and you keep taking chances." Andrea rubbed the rim of her teacup. "Did you have friends when you were growing up?"

"Ouch." I rubbed my neck. "That's a sharp change in the direction of this conversation. I think I got whiplash."

Andrea leaned forward. "Friends, Kate. Did you have any?"

"Friends make you weak," I told her.

"So I'm your first real friendship?"

"You could say that." Jim was a friend too, but it wasn't the same.

"And Curran's your first real love?"

I rolled my eyes.

"You don't know how to cope," Andrea said softly.

"I've been doing well so far. It's bound to go away eventually."

Andrea chewed on her lip. "You know that I'm a big girl and I can take care of myself, and I don't need a man to fight my wars for me. And if I wasn't with Raphael, I would still be totally fine, and good at my job, and happy at times." She took a deep breath. "With that in mind . . . A real broken heart never goes away. You can pull yourself together and you can function, but it's not the same."

I couldn't drag this hurt around me for the rest of my life. I'd implode. "Thanks for the pep talk."

"I'm not finished. The thing is, people have a remarkable potential to injure you, but they also have a great power to help you heal. I didn't understand this for the longest time."

She leaned forward. "Raphael is hot and loaded and the sex is great, but that's not why I'm with him. I mean, those things don't hurt, but that's not what keeps me there."

If I had to guess, it would be respect for Raphael's perseverance. Raphael, a werehyena, or bouda as they preferred to be called, loved Andrea beyond all reason. He courted her for months—unheard of for a bouda—and refused to give up until she finally let him into her life. The fact that he was the son of Aunt B, the bouda alpha, made things complicated but neither Raphael nor Andrea seemed to care.

Andrea smiled. "When I'm with him, I can feel myself getting better. It's like he's picking up broken pieces of me and putting me back together, and I don't even know how he's doing it. We never talk about it. We don't go to therapy. He just loves me and that's enough."

"I'm happy for you," I told her and meant it.

"Thank you. I know you'll tell me to fuck off, but I think Curran loves you. Truly loves you. And I think you love him, Kate. That's rare. Think about it—if he really stood you up, why would he be pissed off about the whole thing? You both can be assholes of the first order, so don't let the two of you throw it away. If you're going to walk away from it, at least walk away knowing the whole picture."

"You're right. Fuck off. I don't need him," I told her.

Andrea sighed quietly. "Of course you don't."

"More tea?"

She nodded. I poured her another cup and we drank in my quiet kitchen.

Later she left.

I took a small dish from the counter, pricked my arm with the point of my throwing knife, and let a few red drops fall into the dish. My blood brimmed with magic. It coursed just beyond the surface.

I pushed it.

The blood streamed, obeying my call, growing into inch-long needles, then crumbling into dust. The needles had lasted half a second? Maybe less.

At the end of the Midnight Games, when I lay dying in a golden cage, my blood felt like an extension of me. I could twist and shape it, bending it to my will, solidifying it again and again. I'd been struggling to replicate it for weeks and had been getting nowhere. I'd lost the power.

Blood was Roland's greatest weapon. I didn't cherish the prospect of facing Hugh d'Ambray without it.

The attack poodle stared expectantly at me. I washed the blood down the drain, sat on the floor so he could lay next to me, and petted his shaved back. If I closed my eyes, I could recall Curran's scent. In my head, he grabbed me and spun around, shielding me as his body shook under the impact of the glass shards.

I felt terribly alone. The poodle must've sensed it because he put his head on my leg and licked me once. It didn't help but I was grateful all the same.

CHAPTER 9

———◆———

AN ODD CHOMPING NOISE CUT THROUGH MY SLEEP. My eyes snapped open.

Pieces of garbage lay strewn across my carpet, next to an overturned trash can. In the middle of it, the attack poodle methodically devoured my trash. As I watched, he tore a piece from a potato peel, raised his muzzle to the ceiling, chewing it with a nirvana-like rapture printed on his face, and bent down for more. A black substance stained his paws and muzzle. It had to be paint. Julie had gone Goth on me a couple of months ago. When she wasn't at the boarding school, she stayed with me. She had picked the library as her bedroom and I'd let her paint it black. The poodle had gotten into her paint can.

"You're so dead."

Chomp, chomp, chomp.

The magic wave was still up and my apartment was freezing cold. I had a hard time sleeping in sweatpants—something about sweats under a blanket just didn't agree with me—but this morning I definitely regretted my decision. My toes were so cold, it was a wonder they didn't break off. I grabbed the blanket, stood up on my bed, and put my hand against the vent. Nothing. The building's boiler was in its death throes.

It had cut out twice in the past month. Even if all of the tenants pooled their money, we still couldn't afford to replace the damn thing. Especially considering that we had already bought coal for the winter.

That left me with plan B. I glanced across the room to a small woodstove, half-covered by stacks of books. Building a wood fire right now seemed impossibly hard, so I bravely dropped the blanket and pulled on sweats as fast as I could.

Once dressed, I checked the head in the fridge. Still no decomposition. This whole investigation took the notion of "normal" undead behavior out back and blew its brains out with a sawed-off shotgun.

I walked the dog, sorted out the garbage, which took nearly twenty minutes, and tried the phone. Dial tone. No rhyme or reason to it, but one doesn't look a gift phone in the mouth. I called to the Casino before the phone line decided to cut out on me. In ten seconds Ghastek came on the phone.

"I sincerely hope you have news, Kate. It's been a long night and I was resting."

This was likely the stupidest thing I could've done, but I had no idea who else to ask. "Are you familiar with the Dubal ritual?"

There was a tiny pause before he answered. "Of course. I've performed it on several occasions. However, I'm surprised you're aware of it."

He wouldn't ask me how I knew about it, but he had to be dying of curiosity. Nobody except my guardian's ex-wife knew I was able to pilot undead. The Dubal ritual required a great deal of raw power and a lot of knowledge. Ghastek viewed me as a thug. The idea that I was capable of it would never cross his mind and that's the way I preferred it. "What would cause the ritual to fail?"

"Describe the manner of the failure."

"Instead of the identity or location of the undead's former navigator, the person performing the ritual saw themselves in the blood."

Ghastek hummed to himself for a long breath. "The Dubal ritual lifts the imprint of the navigator's mind from the undead's brain. The blood streaming from the head isn't central to the ritual; in fact, any dark surface will do. The dark background simply makes the image stand out more. If you stare for a few seconds at a lamp, then close your eyes or look at a dark object, you'll see the glowing outline of the lamp. This phenomenon is called negative afterimage. The same principle applies here, except that the image is acquired from the mental footprint left on the brain of the undead."

I filed that tidbit away for future reference. "Aha."

"There are two factors that could cause the practitioner to see themselves. One, too much time had passed or the undead had been unpiloted. How quickly was the ritual performed?"

"Within two hours of death."

"Hmmm. Then the time lapse shouldn't be an issue. I've been able to pull a reasonably decent image six hours after the termination of the undead. In this case we're left with possibility number two: the navigator's will was much stronger than that of the practitioner. If the navigator realized the undead was about to be terminated, he or she could shock it with a mental surge. We refer to it as searing. A seared brain is difficult to read. Lifting the image becomes a matter of raw power rather than skill. Is there a possibility that the navigator is much stronger than the practitioner?"

"Unlikely." I had little skill, but in the raw power department, I would blow even Ghastek off the scale.

"What makes you say that?"

"I know how powerful the practitioner is."

"So this is someone you know personally?"

Thin ice. Proceed with caution. "Yes."

"Am I to understand that you were in possession of an undead head and you didn't take it to me for identification?"

"Yes." Oh boy.

Silence reigned. "There are four people in Atlanta, aside from the People's personnel, capable of performing the Dubal ritual. I have their numbers in front of me. Of the four, Martina is the best, but she can't match me in either finesse or power. Why would you use someone other than me?"

"I had my reasons."

"I'm waiting to hear them."

"I'd rather keep them to myself."

"You disappoint me."

I grimaced. "Why should you be any different?"

"Was it a vampire head?"

This wouldn't go over well. "No."

More silence. Finally he sighed. "Do you still have it?"

If I brought him the head, he'd lift my imprint from its mind. "It decomposed."

Ghastek sighed again. "Kate, you had a unique undead specimen and you've denied me the opportunity to examine it. Instead, you've taken it to a hack, who's obviously ignorant of the basic necromantic principles; otherwise we wouldn't be engaged in this phone call. I trust you won't make the same mistake in the future. Was there anything else?"

"No."

A disconnect signal beeped in my ear.

I looked at the poodle. "I think I hurt his feelings."

This petition was getting complicated in a hurry. On one side, the Steel Mary attacked the shapeshifters. On other side, undead mages tried to barbeque the Casino and the Guild. They didn't seem connected, except that both the Steel Mary and the undead then attacked the Guild.

Maybe Roland had declared a free-for-all on the Pack and we were getting a flood of bounty hunters who thought they could take the shapeshifters on. But then the attack on the Casino made no sense.

The phone rang. I picked it up. "Kate Daniels."

"It's me," Curran said. "I—"

I hung up.

The phone rang again. I unplugged it from the wall. Talking to Curran was beyond me at the moment.

WHEN I MADE IT INTO THE OFFICE, MOST OF THE coffee was already gone and what remained had cooked down to a syrup-thick brew that smelled toxic and tasted like poison. I got a mug anyway. I also stole a small yellow doughnut from the box of Duncan's doughnuts in the rec room and fed it to the attack poodle in my office. He made a great production of it. First, he growled at the doughnut, just to show it who was boss. Then he nudged it with his nose. Then he licked it, until finally he snagged it into his mouth and chomped it with great pleasure, dropping crumbs all over the carpet. Watching him eat made me feel marginally better, but only just.

Mauro walked into my office, carrying a large paper box plastered with evidence tape. The poodle growled and snapped his teeth.

Mauro smiled. "He's such a good doggie. So fierce."

"He has a mad passion for garbage."

"He probably lived on it for a while. Did you name him yet?" Mauro set the box on the table.

"No."

"You should name him Beau. Beauregard. He looks like Beau. Anyway, this came for you from Savannah."

"Thanks."

He left and I checked the shipping manifest. Evidence pertaining to Savannah Mary #7, aka Steel Mary, aka the Guy in the Cloak. Oh goodie.

I reached over to lift the stack of paperwork out and my fingers grazed something solid. Hmm. I dragged it into the light. A lead box, six inches long, four inches wide, and three inches deep.

In the magic trade, people often referred to lead as black gold. Gold, being a noble metal, was inert. It didn't rust, tarnish, corrode, or decay, and most acids had no effect on it. Magically, lead imitated gold. It resisted enchantment, ignored wards, and absorbed most magic emissions without suffering any consequences.

A lead evidence box had to contain something spiffy. The small sticker in its corner stated, EXHIBIT A, MARY #14, OCTOBER 9TH. I dug in the paperwork. October 5, October 8 . . . October 9. Here you are.

I perched on the corner of my desk and scanned the report. The Steel Mary crashed the monthly cage match held in the bottom floor of the Barbwire Noose, a booze hole on the southern edge of Savannah. The proprietor of the Barbwire Noose, Barbara "Barb" Howell, reported a seven-foot-tall, hairy man walking through the door, wearing nothing except a tattered cloak and what she described as leather Bermuda shorts. Barb proceeded to communicate her refusal to serve the intruder by leveling a Remington 870 pump-action shotgun at the man, accompanied by "No shirt, no shoes, no service."

I liked Barb already.

The man laughed. At this point, the head bouncer decided to get involved. The man put the bouncer's head through the wooden bar, which indicated to Barb that she should use her shotgun. Unfortunately, the magic wave had hit and the shotgun misfired. The man confiscated the shotgun and bashed Barb over the head with it. Her recollection of the following events seemed understandably murky.

One of the regular patrons, one Ori Cohen, twenty-one, got up off his chair and held up a locket to the hairy man. According to Barb, the man "snarled like a dog" and backed away. He continued to retreat and Barb thought that Ori would "walk him right out." Unfortunately, a tall person in a cloak entered the bar through the back door and chopped through Ori's neck with an axe. The hairy man then proceeded to demolish the place, while the second intruder watched.

The descriptions were vague at best. According to Clint, Barb's second in command, the first man was a "giant, shaggy sonovabitch with glowing eyes . . . veins on his arms the size of electrical cords." Not exactly a quality description. "Hi, I'd like an APB on a giant shaggy sonovabitch . . ."

The second man was described as tall. Nobody saw his face.

Because of the unusual height and near naked status of the intruder, the incident was classified as a possible Steel Mary sighting. The Steel Mary had struck in Savannah the night before, and the Savannah Biohazard preferred to err on the side of caution.

The report came equipped with several photographs. I spread them on the desk. Ori, a thin, slight man, curled into a ball in the middle of a trash-strewn floor. The second shot showed the body from the back. Ori's face stared right at the camera, his cheek resting in a puddle of thickening blood. He looked at me with milky dead eyes. His face was clean shaven, narrow, and shockingly young.

Just a kid, really. A kid who saw a bully, stood up to him, and was crushed. The good guys didn't always win.

The third photo showed Ori's toolbox, tucked neatly under the bar. Somehow it survived the destruction. Inside the box lay chisels and brick trowels, stacked, clean, organized. A small wicker box tied with a pink bow sat on top of the tools. Close-up of the box. Chocolate-dipped strawberries.

Masons earned good money, but he was barely old enough to be a journeyman. Chocolate was expensive and strawberries were way out of season. He must've saved up for weeks to buy them. Probably planned to give them to somebody special. Instead he ended up on the filthy floor, discarded like some piece of trash.

"We have to find this bastard," I told the attack poodle. "We'll find him and then I'll hurt him."

I flipped through the stack of pictures. A close-up of Ori's hand. A broken silver chain wound about his dead fingers. Something must've been attached to it. An amulet, an idol, maybe a charm of some sort . . . Something that made the Mary back off.

I flipped through the report to Barb's interview. It mirrored the report summary until I came to the "No shirt, no shoes, no service."

Barbara Howell stated that the hairy man laughed like a woman.

The phone screamed at me. I picked it up. "Kate Daniels."

"I'm done with this game," Curran snarled.

I pushed the disconnect button and pressed Maxine's extension. "Maxine, if he calls again, please don't put him through."

"Dear, that was the Beast Lord."

"Yes, I know. Please screen his calls."

"Very well."

I looked back at the paper. The hairy man laughed like a woman. Just like the undead mage.

Why the hell was Curran calling me anyway?

I picked up the phone and dialed Christy's number. Christy was my closest neighbor—she lived only a few minutes down the road from my house near Savannah. She answered on the first ring.

"Hey, it's Kate. How are you?"

"Fine, fine. What's up?"

I'd regret this later. "I need a favor. Could you go up to my house and see if there is a note anywhere by my door?"

A month had passed. Unless he stuck it under the screen door, which had glass panels, even if the note had been there, it would be long gone.

"Sure. I'll call you back in a few. Your job number, right?"

"No, my apartment is better. Thanks."

I hung up. Even if there was a note, it changed nothing. Nothing at all.

If the big and shaggy man who attacked Barb's bar did laugh like a woman, and if the second intruder was the Steel Mary, it meant they were batting for the same team. Was it a new faction trying to carve a territory in Atlanta? Argh. The deeper I dug, the more confused I got.

I went back to the evidence photos. A wide image of the bar. The inside of the Barbwire Noose had been demolished. Everything that could have been broken was. Splintered chairs. Crushed tables. Shattered glass. Holes in the walls. A chaotic twisted wreck that might have been a pool table at some point. The definition of "fury" in the dictionary had this picture under it.

One of the shots captured an amulet, photographed under wooden debris. Two inches long, the amulet resembled a hollow silver scroll with a piece of paper peeking out on one side. It was a common amulet: the scroll contained a piece of paper or parchment with a protective spell. The caption under the picture said: SEE EXHIBIT A.

I opened the lead box. Inside, in a small plastic bag, waited a piece of parchment. It was two inches wide and about four inches long, with tattered yellow edges that had been creased and torn too many times. Gently I flipped it over.

Blank.

Just once, just once I would've liked evidence that wouldn't make me jump through burning hoops.

The notation stated that the parchment was found inside the amulet and it was blank. Whooptidoo. According to the follow-up, Ori lived alone. One of the carpenters he worked with stated that Ori was afraid of getting sick and carried the amulet as a protection against disease. She didn't know what sort of magic it had or how he got it.

I dug around until I unearthed the lab report. It had *Gone With the Wind* ambitions—at least two inches thick. I started with the first test.

All evidence had to be routinely m-scanned. The m-scanner picked up traces of magical residue and recorded it as colors: blue for human, various shades of red and purple for undead, green for most shapeshifters. The m-scan of my parchment was blank, too. Lovely.

The next item was titled "Franco Emission Test (FET)." I hadn't the foggiest what that was.

I pulled a reference volume of magic laboratory procedure off the shelf. Apparently FET involved placing the object of interest on a white sheet of paper, exposing it to intense chant or an item emitting heavy-duty magic, and then m-scanning it. If the tested object had no enchantment, it would saturate with magic, if only for a few moments, enough to be picked up by m-scan. The copy of the post-FET m-scan showed a pale blue piece of paper with a nice parchment-sized blank space in the middle. The parchment had an enchantment. Surely, one of the tests would nail it down.

Thirty minutes later I had learned way too much useless trivia about what bored Savannah PAD mages did for fun. Their conclusions after seventeen tests on the parchment amounted to: it's blank, it's magic, we don't know what it is, and we can't read it. Toodles.

Something good had to be on the parchment, something that made Ori stake his life on it. I picked up the bag and held it up to the window, letting the light shine through. Nothing but parchment grain.

A door clanged to the left, followed by heavy steps echoing through the hallway. The knight-protector entered my office, growled at my attack poodle, and sat down in my client chair. Wood and metal groaned, accepting his weight. Ted fixed me with his flat stare. "What do you have?"

CHAPTER 10

———◆———

"YOU DON'T HAVE MUCH," TED SAID AFTER I HAD laid out my case.

"I've had the case for thirty-six hours."

"Thirty-eight." Ted leaned forward and glared at me with his lead eyes.

Ted had a fondness for Western clothing. Today he wore jeans, cowhide boots, and a turquoise shirt with black patches on the shoulders, each patch embroidered with a white Texas star. Ted Moynohan, channeling a cattle rustler at the prom.

Trouble was, the knight-protector ran about forty pounds too heavy for the outfit. Not exactly fat, but thick across the chest and carrying the beginnings of a gut, Ted had the build of an aging heavyweight boxer. He wouldn't run up a staircase for fun, but if you slammed a door in his face, he would punch through it and knock you out with the same blow.

Despite the outfit, being on the receiving end of that stare was like peering into the mouth of a loaded .45 with the safety off. I wondered what he would do if I screamed and fainted.

His voice was low, almost lazy. "What is the Order's primary directive?"

"To ensure the survival of the human race."

He nodded. "We keep the order. We force monsters to coexist. We ensure peace. Forty-eight hours ago, this city functioned. As we sit here, the People are paranoid that someone has better undead than they do and is coming after their slice of the pie. The shapeshifters are pondering their own mortality and imagining their children dying of epidemics. The mercs are flailing because the Guild's head has been chopped off. Biohazard wants to declare a citywide quarantine and PAD is shaking down every homeless person in a dirty cloak. The city is headed to hell in a hand basket. Do you know what happens when monsters, thugs, and cops get scared?"

I knew. "They stop playing nice."

"We must restore order. We have to simmer Atlanta down at any cost, or it will boil over with panic and chaos. If I had a female knight more competent than you with better experience and a longer track record, I'd pull you off this petition and give it to her."

What is Andrea, chopped liver? "Thanks for the vote of confidence."

"Assigning this petition to a man is out of the question. I have to rely on an Academy dropout with a discipline problem and a big mouth."

I wanted to jump on the table and kick him in the mouth. "My heart bleeds in sympathy."

Ted ignored me. "You have the full power of the Atlanta Chapter behind you. Fix this mess. What do you need to make it happen?"

The urge to pull off my ID and hand it to him was so strong, I had to fight not to touch the cord around my neck. *Here, you deal with it. You try to run around with the weight of a possible pandemic riding you, you carry the responsibility for people dying, and I'll sit back and tell you where you fall short.* A year ago I might have done it. The memory of Ori's crumpled body flashed before me. But then again, maybe not.

I squished my pride into a ball, sat on it, and plucked the lead case from the evidence box. "This is the parchment that stopped him before. I need to know what was written on it. I need to know what hurts him and who he is."

"You need an expert."

I nodded. "I want to take it to Saiman."

"The polyform. He refuses to work with the Order."

"He's the best"—*narcissistic pervert, sexual deviant, greedy hedonist*—"expert in the city. We don't have time to import anyone else and Savannah PAD has exhausted all the standard test possibilities. Given the proper financial incentive, I'm confident Saiman would work with me."

"How confident?"

"Very confident." *He wants to get into my pants and I've been throwing his flowers away. He would be overjoyed if I called.* "But he doesn't come cheap."

Ted wrote down something and put it in front of me: $100,000. It was an exorbitant sum, even for Saiman. "This is your limit. Call him. Now."

He showed no signs of moving from my chair, making it crystal clear: he didn't believe me.

I reached for the phone. Saiman answered on the second ring.

"Kate," a familiar male voice breathed into the receiver. "I thought I was forgotten."

Ugh. "No, only avoided." I put him on speaker.

"You're as blunt as ever. Shall I save us some time? You're calling because Solomon Red's insides erupted from his body and attempted to infect the city's water supply."

"Yes." That was expected. Saiman dealt in information, he paid well for it, and mercs were always short on cash.

His voice could've melted butter. "Do you require my expertise?"

"The Order requires your expertise."

"Oh, but I won't work for the Order." He laughed. "They're too lawful for my taste."

"My apologies for disturbing you, then. I thought you might be interested. I was wrong."

"But I'll work for you. On my terms."

Here we go.

"In fact, I would be excited to work with you. Your call couldn't have come at a better time."

He sounded happy all over. This would cost me.

"Let's get the simplest things out of the way," Saiman stated. "For the ease of accounting, yours and my own, I will require a flat fee of fifty thousand dollars for my services."

"That's a rather large number."

"I'm a rather expensive consultant."

"Thirty grand."

"Oh please, Kate, don't haggle. Ted Moynohan likely authorized double this amount. I know this because he called me this morning and offered me fifty thousand to consult on the case. Which I refused, of course, given that I dislike him personally and find the Order's fanaticism constricting."

Ted's face was granite-hard.

He went behind my back. My memory served up Mauro, bringing me the box of evidence. Why would Mauro have it? All packages came to Maxine's desk and he never once carried them down to me. Unless the package was in Ted's office and Ted told him to do it.

Ted had gone through my evidence and then sat there with a straight face as I recapped my findings.

"Kate?" Saiman's voice prompted.

I picked up my coffee cup and stirred the coffee with a spoon. I'd read somewhere that doing small repetitive movements like stirring or doodling helped reduce stress and I needed to reduce my stress or it would erupt and smash into Ted Moynohan like a ton of bricks. "I'm thinking."

"Have you noticed that your criminal doesn't target women? Either they possess a natural immunity to his power or he simply doesn't feel they're a threat."

"I've noticed."

"Then you must realize that Moynohan's options consist of you and Andrea Nash. Moynohan despises Nash—I'm not sure why, but I'm sure I'll eventually find out—so you are the only viable solution. In fact, I wouldn't be surprised if he's sitting in your office right now listening in on the conversation just so he can be certain you've ensured my cooperation. Your back is against the wall, Kate. Under these circumstances, a fee of fifty thousand is a gift. Accept it graciously."

The spoon bent under the pressure of my fingers. I pulled it out and began bending it with both hands, back and forth, back and forth.

"Very well," I said. "You will be paid the sum of fifty thousand dollars when we have conclusive proof that the Mary is dead or apprehended."

"Or left beyond your jurisdiction. I don't cherish the prospect of chasing him all over the country."

I bent the spoon some more. "Agreed. What's the real price, Saiman?"

"You will accompany me to an event, Kate. It will be a public function, you will wear an evening gown, and you will be on display on my arm. Think of it as a date."

The spoon snapped in my hands. I threw it into the trash can. "The last time we tried that, I ended up covered in demonic blood."

"I assure you, you will be perfectly safe. In fact, the function in question takes place at one of the safest locations in Atlanta."

"It's not my safety that concerns me. It's your company. You seem very gleeful at the prospect of displaying me. Is there an ulterior motive?"

"There's always an ulterior motive," Saiman assured me. "But aside from that, I find your presence delightful."

I found his presence irritating.

He gave an exaggerated sigh. "I don't wish to force you into a sexual relationship. I want to seduce you. That takes far more skill. I'm afraid I do require an answer. Yes or no?"

"Yes." The word tasted slimy, as if I'd bitten into a rotten orange.

"You say it with such distaste. I count myself lucky to be out of your striking range at the moment. Do we have an agreement?"

"We do."

"Marvelous. I'll pick you up tomorrow at nine p.m. I shall send the gown to your house. It will be there by eight tonight with a matching pair of shoes. Do you require anything else, stockings, intimates . . ."

Chaperoning sexual deviants to parties wasn't on my agenda in the near future. "That's rather short notice. I'm a little busy with an epidemic-spraying maniac trying to break down the city. Can this be postponed?"

"Absolutely not. It has to be tomorrow night or our arrangement is off."

What the hell was so important? "Fine, but I'm wearing my own clothes." There was no telling what crazy outfit he'd come up with.

"I assure you, the dress I've chosen is exquisite."

"Perhaps you should wear it instead. I'm sure you'll be the belle of the ball."

Saiman sighed. "Do you question my taste?"

"The last time you dressed me up as a Vietnamese princess. I'm wearing my own dress."

"Having you wear the right dress is infinitely important to me. I'm taking a huge risk."

"My heart bleeds for you. If you wanted me to wear your gown, you should've covered it in our agreement."

"I propose an exchange." Saiman's voice was smooth as melted chocolate. "You answer my question, and I'll drop the issue of the gown."

"Shoot."

"How do you always recognize me no matter what shape I wear?"

"The eyes," I told him. "They give you away every time."

He was silent for a long minute. "I see. Very well. I should be free in about three hours. I would like to begin my evaluation with the scene of the Steel Mary's last appearance. I'll require the presence of at least five witnesses."

"It will be arranged," I told him. "I'll see you at the Guild in three hours."

"I'm changing my face as we speak. Good-bye." He managed to infuse the word with so much innuendo, I needed a rag to wipe it off my phone.

I hung up and turned to Ted. "You went through my evidence behind my back."

He treated me to his best impersonation of a statue from Easter Island.

"You don't trust me."

The attack poodle snarled, punctuating my words. I glared at him and he lay down.

Ted leaned back. "I don't trust you not to fuck up. You aren't a fast learner and I don't have time to teach you, so I put you on a short leash."

The steady anger inside me flared into a full-blown rage. I worked hard. I pulled my own weight. I'd earned some fucking trust. "I can't work if you stand over my shoulder."

"And that's your problem, Daniels. You have an ego. Every day you walk into this office as if you own it. As if you've earned it. The truth is, you couldn't go the distance in the Academy. You don't have the education and discipline necessary for the job. You aren't a knight and you never will be. You have yet to prove to me that you're worth something."

"I've proved it."

"You fought in the Midnight Games and you led Nash into it."

I stared at him.

"Did the two of you really think that you could fight in front of hundreds of witnesses and it wouldn't get back to me?"

"It was necessary."

Ted rose. His voice dropped low. "The world is full of monsters. They're stronger than us. They have better magic. The only reason why we, humans, remain on top is because of our numbers and because the monsters fear us. That's the order of things. That's the way it has always been and that's the way it must remain. Do you know what the Midnight Games really are? They're a way for the monsters to make humans into prey. They keep seeing us die on that sand, and pretty soon they'll get an idea that we're food and we're easy to take down. They'll stop fearing us and throw this world into chaos. And you went into that ring and fought on the side of monsters. You've betrayed everything the Order stands for. You fucked up."

"I fought on the side of shapeshifters."

"The shapeshifters are cans of dynamite, ready to go loup any moment. They aren't human. It's convenient for us to let them think they're human for the time being, but in the end, there is no place for them in our society. They must be kept apart."

The world slid into crystal clarity. I was a hair away from sliding my sword out and carving a new mouth across Ted's throat. "So you would exile them. Shall it be reservations or labor camps?"

"I would remove them from the picture entirely. They are a threat to us. They can kill us and infect us. To survive, we must retain our dominance."

He would exterminate the shapeshifters. He would kill the lot of them. I could see it in his eyes.

Ted straightened. "I gave you an opportunity to add meaning to your life. You think you got in because you're good. No. I gave it to you, because I respected Greg Feldman. He was one of my best, and to honor his memory, I made sure that you wouldn't embarrass his name. And anytime you forget yourself, or forget our mission, and start thinking that you're hot shit and you know better, come see me and I'll set you straight."

He turned.

I exhaled rage slowly. "Ted?"

He stopped, presenting me with his wide back.

"When you walk a dog on a short leash, she's close enough to bite you. Keep it in mind."

He stepped out. I spun to the window, trying to contain the urge to break something. At the Midnight Games, when I circled the sand with Hugh, he'd asked me why I took orders from people weaker than me. Back then I had an answer. It escaped me now and I grappled with my memory trying to wrench it free, because I needed it badly.

I had to kill the Steel Mary. It was personal now, and I would finish it. But I could track Mary on my own, without the Order's help. I had to get Saiman to analyze my parchment and then I could leave the Order. It would feel good.

If I left, the case would go to Andrea. Ted didn't have anybody else. If the Steel Mary released his magic, Andrea's secret half could panic and run. Best-case scenario, the city would burn up in an epidemic, and she would be exposed and booted from the Order. Worst case, she would be mistaken for a loup shapeshifter, hunted, and killed.

My mind painted a gory picture of Andrea's beastkin body riddled with bullets, with PAD standing over her. "She'd gone loup. Never seen anything like it. Had to put her down."

No.

My mess. I'd handle my own shit.

The phone rang. It was probably Christy. I picked it up. "Kate Daniels."

"I'm in lockup in Milton County Jail," Andrea said. "Come get me."

CHAPTER 11

———◆———

A COUPLE OF HOURS LATER I WALKED INTO BEAU
Clayton's office, carrying a long parcel wrapped in rags.

Beau grinned at me from behind his desk. In 1066, ancient
Saxons met ancient Norwegians in a bloody battle over Stam-
ford Bridge. The legend said that the Saxons surprised their
enemy, and as the Norwegians tried to rally, one of their warriors, a giant of a man, stepped onto the bridge and held it by
himself, killing more than forty Saxons, until someone got
smart and stabbed him with a long spear from below, through
the planks of the bridge. Looking at Beau, I could totally picture him on that bridge swinging a giant axe around. Hulking,
six feet six, with shoulders that had trouble fitting through the
door, the Milton sheriff had the face of a bone breaker. He sat
behind a scarred desk that was organized to within an inch of
its life. The only item out of place was a large can. The label
on the can said, CANNED BOILED GREEN PEANUTS.

I sat in a chair before his desk and put the parcel on my lap.
"Canned boiled peanuts. That's pushing it."

"With a name like Beau, a man has to be careful," he said.
"Someone might mistake me for one of them Northern boys.
The peanuts help to avoid misunderstandings."

He passed me the can. I glanced into it. Spent shell casings.

"Every time I get shot at, I drop the shells in the can," Beau said.

The can was about halfway full. I handed it back to him.

"The last time we met, I did say you would one day need a favor from me." He spread his huge arms. "And here we are."

We'd worked the same case before, I from the Order's side and he from the sheriff's side. He'd asked me to do him a favor, arguing that one day I would need one from him, and I had agreed. You never know on whose door you might have to knock next.

"What did Andrea do?"

He opened a manila folder and glanced at it. "Ever heard of Paradise Mission?"

"No."

"It's a high-class hotel. Built like a Spanish mission, with the courtyard screened in. The roof is glass and they keep the temperature nice and steady."

"Like a hothouse."

"Basically. The courtyard is a beautiful place. Flowers everywhere, a pool, hot tubs. Favorite getaway for rich couples from the city. I took Erica there once. Costs an arm and a leg, but it's worth it. Had to be on the waiting list for four months before we got in."

Beau wasn't in a hurry. Screaming at him would just make him slow down more, so I nodded.

"From what I understand, your girl was staying at the place with her significant other. I've got him in the cell next to hers. Now, I'm completely straight, mind you, but he was likely the prettiest man I ever seen."

Raphael. It must've been their big romantic night. He had probably reserved the hotel room weeks in advance.

"Apparently, they were both in the hot tub."

"Hot tubs are nothing but trouble," I told him.

"Oh, I don't know." Beau shrugged. "With a beer and good company, they aren't bad. Relaxing. Soothing, even. In this case, however, they failed to bring about the desired relaxation. Miss Nash got up to go to the bathroom and get some drinks. When Miss Nash came back, she found a young female talking to her significant other." His eyes sparkled a little. He pretended to check his report. "Apparently, the interloping female was scantily clad."

He must've waited years to use that in a report. "Go on."

"According to the hotel staff, the poor man did try to discourage the femme fatale the best he could, but she was either dense or really hoped to take him for a ride. Having met her, I'd say both."

I sighed. I knew where this was going.

"When Miss Nash approached, her fella informed the scantily clad female that Miss Nash and he were together. He says the female appraised Miss Nash as 'cute.'"

I put my head down and bumped it on the table a couple of times.

The two furry caterpillars Beau used as his eyebrows crept up. "Do you need a minute?"

"No, I'll be alright. Sorry."

"It seems that the young woman made some indelicate suggestion of a threesome. Nobody is quite sure what happened next, but everybody agrees it was damn fast. When I got there, Miss Nash was standing by the hot tub in a small bikini, pointing the business end of a SIG-Sauer P-226 at her fella and concerned members of the hotel staff, while dunking the scantily clad female's head under the water and asking, 'Who's diving for clams now, bitch?'"

My pain must've reflected on my face, because Beau reached into his desk drawer and handed me a small bottle of aspirin. I popped two tablets into my mouth and swallowed, grimacing against the bitterness. "Then what?"

"Well, Miss Nash and I had a conversation. I bet that she wouldn't shoot a badge and I won that bet. She had no ID on her—it was a very small bikini—so we invited her, her fella, and the aggrieved party to be our guests here in this lovely jailhouse. Spending the night with us calmed her down."

Oh, boy. "She had no ID, but she had a gun?"

"Brought it in a towel, from what I understand."

Why wasn't I surprised? "She's a knight."

"I figured that when she called the Order."

I took the parcel off my lap, placed it on his desk, and carefully unwrapped the rags. Beau sucked in a lungful of air in a sharp breath.

A beautiful rapier lay in the rags.

"The schiavona," I said. "The preferred weapon of Dalmatian Slavs, who served in the Venetian Doge Guard in the sixteenth century. Deep basket hilt." I traced the gleaming spider web of deceptively narrow metal strips forming the sword's guard. "Thirty-six-point-seven-inch blade, efficient for both cut and thrust. A genuine Ragnas Dream sword."

I turned the schiavona to the side, letting the light of the feylantern catch the stylized RD on the ornate pommel. Ragnas Dream didn't make swords, he created masterpieces. The schiavona alone would pay the mortgages on both my apartment and my father's house in Savannah for a year. Greg, my deceased guardian, had purchased it years ago and hung it on a wall in his library, the way one would display a treasured work of art. It was the kind of sword that would make a lifelong pacifist look for tall boots and a hat with feathers.

Beau's face acquired a greenish tint.

"Breathe, Beau."

He exhaled in a rush. "May I?"

Every person had a weakness. Beau loved rapiers. I smiled. Once he touched it, I had him. "Feel free."

He got up, took the rapier gently, as if it were made of glass, and slid his big hand around the leather hilt. He raised the sword point up, admiring the elegant steel blade. A deep serenity claimed his face. Beau thrust, a textbook perfect, liquid movement, elegant and precise and so completely at odds with his huge body. "Christ," he murmured. "It's perfect."

"She was never here," I told him. "Her 'fella' was never here. You don't know their names and you've never seen them before."

Beau was a very good cop, because he made himself put the rapier down. "Are you trying to bribe a law enforcement official, Kate?"

"I'm trying to present a law enforcement official with a token of appreciation for his delicate handling of the Order's personnel issues. Knights of the Order are under a lot of pressure. Andrea Nash is one of the best knights I've ever met."

Beau looked at the schiavona. A minute stretched into eternity.

I gave him a wide smile. "Oh, and one more thing." I reached over and touched the pale opal in the base of the hilt.

Three. Two.

One.

The sword hummed a single perfect chime, like a silver bell. A thin line of red grew from the hilt down the blade, branching in curling shoots like an ornate vine until it finally reached the point. Beau turned pale.

"Enchanted blade. Never needs sharpening or oiling. I forgot to mention that part," I said.

Beau tore his gaze from the schiavona. "Take them and make sure they don't come back."

TEN MINUTES LATER ANDREA, RAPHAEL, AND I stepped out of the jailhouse into a frigid overcast day. Both Raphael and Andrea wore the orange potato sacks that passed for Milton Jail uniforms.

"Assault." I counted off on my fingers. "Assault with a deadly weapon. Conduct unbecoming a knight. Endangerment of civilians. Reckless use of a firearm in a public place. Resisting arrest. Drunk and disorderly."

"I was neither drunk nor disorderly." Andrea clenched her teeth.

"No, I'm sure you were drowning her in a completely calm and professional manner. Beau Clayton is a crack shot. You're lucky he didn't empty his clip into your head. You brought a gun to the hot tub. Who does that?"

Andrea folded her hands on her chest. "Don't hassle me about my guns. You drag that sword everywhere. The whole thing was his idea. I wanted to go on a weekend."

I looked at Raphael. He hit me with a dazzling smile. If I had any capacity for swooning, I would've hit the floor like a log. Some men were handsome. Some were sexy. Raphael was scorching hot. Not traditionally handsome, he had dark blue eyes, intense and heated from within by a fire that instantly made you think of sheets and skin. Coupled with his long black hair and the toned, supple body of a shapeshifter, the effect was shocking to all things female. Since he was my best friend's honey bunny, I was pretty much immune to his evil powers, but once in a while he caught me off-guard.

"It was the only night that was available in the next six months," he said, "and I had to call in a favor to get it."

Andrea waved her hands around. "And we spent it in a jailhouse. Do you have any idea how hard it is to go out in public with him? We can't go anywhere, we can't do anything, because he gets hit on all the time. Sometimes women come up to him like I'm not even there!"

"I sympathize, but you can't drown them, Andrea. You're trained to kill and they aren't. It's not exactly a fair fight."

"Fuck fair! Fuck you and fuck him, and whatever."

She strode off.

Raphael was grinning ear to ear.

"Well, you're taking it well."

His eyes shone with a faint ruby sheen. "Mating frenzy."

"What?"

"When two shapeshifters become mated, we go crazy for a few weeks. It's all about unreasonable aggression and irrational snarling at anyone who looks at your mate a second too long."

"And you're loving every moment of it."

He bobbed his head up and down. "I've earned it."

Andrea reversed her course and came up to us. "I'm sorry I was an ass. Thank you. I owe you one."

"No big," I told her.

She looked at Raphael. "I'd like to go home."

He bowed with an exaggerated flourish. "Your wish is my command, my lady. We need to go back to the hotel, scale the wall, and steal our car back."

"That sounds good."

They walked off.

Mating frenzy. The world had gone completely insane on me. I sighed and went to get Marigold. I had an appointment with a sexual deviant and I didn't want to be late.

CHAPTER 12

WHEN I TOLD SAIMAN THAT I RECOGNIZED HIS eyes, I wasn't lying. He looked at the world through a prism of intellect, arrogance, and subtle but smug contempt, and he was unable to hide it. It took me precisely two seconds to zero in on him in a half-deserted Guild Hall, but this time it wasn't his eyes that did it.

Today he chose to appear as a lean male in his early thirties. When I entered, he stood with his face in profile, casually speaking to Bob, Ivera, Ken, and Juke seated at a table. Saiman's black jacket showed a light Mandarin influence with a high collar and a formfitting cut that accentuated his narrow waist and the straight line of his shoulders. Dark pants hugged his legs, showcasing muscular thighs, but his was the smooth, long muscle of a fencer or a runner, not the bulk of a weightlifter or the crisp definition of a martial artist. His hair, the color of dark alder wood, fell down to his waist without a trace of a curl.

Saiman turned at my approach, presenting me with a well-defined oval of a face: crisp jawline, a wide nose with a shallow bridge, and almond-shaped, slightly hooded eyes with shockingly green irises. He oozed professionalism and expertise the way I sometimes emanated threat. Had I not known who he was and met him on the street, I would've thought him one of the high mages from the local college, the type who could decipher three-thousand-year-old runes, speak a half-dozen dead languages, and level a city block with a sweep of his hand. He stood out among the mercs present in the Hall like a professor of medieval studies in a bodybuilder bar.

Saiman smiled, showing even white teeth, and came toward me, gracefully stepping past a large wooden trunk.

"Kate," he said, his voice a smooth tenor. "You look lovely. The cloak, in particular, is an intimidating touch."

"I strive to menace," I said.

"Do you like my working persona?" Saiman asked softly. "An aesthetically pleasing combination of intelligence and elegance, wouldn't you say?"

Aren't we pleased with ourselves. "Are you Chinese, Japanese, half-white? I can't tell, your features are neither here nor there."

"I'm inscrutable, mysterious, and intellectual."

He forgot conceited. "Did you have any trouble getting that ego through the door?"

Saiman didn't even blink. "Not in the least."

"Have you been able to glean any information from the eyewitnesses using your mysterious intellect?"

"Not yet. They do seem ill at ease at the moment."

The Four Horsemen looked like they wanted to be anywhere but here. I surveyed the hall. Out of the twenty or so calls I had made this morning, fourteen people showed up, including Mark, who stood leaning against the wall, a sour look on his face. A lot of familiar faces. The movers and shakers of the Guild had turned out to watch Saiman and me work.

I reached into my cloak and pulled out a plastic bag with a piece of parchment in it.

"What's this?"

"This is a magic parchment."

Saiman took the bag with long, slender fingers, held the parchment to the light, and frowned. "Blank. You've piqued my curiosity."

I took a piece of paper from my pocket. "This is the list of tests ran on the parchment by PAD."

Saiman scanned the list. A narrow smile curved his lips. "Amusing. Twenty-four hours. I'll tell you what is written on it, or I'll tell you who can read it." He slipped the parchment into his inside pocket. "Shall we?"

I turned to the mercs. "We need five volunteers. Don't volunteer if you didn't get a good look at the guy."

Bob raised his hand. "The four of us will do it."

"I need one more," I said.

Mark came forward. "I'll do it."

Juke sneered down her Goth Tinker Bell nose, decorated with a tiny stud. "You weren't even there."

Mark gave her a grim look. "I was there for the end."

They glared at each other.

"Let us not argue," Saiman said. "The five of you will do splendidly."

He knelt by the trunk. It was a large, rectangular trunk, made of old scarred wood reinforced with strips of metal. Saiman flicked his fingers and produced a piece of chalk with the buttery grace of a trained magician. He drew a complex symbol on top of the trunk. A dry metallic click sounded from the inside. Slowly and with great care, Saiman lifted the lid and took out a bowling ball. Blue and green, swirled with a gold marbleized pattern, the ball had seen some wear and tear.

"Have you ever heard of David Miller, Kate?" Saiman asked.

"No."

Saiman reached into the trunk and retrieved a plastic pitcher tinted with hunter green. "David Miller was the magic equivalent of an idiot savant. All tests showed that he had an unparalleled magic power. He constantly emanated it the way an electric lamp emanates heat." He set the pitcher next to the bowling ball. "However, despite numerous attempts to train him, Miller never learned to use his gift. He led a perfectly ordinary life and died a perfectly average death from heart failure at the age of sixty-seven. After he had passed on, it was discovered that the objects he had handled most during his life had gained a magic significance. By manipulating them, their owner can achieve a rather surprising and occasionally useful effect."

Interesting. "Let me guess, you hunted the objects down and acquired them?"

"Not all of them," Saiman said. "Miller's descendants made a concerted effort to scatter the objects, selling them to different buyers. They had agreed that concentrating all of that power in the hands of a single person was foolhardy. But I will collect them all, eventually."

"If they were worried, why sell the objects at all?" Mark asked.

Saiman smiled. "The lack of money is the root of all evil, Mr. Meadows."

Mark blinked. My guess was, nobody ever called him by his last name. "I thought it was 'the love' of money."

"Spoken like a man who never went hungry," Ivera said.

"Besides," Saiman continued, "the family had concerns for their safety. They were afraid they would be robbed and murdered by enterprising parties interested in Miller's collection. Considering the worth of the objects, their worries were quite valid."

He extracted a key chain from the trunk and carefully closed it. "I'll need a pitcher of water and five glasses, please."

A couple of mercs brought over a full glass pitcher from the cafeteria and five glasses. Saiman surveyed the floor and headed to the front door, chalk in hand. He drew a semicircle about ten feet from the doorway, the curve facing the center of the room and chalked an odd symbol into it. Then he crossed to the spot of Solomon's death, drew another larger semicircle, straight side flush against the elevator shaft, and filled it with perfectly round circles. I counted. Ten.

"Bowling pins?" I asked.

"Precisely."

Saiman returned to the table, freed the keys from the chain, and handed each of the five keys to the Four Horsemen and Mark. "Hold them between your hands and try to recall the event in your mind. What did you see? What did you hear? What smells floated in the air?"

Saiman poured the water from the glass pitcher into Miller's plastic one.

Ken, the Hungarian mage, studied the key. "What sort of magic is this?"

"Modern magic," Saiman said. "Each age has its own magic traditions. This is ours. It's unlikely that most of you will see a repetition of this ritual in your lifetime. This magic is extremely rare and very taxing. I only perform it for very special clients." He smiled at me.

Oh good. He just made everyone involved think we were sleeping together.

I smiled back. "I'll be sure to inform the knight-protector that he should be very generous in his compensation." Right back at you. Let them scrub the image of a naked Ted Moynohan out of their brains.

After half a minute, he collected the keys, slipped them back onto the keychain, and dropped it into the pitcher. The keys sank to the bottom. Magic pulsed from the pitcher, breaking against me. It felt like someone had clamped a furry soft paw over my eyes and ears, then vanished.

Saiman poured an inch of water into each glass and glanced at the eyewitnesses. "Drink, please."

Juke grimaced. "That shit ain't sanitary."

"I'm sure you've swallowed much worse, Amelia," Saiman said.

"Amelia," I said. "What a lovely name, Juke."

She scowled at me. "Drop dead."

"Drink the water," I told her.

She skewed her face. "I already told you everything I saw."

"Our memory is much more detailed than our recall," Saiman said. "You might be surprised how much you do remember."

Juke gulped it down.

Bob drank his with a stoic expression. Ivera peered into hers and drained it. Mark tossed his down like it was whiskey. Ken was the last. He drank his water very slowly, in sips, holding each swallow in his mouth, probably trying to glean some sort of knowledge from it.

Saiman picked up the bowling ball. "Please remain sitting through the event. Don't interfere with the illusion in any manner. Kate, you may move if you wish; however, don't intersect the image. Is everyone clear?"

An assortment of affirmative noises answered him. He

strode to the first semicircle, held the ball at his chest for a long moment, bent, and sent it hurtling across the hall's floor. As the ball rolled, a different reality bloomed in its wake, as if someone had pulled a zipper on the world, revealing the past. Solomon's murder took place in the afternoon, and the light slanted at a different angle from the present midmorning sun, clearly marking the edges of the illusion: an oval about thirty feet at its widest stretching through the hall.

The ball smashed into the second semicircle, scattering the imaginary pins. It would've been a perfect strike.

Two men dropped from above into the oval. One was Solomon, his eyes bulging, his face bright red. He landed badly, on his back, but jumped to his feet.

His opponent landed in a crouch. A spear fell next to him.

The Steel Mary straightened to six and a half feet. A cloak hung about his shoulders. His hood was up. From where I stood, I could only see the dark fabric.

I ran along the illusion's edge toward the elevator shaft.

Solomon hammered a vicious kick at the Steel Mary's side. The Steel Mary leaned out of the way, his cloak flaring about him. Solomon's foot passed within a hair of his face. Solomon spun for a back kick, and the Steel Mary backhanded him. Solomon flew through the air, crashing against the elevator shaft just as I braked next to him, at the edge of the illusion.

The Steel Mary picked up the spear and walked to us, each step a deliberate point, like the toll of a funeral bell. The hood shifted back and I caught a glimpse of large eyes, dark, almost black, framed in the thick velvet of long eyelashes and brimming with power.

A woman.

I froze. There was something so hauntingly familiar about those eyes. If I just stood still, I could figure it out.

The Steel Mary opened her mouth. Words poured forth, resonating through me. "I offer you godhood, imbecile. Accept it with grace."

Perfect English. No accent. No clue to nationality. Damn.

The Steel Mary grasped Solomon's shirt with her left hand, jerked him up against the elevator shaft, and thrust. The spear head sliced through Solomon's windpipe. Blood gushed. Solomon screamed, writhing on the spear. Crimson spurted from his mouth.

The Steel Mary raised her right hand, fingers rigid like talons, and thrust it into Solomon's chest. *"Hessad."* Mine.

The power word clutched at Solomon. His body strained, his back arching. He screamed again, a terrible hoarse bellow of pure pain. Blood burst from his chest and collapsed back, sucked inward into the wound. A long exhausted sigh broke from Solomon's lips. He sagged. His eyes rolled back into his head. His body shook once and became still.

The Steel Mary pulled her hand out of Solomon's chest, a wad of red glow resting on her palm. I couldn't feel it but instinctively I knew exactly what it was. It was blood. Condensed blood. All of Solomon's power, all of his magic, his essence contained in a small glowing globe trembling, caged, in the Steel Mary's fist.

The Steel Mary smiled. "Finally."

Her lips stretched in a smile. She turned, carrying the blood, and I saw the twisted lines of a tattoo on the inside of her forearm. The letters burst in my mind, searing it. A power word.

The world burned around me. Heat surged through my blood, spreading through every vein and capillary. My body locked, struggling to overcome the shock.

The Steel Mary turned, slowly as if underwater, and walked away, melting into nothing.

Pain wracked me. I couldn't move, I couldn't speak, I couldn't breathe. Through the tempo of my heartbeat thudding like a sledgehammer in my ears, I heard Juke's voice. "He bitch-slapped Solomon Red! I'd missed that the first time around."

My vision faded, replaced by a fog of blood. The power word was killing me. I clamped it, trying to break through its defenses. It hurt. God, it hurt.

"It certainly is interesting," Saiman said. "Don't you think, Kate? Kate?"

"What's the matter with her?" Ivera asked.

The power word cracked under pressure. Searing light pulsed before me and suddenly I saw, crystal clear, Saiman staring at me from across the room.

The power word hammered at me from the inside, threatening to tear me apart. I had to say it to make it mine.

Something clicked in Saiman's eyes. "Run!"

Too late. I opened my mouth and the power word burst forth on a torrent of magic. *"Ahissa!"*

The magic swept through the room. People screamed and fled, trampling each other. Bob clawed onto the table with both hands, his face a skewed mask of fear, and bellowed like a bull in pain. Ivera collapsed on the floor.

I felt light as a feather. The last echoes of magic whipped about me, bringing the true meaning of the word into my mind. *Ahissa.* Flee.

All of my strength leaked out through my feet. I sagged down and slid against the wall.

The hall was empty, except for Bob breathing like there was an anvil on his chest, Ivera weeping quietly on the floor, and Saiman pressed against the opposite wall. Ice covered his arms. His eyebrows had turned blue-green and the eyes that stared at me from under them were the eyes of a frost giant: cold, piercing blue, like a diamond caught in a sheath of brine. The eyes that belonged to Saiman's original form.

We stared at each other's secret face. It dawned on me that I had just scared the crème of the Guild's crop half to death. They wouldn't forget it. To top it off, I had displayed control of a power word in front of Saiman. His eyes told me he understood exactly what had transpired and he was shocked by it. On a scale of one to ten, this disaster was at a twenty. If I could move, I'd be banging my head against the nice hard floor.

Saiman pushed himself free of the wall. The ice on his arms broke into a thousand tiny snowflakes. His blue-green eyebrows fell out, individual hairs fluttering to the ground. New dark brows formed, matching his hair. The savage intensity of the frost giant's eyes dissolved into calm green irises.

"We seem to have experienced a minor technical difficulty," he said with forced cheer. "My apologies for the inconvenience. This type of magic is yet unproven."

Bob bent down and scooped Ivera off the floor. His face said that he wasn't buying any of it. He grunted, shifting Ivera's tall frame in his arms, and carried her from the hall.

Saiman approached me and knelt. If he tried to kill me now, there wouldn't be much I could do about it. Breathing was an effort. The first time I assimilated power words, I came very close to dying. The second time, I lost about three hours. The third time happened during the flare and it was a rush of pain. Now, with normal magic, I felt completely drained. I didn't pass out and I didn't lose time, so I had to be getting better at it, but I had no reserves left.

Saiman brushed my left arm with his fingertips. "There were words," he whispered. "Hundreds of words written in dark ink on your skin."

Words? What words? "What?"

He caught himself and rose. "Nothing. It's best we go. I'll gather the items."

I watched him pack Miller's collection into his trunk and take it out. By the time he returned, I managed to assume a vertical position and shambled on out of the hall into the daylight. It was my body, my legs, and they would obey me, damn it.

Outside, a group of pale-faced mercs waited, gathered around the Four Horsemen and the Clerk. A few smoked, clutching at the cigarettes with trembling fingers. Nobody spoke, but they watched me like I was a rabid pit bull. Ivera wouldn't look at me at all. I had to get the hell out of there, because right now I was easy pickings and my audience was feeling unfriendly.

"What happened?" the Clerk asked.

"A slight technical malfunction with the spell," Saiman said. "My fault entirely."

He was covering for me. Saiman dealt in information and the price of a secret was inversely related to the number of people who knew it. The fewer people possessed the information, the more valuable it became. I knew this, because Saiman had patiently explained it for my benefit.

"Sorry for the trouble, guys," I said to say something.

"Did you at least get what you came for?" the Clerk asked.

"We got it. Thanks," I said.

"Anytime," Bob said grimly.

"The Guild is always willing to cooperate with the Order," Mark said.

I waved at them and headed out into the parking lot. A woman. Dark eyes. I wished I could've seen her face.

A quick staccato of steps echoed behind me and Saiman caught up. "I'd be delighted if you rode with me," he said. "The engine of my Volvo is wrapped in a layer of mass-loaded vinyl, caught between two layers of polyether foam. It's adequate at attenuation of low-frequency noise."

"Fascinating." Most water cars made enough noise to do permanent damage to one's hearing.

Saiman favored me with a narrow smile. "My vehicle is relatively quiet by enchanted engine standards. If you rode in my vehicle, you could rest."

And he could ask me all sorts of interesting questions. I was tired, but not tired enough to risk a car ride with Saiman.

"Thanks, but I'll pass. I can't abandon my mule. Besides, I come with a passenger."

His eyebrows came together. "A passenger?"

I whistled and the dog popped out of his hiding spot behind Marigold.

Saiman stared at my canine companion with an expression of pure horror. "What is that?"

"That's my attack poodle."

Saiman opened his mouth, closed it, opened it again. A grimace gripped his face. A violent struggle of some sort was obviously taking place inside.

"Are you trying to find something nice to say?"

He looked at me helplessly. "I can't. It's an awful creature."

"If you want me to ride with you, this awful creature has to enter your car."

The pain on his face was priceless. "Can't we just—"

"I'm afraid we can't."

The attack poodle trotted around me and proceeded to vomit an inch from my left boot.

"Delightful," Saiman reflected as the dog, having puked his guts out, urinated on the nearest wall.

"He's a dog of simple pleasures," I told him.

Saiman leaned back, stared at the sky, exhaled, and said, "Very well. Your taste in dogs is as appalling as your taste in wine. It's a wonder you didn't name it Boone."

It had been a long time since I had tasted Boone's Farm. Drinking was no longer my preferred entertainment. "It's a he. Please don't insult my faithful canine companion."

Saiman turned and strode to his sleek, bullet-shaped vehicle, disfigured by the bloated front end containing the enchanted water engine.

I petted the poodle. "Don't worry. I'll let you bite him if he gets out of line."

The dog wagged his tail. Either Saiman smelled tasty, or my poodle had good instincts.

I mounted, swaying a bit, and nudged Marigold into action. Even if I did fall along the way, I'd likely land in a snowdrift. Any landing you could walk away from was a good landing.

CHAPTER 13

THE MAGIC WAVE KEPT GOING. MY APARTMENT would give any meat freezer a run for its money. I couldn't avoid the woodstove forever.

I'd been thinking about the female Steel Mary the entire time I rode to my apartment and was getting nowhere. A woman's voice came out of the undead water mage's mouth but I couldn't recall it well enough to compare it to the Steel Mary's. So either there were two women working together, or there was only one woman, six and a half feet tall, expert with a spear, with the ability to pilot the undead, use power words, and create pandemics.

Nothing I'd read even remotely fit that scenario. I'd have to rely on Saiman's ability to read the parchment.

I pulled my shoes off and trudged into the kitchen. The red light on my answering machine was blinking.

I pushed the button.

"Got your note," Christy's voice said. "Someone ripped out the lock on your screen and pinned the paper to your front door with a nail. It's rain-stained, but I think it says, 'I'm here, you're not. Call me.'"

He did come to see me with broken bones. A day too late and a dollar short.

The second message was from Andrea.

"Hey. It's me. Raphael says that Curran's been a real bastard since about mid-November. He's in a bad mood, he's snarling at everything and everyone, and he stopped hearing petitions. The big items that have to be done get done, but no new projects have been approved. Raphael's been trying to get financing from the Pack to buy out a competing business. He says the last time he brought it up, Curran almost bit his head off. He apparently stalks the Keep halls at night, looking for someone to chew out."

"He needs to get laid!" Raphael's voice called out from a distance.

"Shush. Raphael's mad because he can't get his thingie approved."

"My *thingie* would make us money," Raphael yelled. "Not getting it approved is costing us money we could be making."

"*Anyway,*" Andrea said, "I thought you ought to know."

The message ended.

The answering machine was still blinking. There was another message and I had a pretty good idea who it was from.

For a while I sat in the kitchen and petted the attack poodle, deciding whether I should listen to the message or just erase it. Finally I pushed the button and Curran's voice filled the room.

"You can run, but it won't matter. I will find you and we will talk. I've never asked or expected you to deal with me on shapeshifter terms, but this is juvenile even by human standards. You owe me an answer. Here, I'll make it easy for you. If you want me, meet me and I'll explain my side of what happened. Or you can run away from me the way you always do, and this time I won't chase you. Decide."

"You've lost your mind," I told the answering machine.

I played the message a couple of times more, listening to his voice. He'd had his chance and blown it. I'd paid for it. It would be stupid to risk this kind of pain again. Plain stupid.

I slumped in my chair. The rock in my chest cracked into sharp pieces. Thinking about letting him go hurt. But then he wasn't mine to let go in the first place.

My father taught me many things. Guard yourself. Never become attached. Never take a chance. Never take a risk if you don't have to. And more often than not, he proved right. Taking stupid risks only landed you into hotter water.

But if I let Curran go without a fight, I would regret it for the rest of my life. I would rather drag a dozen rocks in my chest and know that he wasn't my chance at happiness, than walk away and never be sure. And that's all he wanted—to be sure. We both deserved to know.

As much as it pained me to admit it, Curran was right. I never made allowances for him being a shapeshifter. I always expected him to deal with me as a human. He didn't think I could meet him on his home turf and play by his rules.

Big mistake, Your Majesty. You want me to act like a shapeshifter? Fine, I can do that. I pulled up the phone and dialed a number from memory.

"Yes?" Jim answered.

"I was told that shapeshifters declare their romantic interest by breaking into each other's territory and rearranging things."

There was a slight pause. "That's correct."

"Does the cat clan use this ritual?"

"Yes. Where are you going with this?"

When on shaky ground in negotiations, shovel on some guilt. "Do you remember when I stood by you during the Midnight Games, even though you were wrong and your people attacked me?"

He growled quietly. "Yes."

"I need access to Curran's private gym for fifteen minutes."

Silence stretched.

"When?" he asked.

"Tonight."

Another pause. "After this, we're even."

Jim was an ass but he paid his debts. "Deal."

"He's in the city tonight. I'll keep him here. Derek will meet you at the Keep in two hours."

I hung up and punched in the second number. What do you know, I actually pulled it off.

"Teddy Jo," a gruff voice answered.

"You owe me for the apples," I said into the phone. I was calling in all favors tonight.

"That's right. What can I do you for?"

I smiled. "I need to borrow your sword."

THE NIGHT WAS FREEZING AND I TOOK KARMELION, my old, beat-up truck of a bile green color. It was missing the front light assembly and had more dents than a crushed Coke can, but it ran during magic waves and it would keep me warm. It also made enough noise to wake the dead, but I didn't care. Being warm won.

It took me two hours to get the sword and leave Atlanta behind. Before the Shift, many of Atlanta's residents had had the luxury of commuting from nearby towns, driving in through the countryside. Aided by magic, nature had reclaimed these undeveloped stretches with alarming speed. Living things generated magic by simply being, and when put against inert concrete and steel, plants had the advantage. What once were fields now had become dense forest. It swallowed gas stations and lone farmsteads, forcing people to move closer together. Trees flanked the road, their branches black and leafless, sharp charcoal sketches in the snow.

I peered into the dark and petted the attack poodle. I had to lay the front seat flat for him—he was too big. "I always miss the damn road."

The poodle made a small growling noise and curled up tighter.

A long howl of a lone sentry rolled through the night, announcing our arrival.

We made a sharp turn, picking up a barely perceptible narrow road between the thick oaks. The trail veered left, right, the old trees parted, and we emerged into a wide clearing. The enormous building of the Keep loomed before us. A hybrid of a castle and a modern fort, it jutted over the forest like a mountain, impregnable and dark. It was built the old-fashioned way, with basic tools and superhuman strength, which made it magic-proof. Since I'd been here last, most of the north wing had been completed, and the wall of the court-yard now rose about fifteen feet high.

I steered through the gates into the courtyard. A familiar figure sauntered to the truck. Derek. I'd know that wolf gait anywhere.

Three months ago Derek had been handsome. He'd had one of those perfect male faces, fresh, almost bordering on pretty, and dark, velvet eyes that made women wish to be fif-teen again. Then rakshasas poured molten metal on his face. It healed. He wasn't disfigured, although he thought he was, but his face had lost its perfect lines.

His nose was thicker, his jaw bulkier. His eyebrow ridge protruded farther, making his eyes appear more deep set, the result of the Lyc-V thickening the bone and cartilage in response to trauma. The skin along his hairline on the left temple showed permanent scarring, where bits of his shat-tered skull had become lodged in the muscle. I touched it once and it felt like grains of salt under the surface of the skin. With longer hair, it would be practically invisible, but Derek kept his hair short. There were other small, minute things— the slight change in the shape of the mouth, the network of small scars on the right cheek. His face now made you want to call for backup. He looked like an older, scarred, vicious version of himself.

And his eyes were no longer velvet. One look into those eyes and you knew their owner had been through some heavy shit and, if he got pissed off, you wanted to be miles away.

I shut off the engine. The sudden silence was deafening.

Derek opened the door for me. "Hey, Kate." He had a wolf's voice, raspy, harsh around the edges, and occasion-ally sardonic. The ordeal at the Midnight Games had perma-nently damaged his vocal cords as well as his face. He'd never howl at the moon again, in fur or out, but his snarl made you cringe.

He looked my truck over. "Nice vehicle. Inconspicuous. Stealthy even."

"Spare me." I got out, carrying Teddy Jo's sword wrapped

in flame-retardant cloth, and shut the car in the poodle's face. "Stay."

Derek nodded at the vehicle. "Who is that?"

"Your replacement."

He led me away from the front gate to a narrow side door.

"You replaced me with a shaved poodle?"

"He's got mad skills."

Derek's eyebrows crept up.

"He can vomit and urinate at the same time and he doesn't make fun of my car."

He laughed under his breath.

We entered the door and started up a long winding staircase. "Let me guess, he's up at the very top."

Derek nodded. "Curran has the top floor to himself."

"It's good to be the Beast Lord."

We kept climbing. And climbing. And climbing. Five minutes later the stairs finally ended in a large door. Derek opened it, inviting me into a small room, ten by ten. Another door blocked the exit at the far wall.

Derek waited a moment.

The second door swung open, revealing two shapeshifters, an older bald man and a woman about my age, both in superb shape. They gave me the evil eye.

Derek nodded at them.

They plainly didn't want to let me in.

Amber rolled over Derek's eyes. "Move," he said quietly.

They stepped aside. Derek motioned me in. "Please."

The boy wonder had moved up the ranks.

We passed between the shapeshifters into a hallway. On the left was a small room. A third shapeshifter, a man about Derek's age, sat there.

We strode down the hallway, the older man and the woman shadowing us. Curran's guards definitely had doubts about my presence here. They were right. I was up to no good.

"The gym will be on the left." Derek nodded at the hallway, where the stone wall ended, replaced by glass. "His living quarters are upstairs. There is a small stairway down the hall."

He pointed to the doors as we passed them. "Private meeting room. Sauna."

"And that?" I nodded to another door.

The bodyguards looked like someone had stepped on their feet.

Derek's face turned perfectly neutral. "It's reserved for the female guests."

I opened the door. A huge canopied bed occupied most of the room, gauzy curtains drawn up like clouds above the snow-white comforter. The furniture was pale, blond oak with golden accents, elegant and light, almost floating above the polished wooden floor. A large dresser stood against the wall, next to a vanity table with a three-panel mirror. The middle of the floor was taken over by an overstuffed sofa facing a fireplace with a thick white rug by it. A flat screen hung on the wall above the fireplace. The far wall was frosted glass, strategically interrupted by clear stretches forming a bamboo design. The door stood ajar and through it I saw a pristine hot tub.

"Where is Barbie?"

The female shapeshifter snickered and choked it off.

"Is there a stripper pole?"

The older man winced. Derek looked pained. "No."

"Speakers for the mood music?"

Derek pointed at the corner above a small refrigerator. I bet there was cold champagne in that fridge.

I stepped out, shut the door, and pulled on an oven mitten. The shapeshifters watched me with great interest. I untied the cord securing the flame-retardant cloth on Teddy Jo's sword and handed it to Derek, revealing a thick, asbestos-lined scabbard. "Hold this, please."

He took it.

I grasped the onyx-colored hilt and pulled the sword free. It was a classic Hoplite blade, leaf-shaped, about two feet long. A spark ran down the metal, from the hilt to the point. The blade burst into blinding white fire.

The shapeshifters jerked back.

Derek's eyes went wide. "Where did you get this?"

"It's a loaner from the Greek angel of death." I aimed the sword at the lock and touched it to the door. Blue sparks flew.

"What are you doing?" the female bodyguard snarled.

"I'm welding the bimbo room shut."

She opened her mouth and clamped it closed without a word.

I lifted the sword. The lock had melted into a blob of quickly cooling metal. Lovely. I held the sword straight up and turned to Derek. "Where did you say the gym was?"

They led me down the hallway into a large room. The gym was state of the art: a free-weight rack, filled with custom dumb-bells, a curl bar for working the biceps, a station for dips and leg raises, and in the middle of the floor the bench press—a leather bench with a bar rest. You lay flat on the bench and raised a bar loaded with weights above your chest. Curran's bar was already loaded. I checked the numbers etched on the disks—custom made, two hundreds and a fifty on each side. Five hundred pounds. The bar had to be specially made to support the weight. Curran truly was a scary bastard.

I smiled and lowered the flaming sword.

THE PHONE SCREAMED. I CLAWED MY EYES OPEN. Twelve minutes after 2 a.m. I had gotten in about two hours ago—Teddy Jo wanted to chat, and while we chatted, the magic crashed. It took me forever to get home, and my skull hummed like someone was beating a kettle drum between my ears.

I yawned and picked up the phone. "Kate Daniels."

"That was a custom weight bench!" Curran snarled.

My voice dripped bewildered innocence. "I'm sorry?"

"You welded the press bar to my bench."

"Perhaps it would help if you started at the beginning. I take it someone broke into your private exercise facility in the Keep?"

"You! It was you. Your scent is all over the bench."

"I have no idea what you're talking about. Why would I vandalize your bench press?" Think, Curran. Think, you idiot.

A lion roar burst through the phone. I held it away from my ear until he was done. "Very scary. I feel it's my duty to remind you that threatening a member of law enforcement is punishable by law. If you would like to file a petition regarding your break-in, the Order will gladly look into the matter for you."

The phone fell silent. Oh God, I gave him an aneurysm.

Curran made an odd noise, halfway between a snarl and a purr. "There is catnip all over my bed."

I know, I dumped my entire supply on your comforter. It was a hell of a bed, too, enormous, piled with thick mattresses until it was almost four feet tall. I had to literally climb onto it.

"Catnip? How peculiar. Perhaps you should speak to your head of housekeeping."

"I have to kill you," Curran said, his voice oddly calm. "That's the only reasonable solution."

Apparently, I had to spell it out. "There's no need to be so dramatic. I understand that having someone enter your extremely well-guarded private territory, wreak havoc in it, and then escape, unscathed, can be quite upsetting."

He said nothing. He didn't get it. I treated him to a pass on his terms and he didn't get it. I had just made a fool of myself again.

"You know what, never mind. You're dense like a rock." I'd chased him as he had chased me and he couldn't even figure it out.

"I'm leaving the catnip where it is," he said. "You will remove every piece of it. And you'll do it naked."

"Only in your dreams." And I meant it, too.

"Of course you know this means war."

"Whatever." I hung up and exhaled.

The attack poodle gave me a bewildered look.

"I'm in love with an idiot."

The dog turned his head to the side.

"Just wait until he figures out I shut him out of his slut hut." The poodle whined softly.

"I don't need any criticism from you. If you can go a day without barfing or destroying my house, then I might listen to what you have to say. Until then, keep your opinions to yourself."

I fell back into my bed and put a pillow on my head. I'd just had a conversation with a poodle and accused him of criticizing me. Curran had finally driven me out of my mind.

CHAPTER 14

—◦◦◦—

I WOKE UP EARLY AND LAY IN BED FOR ABOUT TEN minutes, thinking of various ways I could kill Curran. Unfortunately, I still had the Steel Mary to catch, so I dragged myself out of bed and got dressed.

Outside the world had turned completely white. The snow must've started shortly after I got in and at least three inches of powder covered the asphalt. Thick gray clouds smothered the sky. Cold burned my face. Winter had taken Atlanta into its mouth and bit hard.

I looked at the attack poodle. "Are you cold?"

He wiggled his shaved butt at me.

I went back inside and added a T-shirt under my turtleneck and a green sweatshirt on top of it. Together with my old cloak, the layers would keep me warm. Next, I retrieved an old torn-up black sweater from the closet, cut off the sleeves, and stuffed the poodle into it. Since I'd shaved him, I now had to provide the artificial fur. He looked . . . cute. Some people got vicious Dobermans. I got a shaved attack poodle in a black sweater. His tough, spawn-of-hell image had taken a fatal blow, but at least he would be warm.

We headed to the Order. The snow crunched under my

feet. Saiman would love it. Being a frost giant, he lived for winter. For me, the winter meant high heating bills, eating lean, and freezing as I tried to conquer snowdrifts. The colder the weather, the more poor people would die of exposure.

We turned a corner onto a narrow path between two rows of decrepit office buildings. The magic hit hard here. Some offices had crumbled and spilled onto the street in huge piles of bricks and mortar. Some teetered on the brink of collapse, looking over the edge but not quite willing to take a plunge. Once the entire street crumbled, the city would clear the rubble out and rebuild—the location was too close to the Capitol to remain vacant for long.

A male voice floated from behind the bend. ". . . just walk right on. Gotta pay."

A shakedown. I picked up speed and circled the pile of debris.

Two men and a woman crowded an older woman toward a concrete building, all three with a familiar hungry look in their eyes. Not professional thugs, just opportunists—saw an easy mark and took a chance. Bad idea.

The older woman saw me. Short, stocky, she was swaddled in a dark garment. An indigo mesh veil covered her dark hair and forehead. Two deep-set eyes looked at me from a face the color of walnut. She showed no expression. No fear. No anxiety.

I headed toward them. The attack poodle trotted next to me, amused.

"It's our turf," the younger woman barked.

"Actually it's my turf."

The thugs spun to me.

"Let's see . . . You're hassling people in my territory, so you owe me a fee. A couple of fingers ought to do it. Do we have a volunteer?"

The small thug pulled a bowie knife from a sheath on his waist.

I kept coming. "That's a mistake."

The thug crouched down. He clenched his knife, like he was drowning and it was a straw that would pull him out. A little crazy light danced in his eyes. "Come on, whore. Come on."

The oldest bluff in the book: get a crazy glimmer in your eyes, look like you're ready to fight, and the other guy might back off. Heh.

"That might work better for you if you held the knife properly. You were doing okay until you pulled the blade. Now I know that you have no clue how to use it and I'll have to chop your hand off and shove that knife up your ass just to teach you a lesson. Nothing personal. I have a reputation to uphold."

I pulled Slayer out. I had years of practice to back me up and I made the draw fast.

The two bravos behind the knife-wielding thug backed away.

I looked at Slayer's blade. "Well, check this out. Mine is bigger. Let's go, knife-master. I don't have all day."

The knife thug took a small step back, spun on his heel, and peeled out like his life depended on it. His friends chased him down the alley.

I sheathed Slayer. Their would-be victim didn't move. Her eyes stared straight at me, unblinking, the irises so dark, I couldn't tell where her pupils were. She smiled, wide lips stretching, her mouth opened, and she laughed. It was a throaty, genuine laugh, deep for a woman.

She wasn't laughing at the thugs. She was laughing at me.

"Are you alright, ma'am?"

She gave no indication of having heard me.

I shook my head and kept going. The attack poodle followed. The woman's laughter floated after me. Even after we turned off onto the side path, I could still hear it.

"It doesn't matter if she's a creepy old lady," I told the attack poodle. "We still had to do our job."

Ten minutes later we stepped through the door of the Order's building. Andrea exploded out of the staircase, her eyes huge.

"Someone broke into Curran's private quarters in the Keep and welded his weight bench together. They also melted the lock on the room where he entertains his women. Was it you?"

"He's making a big deal about never expecting me to behave like a shapeshifter. So I did."

"Are you out of your mind?"

It's not polite to lie to your best friend. "It's a possibility."

"You challenged him. The whole Keep is talking about it. He'll have to retaliate. He's a cat, Kate, which means he's weird, and he never courted anyone that way. There is no telling what he'll do. He doesn't operate in the same world you do. He might blow up your house because he thinks it's funny."

I waved my arm. "It doesn't matter. He didn't get it."

Andrea shook her blond head. "Oh no. He got it."

"How do you know?"

"Your office smells like him."

Oh crap.

"Can you sniff out what he did?"

Andrea grimaced. "I can try. But no promises."

THE OFFICE LOOKED PERFECTLY NORMAL.

Andrea wrinkled her nose and surveyed my working space. "Well, he definitely was here. I'd say about two hours ago."

She closed her eyes and moved to my desk. "He stood here for a while." She turned, eyes still closed, and paused by my bookshelves. "Yep, here, too." She opened her eyes and pulled a book from the far end. The cover showed a drawing of a lion sprawled on a rock outcropping. "You're reading about lions?"

"Research," I told her. "In self-defense."

"Well, he flipped through it."

Probably chuckled to himself, too.

"I'm not sure how he came in . . ." Andrea frowned.

"Through the window," I told her.

Her blond eyebrows came together. "How do you figure?"

"The bars are missing." He must've disabled the alarm, too. If the magic had been up, he wouldn't have gotten through the wards in a million years.

She stared at the window, where the fastenings of a once mighty metal grate jutted sadly into the empty space. "Good call."

"Thank you, ma'am. I'm a trained investigator—that's just the way we roll."

Andrea rolled her eyes. "If he did anything, I don't see it. Sorry."

"Thanks anyway."

She left. I trudged down to the rec room and got a small doughnut and a cup of coffee. On my return, the office didn't look any different. Nothing out of place. Nothing jumping out at me. What the hell did he do? Maybe he did something to my desk. I sat into my chair and checked the drawers. Nope, all my magic crap was still where it was supposed to be.

The phone rang. I picked it up.

"Are you sitting down?" Curran's voice asked.

"Yes."

"Good."

Click.

I listened to the disconnect signal. If he wanted me to sit, then I'd stand. I got up. The chair got up with me and I ended up bent over my desk, with the chair stuck to my butt. I grabbed the edge of the chair and tried to pull it off. It remained stuck.

I would murder him. Slowly. And I'd enjoy every second of it.

I sat back down and tried to push from the chair. No dice. I clamped the sides of the table and tried to twist myself off. The chair legs screeched, scraping across the carpet.

Okay.

I picked up the phone and dialed Andrea's extension.

"Yes?"

"He glued the chair to my ass."

Silence.

"Is it still . . . attached?"

"I can't get it off."

Andrea made some choking noises that sounded suspiciously like laughter. "Does it hurt?"

"No. But I can't get up."

Choking turned into moans.

"*Visitor,*" Maxine murmured in my head.

That's just perfect. I hung up and crossed my arms over my chest. When your butt is permanently attached to a chair, the only thing you can do is sit and hope to look professional.

A familiar man stepped into my office. Of average height and average build, he had a pleasantly unremarkable face, well formed, but neither handsome, nor affected by any strong

emotion. If you passed him on a street, you might overlook
him the same way you would overlook a familiar building.
He was a perfect blank slate, except for the eyes and his black
overcoat. Elegant and soft, it was made of some wool I'd never
seen before.

"Hello, Saiman."

"Good morning."

He paused, probably hoping I'd get up to greet him. Fat
chance.

"What can I do for you?"

Saiman sat in my client chair and surveyed my office. "So
this is where you work?"

"This is my secret HQ."

"Your Batcave?"

I nodded. "Complete with Robin."

The attack poodle showed Saiman his teeth.

"He's delightful."

"What is your coat made out of?"

Saiman gave me a blank look. "Cashmere."

I didn't know they made coats out of cashmere. "Is it
warm?"

"Very." He sat back.

"So why do you need it?" I'd seen him dance naked in
the snow before, with snowflakes chasing him like happy
puppies.

He shrugged. "Appearances are everything. Speaking of
appearances, your Batcave looks . . . what is the word I'm
looking for?"

"Sparse, functional . . ."

"Shabby."

I hit him with my hard stare. "Shabby?"

"Shopworn. Which brings me to my point." He reached
into his spiffy coat and pulled out the petition report I'd given
him the day before. My summary of the case so far, listing
facts, research, and theories. "I've read your summary."

"And?"

"It's not incompetent."

Be still, my heart, so I don't faint from such faint praise.
"Did you expect it to be written in crayon?"

Saiman grimaced and raised his hand. "Hear me out.

You've surprised me. This analysis is mercifully free of the amateurish enthusiasm and faulty reasoning I expected from you. If you can forgive a colloquialism, you do project the image of brawn over brains. Which isn't to say that your native intelligence isn't evident; on the contrary, but there is a great deal of difference between a naturally agile mind and a mind trained in logical deduction."

I rubbed my face. "For a man trained in logical deduction, you should be able to deduce the consequences of insulting a person of brawn in her shabby office."

He shook his head. "You know what you could be, Kate? An expert. You have the potential to become a true professional. All you need are the proper tools and freedom to use them. Here is my offer to you: I will lease and furnish a space, providing starting capital for, let us say, six months to a year. The main expense will come in the form of equipment. You'll need a quality m-scanner." He counted off on his fingers. "A working computer with a printer station, and a well-stocked herbal and chemical supply room, and an arsenal, all of which I'll obtain for you. We'll set up a relaxed repayment schedule. You can be completely independent. You can pick and choose your clients, provided that, when needed, my professional needs take precedence over the rest of your client list. You have a solid reputation, and with my backing, you can capitalize on it and be very successful. This is a professional offer, Kate. Strictly business, with no personal strings attached."

"Why, thank you, that lovely beachside property in Kansas you're selling sounds wonderful."

"Your abilities complement my own. I can use you, and I would much rather rely on you than on the people I employ now, because you can do it better and you're chained by a code of ethics, which, while bewildering, would prevent you from betraying me. My offer makes more sense than working long hours for an organization that is refusing to provide you with the resources and authority to adequately do your job."

A small part of me actually sat up and thought, *This sounds good*. Ted must've gotten deeper under my skin than I'd realized.

At the core, Saiman was right. I was paid a fraction of what a knight made, my professional designation was precarious at best, and my half-assed status barred me from most of the resources available to a full-fledged member of the Order. If I took a cynical view, and it was probably right on the money, Ted had placed me into this position of "neither here nor there" on purpose. It was a bait-and-wait. Show me things I could have, give me a taste, and wait until I got frustrated enough to demand the whole enchilada and agree to joining the Order permanently. Except that he decided I betrayed the human race in the Midnight Games.

I looked at Saiman. "How do you decide if someone is human?"

He braided his long, slender fingers on his bent knee. "I don't. It's not up to me to assess someone's humanity. Being human in our world is synonymous with being included into the framework of society. Humanity entitles one to certain rights and privileges, but also implies voluntary acceptance of laws and rules of conduct. It transcends mere biology. It's a choice and therefore belongs solely to the individual. In essence, if a person feels they are human, then they are."

"Do you feel you're human?"

He frowned. "It's a complex question."

Considering that he was part Norse god, part frost giant, and part human, his hesitation was understandable.

"In a philosophical sense of the concept, I view myself as a person, a being conscious of its sentience. In the biological sense, I possess the ability to procreate with a human and produce a viable offspring. So yes, I consider myself a type of human. A different species of human perhaps, but human nonetheless."

I considered myself human. I knew Andrea did, too. Derek was human to me. So were Jim and Dali. And Curran. Ted Moynohan did not see them as humans. He wasn't alone. I'd glimpsed similar views within the Order during my time at the Academy. That, more than anything else, made me want to leave.

"Back to my offer—being your own boss has its advantages," Saiman said. "Money doesn't purchase happiness, but it does provide comfort, cashmere coats, and chocolate. Think about it."

Thank you for that demonstration of your steel-trap

memory. The only time he caught me drooling over chocolate was almost three years ago, when we first met. Saiman forgot nothing. "It's a good offer. But I would be trading the Order's leash for the chain of being in debt to you."

His voice gained a soft velvet quality. "Being in debt to me wouldn't be taxing."

I matched his voice. "Oh, I think it would. A leash is a leash, whether it's silk or chains."

Saiman smiled. "It wouldn't have to be silk, Kate."

Full stop. Change of subject before we got to a place I didn't want to go. "Were you able to crack my parchment?"

Saiman assumed a martyred expression. "I should be insulted that after all this time you still doubt me."

I knew what was coming—the Saiman show. He'd cracked it and now he wanted to show off.

Saiman reached into his coat and produced a narrow lead box. "Are you familiar with the Blind Monk's Scrolls?"

"No."

"Twelve years ago, an Eastern Orthodox monk by the name of Voroviev attempted to exorcise what he perceived as a demon, which had taken over the local school. He sought to banish the deity. The creature had attacked him during the exorcism, blinding him, and he defended himself by means of an ancient religious scroll containing a prayer. When the exorcism was completed, the scroll went blank. It was placed into a glass case, and over the course of the next three years, the writing gradually reappeared."

"What happened to the monk?"

"He died of his injuries. The question before us is why did the writing on the scroll vanish?"

I frowned. "I'd guess that the scroll's enchantment was exhausted by coming into contact with the creature. If the writing itself was magic, it would vanish."

"Precisely. The scroll slowly absorbed magic from the environment, and when it replenished its magic reservoir, the writing reappeared. Your parchment is of the same ilk. The writing is still there, it's simply weakened beyond the level of our detection." He snapped his fingers. A black oblong stone about the size of my middle finger popped into his hand. Saiman the magician. Oy.

He turned the stone. A rainbow danced across the smooth black surface. He wanted me to ask a question. I obliged. "What is it?"

"A tear of rainbow obsidian retrieved from under a ley line. Very rare. When properly positioned, it picks up residual magic, amplifies it, and emits it. I placed your parchment on one side of it and a piece of true vellum, calfskin, on the other. The vellum was cured with chanting over a period of two months. It's extremely magic sensitive. A scroll of this vellum costs upward of five thousand. As I've mentioned, my fee is a mere pittance."

"You're making more on this job than I make in a year."

"A disparity I have offered to remedy."

Not in this lifetime. "So the obsidian picked up the weak magic from the parchment and radiated it onto the vellum. What was the result?"

Saiman opened the box and held up a small square of vellum. Blank. All except a corner, where eight tiny lines crossed each other: four vertical and four horizontal, forming a square sectioned off into nine smaller squares, like a tic-tac-toe field. Numbers filled the squares: 4, 9, 2, 3, 5, 7, 8, 1, 6.

I'd seen this before. The sum of each row, column, or diagonal would be equal. "Zahlenquadrat. Magic square."

Saiman cleared his throat. He must've expected me to be baffled and I stole his thunder.

"Yes. The magic square is quite old. It was used by Greeks, Romans, Chinese, Hindus—"

The wheels in my head started turning. This was the area of magic I knew very well, because it related to my biological father. "It's a nine square, three by three. Five in the middle, the sum is fifteen. The Jews employed Hebrew letters as numerals. The center number, five, corresponds to the Hebrew letter *heh*, which is a symbol for Tetragrammaton, YHWH, the holiest of the names of God. The sum, fifteen, is the Hebrew *yah*, which in itself is a name of God. This is a Jewish magic square."

Saiman's handsome face jerked. "I had no idea you've studied Jewish mysticism. How interesting . . ." He let his voice trail into silence.

Jewish scholars wrote down everything and hoarded their

records as if they were made of gold. Half of what I knew about my family came from those scrolls and I had studied them since Voron taught me to read.

I looked at him. "Is there a way to restore the rest of the parchment now that we know to whom it belongs?"

He leaned back. "The Temple on Peachtree possesses a secret room. Within the room there is a magic circle. If you stand inside the circle, provided you're strong enough, it will use your magic to restore the writing to its original form. The chances of success are much higher if the writing is of Hebrew origin."

Finally. I'd get a fix on the Steel Mary. About time, too.

"Of course, you have to wait until the magic is up for the circle to work, and given that the wave ended early this morning, I'd say getting into the Temple today isn't likely. A word of warning. First, the circle may drain you dry; second, there is a price for using the circle, and I won't be able to help you. I'm afraid I'm a persona non grata in Jewish houses of worship. I do suspect that if I were to venture into Toco Hills or Dunwoody and were discovered, I may have to fight my way out."

I blinked. "What did you do?"

Saiman shrugged. "Let's just say that a certain young rabbi was rather zealous in his study of sin. He was happy to trade privileged information for that knowledge and I was happy to instruct him."

Ugh. "You seduced a rabbi."

Saiman smiled. "I seduced several. But the last affair was the only one to have exploded into the public eye. A pity, too. He was a proverbial font of sensitive information."

I almost laughed. "So why not go as someone else?"

Saiman wrinkled his lip in disgust. "They have a golem. It sniffs the odor of your magic, and it is, alas, infallible. I've tried. Have I proven my usefulness to your satisfaction?"

"Yes. Don't worry, I remember. Dress, tonight, your company."

"Actually that's not what I had in mind. I hope to receive an answer to a question."

I arched my eyebrow at him.

"What is wrong with your chair?"

Perceptive bastard. "I'm sorry?"

Saiman leaned forward. "You move while you sit, Kate. You touch your sword to make sure it's there, you change the angle of your body, and so on. You're chronically unable to sit still. But you haven't moved since we began our friendly chat."

I raised my head. "My butt is glued to my chair."

"Literally or figuratively?"

"Literally." *Say something. Make my day. I could still kick your ass even with the chair on my butt.*

A little light danced in Saiman's eyes. "How peculiar. Was it a practical joke?"

"Yes, it was." And the joker would get a piece of my mind as soon as I managed to detach myself from the furniture.

"I found that, in cases like this, the easiest way out is to remove the trousers. Of course, it might be a soluble glue. Would you like me to take a look?"

"No, I would not."

Saiman's lips quivered a little. "If you're positive."

"I am."

"It really is no trouble."

"Examining my butt is not included in our agreement. My parchment, please."

Saiman passed me the plastic bag and rose. "Do let me know how it turns out."

"Go away."

He chuckled to himself and departed. I took a gulp of my coffee. Cold. Eh. At least my blueberry doughnut would taste the same hot or cold. Except for one small problem—I'd left the doughnut on the outer side of the desk and getting to it would require me to get up.

My phone rang. I picked it up.

"Acetone," Andrea's voice said. "Dissolves everything. I found a gallon of it in the armory. We soak the chair and you're good to . . . Oh shit. Incoming!"

I dropped the phone and grabbed my sword.

Curran stepped through the doorway.

"You!"

My attack poodle surged off the floor, teeth on display.

Gold sparked in Curran's eyes. He looked at the poodle. The dog backed away, growling under his breath.

I ground the words through my teeth. "Leave my dog alone."

Curran kept looking.

The dog backed into the wall and lay down.

Curran strolled in, carrying some sort of garment. "Nice dog. Love the sweater."

I'd mince him into tiny, tiny, tiny pieces . . .

"I changed my mind about the catnip." He held up the garment. A French maid outfit, complete with a lacy apron.

Slayer's hilt was smooth in my fingers. Beast Lord or not, he did bleed.

The poodle growled.

Curran hung the outfit on the back of the door and approached my desk. That's right, come closer. Closer. Closer . . .

He struck at the desk, preternaturally fast. Tiny hairs rose on the back of my neck. I barely saw it. One moment his hand was empty, the next it held my doughnut. He bit it. "Mmm, blueberry."

In my mind, his head exploded.

"Hard to protect your food with your ass anchored." He saluted me with the doughnut. "When you're ready to talk, call me. You know the number."

He walked out.

CHAPTER 15

THE MOMENT ANDREA SQUIRTED ACETONE INTO my chair via syringe, the glue decided to have a chemical reaction, which set my behind on fire. It took me less than five seconds to cut through my pants. It took approximately half an hour before I dared to land again and I had to spend my day sitting on a bag of ice, which I had chipped from the street outside. The ice was cold and my ass hurt.

The tech held for the entire day. I called the Temple and requested an appointment, tentatively scheduled for tomorrow noon, if the magic was up. After being put on hold twice, I was told that the rabbis would see me. Kate Daniels, master of the phone.

I spent the day poring over the Steel Mary case history and learned pretty much nothing new. A check with Biohazard and PAD revealed no new developments. The magic was down and the Steel Mary stayed dormant. We all sat on our hands, or in my case, on ice, and waited for the trouble to start.

At the end of the day I went home and took a nap. When I awoke, the sun had set. The city beyond my barred windows lay silent, frozen in the winter gloom.

Time to get gussied up for Saiman's date. Oh joy.

I owned only one formal gown. I bought it a few years back, and my guardian's ex-wife, Anna, helped me choose it. The dress waited for me in the closet. I pulled it out, wrapped in plastic, and put it on the bed. Thin silk shimmered in the light of the electric lamp. An odd shade, neither yellow nor gold, with a hint of peach. A touch too yellow and it would be bordering on lemon, a touch too gold, and it would've been gaudy. As it was, it looked radiantly beautiful.

I slipped it on. Artfully draped, the front of the dress clung to my breasts, cascading down into a V before twisting at my waist and falling to the floor in a waterfall of fabric. The layered silk added softness to my body, tricking the eye into seeing curves rather than muscle. The sunlight gown, Anna had called it. It still fit, a little more snugly than it used to, which wasn't a bad thing. Thanks to the Order, I didn't starve as much.

The last time I had worn the gown, I was going on a date with Max Crest. Now I would wear it to go with Saiman. Just once I would've loved to wear it for a man I actually wanted to see it.

I pulled my hair back from my temples. It made my face look hideous and showed a scar near my left ear. Two for the price of one, yay. I settled for brushing all the tangles out and massaging it in place with styling gel. It hung over my back in a long glossy wave. I'd never pierced my ears—I'd ripped enough earrings out of people's ears to know how much pain that could deliver. I didn't own any jewelry, but I did have a pair of shoes that matched the dress, narrow, yellow, and equipped with small stilts instead of heels. I'd bought the shoes for the dress. Looking at them hurt. Walking in them was comparable to Chinese water torture.

They would have to do.

In the past year, I'd had a chance to put on makeup exactly twice, so the higher levels of the art were way out of my reach. I brushed on blush, darkened my eyelids with brown shadow, and put on mascara. No matter what shade I chose, mascara always catapulted me into exotic territory. I brushed on pink lipstick and put the war paint away.

No sword. No place to hide my needles. It should've worried me, but it didn't. The biggest threat would come with the magic wave, and magic rarely hit twice in a twenty-four-hour period. Anything else I was willing to take on with my bare hands. In fact, hurting someone with my fists might prove therapeutic, considering my current state of mind.

At four minutes to eight a knock echoed through my apartment, sending the attack poodle into hysterics. I put him in the bathroom, where he could cause minimal damage, and opened the door.

Saiman wore a suit and an updated version of Thomas Durand. The original Durand, the one who owned one seventh of the Midnight Games, was in his fifties. This version was in his thirties, wide in the shoulder, masculine, and perfectly groomed. Just as before, the aura of wealth emanated from him, from his expensive shoes to his patrician profile and artfully cut dark blond hair. He looked like the favorite son of his former self.

He opened his mouth and simply stopped, as if someone had thrown a switch.

Earth to Saiman. "Hi."

He blinked. "Good evening. May I come in?"

No. "Sure." I stepped aside and he walked into my apartment. He took a long moment to survey my residence. His gaze lingered on my bed.

"You sleep in your living room?"

"Yes."

"Why?"

Because I had inherited the apartment from Greg, my guardian. He'd turned the only bedroom of the apartment into a makeshift library/storage room and slept there, surrounded by his books and artifacts. Greg was murdered less than a year ago. Sleeping in his bed was out of the question, so I bought a daybed and put it in the living room. I slept there, with the door to the real bedroom firmly closed. And when Julie came along, I gave it to her.

Explaining all of this was tedious and unnecessary. I shrugged. "It's a habit."

Saiman looked like he wanted to ask something else but changed his mind.

I slipped on my shoes, wrapped a crocheted shawl around myself, and picked up Slayer. "I'm ready."

Saiman didn't look like he wanted to leave. I opened the door and stepped out onto the landing.

He followed me. I locked the door. He offered me his arm and I rested my fingers on his sleeve. It was covered by our agreement after all. We descended the grimy stairs. Outside, the cold bit at me. Small white flurries drifted from the night sky. Saiman raised his face to the sky and smiled. "Winter," he said softly. When he turned to me, his eyes luminesced, like two chunks of ice lit by a fire from within.

He opened the car door for me with a deep nod that resembled a bow. I got in and put the saber across my lap. He shut the door and slid into the driver's seat, producing a carved wooden box. "I brought these for you," he said. "But you don't need them. You look divine."

I opened the box. A yellow topaz bracelet, earrings, and a necklace lay on the green velvet. The necklace was by far the most stunning—an elegant thin chain crowned with a fiery drop of a stone. "Looks like the Wolf Diamond," I said.

"Indeed. It's a yellow topaz. I felt it was fitting, but your naked neck is shocking. You're welcome to them, of course."

I closed the box. "I better not."

Saiman pulled away into the night. The city slid by. Ruined buildings stared at me with the black holes of their windows.

"Do you like winter, Kate?"

"In theory."

"Oh?"

"The kid in me likes the snow."

"And the adult?"

"The adult says: high heating bills, people freezing to death, burst water pipes, and clogged roads. What's not to love?"

"I find you so immensely entertaining." Saiman glanced at me.

"Why do you persist with this nonsense? I made it clear that I don't like you romantically and never will."

He shrugged. "I don't like to lose. Besides, I'm not interested in a fling. What I offer is infinitely more stable: a partnership. Infatuation is fleeting, but a relationship based on mutual benefit would survive years. I offer stability, loyalty, my resources, and myself. I'll never bore you, Kate. I'll never betray you."

"Unless it suits your interests."

He shrugged. "Of course. But the gains would have to outweigh the risks. Having you on my side would have a lot of value to me. If I did find something more valuable, I would have to make sure you never found out about the cancellation of our arrangement. You're a very violent woman, after all."

"In other words, you'd kill me, so I couldn't punish you for your betrayal."

"'Kill' is such an ugly word. I'd simply make sure that I was out of your reach."

I shook my head. He was hopeless. "What woman wouldn't jump on that offer?"

"I would never lie to you, Kate. It's one of the perks I offer you."

"I'm overcome with gratitude. Have you ever loved anyone, Saiman?"

"No."

This was a pointless conversation. "I know a man who is in love with my friend. He loves her absolutely. The only thing he wants in return is for her to love him."

Saiman arched his eyebrows, imitating me. "And?"

"You're the exact opposite of him. You lack the capacity to love, so you want to smother mine as well."

He laughed. His laughter rang inside the vehicle, an eerie soundtrack to the crumbling city.

CHAPTER 16

⸻

FORTY MINUTES LATER SAIMAN PULLED INTO A parking lot before a large mansion. We'd climbed north, far into the affluent part of Atlanta, but this house made "affluent" sound like an insult. Too large for its lot, the building sprawled, rising two oversized stories into the night and edging its southern neighbors out of the way. When Atlanta's rich built new houses, they typically imitated antebellum Southern style, but this monster was decidedly English: redbrick, huge windows, dark ivy frosted with new snow, and a balcony. All it needed was a fresh-faced English miss in a lacy dress.

"What's this?" I eyed the windows that spilled yellow electric light onto the snow.

"Bernard's." Saiman sank a world of meaning into the word, which whistled happily over my head.

I glanced at him.

"It's a party house."

"I hope for your sake it's a very tame party." If he had taken me to some sort of sex orgy, he would fly right through one of those pretty windows, headfirst.

"Not that kind," he assured me. "It's a place where Atlanta's rich and influential gather to be seen and to be social.

Technically it's a restaurant, but the patrons are the real draw, not the food. The atmosphere is informal and most people mingle, drink in hand."

Oh boy. Rich and influential. Precisely the crowd I wanted to avoid. "And you brought me here?"

"I warned you that you would be on display. Please don't grind your teeth, Kate. It makes your jaw look more square."

Saiman parked at the end of the lot.

"No valet?"

"People who patronize Bernard's rarely relinquish control of their cars."

I slid Slayer between the seats and opened my car door. Getting out without catching the heel of my shoe on my hem took a moment, and by the time I had accomplished this feat of dexterity, Saiman was there with his arm and his smile.

Why did I agree to this again? Aaah yes. Because I had no choice.

I let Saiman walk me up the steps. Above us a couple on the balcony laughed at something. The woman's laughter had a slightly hysterical pitch.

We negotiated a vestibule and a luxurious staircase, and Saiman escorted me to the second floor, where a number of small tables dotted a wide room. A smiling hostess in a tiny black dress led us to a table. I sat so I could see the door and surveyed the crowd. Expensive women and expensive men traded pleasantries. A few glanced at us. No hired help. Odd.

"Where are the bodyguards?" I murmured.

"Bernard's is a sanctuary," Saiman said. "Violence is strictly prohibited. Should someone break the rule, the entirety of Atlanta's elite would rise to bring him down."

In my experience, when the violence broke out, the entirety of Atlanta's elite scattered and ran for its life.

Saiman ordered cognac, I ordered water. The drinks arrived almost immediately. Saiman picked up his heavy crystal glass, warming the amber liquid it held with his palm. Déjà vu. We'd done this song and dance at the Midnight Games.

"Just so you know: if a rakshasa shows up, I left my sword in the car."

Saiman's affable expression gained an edge. "It was a dreadful affair. Thankfully it's behind us."

He drained his glass. In seconds he had another, emptied that one as well in a single swallow, and was brought a fresh one.

I leaned forward and nodded at the cognac about to chase its fellows down Saiman's throat. "What's the rush?"

"It's simply sugar." He shrugged and emptied the glass. "I exerted myself earlier today and need to replenish my resources."

The waiter flittered by and deposited a huge square bottle of cognac on the table. "With our compliments, sir."

Saiman nodded and splashed cognac into his glass. His hand shook slightly. Saiman was nervous. I scrutinized the set of his jaw. Not just nervous, but angry. He was psyching himself up for something and fueling it with liquid courage. Not good.

He noticed me looking. Our eyes met. His lips curved in a smile. Unlike the self-satisfied smile of an expert taking pride in his accomplishment, this was the smile of a man looking at a woman and fantasizing.

I gave him my flat stare. Down, boy.

"You look so surprisingly striking, Kate," Saiman murmured and gulped cognac down like it was water.

"Slow down."

Saiman leaned forward. "I would buy you a new dress every weekend just for the privilege of sliding it off of you."

Not in this lifetime. "You're drunk."

"Nonsense." He poured more liquor. "It's my third glass."

"Fifth."

He studied the amber liquid. "Do men often tell you you're enchanting?"

"No. Men often tell me I hit very hard." Hint, hint.

"Every woman should be told she's attractive. Men are seduced by their eyes, women by their ears. I would tell you every night and every morning."

He was just going and going. "That's nice."

"You would like it." Half of the cognac was already gone. Even with his racehorse-on-crack metabolism, he had to be wasted. "You would like the things I would say. The things I would do."

"Sure, I would." Maybe if Mr. Casanova drank himself under the table, I'd get the waiter to help me carry him down to the parking lot and we'd call it a night.

Worry nagged at me. I'd never seen Saiman drunk. Drinking, yes, but not drunk.

I glanced behind me. At the far wall sat a large table full of hors d'oeuvres. If I couldn't prevent him from drinking, perhaps I could distract him with food.

"Would you mind if I helped myself to some?"

He rose, as expected. Drunk or not, Saiman's manners were flawless. "Allow me to escort you."

We strolled to the appetizers. I positioned myself so I could have a better view of the floor. Saiman loitered next to me.

"Aren't you hungry?" I asked him.

"Not particularly."

"What about replenishing your resources?"

"Ah yes! Thank you for reminding me." He raised his empty glass and within seconds a waiter brought him a full one.

Bernard's six, Kate zero.

I surveyed the food. Directly in front of me was a silver platter filled with tiny fried squares. Each square supported a cube of minced meat, flecked with tiny pieces of green onion, sesame seeds, and what might have been grated ginger.

"Tuna tartare," Saiman told me. "It's delectable."

I picked up a square and popped it into my mouth. Saiman's gaze snagged on my lips. A few more drinks and he might strip naked and offer to dance with me in the falling snow outside. How the hell did I get myself into these things?

"Do you like it?" he asked.

"It's go—"

Jim walked through the door, wearing a black cloak and a scowl.

Oh, hell.

He paused in the door, surveying the crowd and radiating menace. In the gathering of Atlanta's glittering elite, the alpha of Clan Cat stood out like a solid block of darkness. He saw me and reeled back, wide-eyed, looking like a cat who'd been unexpectedly popped on the nose—shocked and indignant at the same time.

I would never live this down.

Behind him, Daniel and Jennifer, the alpha wolf couple, strode through the door. Interesting.

Jim flashed his teeth. A young man quickly detached himself from the opposite end of the room and hurried over.

A bulky form blocked the doorway next. Mahon. The Bear of Atlanta, alpha of Clan Heavy, and the Pack's executioner. What the hell was going on?

Jim drew the young man aside. Green rolled over his eyes. He said something. The man glanced at me. His eyes widened.

A tall, handsome man came through the door, side by side with a leaner, darker man a few years younger and pretty enough to be stunning. Robert and Thomas Lonesco, the alpha rats. More people followed, all with the liquid grace of shapeshifters.

Houston, we have a problem. "We need to leave."

"Oh no." Saiman's eyes flared with a crazy light. "No, we must stay."

Jim continued his fierce chewing-out. It was a very one-sided conversation.

A plump middle-aged woman stepped through the door next, registered me, and pursed her lips. Aunt B, the alpha of the boudas. Saiman had dragged me into a restaurant where the Pack Council apparently had dinner. Alphas from every clan were in attendance . . .

My ears caught a voice I knew very well. I couldn't have possibly heard it all the way from across the room, but I sensed it all the same. My fingers turned ice-cold.

A familiar muscular figure walked through the door.

Curran.

He turned his blond head. Gray eyes looked at me.

Time stopped.

The floor dropped down from under my feet and I floated, disconnected, seeing only him. For a second he looked as if he'd been slapped.

He thought I'd rejected him.

Curran's gaze shifted to Saiman. Molten gold flooded his irises, burning off all reason and turning it into rage. Shit.

Jim said something at Curran's side, then said something else.

Curran gave no indication he heard him.

He wore khakis, a black turtleneck, and a leather jacket. For him, that was the equivalent of formal wear. He must've come here for some special occasion. Maybe he wouldn't rip Saiman to pieces in public. Maybe pigs would fly.

Next to me, Saiman smiled. "We all want what we can't have, Kate. I want you, you want love, and he wants to break my neck."

Dear God. The fool had actually orchestrated the whole thing. I was on display for Curran's benefit. I opened my mouth but words failed to come out.

"He can do nothing here." Saiman sipped from his glass. "After the Red Stalker affair, the People and the Pack instituted a monthly rendezvous held here in neutral territory, to keep the lines of communication open and discuss business. Any deviation from the protocol would mean war. He can't move a finger out of line."

Jim was still talking, but Curran wasn't listening. He was looking at us with that unblinking focused stare.

I finally forced my voice to work. "You brought me here to humiliate the Beast Lord? Are you out of your mind?"

An ugly grimace skewed Saiman's features. The civilized mask slid off his face. His voice was a rough snarl. "Would you like to know what humiliation is? Humiliation is being forced to sit quietly and mind your manners sandwiched between two brutish animals at your own venue. Humiliation is being told when to leave and when to arrive, to be confined to your quarters, and to have claws on your neck at the slightest deviation from your orders. That's what he did to me at the Midnight Games."

Saiman had spent the tournament sitting between Aunt B and Mahon. So that's what this was all about. His towering arrogance couldn't take it. He must've seethed for weeks, and I had played right into it. That's why he'd drunk his weight in booze. Curran was pressurized violence and Saiman had expected a confrontation.

"Of course, you know that he wants you." Saiman grinned, a savage bearing of teeth.

"He can hear you." Shapeshifter hearing surpassed human, and Curran had to be straining every nerve to catch our voices.

"I want him to hear. I'm an expert at lust and he lusts after you. He's possessive. He would've tried to claim you and you must've rejected him the way you had rejected me; otherwise you wouldn't be available to join me here. I wanted him to see it. To drink it in. I have you and he doesn't."

Idiot. "Saiman, *be quiet*."

Curran's face was unreadable.

Saiman bent toward me. "Let me tell you about love. I once seduced a bride and a groom on their wedding night. I had him before the reception and her afterward. I did it solely for fun, to see if I could do it. Two people at the start of their new life together, having just promised to forsake all others. If that's not proof of the impermanence of love, what is?"

Curran graduated to a full alpha stare. It was the primeval, merciless glare of a predator sighting his prey. It slammed my senses. I stared right back into the golden irises. Bring it. I have a lot of pent-up aggression I saved just for you.

Aunt B turned to the two rats, said something with a smile, and together they walked into the side room marked PRIVATE PARTY. One by one the alphas followed her.

Saiman laughed softly. "We aren't without similarities, Curran and I. We both fall prey to lust. We both guard our pride and suffer from jealousy. We both employ our resources to get what we want: I use my wealth and my body and he uses his position of power. You say I want you only because you refused me. He wants you for the same reason. I remember when he became Beast Lord. The boy king, the perpetual adolescent, suddenly at the head of the food chain, granted access to hundreds of women who can't say no. Do you think he forces them into his bed? He had to have done it at least a few times."

A muscle jerked in Curran's face.

At the corner Jim nodded, and a couple on our left and the recipient of Jim's chewing-out followed the Pack Council. Jim had pulled his people in. They were giving Curran a clean playing field. No Pack witnesses, so no shapeshifter could be forced to testify against the Beast Lord. Nice.

Curran's eyes promised murder. I could practically see the headline: ORDER'S CONSULTANT TORN APART BY BEAST LORD IN EXCLUSIVE NORTHSIDE RESTAURANT. I had to keep Saiman alive. I needed him to help me with my petition, and I had extended the Order's protection to him when I agreed to this idiotic date.

I had no sword, no needles, nothing.

Saiman signaled for a new drink. "There is only one difference between us. The Beast Lord will lie to you. He'll tell you he loves you, that you'll always be the only one, that he'll sacrifice everything to be with you and keep you safe. I won't lie to you. I won't make promises I can't keep. Honesty, Kate. I offer honesty."

How could a man so smart be so stupid? It was like he couldn't stop himself. He'd gone beyond the point of reason. "Saiman, shut the hell up."

"You're all mine tonight. Kiss me, Kate. Let me nuzzle your neck. I bet it would send him over the edge."

Saiman reached for me. I sidestepped.

Something snapped in Curran's eyes. He started toward us, moving in an unhurried, deliberate fashion, his gaze fixed on Saiman.

If Curran got his hands on him, he'd kill him. I had seconds to prevent it.

I stepped in front of Saiman. "Stay behind me."

"He won't hurt me. Not here. It would mean repercussions."

"He doesn't care." Saiman knew that society operated by certain rules, and as long as he stuck to those rules, he would be safe and respected. No emotion ever touched him deep enough to contemplate breaking those rules. He couldn't fathom the fact that Curran could throw everything out the window just for the chance to grip Saiman's throat.

Curran wove his way between the tables. I started toward him. Weapon. I needed a weapon. On my right a couple was laughing at the table, a mostly empty bottle of wine sitting on the white tablecloth next to them. I swiped the bottle and kept moving.

Curran's eyes shone.

I showed him the bottle. *You can't have Saiman. I'm guarding him.*

He picked up speed. *I don't care.*

I hefted the bottle and picked a spot between two tables. *Fine. Keep coming. You wanted to talk. We'll talk.*

A man entered the room. Slight of build, he wore a sherwani, a long Indian coat, heavily embroidered with scarlet silk and golden thread. Glittering gems punctuated the twists of the embroidery. His dark head was bare. He carried a cane tipped with a gold cobra head, which, knowing him, was probably the genuine article. Nataraja, the resident big kahuna of the People. He handled the People's interests in Atlanta, reporting to Roland's inner circle.

Behind him the gaunt figure of Ghastek emerged, next to Rowena, a stunning redhead, wrapped in a mind-numbingly beautiful indigo dress. Other Masters of the Dead followed. The People had arrived.

Nataraja saw Curran, grimaced, and called out in a slightly bored voice, "The People greet the Beast Lord."

Curran stopped in midstep. The fury in his eyes simmered. He choked it back, bringing himself under control. It must've taken a monumental effort of will. It scared the shit out of me.

Curran mouthed a word at me. *Later.*

I tapped the bottle against my palm, and mouthed back. *Anytime.*

Slowly Curran turned his back to us. His voice was even and clear. "The Beast Lord greets the People."

He held out his hand toward the private room and together he and Nataraja strolled into it side by side.

"WE HAVE TO LEAVE," I GROWLED.

Saiman shrugged with elegant nonchalance. "You worry too much."

Twenty minutes had passed since the People and the Pack Council had gone into their private room and I couldn't for the life of me pry Saiman free. He kept drinking. Before he'd drunk to build up his courage, now he was drinking to commemorate surviving the ordeal.

Saiman lived in the bubble of his own egocentrism. Nothing was more important to him than money and influence. Breaking the rules of Atlanta's elite would cost the offender both. No strong emotion disturbed or troubled Saiman enough to make him break the rules. He simply couldn't comprehend that Curran would sacrifice everything for a chance to sink his claws into Saiman's throat.

More, Curran was obligated to violence. Saiman had delivered a colossal insult in front of Pack members. Right now Curran sat in that private room, fantasizing about redecorating the dining room with garlands of Saiman's guts. Sooner or later, he'd come out and I didn't trust myself to keep Saiman safe.

I wanted a confrontation. I wanted to break the bottle over Curran's head. But once we started at it, I'd forget Saiman was even there. I would be so intent on hurting Curran, I'd become oblivious to all else. There was a reason why the first rule of bodyguard detail said, "Know where your 'body' is at all times." The moment you lost sight of the body you were protecting, he became vulnerable. Curran was a lethal bastard. I couldn't afford to risk Saiman's safety.

I tried reasoning. I tried threats. Saiman remained rooted to his chair, hell-bent on ensuring I ended the night cradling his corpse. Leaving him and walking out, hoping he'd follow me, was out of the question. For all I knew, Curran would burst out of that room the moment I stepped out of sight. And Saiman was too heavy for me to carry him out. Of all the times not to have supernatural strength. If I had Andrea's strength, I'd sling him over my shoulder and drag his ass out.

Jim strolled out of the private room and headed our way. He moved with casual grace, just a friendly tough guy on the prowl. People discreetly shrank from him. It's hard to shrink when you're sitting down, but they managed.

He stopped by our table and stared at Saiman. Jim's voice was melodiously smooth and he spoke softly, but his words dripped malice. "If you leave now, alone, the Beast Lord will grant you safe passage."

Saiman laughed, a quiet humorless sound. "I hardly need his assurances. I'm very much enjoying my date, and I plan to enjoy the rest of my night in Kate's company."

Jim leaned to me, pronouncing the words with crisp exactness. "Do you require assistance?"

Yes. Yes, I do. Please whack the dimwit next to me upside his head, knock him out, and help me carry him out of here. I unclenched my teeth. "No."

A triumphant smile played on Saiman's lips. Just one sucker punch and he'd be picking his teeth out of that perfect hair.

Jim leaned closer. "If you want to leave without him, I'll make it happen." A green sheen rolled over his eyes.

"I'm obligated to stay with him for the evening. But I appreciate the offer."

Jim nodded and withdrew.

If fury generated heat, I'd be boiled from inside out. Desperate times called for desperate measures. I scraped together what little feminine wiles I had left and touched Saiman's hand. "Saiman, please let's go. As a favor to me."

He paused with a glass halfway to his mouth. "I'm looking forward to tormenting him a bit more, once he emerges."

Idiot, idiot, idiot. "You've made your point already and I'm tired and stressed out. I just want to go and have a cup of coffee in my kitchen."

His mind took a moment to work through the alcohol daze. He arched his eyebrows. "Are you inviting me for a private cup of coffee at your place?"

"Yes." I'd give him a cup of coffee and a big helping of a knuckle sandwich. Generosity was a virtue and I was in the mood to be extremely virtuous.

Saiman made an exaggerated sigh. "I recognize it's a bribe, but I would be a fool to decline."

"You would."

He paid the bill. With luck, the People and the Pack would remain cloistered for a little while longer.

We started down the staircase. I watched him like a hawk, expecting him to trip on the stairs, but he managed to descend with his usual elegance. Outwardly he showed no signs of inebriation. He didn't stumble and his speech didn't slur, which worked against him. Curran might be able to forgive a drunken man but not a sober one.

Outside, snow fell from the black sky, hiding the ground in a soft white blanket. Saiman raised his hand, and snowflakes swirled to his skin, trailing his fingers.

"Beautiful, aren't they?"

"Very pretty." I steered him to the vehicle.

We finally negotiated the parking lot. Saiman snapped his fingers, pulling the keys out of thin air.

"You shouldn't drive," I told him.

"On the contrary, I should."

A normal human would be dead of alcohol poisoning by now. He wanted to drive. "Give me the keys."

He considered it and dangled the keys before me. "What do I get if I let you drive?"

I felt the weight of someone's gaze, as if a sniper had sighted my back through a rifle scope. I turned. The building loomed about thirty yards away. The double glass doors leading to the balcony swung open, and Curran walked out.

"What do I get if I let you drive, Kate?"

I grabbed the keys from his hand. "To live! Get into the car."

"Now, now . . ."

I snapped the locks open, jerked the passenger door ajar, and shoved him into the seat.

Curran's eyes glowed with gold. He shrugged off his leather jacket, grabbed the neck of his turtleneck with both hands, and ripped it in half.

I dived into the car and floored the gas pedal.

In the rearview mirror Curran tore apart his pants. His flesh boiled, and a monster spilled forth.

"What's the rush?" Saiman wondered.

"Look back."

The man was gone. In his place stood a beast, dark gray and corded with muscle. I caught a glimpse of huge fangs on a face neither lion nor human, and then he leapt off the balcony onto the neighboring roof.

"He's chasing us." Saiman stared through the rear window. "He's actually chasing us!"

He's chasing you. He wouldn't hurt me. "Well, what did you expect?"

Shock stamped Saiman's face. "He's abandoned all pretenses at humanity."

I took a sharp corner. The tires skidded. The vehicle slid, brushing a snowdrift. I wrestled with the wheel, righting the car, and we hurtled down the street.

Curran appeared above the building behind us. He sailed through the night sky like he had wings and landed on the shingles. The moonlight clutched at his shaggy mane. He took a running start, cleared another gap between the buildings, and followed us, bounding from roof to roof in great leaps.

I tried to speak clearly, hoping it would penetrate the fog of Saiman's brain. "We go to my place. I get out. You get behind the wheel and drive as fast as you can. It's your only chance." And my only chance to settle all that ailed me without outside interference.

Saiman didn't answer. Flesh flowed on his face and hands, changing into a new shape and instantly shifting into another, as if his body had gone liquid.

"What are you doing?"

"Burning off the alcohol." He glanced back. "He's still there!"

"Help me navigate. I don't know where I'm going."

"Take the next left. You'll see a bridge. Go up."

I made the turn, praying the tech would hold. If the magic hit us, we'd be in deep shit.

CHAPTER 17

———

THIRTY MINUTES LATER WE SCREECHED TO A halt before my apartment building. I jumped out into the snow, Slayer in hand. Saiman lunged into the driver's seat. The wheels spun, spraying snowflakes. I jumped back. The car reversed, rolling over the spot where my feet were half a second earlier, and sped into the night.

He almost ran me over. Coward. Let's have a partnership, Kate. I offer honesty, Kate. I don't have to outrun the Beast Lord I just pissed off, Kate. I only have to outrun you and hit you with my car as I hightail it out of here.

The dogs down the street exploded with frantic barking. Speak of the devil . . .

I needed to attract His Majesty's attention and take this off the street. In the open, he could take a running start and bulldoze over me. In my apartment, he'd have a harder time maneuvering and I'd have the home turf advantage.

I hiked up my dress and ran into the building, taking the stairs two at a time. It took me three precious seconds to get the door open. I burst inside, dropped the sword, ran to the living room window, and slid it open. A thick grate of steel and silver bars guarded my window. I grabbed the two handles and twisted. The lock snapped open. The grate swung to the left and I saw him, a nightmarish beast charging up the roofs across the street, like a demon caught between the black sky and the white snow.

Dear God.

He saw me and changed direction in midleap. That's right. Come let me kiss you with my fist, baby.

I backed away from the window. Shoes. I had spiked heels on. I pulled them off and tossed them into the hallway. If I had to kick him, the heel would go right into the body like a knife. It would hurt, but not enough to stop him, and I'd have a hell of a time getting free.

Curran dropped off the roof and dashed across the street to my building. I backed away, giving myself room to kick. My heart hammered. My mouth went completely dry.

A second passed.

Come on. Come on.

A clawed half-paw gouged the windowsill. Curran lunged through the window.

He was huge, neither a man, nor a lion. Curran's usual warrior form stood upright. This creature moved on all fours. Enormous, bulging with muscle under a gray pelt striped with whip marks of darker gray, six hundred pounds at least. His head was lion, his eyes were human, and his fangs were monster.

So that's what the Beast Lord with no brakes looked like.

He landed on the floor of my living room. Muscles twisted and crawled, stretching and snapping. The gray fur melted, fading into human skin, and Curran stood on my carpet, nude and pissed off, his eyes glowing gold.

His voice was a deep snarl. "I know he's here. I can smell him."

I felt an irresistible urge to brain him with something heavy. "Did you lose your sense of smell? Saiman's scent is two hours old."

Golden eyes burned me. "Where is he?"

"Under my bed."

The bed went airborne. It flew across the living room and slammed into the wall with a thud.

That was just about enough of that. "What the hell do you think you're doing?"

"Saving you from whatever mess you got yourself into this time."

Why me? "There is no mess! It's a professional arrangement."

"He's paying you?" Curran snarled.

"No. I'm paying him."

He roared. His mouth was human, but the blast of sound that shot out of it was like thunder.

"Ran out of words, Your Majesty?"

"Why him?" he growled. "Of all the men you could have, why would you hire him for *that*?"

"Because he has the best equipment in the city and he knows how to use it!"

As soon as I said it, I realized how he would take it.

The beginnings of another thundering roar died in Curran's throat. He stared at me, mute.

Oh, this was too good. I threw my hands up. "The lab! I'm talking about his lab, not his dick, you idiot. He's the only one I know with a Class Four lab in the city. He can take a blank piece of paper and read an invisible incantation on it."

It must've penetrated, because he regained his ability to speak. "That's not what I was told. Don't lie to me, Kate."

"Get out of my apartment!"

"I know he was planning a long night and you had no choice about it."

The next time I saw Jim, I'd kick him in the throat. "Do I look like a fragile flower to you? I can kill Saiman three times before his body ever hits the ground. If I don't want to sleep with him, no force on earth would make me. See, in our world, we have this pesky thing called reality. Before you ran over here in your beastly glory to rescue me, did that concept ever cross your mind?"

He opened his mouth.

"No!" I growled, pacing back and forth. "I'm not done. I need him for the Order's investigation. He made going out with him a condition of his services, because you made him spend the Midnight Games between Mahon and Aunt B and this is his petty version of revenge. You knew I was guarding him, and you still went after him. You fucked up my personal life, now you're trying to destroy my professional one. If you kill him tonight, I swear to God I will murder you."

"Is he forcing you to sleep with him?"

One-track mind, Your Majesty. "No. But even if I wanted to jump into the sack with him and screw his brains out, you have no right to an opinion on it."

Rage shivered in the corners of Curran's mouth. He stalked back and forth like a caged cat. "I have every right."

"Who says?"

"You. You gave me that right when you dumped catnip all over my bed."

I opened my mouth, but nothing came out. He had me there. "I changed my mind."

"What, again? Why am I not surprised?"

"What do you mean, again? You stood me up, remember?"

"You were relieved I didn't show up."

Argh. "Let's review. I cooked the dinner. I made you a pie. I set the table. I took a shower. I put on *makeup*. I bought condoms, Curran. And then I sat in my kitchen for hours, waiting for you. I sat and waited for three hours. Then I called to the Keep and was told not to contact you again. And you have the audacity to snarl at me?"

He showed me his teeth. "The phone call came when Doolittle was setting my bones. It went to Mahon, who thought it wasn't important. It never got to me. I had no idea you had called. It was a fuckup, it happened on my end, and I accept full responsibility for it. I'm sorry. It won't happen again."

"On that we're in complete agreement."

His eyes flashed. "But you, you didn't even try to find me and figure out what happened."

"You made me feel this small." I held my thumb and index finger barely apart. "Was I supposed to crawl to the Keep, collapse at your feet, and beg you to take me?"

He snarled. "You were supposed to march to the Keep and punch me in the face. That would've been fine. But you ran away."

The fury in his eyes made the hairs on the back of my neck stand up.

"I was trying to avoid a conflict between the Pack and the Order, you stupid idiot!"

"Bullshit." He kept going like he didn't hear me. "You could've found me. You could've demanded an explanation. Instead your bright idea to deal with this mess was not to talk to me. Do you get off on having me chase after you like some sixteen-year-old?"

"Twelve tops. Sixteen is giving you too much credit."

He bit the air. "Look who's talking."

My voice was so bitter I could taste it. "It doesn't matter. I thought you wanted to be with me. You made me want"—I struggled with words—"things I didn't think I would ever get. I thought we had a chance. But it's over now. Thank you, Your Majesty, for curing my temporary madness and showing me how it was all my fault. I apologize for trashing your love-me gym. It was a mistake on my part. I will replace your bench and comforter. You can leave now."

He stared at me. If he didn't leave, I would kill him.

"Do you want me to spell it out? I'll speak slowly. You broke my heart and now you're stomping on it. I hate you. Get the hell out of my apartment, or I swear I'll beat you bloody."

His face was dark. "You want me to grovel? Is that it?"

"Come to think of it, groveling would be nice, but no, I just want you to go. Leave."

His eyes flashed at me. "Make me."

I lunged left and kicked him. He made no move to avoid it. My foot smashed into his stomach. Like kicking a tree sheathed in rubber. The kick knocked him back a couple of steps. He grunted. "That's it, baby?"

I whipped about, picking up momentum, and kicked him in the head. He staggered back, looking a bit unfocused.

I forced a grin out. "Rang your bell, *baby*?" Shit. I'd hit him with everything I had and he didn't go down. He should've been out like a light.

Curran shook his head and spat blood onto my carpet. The gold in his eyes burned me. He started toward me, his jaw set.

He wouldn't take another kick to the head, and kicking his body was useless. I snapped a sidekick to his knee. He knocked my foot aside and grabbed at me. I dodged and hammered a punch into his side. He turned into it and my fist bounced off his back. Ow. I sank my heel into his knee again, driving it with all my power. He grunted, but kept coming. I grabbed a lamp off the nightstand and bashed him with it. He caught it, ripped it out of my hands, and tossed it aside.

I was almost to the wall. My room to maneuver shrank to nothing.

I smashed my knuckles into his solar plexus. He exhaled in a sharp breath and drove me into the wall. His forearm pinned my left arm. I hammered my right fist into his ear. He growled, caught my wrist, and locked it against the wall above my head.

I had no room to move. Game over.

He crushed me against the wall, bracing me with his body. I strained, trying to break free. He might have been made of stone for all the good it did me. Except he was made of flesh and he was stark naked.

I strained every muscle I had. Nothing. Outmuscling him was beyond me.

"Feel better?" he inquired.

"Lean over to the left, Your Majesty."

"Want a shot at my jugular with your teeth?" He leaned to the right, exposing his thick neck. "Carotid's better."

"My teeth are too small. I wouldn't cause enough damage for you to bleed out. Jugular is better—if I rip it a bit and get air bubbles into the bloodstream, they'll be in your heart in two breaths. You would pass out at my feet." A normal human would die, but it took more than an air embolism to bring a shapeshifter down permanently.

"Here you go." He leaned his head to me, his neck so close to my lips, I felt the heat coming off his skin. His breath was warm against my ear. His voice was a ragged snarl. "I miss you."

This wasn't happening.

"I worry about you." He dipped his head and looked into my eyes. "I worry something stupid will happen and I won't be there and you'll be gone. I worry we won't ever get a chance and it's driving me out of my skull."

No, no, no, no . . .

We stared at each other. The tiny space between us felt too hot. Muscles bulged on his naked frame. He looked feral.

Mad gold eyes stared into mine. "Do you miss me, Kate?"

I closed my eyes, trying to shut him out. I could lie and then we'd be back to square one. Nothing would be resolved. I'd still be alone, hating him and wanting him.

He grabbed my shoulders and shook me once. "Do you miss me?"

I took the plunge. "Yes."

He kissed me. The taste of him was like an explosion of color in a gray room. It was a fierce, possessive kiss and I melted into it. His tongue brushed mine, eager and hot. I licked at it, tasting him again. My arms slid around his neck.

He growled, pulling me to him, and kissed my lips, my cheeks, my neck . . . "Don't make me leave."

Not a chance. I gulped to catch my breath. "If you leave, how will I strangle you?"

He hoisted me up onto his hips and I molded myself to him and kissed him on the mouth, stealing his breath. I didn't want to let go. His hands slid over my body, caressing my neck, moving to my shoulders, then my breasts. His fingers brushed my nipples, sending shivers through me. I arched my body, grinding into him, faster and faster.

He made a noise, halfway between a growl and a purr. It triggered something deep, on a primeval female level, and I pressed tighter to him, running my hands over the cords of the muscles on his back, licking his neck, kissing him over and over, so he would make it again.

Curran swung me off the wall and carried me across the room, bumping into things. We stumbled onto the bed, tipped over at an angle. Curran pulled it down with one hand and we fell on it, his big body on top of mine. He dragged his mouth from my lips and kissed my neck, painting heat down my throat. My nipples ached. He pulled the gown down off my shoulder and sucked on my breast. Heat shot through me, making me hyper and impatient. I felt so empty and I wanted to be full of him. His scent and the heat coming off him made me drunk.

Curran caught my arms and pushed them above my head. His left hand closed on my wrists. He kissed me with a low hungry growl, teeth nipping at my skin. His hot hand slid up my thigh, sending me into shivers, and I heard my underwear rip. He tossed it aside, thrust his hand under my butt, lifting my hips, and bent down between my thighs.

Oh, my God.

I screamed.

He licked me, sucking, and all of me faded except for the hot knot of pleasure down below. Every stroke, every touch of his tongue, made it grow hotter and hotter, building the pressure, unbearable, wonderful, overpowering. Finally it burst through me in a searing jolt, from inside all the way to my skin. Curran released me. I cried out and grabbed at him. The heat dissolved into a cascade of waves.

"Condoms," I breathed.

"Where?"

I pointed past him to where the bed used to be.

He strode off and I almost growled. I didn't want him to let go of me. The world reeled. I was light-headed, as if drunk.

Curran reappeared with a condom.

He peeled open a packet. For an absurd second I thought the condom wouldn't fit. Somehow he got it on, loomed over me, and kissed my neck. His teeth grazed my skin. He clenched me to him.

I swung my legs around his hips.

The huge muscles of his back bulged under my hands. He thrust, and I cried out again as he slid inside me, filling me, hot and hard. My body shuddered. He thrust again and again, building into a smooth rhythm, and I moved with him, rocking and trying not to pass out from bliss. Another orgasm exploded in me, tearing a scream from my mouth. Curran thrust deep. My body clenched around him. He growled and emptied himself, and we collapsed onto the blankets.

I was out of breath.

It had to be a hallucination, but I was so happy, I didn't care.

He pulled me to him, and I put my head on his chest. His

hand caressed my hair. His heartbeat was even and strong. We lay together as the sweat slowly cooled on our skin.

I rolled over and punched his ribs. He grunted.

"That's for that damn phone call."

He caught me into a hug, pinning my arms. "I think a mosquito bit me."

I tried to pull away but he had me wrapped up.

Gray eyes looked into mine. "Why didn't you come to the Keep?"

"Oh, I planned on it. Had my boots on, ready to go, when I remembered it would cause an interagency disaster. I was being responsible."

He shook with laughter.

"What?"

"You? Responsible?"

"Shut up. How was I supposed to know that you let two little bears hurt you, Goldilocks?"

"Ah, yes, that mouth. I missed it." He crushed me to him in a fierce hug. "All mine now." My bones whined.

"Can't . . . breathe," I squeaked.

"Sorry," he whispered, letting me go just enough to inhale.

We lay together for a while, until the cold air from the open window got to me and I shivered.

"You're cold." He rose and went to close the window.

My gown clung to my legs and bunched around my waist. I wriggled and slid it off.

"We've ruined your Princess Buttercup dress," he said.

"I have the worst luck with that dress." I raised myself on the elbow to kick it off and caught sight of my apartment. We'd wrecked the place. "At least the building is still standing."

"I pride myself on restraint," he said.

I laughed.

We picked the pillows up off the floor and found the blanket. He slid into bed next to me, and I wrapped myself around him, my head on his chest.

"What the freak said, it's not like that," Curran said.

"I know," I told him and kissed the corner of his jaw.

"I've never forced anyone and I don't lie to you."

"I know."

A long, sad whine rolled through the apartment.

Curran frowned. "Is that your mongrel?"

"He's an attack poodle. I found him at an incident scene, washed him, shaved him, and now he guards the house and barfs on the carpet."

"What's his name?"

I stretched against him. "Grendel."

"Odd name for a poodle." He turned, taking full advantage of the fact that my breasts were squished against him.

"He came into a mead hall full of warriors in the middle of the night and scared them half to death."

"Ahh. That explains it." His hand caressed my shoulder, then my back. It was a deceptively casual caress, and it made me want to rub myself against him. He leaned in closer and kissed me. His teeth grazed my lower lip. He kissed my chin and began working his way down my neck. Mmmm . . .

"I read lions can have sex thirty times a day," I murmured.

He raised an eyebrow. "Yeah, but it only lasts half a minute. Would you prefer the twenty-second special?"

I rolled my eyes. "What woman could pass on that offer?"

His hand cupped my breast. His fingers brushed my nipple and I shivered.

"I'm not all lion," Curran said. "But I do bounce back quickly."

"How quickly?"

He shrugged. "Two minutes."

Oh, boy.

"I do slow down eventually," he said. "After the first couple of hours or so."

Couple of hours . . . I slid my hand down his chest to his stomach, feeling the hard ridges of muscle. I'd wanted to do that for so long. "It's good that we have a whole box of condoms."

He laughed low, like a satiated predatory cat, and swung me on top of him.

CHAPTER 18

——◆——

I OPENED MY EYES, SAW LIGHT, AND JERKED UP-right.

The magic was still down. Thank the universe.

The bed was back in its rightful place. Oh, good. I'd dreamed the whole thing up.

Curran walked into the room. He wore Pack sweatpants he must've gotten out of my closet and nothing else. Toned muscle bulged on his chest and arms, hardened by constant exertion. He had the build of a man who fought for his life—neither too bulky, nor too lean, a perfect combination of strength and supple quickness.

And he grinned like a man who'd had a rather long and exciting night.

Nope. Not a dream.

I did sleep with him. Dear God.

Curran's gray eyes laughed at me. "Morning."

"Tell me I'm still sleeping."

He showed me the edge of his teeth. "No."

I lay back down and pulled the sheet on top of me. I couldn't have been that reckless.

"It's too late for that," he said. "I've already seen everything. Actually I'm pretty sure I've already touched and tasted everything, too."

"I just need a moment to cope with this."

"Take your time. I'm not going anywhere."

That was what I was afraid of.

It occurred to me that I didn't hear any barking. "Where is my dog?"

"I let him out."

I jerked up. "On his own?"

"He'll come back once he's done. He knows where the food is."

Curran strode over to the bed, moving silently, his bare toes gripping the floor lightly as he walked, as if he still had claws. He really was an incredibly attractive bastard. He leaned over the bed. His lips brushed mine. He kissed me. And I kissed him back. He tasted of Curran and toothpaste. Clearly, I had lost my mind.

"Did I hurt you last night?"

I could've used many words to describe last night, but pain wasn't one of them. "No."

"I wasn't sure since you told me to stop."

"Yes, at five in the morning." He just kept going and going, and at about five o'clock, my body gave out. "I had to have sleep. But I'm nice and rested now." Why did that just come out of my mouth?

He looked like a cat who'd gotten into a pantry and had himself a cream and catnip party. "Is that a hint?"

"Would you like it to be?" I just couldn't stop myself.

He grinned and slid into the bed next to me. "Yes."

Half an hour later, I escaped and started looking for my clothes. The air smelled of java—he'd made coffee for me.

I got dressed and went into the kitchen to fry an omelet and call Andrea for updates.

"You're two hours late," she told me. "Are you okay? You're never late. Do you need me to come and get you?"

"No. I'm fine. Just tired."

Curran loaded bread into the toaster.

"Any news of my Mary?" I asked.

"Nothing."

We dodged the bullet. "Thanks."

"Wait, don't hang up."

"Yes?"

Andrea lowered her voice. "Raphael found out more gossip about the gym thing."

Curran glanced at me.

I had to head her off at the pass before she said something Raphael would regret. "Now isn't the best time . . ."

"Look, you, I'm hiding in the armory with the phone, watching the door, and whispering so nobody will overhear me. I feel like a kid cutting class hiding in the bathroom with a joint. The least you can do is hear me out. Raphael says that Curran lay there on the weight bench for fifteen whole minutes trying to lift the damn bar, even though it was welded on there."

Curran's face took on an inscrutable impression.

"Aha," I said. "Aha" was a good word. Noncommittal.

"He broke it."

"I'm sorry?"

"He broke the bar off. And then he smashed the bench with the bar. Bashed the thing to pieces."

Just kill me now. "Aha."

"He must have a lot of frustration. The man's unstable. So watch your back, okay?"

"Will do. Thanks."

I hung up and looked at him. "You broke the bench."

"You broke it. I just finished the job."

"It wasn't one of my brightest moments."

He shrugged. "No. I just didn't get it until I saw the catnip. I thought you were taunting me. It was unexpected." He growled under his breath. "I'm going to muzzle Raphael."

"He just wants his financial machinations approved."

"Are you asking me to do this for him?"

"No."

I turned the gas off and got out two blue metal plates. I'd given up on breakable plates after the last time my front door got broken and demonic mermaids wrecked my kitchen. I split the omelet between the plates and stopped when Curran's arms closed about me. He pulled me against him, pressing my back against his chest. I heard him inhale my scent. His lips grazed my temple. Here we were, alone, in my kitchen, holding each other while breakfast cooled on the table. This was some sort of alternate universe, with a different Kate, who wasn't hunted like a wild animal and who could have these sorts of things.

"What's up?" I asked softly.

"Just making sure you know you're caught."

He kissed my neck and I leaned against him. I could stay for days wrapped in him like this. I'd sunk in way too fast and way too deep. Yes, this was all well and good, but what happened when he saw the next conquest on the horizon? The thought cut at me. Apparently, I was still fragile. "I didn't break any bones last night, did I?"

"No. But that was a hell of a kick. I saw pretty lights for a moment or two."

"Served you right."

We broke apart, slightly awkward. He checked the fridge. "Is there any pie?"

"In the bread box."

He extracted the pie from the box and sniffed the crust. "Apple."

"Made it yesterday." Magic apples thawed well.

"For me?"

"Maybe."

"Before or after the chair?"

"After. Although I was really pissed off at you. What the hell did you use?"

"Industrial glue. It's inert until you add a catalyst to it. I took off the fabric and filled the chair with a bag of glue in thin plastic, covered the plastic with catalyst, put sponges on top, and reupholstered the thing."

That was why it didn't feel weird sitting on it. The moment I sat down, the bag broke, glue and catalyst mixed, and the sponges stuck to my butt. "That must've taken a long time."

"I was very motivated."

"Did you know the glue produces heat when mixed with acetone?"

His lips curved. "Yes."

"Would it have killed you to mention it?"

He chuckled.

"Oh, get over yourself," I growled.

Curran dug into his omelet. I drank my coffee and watched him try my cooking. Most shapeshifters avoided spicy food. It dulled their senses. I'd used half of the salt I normally stuck in there, and none of the jalapeños made it in.

For some reason it was terribly important that he liked it.

He hooked a piece of omelet with his fork and chewed it with obvious pleasure. "Did Doolittle talk to you about the body?"

"No. Any news on the missing shapeshifters?"

Curran nodded. His face turned grim.

"Bad news?" I guessed.

"They went wild."

I stopped with the coffee cup halfway to my mouth. It was often said that the shapeshifter had only two options: going Code or going loup. The first demanded sacrifice and iron discipline, the second catapulted them down the path of wild abandon, turning them into murderous cannibalistic maniacs. There was the third option, which almost never happened. A shapeshifter could forget their humanity completely. It wasn't loupism in the strict sense, because loups shifted into human shape frequently, if only to taunt their victims while they ripped them apart. Wild shapeshifters regressed so deeply into their animal forms that they lost the ability to transform, to speak, and probably to form coherent human thoughts. Going wild was so rare, I could count the known cases on the fingers of one hand. It usually happened when a shapeshifter was forced to maintain animal form for extended periods of time—months, sometimes years.

Unfortunately wild shapeshifters still carried Lyc-V. If they bit a human and the human became a loup, the Pack would bear responsibility for it. That was the greatest burden of the alphas. Sometimes they had to kill their own people.

"Did you . . . ?"

"It wasn't me, but it was done. The bodies are being brought to the Keep today."

"What would cause them to go wild?" I stirred my coffee.

Curran reached over and brushed my hand with his fingers. "Sometimes fear does it. When little kids get startled, they often go furry to run away."

"So she terrified them to the point they forgot they were human?"

Curran stopped. "She?"

Thin ice. Proceed with extreme caution. If I mentioned Saiman, it might set him off. "I think it might be a woman. She pilots the undead mages the way navigators pilot vampires."

He chewed on that. "One of Roland's?"

"I don't know yet. You'll know the second I do."

Curran cut two pieces of pie and put one in front of me. "How long will you need to pack?"

And the happy morning screeched to a halt. "Why would I need to pack?" I asked casually.

"Because you're coming to the Keep with me." He delivered it as a fact. His face wore the familiar blank expression I'd come to define as the Beast Lord's "my way or the highway" look. He was actually serious about this.

"Why?"

"She saw you at the Guild. She could track you down here. It's not safe here."

"Nice try. She's targeting you, not me." If I gave him any hint Roland was after me, he would carry me to the damn Keep and hide me in an armored room.

"I want you with me," he said. "It's not a request."

"Too bad. You must've forgotten, Your Fuzziness, that I don't do well with orders."

We locked stares over the table.

"You have no sense of self-preservation."

"And you expect me to commute two hours each way from the Keep to the Order." I kept my voice mild. "I suppose I won't be needing my job, my house, or my clothes anymore."

"I didn't say that. Although let me get back to you on the clothes. It's still under consideration."

"Look, you don't get to run my life. We slept together once—"

He held up seven fingers.

"Fine," I squeezed through my teeth. "We had sex seven times in a twenty-four-hour period. Just because I'm your lover—"

"Mate."

Words died in my mouth. In shapeshifter terms, mate meant monogamy, family, children—a union, civil, physical, and spiritual. It meant marriage. Apparently he hadn't given up on that idea.

"Mate," I said finally, tasting the word.

He winked at me. Dear God.

I gave him my hard stare. "You're a control freak and I fight all authority. And you want us to mate?"

A wicked spark lit his eyes. "Many, many times."

"What's wrong with you? Did I hit you too hard on the head?"

"My mate lives with me," he said. "In the Keep."

"Have you had many mates before?"

He gave me a look reserved for the mentally challenged. "I had lovers."

"So this is a new rule you made up on the spot?"

"That's a perk of being the Beast Lord. You get to make up rules."

Going to the Keep was out of the question. They were already in danger, but it would be nothing compared to what would happen if I moved in. Curran protected his people, and I endangered them. I forced my voice to sound normal. "Any other Curran rules I need to know about? Might as well get them out now, so I can veto all of them."

"You don't get to veto my rules," he said.

I laughed. "This will never work."

We looked at each other.

"Let's trade," he said. "You tell me what you have to have and I'll tell you what I want."

He was trying to negotiate. I must've won a victory somewhere. Either that or last night was as good for him as it was for me. "Okay."

He invited me with a wave of his fork. "You start."

"The Order is off the table," I said. "I'm not quitting."

"I didn't say you had to." He leveled a heavy stare on me. "But since you insist, I agree. The Order is off the table. My turn."

Danger, danger . . . "Okay."

"Monogamy," he stated flatly. "While you're with me, I'm the only one. Anybody else touches you and I'll kill them."

"What if I accidentally bump into someone?"

Gold flashed in his eyes. "Don't."

Apparently he refused to feel humorous about this situation. "I'll keep that in mind."

"You said yourself, I'm a control freak. I'm a jealous, possessive bastard and I'm not as human as some. You have no idea what last night cost me. Betray me and I'll kill him. If you don't want to be with me, tell me. Don't go behind my back. I'm trying to be as honest as I can. So there are no surprises."

"You do realize that killing the other male makes no sense. If I cheat on you, I'm at fault, not him. He didn't promise you anything."

"It's not about logic. That's the way Pack works. I would be within my rights to kill anyone trying to take my mate. I would be expected to do it, I'd want to do it, and I would do it."

I pointed the fork at him. "Fine. But the parade stops now."

"What parade?"

"Your girlfriend parade."

His eyebrows crept up. "Girlfriend parade?"

"Curran, you cheat on me and we're done. That's fair."

"Kate, it goes both ways. If anyone tries to make a pass at me, you're welcome to their throat."

"I don't care about people making passes at you. I only care if you act on it."

"Agreed. The girlfriend parade stops." He bared his teeth in a happy feral grin. My own personal psycho. "I kind of figured that out when you melted the lock on my guestroom in a fit of jealousy."

"You don't say." I picked at my omelet.

"My turn. The not-talking thing—we'll never do that again."

"Boy, that really bugged you, did it?"

He growled. "Yes, it did."

"Okay. I promise never to stop talking to you. You may come to regret this."

He grimaced. "I'm sure. We can discuss it in more detail, at the Keep."

"And what will the rest of your subjects think about that?"

He shrugged. "The Pack functions best when hierarchy is clear. Right now most people don't know why I was irritable, and those who do know are unsure where we stand, so everyone is walking on eggshells. It will be better once the Pack sees us together."

No matter what rocks I threw at him, he refused to deviate from his course. I chose my words very carefully. "I'd rather they didn't."

He sat completely still. His voice gained a low dangerous edge. "Are you ashamed of being with me?"

"No."

His face slid into a flat unreadable expression. "Is it because I'm a shapeshifter?"

"No, it's because you're the Beast Lord."

He leaned back. "Care to elaborate?"

"My value is in my impartiality. I can approach the People, the Pack, the druids, or the Witch Oracle, because it's clear I don't take sides. I'm able to function effectively only if I'm neutral. Sleeping with you destroys my impartiality. You won't tolerate someone who isn't loyal to you, so the moment I acknowledge being with you, everyone who ever had a problem with the Pack will stop talking to me. That's only part of the issue."

"Is there more?"

If I had any hope for the two of us, I'd have to tell him everything.

The thought froze me in my seat.

"Kate?" he asked softly.

I opened my mouth and tried to make words come out. They didn't.

He reached over and covered my hand with his.

I couldn't tell him. Not yet.

I had to find some other reasons and so I stuck to things that had gotten me through the misery of the last few weeks. "How many women have you slept with?"

He pulled back and crossed his arms, making his biceps bulge. "Don't do this."

"It's a legitimate question," I said.

"How many men have you slept with?"

"You're my third. Answer the question."

"Well, are we counting long-term partners or one-night stands?"

I sighed. "Would you like to count partners only?"

He grimaced. "Less than twenty."

"Would you care to elaborate?"

He mulled it over. "Eighteen."

"And how many of them lived in the Keep with you?"

The answer came a little quicker. "Seven, but none shared my rooms."

"What do you mean, they didn't share your rooms? Where did you . . ."

"In their quarters."

I laughed. "Oh, so you graced them with your nocturnal presence in the bimbo room, Your Majesty? Like Zeus, in a blaze of golden light?"

He showed me the edge of his teeth. "They liked it."

Arrogant ass. "Sure. So why don't you let women in your rooms?"

"Because being in my rooms means being in a position of power."

If he thought I would stay in a bimbo room when this was over, he was out of luck.

I would be dead when this was over.

"In the public eye, there is a huge imbalance of power between you and me. If I went to the Keep with you, Atlanta would stop viewing me as Kate Daniels, agent of the Order, and would perceive me as Beast Lord's Girlfriend Number Nineteen. Or Number Eight, depending on how they chose to look at it. What little reputation I've earned would be wiped away and you can bet that the Order will take me off the current case faster than you can snarl."

"We both have to give up some things," he said.

I crossed my arms. "I'm so glad you see it my way, Your Majesty. Quit being the Beast Lord, give up the Pack, and come live with me in my apartment."

"You know I can't do that."

I smiled at him.

"I get it," he said. "Point made. It's not fair. But the Pack is who I am. I built it for my people. The Order isn't who you are. Half of the time you're trying to figure out how to hide what you find from them. I've read your report of the flare. If there was a lying competition, you'd win it hands down."

That hit really close to home. "The Order is where I choose to be right now. If I'm taken off this petition, it will go to Andrea. She's my best friend. If she collides with the Mary's magic, she might be exposed. It'll destroy her. In any case, I don't have to justify myself to you."

"Andrea knew the risks when she became a knight. You didn't put her into this situation, she did it herself. You're just delaying the inevitable. She's trying to live in two worlds at once and she can't."

Ouch. That hit really, really close to home.

He kept going. "You don't want to justify yourself. I respect that. But you want me to be your dirty secret. To skulk about and pretend that you're not mine in public. I won't do it."

"I'm asking you to be discreet."

"No."

"Would you like to borrow a pair of my panties to wave around at the next Council meeting to get the point across?"

His eyes flashed. "Got any to spare?"

I could've picked somebody rational. But no, I had to fall in love with this arrogant idiot. Come to the Keep with me, be my princess. Mourn me when your crazy dad kills me. Yeah, right.

He got up, took the phone from the counter, and set it before me. "I said we both had to give up something."

"So far I'm the one expected to give up things. What's your sacrifice?"

He nodded at the phone and rattled off a number. "That's the phone of the Keep's steward. His crew makes all the sleeping arrangements. I called him this morning to tell him I would be coming in. Call him. See if I requested a room to be prepared for you."

The phone rang.

We both looked at it.

It rang again and I picked it up. "Yes?"

"Kate?" Saiman's voice sounded mildly anxious. "I see you survived the night."

"Barely."

Curran picked up his empty plate.

"Are you injured?"

"No." Just tender in some places.

"That's good to hear."

The sound of tortured metal screeched through the kitchen. Curran was slowly, methodically rolling the metal plate into a tube.

"What is that noise?" Saiman said.

"Construction."

"Are you planning to visit the Temple today?"

"If the magic complies."

"I would be interested in learning what you find out."

"Your interest has been noted."

I hung up. Curran dropped a chunk of nearly solid metal that used to be a plate onto the counter.

I looked into his gray eyes. "Curran, if you attack him, I'll have to defend him. There is no competition there. If I had wanted to be with him, I could have." Crap. That didn't come out right.

He took a deep breath.

"What I meant to say was, he offered and I declined."

"Come with me."

"I can't."

A shadow passed over his face. "Then we're done."

"So it's all or nothing?"

"That's the only way I can do it." He turned his back to me and walked out.

CHAPTER 19

———◆———

THE MAGIC HIT TEN MINUTES AFTER CURRAN LEFT. I grit my teeth, got dressed, saddled Marigold, and headed to the Temple.

All or nothing. Hello, Your Fuzzy Majesty. My name is Kate Daniels, daughter of Roland, Builder of Towers, the living legend, and coincidentally, the man who is trying to eradicate you and your people. If you take me in, he will move heaven and earth to kill you and me, when he finds out who I am. Even now, I'm being hunted. And if you keep sleeping with me, you'll never be the same.

That was what all or nothing really meant. And I wanted so badly to ignore it and go with him to the Keep. When had I become so attached to that arrogant bastard? It wasn't last night. Was it all the times he'd saved me from myself? At least, I knew when it started—when he tried to trade the lid wanted by a horde of sea demons for Julie's life.

I would kill to stay with him. Now there was a scary thought.

The temperature continued its suicidal plunge. Despite all the layers of fabric, I could barely feel my arms, and my thighs were frozen solid. Grendel and Marigold seemed no worse for wear, but then they'd run the whole way.

Bordered on three sides by a low brick building and by a brick fence on the fourth, the Temple looked almost cheerful against the stark landscape of ruined buildings: bright red walls, snow-white colonnade, and equally white stairs perched upon a snowy lawn. Just a few yards to the left, Unicorn Lane lay in wait. An area of deep violent magic, Unicorn Lane cut across the battered Midtown like a scar. Things that shunned the light and fed on monsters hid there, and when desperate fugitives fled there, neither PAD nor the Order bothered to follow them. There was no need.

Unicorn Lane ran straight as an arrow, except when it reached the Temple grounds, where it carefully veered around the synagogue. Mezuzot, verses from the Torah, written by a qualified scribe and protected by pewter cases, hung along the perimeter of the Temple wall. The wall itself supported so many angelic names, magic squares, and holy names, it looked as if a talismanic encyclopedia had thrown up on it.

Four golems patrolled the grounds: six feet tall and red like Georgia clay. The shapeless monstrosities of the early days, just after the Shift, were gone; these guys had been made by a master sculptor and animated by a magic adept. Each had the muscled torso of a humanoid male, crowned with a large bearded head. At the waist the torso seamlessly merged into a stocky animal body, reminiscent of a ram and equipped with four powerful legs with hoofed feet. The golems stalked back and forth, carrying long steel spears and peering at the world with eyes glowing a weak watery pink. They paid me no mind. If they had, they wouldn't be difficult to kill. Each was animated by a single word—*emet*, truth—cut into their foreheads. Destroy the first letter and *emet* became *met*. Death. An end to the golem. Judging by their slow gait, I could waltz in, take the letter off, and skedaddle before they could bring those big-ass spears around.

Everyone had their own method of manipulating the magic. Witches brewed herbal potions, the People piloted vampires, and rabbis wrote. The surest way to disarm a Jewish magician was to take his pen away from him.

As I approached, a woman stepped out of the Temple and

came down to the bottom of the stairs. I tied Marigold's reins to a rail welded to the fence and jogged up the stairs.

The woman was short and happily plump. "I'm Rabbi Melissa Snowdoll."

"Kate Daniels. This is my poodle."

"I understand you have an appointment with Rabbi Kranz. I'll take you to him, but I'm afraid the poodle will have to wait outside."

The attack poodle expressed doubts about waiting, and he liked the chain even less, but after I growled at him, he decided it was in his best interest to play it cool.

The rabbi raised her hand and stepped forward. A pale glow clamped her fingers and drained down in a waterfall of light, as the protective ward on the Temple opened to let me pass.

"Follow me, please."

She led me inside. We passed by the open doors of the sanctuary. Enormous arched windows spilled daylight onto rows of cream pews, equipped with dark red cushions. Soothing cream walls climbed high to a vaulted ceiling, gilded with gold designs. On the east wall, in front of the pews, a pale feylantern illuminated a raised platform and on it the holy arc, a gold case containing the scrolls from the Torah.

The contrast to the bleak outside was so startling, I wanted to sit down on the nearest cushion, close my eyes, and just sit for a long moment. Instead I followed Rabbi Melissa down the hall to a small staircase into a narrow room. A square bath occupied the far end of the room. A mikvah, a place where Orthodox Jews came to purify themselves.

The rabbi approached the right wall, placed her hand on it, and murmured something. A section of the wall slid aside, revealing a passage stretching into the distance. Pale blue tubes of feylanterns lit stone walls. "There we go," she said. "Just keep on straight, you can't miss it." I stepped inside. The wall closed behind me. No way to go but forward.

THE PASSAGEWAY BROUGHT ME TO AN EMPTY round office. I passed through it and kept walking. Another office waited ahead, this one with a heavy stone desk and two men standing behind it. The first was in his forties, tall, thin, with a long face, made longer by a short beard and a receding hairline, and smart eyes behind wire glasses. The second was older by ten years, heavier by seventy-five pounds or so, and had the square-jawed face and the eyes of a cop, skeptical and world-weary.

The taller man came out from behind the desk to greet me. "Hello, I'm Rabbi Peter Kranz. This is Rabbi John Weiss."

I shook their hands and handed them my Order ID. They looked at it for a while and gave it back to me.

Peter folded his long frame back behind the desk. "Sorry about the dungeon atmosphere."

"No problem. As dungeons go, I've seen worse."

The two of them chewed on that remark for a bit. I looked past them. Hebrew script decorated the walls of the office, lines and lines of text inked on the wall in thick black lines. It drew the eye. I tried not to stare.

"I understand you wish to access the circle." Peter folded his long fingers in front of him.

"Yes."

"We would like to know why."

I explained about the Steel Mary and produced the bag with the piece of paper.

The two rabbis looked at each other. I looked at the wall. There was something about the Hebrew text. My eyes almost itched when I looked at it. If I squinted just right . . .

"You must understand, of course, we do wish to cooperate with the Order," Peter said. "However, we don't advertise the existence of the circle. You might even say we strive to keep it a secret. We're most curious as to how you learned about it."

Mentioning Saiman would get me thrown out. "The Order has its sources."

"Of course, of course," Peter said.

The rabbis exchanged another look.

The black lines blended, like the old stereograms that hid a 3-D image in an ordinary picture. The impact punched my brain and I saw a word, written in a language of power. *Amehe.* Obey.

The word sizzled in my brain. I already owned this one, but seeing it written still set my mind buzzing.

It made sense that it would be written on a wall full of names of God. Rabbis specialized in written magic and Yahweh was all about obedience, if the Torah was anything to go by.

"People study for years and years to access the circle," Weiss said. "Some Johnny-come-lately can't just waltz in and demand to see it."

"I'm not some Johnny. I'm the Johnny with an Order's ID and a sharp sword, who's trying to save the city from an epidemic." If they thought their mezuzot would protect them from the Steel Mary, they would be deeply disappointed.

The corners of Peter's mouth sagged. "What Rabbi Weiss means is that we're dreadfully sorry, but your lack of qualifications prevents us from granting you access. It's unfortunate."

On that we were in agreement. "Would you like me to read what's written on the wall behind you to prove that I'm qualified?"

Peter gave me a sad smile.

Weiss sighed. "These are the many names of God. Knowing how to read Hebrew won't get you in, but go ahead if it makes you feel better."

"It says: 'Obey.'"

A long moment passed and then Peter closed his mouth with a click.

Weiss's eyes turned cold. "Who told you about that?"

"Would you like me to pronounce the word in the original language?" There was no telling what the word would do to them. I mostly used it to control magic, but it could be used to control people. I'd done it once—to Derek—and I would never do it again. But they didn't know that.

The rabbis paled. I'd managed to terrify holy men. Maybe I could beat up a nun for an encore.

"No!" Peter raised his hands. "No, that's not necessary. We'll take you to the circle."

THE GOLEM WAS SEVEN FEET TALL AND SIX FEET wide. Unlike the golems outside, who had been shaped with finesse like Greek statues, this brute was pure power. Broad, crude, and hewn together with thick slabs of clay muscle, it stood at the end of a narrow hallway before a door shaped like an open scroll. It wore a steel helmet, an armet with visor removed. The metal guard covered its mouth and a layer of steel shielded its forehead. No scratching off letters here. I wondered what they would do if they ever had to deactivate it. Shoot it with a tank maybe.

Next to me, Peter pointed to the floor, where a small stone fire pit with the fire already laid out waited before the golem. To the side sat a box of matches. "There is a price for using the circle."

"What is it?"

His voice was soft. "Knowledge. That is the keeper of the circle. You must light the fire and tell it a secret. If your knowledge is worthy, the golem will open the door for you."

"And if the golem doesn't like the knowledge?" Was it too much to hope it would chide me and send me to bed without my supper?

"It may kill you," Weiss said.

"If you lie, it will know," Peter said. "The flame will turn blue."

Lovely. The golem's fists were bigger than my head. All it had to do was grab me and squeeze and my skull would crack like an egg. The hallway was too narrow to maneuver. My speed wouldn't do me any good.

"We will wait here." Weiss pointed to a small stone bench a few yards away. It faced the golem so they would have front row seats if it decided to use me as a punching bag.

"It's not too late to change your mind," Peter murmured.

And stare into Ori's dead eyes every time I closed mine? No, thank you.

I crossed the floor, picked up the matches, and struck one. A tiny flame flared. Carefully I brought it to the fire and let it chew on the piece of paper in the center of wooden kindling.

A low rumble started in the center of the golem, a rough grating sound of rock grinding against rock. Two pinpoints of sharp light flared in its cavernous sockets.

I sat on the floor.

The golem shuddered. One huge columnar leg lifted and stepped forward, shaking the floor.

Boom.

Boom.

Boom.

The golem stopped before the fire and bent down. Tiny flecks of stone or dry clay broke from its shoulders and fell into the fire, igniting into brilliant white sparks. Slowly, ponderously, it crouched, its steel mouth guard only three feet from me.

I looked into its eyes. "Let me into the circle, and I will tell you the story of the first vampire."

Behind me, clothes rustled as the two rabbis sat on the bench.

I picked up a stick and poked the fire with it. "Long ago there lived a man. He was a great man, a thinker, philosopher, and magician. We'll call him Roland. Roland once had a kingdom, the most powerful kingdom in the world, a realm of magic and wonders. His ancestors brought people out of savagery into an age of prosperity and enlightenment and he was very proud of what his family had achieved.

"Roland had many children, for he had lived a very long time, but his favorite was his youngest son, let's call him Abe. He was Roland's only child at the time. You see, Roland had a habit of killing children when they rose against him, so Abe was the only one left.

"Everything went along splendidly, but the kingdom's people had pushed their magic too far. They disrupted the balance between magic and technology. Tech came, interrupting the flow of magic. The waves of technology attacked Roland's kingdom, pulling it apart the way magic now pulls apart our world. He counted on his son to help him. But Abe saw it as his chance for freedom. In the chaos of tech waves, Abe betrayed his father and fought him for power. The war between them ripped their kingdom to shreds. Abe lost, and took his followers into the wilderness, proclaiming he would make his own nation, greater than his father's fallen realm.

"Eventually Roland failed his people. The mighty kingdom had fallen and its ruler lost everything. He hid from the world, choosing to live alone on a mountain, spending his days in meditation.

"Meanwhile Abe's nation of nomads grew larger. They lost

most of what they knew. Philosophy and complicated magic were no longer important—survival was. Abe had a son and his son had sons, two boys. We'll call them Esau and Jacob. Esau was the oldest. He prided himself on being a great warrior and a hunter of men and beasts. Truth is, Esau was a thug, but he was stronger and more powerful than ordinary thugs and he made the best of it.

"The older nomads told stories of the wonders of Roland's fallen kingdom. Rumor had it that when Roland went to his mountain, he took the treasures of his realm with him. Among these treasures was a set of clothes made from the skin of a mythical beast and permeated with the fragrance of a lost valley. A hunter who wore this garment could hunt and capture any animal he wished. Esau, being an enterprising guy, decided to get his hands on these clothes. After all, how much trouble could one old guy be? So Esau got his supplies together and headed for Roland's mountain.

"Put yourself into Roland's shoes. Here he was, a man who'd lost everything, and now his own great-grandson shows up and tries to rob him. And more, his great-grandson, the fruit of his family tree, is an ignorant thug. In Esau, Roland saw the reflection of his people's fate—all of their knowledge lost, all of their achievements squandered, as they reverted to primitive brutality.

"Roland saw red, and Esau died before he could land a single blow. But that wasn't enough. Roland had a lot of frustration to vent. He raged at his great-grandson, at his fallen kingdom, at the world. He wanted to kill Esau again, and so he dragged him back from the brink of death and murdered him a second time. Again and again Esau died, until finally Roland stopped to take a breath and realized that Esau was gone. His body remained, but his mind had died. Instead Roland found a mindless creature, neither alive nor dead. An undead with its mind completely blank, like a white page.

"Roland discovered that he could control this empty brain with infinite ease. He could speak through Esau's mouth and hear what the undead heard. A host of possibilities occurred to Roland and he decided it would be convenient for him if people thought that Esau had murdered him. He dressed the creature that used to be his great-grandson into the magic garment Esau had come for and sent the undead back to its family, controlling its every move and spinning wild tales of his own death. He used Esau to torment Abe's nomads. He wanted to destroy Abe and all of his descendants.

"Eventually Esau grew fangs and developed a terrible thirst for blood. Years later the once-king put those fangs to a test. He lured Esau's brother to a meeting under the pretense of reconciliation, and there he unleashed the full fury of the undead on Jacob, letting Esau tear into his brother's neck. But Jacob had worn an ivory collar and Esau's fangs failed to sever his jugular.

"With time, Esau's body changed. He grew claws. His hair fell out. His body turned gaunt and he scuttled about on all fours like an animal. Roland released him into a cave, where the bodies of his ancestors and his children lay interred. Starving, the first vampire haunted the cave until a brave man finally put it out of its misery.

"Such is the true story of the first vampire." I got up. "It's not really all that secret. There are echoes of it in the Bible and in the Jewish scholarly writings. Abe is gone, and so are his children. But Roland, he still lives. Outlived them all, the old bastard. He's made more undead and he's rebuilding his power, waiting for a time to resurrect his kingdom."

I pricked my finger with my throwing knife. A single drop of red swelled on my skin. I leaned toward the golem and whispered so quietly, I could barely hear myself. "And his blood lives on as well."

I touched the blood to the golem's chest. It rocked back, as if struck. Stone screeched, dust puffed. The golem spun, backed to the door, grasped the stone with its massive hand, and pushed it aside, revealing a dark room beyond it.

I walked past it into the darkness. Behind me the stone door slid shut.

PALE BLUE LIGHTS WINKED INTO EXISTENCE ON the walls. I counted. Twelve. They pulsed, fading and flaring brighter and brighter, until they finally illuminated the floor in front of me: two circles, the first six feet wide, the next a foot wider, carved into the stone. Twelve stone pillars surrounded the circle, each five feet tall. On top of each rested a glass cube. Within the cube lay a *sefirot*, a scroll.

I approached the circle. Magic pulsed between the scrolls, like a strong invisible current. A ward, and a very powerful one. Wards both protected and contained. For all I knew, stepping into the circle would result in some weirdness manifesting in the middle of it and squeezing me like a juice orange.

I pulled Slayer from its sheath and circled the lines. No mysterious runes on the walls, no instructions, no warnings. Just the weak gauzy blue light of the lantern, the scrolls resting in their transparent cases, and the double circle on the floor.

I'd come this far. No turning back now.

I slid Slayer under my arm, pulled the paper out of the Ziploc bag, and stepped into the circle.

A silver light ignited in the spot I crossed. It dashed along the carved outline of the double circle, igniting it. Magic roiled between the scrolls. A wall of silvery glow surged up, sealing me from the outside world. All I needed now was for some monstrous critter to manifest and try to eat me.

Dear rabbis, I'm so sorry, I nuked your circle dude. Here is his head as a souvenir. Yeah, that would fly.

Magic nipped at my skin in tiny sharp needles, as if testing the waters. I tensed.

Hairline cracks spread through the floor. Pale light stabbed through the gaps. Something was coming. I swung Slayer, warming up my wrist.

Power burst under me. Magic punched through my feet and tore through my body in an agonizing torrent, grating at my insides as if every cell of my body had been stripped bare. It ripped a scream from me and the torrent burst out of my mouth in a stream of light, so bright I went blind. My head spun. Everything hurt. Weak and light-headed, I clenched my sword.

Breathe. One, two, three . . .

Slowly my vision cleared and I saw the translucent ward and beyond it the scrolls glowing on their stone pillars. Deep blue currents of magic slid up and down within the glow. What the hell? I looked up. The last of the magic torn from me floated above in a cloud of indigo, slowly merging with the ward.

Damn it. The perimeter wall of the circle wasn't a ward, although it looked and felt like one. It was an *ara*, a magic engine. I'd read about them but never encountered one. It lay dormant until some idiot, like me, stepped inside it and donated some magic juice to get it running. It absorbed my magic and turned blue. If I'd been a vampire, the glow would've become purple.

It occurred to me that my feet were no longer touching the ground. Out of the corner of my eye I could see the place where the floor used to be and it wasn't there. I glanced down. The floor had vanished. In its place gaped a black pit and I floated above it, weightless.

Oh, great. Just great.

I opened my hand, revealing the parchment. A feather of light swept it off my palm and dragged it into the air to my eye level.

The magic buckled. Long veins of indigo streaked through the *ara* and struck at the parchment. It shivered, caught in the spider web of blue tendrils.

It was good that the Temple was shielded by a ward; otherwise anyone with an iota of power would be able to sense these fireworks.

The tendrils clutching the parchment turned a darker blue. The circle picked up the parchment's magic and now it spread through the glow.

A powerful magic pulse ripped through the *ara*.

The center of the parchment turned smooth. The worn lines creasing the rough paper vanished. Ink appeared, slowly, like a developing photograph. A magic square formed in the corner. An assortment of geometric figures: spirals, circles, crosses . . .

The magic pulsed again and again, like the toll of a great bell. My whole body hummed with the echo. *Hurry up, damn you.*

The ragged edges of the parchment grew as the web built onto it. The parchment must've been only a small piece of the original scroll, a top left corner, and now the circle was reconstructing it as it once had been.

Words appeared, written in Hebrew. Between them, smaller lines written in English came through.

I devastate the land and shatter it to dust,
I crush the cities and turn them into waste,

This was familiar. I knew this.

I crumble mountains and panic their wild beasts,
I churn the sea and hold back its tides,

I squeezed my memory, trying to pinpoint where I'd read this before.

I bring stillness of the tomb to nature's wild places,
I reap the lives of humankind, none survive,

Come on, come on. Where did it come from? Why was it lodged in my brain? Words kept coming, faster and faster. I scanned the lines.

I bring dark omens and desecrate holy places,
I release demons into sacred dwellings of the gods,
I ravage palaces of kings and send nations into
     mourning,
I set ablaze the blooms of fields and orchards,

A final phrase ignited at the end of the scroll. It pierced my mind. Cold bit my fingers.

I let evil enter.

Oh no.
The words glared at me. *I let evil enter.*
Oh no, you don't. I knew this—this was a part of an ancient Babylonian poem, used as an amulet against a man once worshipped as the god of plagues. He'd brought panic and terror to the ancient world and decimated its people with epidemics. His wrath was chaos, his temper was fire, and ancient Babylonians feared him so much, they were too afraid to build him a temple.
I read all about him when I was ten years old. His name was Erra.

But the Steel Mary was a woman. I was absolutely, positively, one hundred percent sure she was a woman. I saw her with my own eyes. A huge six-foot-six woman, but unmistakably female. I had a round hole, and no matter how the universe tried to get me to shove a square peg into it, it wasn't going to happen.

The tendrils curled back, withdrawing into the circle. The scroll snapped taut and disintegrated into a cloud of glowing sparks. The piece of parchment, once again ancient and blank, landed into my hand. The power of the circle vanished and I dropped to the stone floor.

The door slid open and I saw Peter's pale face. He wheezed, catching his breath. "We're under attack."

CHAPTER 20

———◆———

I DOUBLE-TIMED IT THROUGH THE PASSAGEWAYS
of the synagogue. Peter jogged next to me.

"What do you mean, there is no way to hide the circle's
magic? You said you keep the circle secret."

He huffed. "The particulars of the circle are secret. Its
power isn't. One doesn't hide the power of God. The light of
knowledge must shine through."

It shone alright. It shone real well. It shone so well that the
Steel Mary had sensed the parchment and sent the cavalry to
investigate.

A thud shook the walls of the old building. I dashed up the
stairs, through the hallway, and to the front. Several people
stood before the door on the stairs.

On the snow-buried lawn a six-foot-tall blood-red man
grabbed a golem by the hind leg. He jerked the golem up,
swung it, and smashed it on the ground, sending a spray of
snow into the air. The golem slid, scrambled up, and galloped
away, leaping over the broken body of its twin. All around the
Temple crushed clay bodies littered the grounds. At least ten,
maybe more. It looked like a war zone and only one side had
suffered casualties.

A red aura flared from the man, ruby bright against the white snow. The sun was a pale glow behind the clouds. It was almost five and the night would pounce soon. I didn't want to fight him in the dark.

"Is he alone?"

Nobody answered.

"Did he come alone?"

"Yes." Rabbi Weiss swung into my field of vision. "What was on that parchment? What is he?"

You don't want to know. "In ancient Babylon there was a god called Erra, also known as Nergal. He was the god of plagues and chaos." And fear.

Except he wasn't really a god. I would've preferred a god, but Erra was something much, much worse.

Another golem galloped from the back and hurled its spear at the man. The man batted it aside.

"Erra had seven warriors at his disposal." I flipped Slayer, warming up my wrist. "Darkness, Torch, Beast, Tremor, Gale, Deluge, and Venom. Deluge is dead. The Beast Lord killed him three days ago."

The golem charged the red man and reared, kicking with its hoofed legs.

I watched the charge. "This would be . . ."

The man stomped. Thunder rolled through the yard, like the sound of a colossal sledgehammer. The ground yawned. He grabbed the golem and thrust it into the forming hole. It sank up to its waist, still kicking. The man swung his huge fist and hammered a punch to the golem's sternum. The clay chest shattered like an egg shell. The golem's head fell to the ground.

"Tremor." Power of earth. Lovely. By all rights, he shouldn't have been able to make sinkholes, given that the ground was frozen solid, but apparently someone forgot to mention it to him.

Tremor surveyed the grounds, looking for the next target.

"He'll never break the ward," someone said to my right.

Oh yes, he will. Trust me on this. "I wouldn't count on it. Your wards are very strong but your magic is too young for him."

A gray-haired woman gave me a pitying look, usually

reserved for imbeciles. "Our wards are written in a language that was twelve hundred years old before the Common Era began. Even Unicorn Lane can't breach them."

I pointed at Tremor. "Twelve hundred years before the Common Era, Erra was thirty centuries young. He predates your language."

A bout of hysterical barking came from the left. Idiot dog, making himself a target.

"Open the ward." I started down the stairs.

"That isn't wise," Peter called out. "The spell will hold."

"Out of the question. It's too dangerous." The older woman crossed her arms. "We won't be held responsible for your death or damage to the Temple."

Tremor took a step toward my poodle.

"Open the damn ward, or I will break it!"

Tremor turned away from the dog, swiped the golem's head off the snow, and hurled it at the Temple. It flew through the air, cleared the ward in a flash of silver, and shattered against the Temple's door. Of course—the golems belonged to the Temple and the ward was keyed to them, so they could pass through it. He'd pelt the Temple with golem remains, and when he'd run out of bodies to throw, he'd stomp over here himself.

The rabbis stared at the shards of the broken head. Tremor reached for another body.

The gray-haired woman looked up. "Peter, open the ward!"

White light streamed down. I stepped through, and the ward surged shut behind me. I started toward Tremor, pulling on the clasp of the cloak.

Tremor turned to face me. He wore the face of Solomon Red. Surprise, surprise.

The cloak slid off my shoulders and fell on the snow. I kept walking. Nice and slow.

Solomon regarded me with a condescending grin. He never smiled. Like a drunk straining every muscle to appear sober, Solomon did his best to hide the fact that he couldn't read behind a mask of grave importance. But now he smirked at me with obvious contempt. An agile intelligence lit his eyes. Erra's intelligence.

Solomon opened his mouth. A familiar female voice spilled forth. "You again. This is the best the priests can do? Or are they trying to entertain me?"

I swung my sword, warming up my wrist. "Why are you a woman?"

"Why can't I be a woman?"

Because it fucks up my family tree. "Because Erra's poem says you're a man."

Solomon shrugged. "You shouldn't put your trust into the ramblings of senile temple rats."

"I'll keep that in mind. Any other pearls of wisdom?"

"None that would help you live through the next minute." Solomon spread his arms and pulled them together as if pushing a great weight before him.

The ground shook beneath my feet.

I leapt up and to the left. A sinkhole gaped where I'd stood. I landed and jumped again, barely avoiding another pit. All around me holes opened, like greedy black mouths in the snow, and I hopped between them like a chicken on hot tin. I dashed right, then left. Unless I learned to fly, I'd never get to him.

Solomon laughed in Erra's voice.

Usually I saved my magic as a last resort, but this was the old power and now wasn't a good time to screw around. I had to hit him now and hit him hard.

I took a deep breath and barked a power word. *"Ossanda."* Kneel.

The world reeled in a haze of pain. Like grabbing a handful of my own flesh and ripping it out. I reeled, but didn't go down.

Solomon's mouth gaped open. A dull roar like the sound of a rockslide spilled from his lips. His knees hit the dirt. *Who's laughing now?*

The holes in the ground closed. I ran.

The power word had drained too much of my magic, and every step turned into a battle of will. Like dragging lead chains. I kept running.

Snow flew under my feet. Solomon shuddered. Thick cords of muscle bulged on his thighs.

Ten feet.

Six.

Three.

I struck in a classic overhead blow designed to cleave through his neck. As I swung, dirt thrust between us. The saber's blade sliced through soil and came away clean. Missed. Shit.

A thick mound jutted where Solomon had knelt. Trying to thrust through it would break the blade and accomplish nothing.

"First, you kneel, then you hide. So far I'm not impressed."

The mound exploded. Chunks of dirt pelted the snow. Solomon lunged at me, laughing.

I dodged and carved at his side. Slayer sliced a narrow line just under Solomon's ribs. Red gushed. Solomon whipped about and backhanded me. The punch smashed into my chest. I flew, slid through the snow, and crashed against something. Cold sliced my right side, as if someone had thrust an icicle into my kidney. My lungs burned. Colored circles swam before my eyes. I must've hit my head.

I squinted—the body of a broken golem. Warm sticky liquid wet my side. I wanted a shower to wash it off . . . Yep, definitely hit my head.

"Shake it off," Erra said. "Come on. Up you go."

I jerked myself free. The golem's spear jutted out, propped by its corpse, and its spearhead was red with my blood. Just what I need.

"Have your eyes cleared yet?"

"Hold your horses. I'm coming." Yeah, not so much.

"From where I stand, you're just breathing laboriously."

The snow swam in and out of focus. "Breathing hard. Are you coming or just breathing *hard.* You've got to get your one-liners straight."

"Thanks. I'll remember that."

The blurry haze cleared and I saw Solomon charging at me on all fours.

No time. I braced my back against the golem and gripped Slayer with both hands.

Solomon loomed over me. "Time to pray."

I kicked my leg up, catching him in the gut, and thrust into his chest. Slayer slid into the flesh between his ribs. The point met resistance and it vanished.

Solomon's huge hands tried to grip at me, but my foot on his stomach held him back. Pressure ground at my bones. God, he was a heavy bastard. I twisted the blade, trying to rupture the heart.

"Give it up," I squeezed out. "I hit the heart."

Erra snorted. "I know. Do you have any idea how many bodies I had to go through to get him?"

The light shrank. Earth piled around us. A few moments and we'd be buried.

The wound gnawed at my side. My saber was caught, and sinking silver needles into the undead would be like poking him with toothpicks—slightly painful but ultimately futile.

Solomon dug his feet in. His fingers scratched my neck.

There wasn't enough air. "Would you just let him die already?"

"He doesn't have much left, don't worry. You do talk a lot. Like a little squirrel in a tree, chirp-chirp-chirp."

I barely saw the light above us. If the earth built up any more, Solomon would collapse on me when he died for the second time. I would suffocate, buried alive. "Your animal impressions are stunning."

Solomon jerked right. His hand grasped my arm, he ducked his head, and pain clenched my forearm.

She made her undead bite me. "What the hell?"

Solomon grinned. "Little squirrel! You taste like family."

Oh, shit.

A shaggy shape hit Solomon, snarling and snapping teeth. Solomon jerked and extra weight pressed on me as the dog tore into Solomon's back. I cried out. Solomon swiped with his arm, knocking the poodle aside. His weight shifted, and I grabbed my throwing knife.

"Don't touch my dog."

Solomon laughed. "How curious. Hugh's been keeping secrets. No wonder. That's the trouble with hired help: without ambition, they are useless, with ambition—"

I stabbed my throwing knife into Solomon's throat. "Severed carotid. Enjoy."

Blood gushed from Solomon's mouth, drenching my face. "See you soon," he gurgled.

Solomon's eyes went blank. He shuddered once and crashed on top of me.

Erra had bailed.

I strained and pushed Solomon's corpse to the side, into the dirt.

A moment later a smelly tongue licked my face, covering my skin with the fine perfume of day-old roadkill.

I hugged the furry neck. "Okay, okay. Let me up now."

The poodle leaped away, excited. I got to my feet. The cut in my side screeched in protest. An earthen wall rose up to my waist. I clutched on to it, so I wouldn't tip over.

Solomon lay facedown. I kicked him. It didn't make me feel that much better. I kicked him again, just in case, and realized I was looking at a spear sticking out of his back.

The ward went down. People rushed from the Temple, heading toward me.

Where the hell had the spear come from?

A man reached me. "Are you hurt?"

"Who threw the spear?"

He shrank back. "I'm a medic. I can help you."

I tried to speak slowly in my nonthreatening voice. "Where did the spear come from?"

He blinked. "I don't know, I didn't see."

I grabbed the spear and strained. Sonovabitch, really in there. I put my foot on the body, crushing a few black needles, and pulled hard. The spear came free. It used to belong to one of the golems. Someone had picked it up and hurled it. Someone with great strength.

Someone had reported my crawling around the pole with Joshua's body on it. Someone had watched me from the ruins. And now someone had skewered Solomon and vanished. I was really getting tired of all the secrecy.

Little squirrel. You taste like family. See you later.

She recognized the blood, but she didn't know who I was. If I were her, I'd track me down. I'd get into my house, learn anything I could about me, and look for anything I could use as leverage. I knew this would eventually happen and it finally did. All my friends had just acquired a huge bull's-eye on their backs.

Julie. I had Julie's pictures in the house.

I had to get home.

I had to warn the Pack.

I spun around and saw Marigold lying on her side in red snow.

Oh, God. I stumbled toward her and broke into a run.

"Wait!" the medmage chased me.

Marigold lay unmoving, her head jerked high. The twisted wreck of a golem's spear jutted from her neck. She must've been hit when Erra was throwing shit around.

I dropped into the snow and grabbed her head. Her eyes stayed dark. Her long eyelashes didn't move.

"Can you fix her?"

"She is dead," the medmage said.

She killed my Marigold. The bitch killed my Marigold. I'd used this mule for a year. I'd brought her carrots, brushed her out, and relied on her to carry me into a brawl or storm. Now she was dead, killed as an afterthought.

I staggered to my feet. I had to get to the phone.

People jumped out of my way. I marched up the steps and grabbed the first warm body. "Phone?"

"Inside, to the right."

I ran inside, made a right into a small room, and grabbed the phone. Work. Work, damn you, work, *work*.

Dial tone. Yes!

I dialed the Keep. A man picked up. I barked, "Curran. Now."

"Who is this?"

"Kate Daniels. I'm the agent of—"

The phone clicked and Curran's voice filled the phone. "Leave a message."

"The Steel Mary's name is Erra. If any of your people fight her, she will make you go mad. It's her specialty. She served Roland, which means she came here to kill the Pack. Be careful. Don't fight her directly if you can—"

The call cut out. I'd reached the message limit.

I dialed the Order. Maxine came on the line.

"I need a pickup at the Temple."

"I'm sorry, dear, but everyone is out."

"Andrea?"

"She's out helping Mauro."

I hung up and punched in Jim's number. He picked up on the second ring.

"I need help."

"You just now figured this out?"

I tried to speak calmly. "I'm at the Temple. I just ran into the Steel Mary and I need to get home before she makes it there."

"I'll have a car there in twenty minutes."

"Thank you."

I went outside. Three rabbis approached me. The older woman, Weiss, and a man who had to be in his seventies. With long pure white hair and an equally white beard, he looked positively ancient and he walked with a limp, leaning on an ornate staff.

"You've brought this to the Temple." He indicated the golem graveyard with the sweep of his hand. "You are no longer welcome here. Leave."

Oh, that's just peachy. I pointed to Solomon. "Burn the body. Don't touch the blood. If you experience any symptoms of illness, immediately contact Biohazard." I pointed at the medic. "You! Patch me up."

"Did you not hear?" The woman stared at me, incredulous.

"I have a Mary with pandemic potential who pilots undead mages and who is fixing to raid my house. Everyone I've ever known is about to become a target. Being banned by the Temple is the least of my worries."

EVERY STEP I TOOK JABBED A DULL, COLD PAIN INTO my side. My skin felt wet under the dressing. The wound had come open. The Temple medic was very good, but the cut simply hadn't had enough time to heal. At least the dressing had been well applied, so the blood should stay put.

I made it to the bridge and slumped into the snowdrift. Grendel licked me and ran away to paint the snow yellow.

I had to get home.

A car shot across the bridge way too fast. Metallic black, it had the body of a hot rod that had somehow sprouted Indy-racer-style front wheels. Painted red flames stretched from its front over the hood, licking a bizarre horned skull with the words DEMON LIGHTNING painted above it. Its backside bubbled up, struggling to contain a monster of an enchanted water engine.

The car hurtled past me, braked in a spray of snow, and stopped two feet away. The driver side window slid down, revealing a tiny Indonesian woman. I'd met her before. She was the Pack's resident mythology expert. She was also a vegetarian, and when she turned into her animal, which happened to be a cross-eyed white tiger, she refused to bite anything that would bleed into her mouth.

She was also blind as a bat.

Dali peered at me through her glasses and nodded at the car. "Get in!"

I opened my mouth but nothing came out.

"Get in, Kate!"

"What the hell is this?"

"That's a 1999 Plymouth Prowler. Also known as Pooki."

I bet Jim thought he was funny. "Dali, you can barely see. You can't drive."

Dali stuck her nose in the air. "Watch me."

No choice. I screamed for Grendel, stuffed him into the car, got in, and buckled my seat belt.

Dali floored it. Snow burst on both sides of the car and we shot forward. The wooden planks thudded under the Prowler's weight. The bridge curved ahead. Dali showed no indication of slowing down.

"Dali, there is a turn."

The turn rushed at us.

"Dali . . ."

The Prowler sped up, straight as an arrow.

"Turn! Turn left!"

The wooden rail loomed before us. The Prowler veered left, turning so sharply it almost careened. I held my breath. For a second we were weightless, and then all four wheels landed on solid ground.

"I saw it." Dali pushed her Coke-bottle glasses up the bridge of her nose. "I'm not blind, you know. Hold on to your seat, there is another turn coming up."

If I survived this, I'd kill Jim with my bare hands.

The car squealed and missed the rail by a hair.

Dali's happy face swung into my view. "I know your kryptonite."

"What?"

"Kryptonite. It's the rock that could take down Superman?"

I stared at her.

Dali grinned. "You're scared of my driving."

It wasn't driving. It was suicide by car. "I need to tell you about Erra." I clenched my fists as the car fishtailed. "So you can tell Jim."

Dali made a face. "Why do I get the privilege?"

"Because you're a Pack expert with a proven record and you can back up what I say with your own research. He'll listen to you and I don't have time to explain things to him myself right this second."

She looked at me. "Kate? Is this something really, really bad? Because you have that clenched-teeth look . . ."

"Watch the road!"

She swerved, avoiding an overturned wreck of a truck. "I have it under control."

"What do you know about Babylon?"

"Not much. My expertise is in the Asian region. It was a Mesopotamian city-state that sprung up around the third millennium BCE and eventually grew into an empire. Sargon of Akkad claimed to have built it. Mesopotamia is considered to be the cradle of civilization and Babylon is mostly famous for the Code of Hammurabi, which was the first written code of laws, and the Hanging Gardens, which was the first time a man had to restructure the city to get laid. I think the name means 'Gateway of the Gods,' although nobody quite knows why."

Her definition of "not much" needed work. "It was called Gateway because it was the first city built after Eden."

She turned back to the windshield. "Babylon dates back to three thousand years before the Common Era. It's too recent."

"That's the new Babylon. The old Babylon was almost completely built with magic, and when the tech came, it crumbled to the ground, just like that." I pointed at Downtown's architectural graveyard through the window. "The old Babylon was over twelve thousand years old when the Common Era rolled around."

"How do you know this?"

"Not important. Have you ever read the poem of Erra?"

"No."

"It's a poem that acts as an amulet against diseases in general and a god called Erra in particular. It was found chiseled on stone tablets all over Babylon. More copies of it exist than there are copies of the Gilgamesh epic."

Dali whistled. "Gilgamesh was their big daddy."

"Yes, but they weren't that scared of him. They were very scared of Erra, so scared, they cut the poem into every available stone surface. According to the story, Erra was the god of plagues, fear, and madness. He had seven warriors at his disposal: Torch, Tremor, Deluge, Gale, Beast, Venom, and Darkness. The first four had elemental powers."

"Fire, Earth, Water, and Wind." Dali nodded.

"Beast was a monster. Venom is self-explanatory."

"And Darkness?"

I shook my head. "Nobody knows."

She wrinkled her nose. "Don't you just love when that happens?"

"The poem goes on about how Erra and his advisor called Ishum came to Babylon and destroyed it. The poem is also wrong. Erra wasn't the one in charge, Ishum was. The Babylonians were so terrified of Erra, they put him in charge just to be on the safe side. They also made him male."

"Wait, Erra was a girl?"

"Yes. Erra is a woman and Ishum is Roland."

Dali said nothing. She clenched the wheel tighter—her knuckles turned white.

I kept going. "About 6200 BC, Roland and Erra were running around and conquering Mesopotamia. They were young and this was their first big war. They came across Babylon, which was ruled by Marduk, who was unimaginably ancient by this point. He used to be monstrously powerful, but he had grown old and senile. The world moved on. Marduk didn't and he knew it. He was content to rule Babylon, his last city, the gem of the ancient world. It was a large thriving metropolis, built almost entirely with deep magic, and he was very proud of it.

I knew this story very well. Voron had told it to me long ago, except in his version Erra was a man. Even Roland's Warlords didn't know everything about him.

"Roland decided they didn't have the troops to hold the city. Marduk was greatly revered, so they'd have to put up with a lot of native resistance and the infrastructure was too complex to easily take it over. Roland makes war to acquire, not to subjugate. He wants to take cities with minimal damage, install his own government, and build them up to make them better. He moved on. But Erra dug her heels in. Something about Marduk must've rubbed her the wrong way.

"Erra took a chunk of Roland's army, and along with her seven, they invaded Babylon. She took the city and ran Marduk out, but the Babylonians refused to bend over and take it. Erra decided to break Babylon. She bombarded them with plagues and let the seven run amok in the city. Halved the population, wrecked the holy places, engaged in unbelievable atrocities. It was hell on earth. When there was nothing left to hold, she left. Marduk later came back to the city and rebuilt it, but it took centuries for it to rise to prominence again. What we know now as Babylon from archaeological records is a pale imitation of what once was." I looked at Dali to make sure she understood. "They had magic defenses that we can't even dream of. And Erra crushed them and walked away laughing. I need you to tell this story to Jim."

Dali swallowed. "Why?"

"Because Erra is here. Curran killed Deluge and I just took out Tremor."

"Is she after us?"

"I think so. She has her seven warriors with her. They are undead. She pilots them like vampires."

Dali shrugged her shoulders, as if shaking off dread. "How sure are you of this?"

"I'm very sure. Erra makes plagues. In ancient times, she walked before Roland's army. She'd pass through the place and the next morning there would be nothing but corpses. A few days later, once the land aired out, Roland's troops would roll in. We know that Roland wants to do away with the Pack. Erra is the perfect person to do that. She has the power to panic animals and it works on shapeshifters."

"You're joking."

I quoted, " 'I devastate the land and shatter it to dust, I crush the cities and turn them into waste, I crumble mountains and panic their wild beasts.' She drives shapeshifters mad, Dali. She makes you go wild. You've heard about the witnesses to the fight at the Steel Horse. All of them went wild. You can't fight her. Explain this to Jim. I don't know if it's her personal power or if she's using one of the warriors to do it, but she has the Old Magic, the kind that the Pack can't counter. You can't engage her, because she will make all of you insane."

The car skidded to a halt and I realized we had reached my apartment. I jerked the door open and jumped out. Grendel followed.

"Kate?" Dali's eyes were huge on her face. "How do we fight her?"

"I don't know. You can't fight her directly and I'll do everything in my power to make sure you don't have to."

I slammed the door closed and ran into my building.

CHAPTER 21

———— ◆ ————

I CHARGED UP MY APARTMENT STAIRS, SLAYER
in hand and my sweatered demon spawn in tow.

My apartment door. In one piece. No sign of a break-in.

I forced myself to slow down, slid the key into the lock,
and swung the door open. The poodle trotted in. I followed
softly on my toes.

Kitchen. Clear.

I nudged the bathroom door with my fingertips. Clear.

My living room. Clear.

Library/Julie's room. Clear.

Clear. The apartment was clear.

I had to hide Julie.

I scanned the apartment. Too much. I could throw away
the pictures, but signs of her were all over my place. Clothes,
teddy bear with vampire teeth, half-painted black bedroom
with a big KEEP OUT stenciled on the wall . . . Sooner or later
Erra would make it into my apartment, and she would find
something I'd missed. She would look for Julie, and if she
found her, she would kill my kid and she'd do it slowly to
torture me with it.

Think. Think, think, think . . .

I grabbed scissors, marched into Julie's closet, and pulled out her favorite Goth dress. Two snips, and I had two pieces of black ribbon. I snatched glue out of the utility drawer and fixed black ribbon over the corner of two photo frames.

Funeral pictures. That was what Voron did when Larissa died. She was a wererat, who traveled with us for a while, and when she died, he fixed the ribbons on her photo. I had a kid, but she died and I kept her funeral pictures in plain sight.

I pulled the paper drawer open, took the folder with Julie's school papers, and pushed the books off the woodstove. A bit of kerosene, some crumpling, and two minutes later Julie's school records went up in flames.

Okay. I had the phone number of the school memorized. There was no record of it. And if Erra thought Julie was dead, she wouldn't look for her. I grabbed the phone and dialed the school's number. In ten seconds I was patched through to security and gave detailed instructions: Julie was not to leave the grounds. She was not to contact me until I contacted her.

I ended the call, dialed the Order, and hung up. If Erra knew how to use redial, it wouldn't lead her to Julie either.

The papers burned to ash. I sat on the floor and stared at the flames.

I beat her. If she broke in now, Julie would be safe.

Grendel wandered over to me and whined softly.

"Give me a minute," I told him.

All my life had been focused on avoiding this moment. My family had found me. Even if I killed her, which was a huge "if," it wouldn't exactly go unnoticed.

I had to go. I had to grab my shit and take off into the wilderness, where she couldn't track me. I knew where to hide. Voron and I had planned out several escape routes years ago.

What about Julie? She was safe at the school but she wouldn't understand. She would think I'd abandoned her. Taking her with me was out of the question. Julie wasn't me. I could take a knife, melt into the forest, and come out on the other side weeks later, leaner, but no worse for wear. Julie wouldn't be able to handle it. The responsible thing would be to leave her where she was.

She'd run away and go looking for me. She'd run away in a heartbeat.

All I could do would be to send a message to the school and tell them that I had to go and she had to stay and trust them to keep her there.

No good choices. When you care about people, they tie you down.

Suppose I did take off and Erra lost my trail. The Pack would be her next target. She would demolish the shape-shifters. Once she was done with them, she'd have the city to play with. If she really did what she was famous for, Atlanta would become the land of diseased corpses.

Erra was made out of my childhood nightmares. For the first time since I reached adulthood, I wanted my dad to be alive, in the way a child wants his parent to come into a dark bedroom and turn on the light. Except Voron was dead. Besides, I knew what his response would be: Run. Run as fast and as far as you can. I had a window of opportunity now, before she found me again. Once I let it slip, my avenue of escape was gone forever. Show over.

I picked Slayer off the floor and dragged my fingers across the blade, feeling magic nip at my skin. The need to run gripped me. The walls closed in, as if my apartment had shrunk.

This wasn't me. I didn't panic. I needed to be sharp for this.

I closed my eyes and let it all go. I pictured the worst pos-sible scenario. Julie dead, her little face bloody. Curran dead, his body broken, gray eyes staring into nothing, all of the gold gone. Jim, Andrea, Raphael, Derek, dead, their bodies torn apart.

My hands turned ice-cold. My pulse raced. My heartbeat thudded in my ears, too loud.

Atlanta dead. Corpses on the streets. Vultures that circled but wouldn't land because the corpses were poison.

I soaked it all in. It hurt. Sweat broke out on my face.

A long moment passed.

Gradually my heart rate slowed. I breathed in deep and let it out. Again. Again. Fatigue rolled over me in a sluggish wave. The poodle licked my hand.

I'd tricked my mind into thinking the worst had happened

and I had lived through it. Everyone was still alive. I still had a chance to shield them.

My breathing evened out. Dread and fear fell away from me. Fear drained resources. One could be afraid only so much before the body shut it off in self-defense. I'd overloaded the circuits. Calm came. My mind started slowly, like a rusty clock. "I had my fun. I made friends, adopted a kid, fell in love. It's time to pay the piper."

Grendel tilted his head.

"Besides, the bitch killed Marigold. We've got to nuke her. Are you game?"

The poodle turned around, trotted into the kitchen, and brought me his food dish.

"What happened to your altruism? Fine. I'll pay you in meat if you help me kill her."

The dog barked.

"You've got yourself a deal. Here, let's see what we can scrounge up." I grinned and pushed off the floor. Everything hurt. I was spent. The power word and the fight had cost me and the wound didn't help. It felt like I was dragging steel chains.

My invisible chains and I made it into the kitchen. I opened the fridge, tossed the undead head into the garbage, and tried to find something to eat.

A knock sounded through my apartment.

I PUT GRENDEL IN THE BATHROOM AND OPENED the door.

Erra stood on the landing, wrapped in a fur cloak, her face hidden by a hood. I was about five seven. She topped me by at least ten inches.

Would it have killed her to wait a couple hours and let me catch my breath?

I held the door open. "I get a visit in person. I'm so honored."

"You should be. There is a ward on the door. Yours or did you pay someone?"

"Mine."

She held out her hand, giving me a glimpse of calluses at the base of her fingers—from sword use. Man-hands, Bob had said. I could see why he'd think that.

The ward clutched at her skin in a flash of blue. It had to hurt like hell.

She clenched her fist.

The blue glow solidified around her hand. Hairline cracks dashed through it. For a long second it held, like a pane of translucent blue glass, and then it broke. Magic boomed inside my skull, exploding into a crippling headache.

Message received. Whatever I could make, she could break. Subtle "R" Us.

Pieces of the ward fluttered down, melting in midair. Erra shook her hand with a grimace. "Not too bad."

My skull wanted very much to split open. "Shall we fight now or fight later?"

"Later." She strode into my apartment. Apparently she wanted to talk. That was fine. I could always make her bleed later. I closed the door.

Erra pulled back the hood, revealing a mass of dark brown, nearly black hair, slipped her cloak off, and tossed it on my bed. She wore loose black pants and a tailored leather jerkin studded with metal. A simple longsword hung at her waist. No frills, functional hilt, double-edged blade about twenty-eight inches long. Good for thrusting or slashing. The kind of sword I'd carry. Her calluses said she knew how to use it. My vision of facing a spear fighter just went up in flames. She cracked wards like walnuts, she was a giant, and she was good with the blade.

"You don't spit fire, do you?"

"No."

"Just checking."

Erra faced me. She looked older than me by about ten years. Her sharp nose protruded farther, almost Roman in shape, and her lips were fuller than mine. Looking into her dark eyes was like being shocked with a live wire. Magic churned in her irises, fueling towering arrogance, intelligence, and white-hot temper. The tiny hairs on the back of my neck rose.

Her eyes narrowed. She scrutinized me.

I raised my chin and stared back.

Erra laughed softly. "What do you know? Blood ran true. A little remainder of my own mortality. Thousands of years and godlike power, and here I am, getting challenged by a babe who looks like me."

She had me there. Nobody with an iota of sense would have any doubt that we were related. Same skin tone, same eyes, same shape of the face, same smirk, same build, except she was huge. We even wore similar clothes.

The Dubal ritual suddenly made sense. I hadn't seen myself in the smeared cloudy liquid. I'd seen her. The second anyone viewed us side by side, the jig would be up.

Erra surveyed the apartment. "This is where you dwell?"

"Yep."

"It's a hovel."

What was it lately with everyone commenting on my accommodations? My office was shabby, my apartment was a hovel . . .

"How old are you?"

"Twenty-six."

She blinked. "You *are* just a baby. When I was your age, I had a palace. Servants and guards and teachers. You never forget your first one."

"First what?"

"Your first palace."

I rolled my eyes. "Thanks."

"You're welcome." Erra strolled into the back and glanced into the library. "I like your books." She picked up Julie's picture off the shelf. "Who is the child? She isn't of the family."

"An orphan."

Erra's fingers slid across the black ribbon. "What happened?"

"She died."

"Children often do." She turned and nodded at the kitchen. "It's cold. Do you have anything to drink?"

"Tea." This was surreal. Maybe if I fed her some cookies, she would postpone turning Atlanta into a wasteland.

"Is it hot?" Erra asked.

"Yes."

"That will do."

I went into the kitchen, made tea, poured two cups, and sat.

Slayer was waiting for me on the chair. I slid it on my lap and looked at Erra. She folded herself into a chair across from me and dumped half a cup of honey into her tea.

Of all the people I knew, I had the best shot at taking her down. I wasn't at my best right this second, but we don't get to pick the time to fight for our lives.

"What are you thinking?" she asked.

Thinking that you have better reach but I'm faster. "Why a sword and not a spear?"

"The spear is good to pin things in place. Swords tend to break under the weight. I've seen you fight and you deserve a sword." A corner of her mouth crept up. "Unless you plan to stand still while I skewer you."

I shrugged. "The thought did cross my mind, but I have a reputation to uphold."

Erra chuckled. "I figured out who you are. You're the lost child Im carries on about, when he gets his attacks of melancholy."

Melancholy, right. He mourns the fact he failed to kill me—how charming. "Im?"

"A childhood nickname of your father's. Do you know who I am?"

"The scourge of the ancient world. Plaguebringer. City Eater. My aunt." Roland's older sister.

Erra raised her cup. "Shall we celebrate our family reunion?"

I raised my spoon and twirled it in the air a couple of times. "Whooptidoo."

She smiled. "You're too funny to be his. His children tend to take themselves absurdly seriously."

I sipped my tea. The longer we chatted, the more I rested. "You don't say."

"You're much more like my brood, but I only woke up six years ago so you can't be mine. Too bad. Another time, another place, I could possibly make you into something suitable."

I couldn't resist. "What were your children like?"

"Impulsive. And violent. I mostly made boys, and they tended toward the simple pleasures in life: drinking, whoring, and fighting, preferably all three at once." She waved her fingers. "Im's offspring stare at stars and make clocks that calculate useless happenings like the angle of a hawk's claws as it strikes its prey. They demonstrate their contraptions and everyone marvels. My children get drunk, confuse a herd of cows with an enemy regiment, and slaughter the lot, screaming like lunatics until the entire army panics."

That sounded like big Ajax, one of the Greeks who besieged Troy. Must've been during her "Greek" period.

Erra took a drink. "One dimwit dragged the city gates up a mountain. I asked him why he did that. He said, 'It seemed like a good idea at the time.'"

I blinked. "Did he also refuse to cut his hair?"

Erra grimaced. "He was balding. That was his master plan: grow out a mane so nobody would notice. His father was gorgeous. Dumb as a pigeon but gorgeous. I thought my blood would compensate for his lack of brains."

"How did that turn out for you?"

My aunt grimaced. "He was the dumbest child I ever produced. Killing him was like curing a headache."

I sipped my tea. "You killed your own son?"

"He was a mistake, and when you make a mistake, it must be corrected."

"I thought he committed suicide." At least according to the Bible.

"He did. I just helped him along the way."

"Ajax killed himself, too."

She sipped her tea in a gesture so similar to mine, I had to fight not to stare. "You don't say."

That's my family for you. Oh, so pleasant.

I refilled my cup.

My aunt glanced at me. "Do you know what your father does when his kids disappoint him?"

"I'm sure you'll tell me."

"He calls me. Im's too sentimental to remedy his mistakes. He's done it a few times, but they have to do something truly asinine for him to kill them personally."

"I'm excellent at asinine."

She smiled, sharp enough to cut. Like a sword coming out of a scabbard. "That I can believe."

We looked at each other.

"Why the Pack?" I asked.

"Five half-breeds are easy to dispatch. Throw enough troops at them and they will be overwhelmed. Fifty half-breeds will slice through five times their number. They're fast and those they don't kill, they panic. Five hundred half-breeds can take on an army ten times their size and triumph." She sipped her tea. Her face turned cold. "I saw it happen thousands of years ago. This new kingdom of the half-breeds is in its infancy. It must be crushed before they learn to walk."

I looked into her eyes. A ruthless intelligence looked back.

"Why call them half-breeds?"

"It's a convenient term. It drips with contempt. You're a soldier who faces a monstrosity. It's stronger and faster than you, it looks like a nightmare, and when it takes a wound that would kill a normal man, its fellows push you back and fifteen minutes later the creature you wounded is back on its feet. Where will your courage come from?"

I leaned toward her. "But if you think the creature is an abomination, a half-breed, who is less than you, you might reach deep inside and find a pair."

Erra nodded. "Exactly."

"Why not just declare them unclean and turn it into a crusade, then?"

She pointed her spoon at me. "You want to stay away from religion. Once you bring prayers and worship into it, your troops start thinking you're a god. Faith has power during magic. You begin getting urges that aren't your own. That's why I warned Babylon that if they ever built a shrine to me, I'd raze the city down to a nub and salt the ground it stood on. In any case, the half-breeds must be scattered. They're too organized and they have a First."

I toyed with my cup. "What's a First?"

"The First were there first. They have more power, better control, and the rest of the half-breeds flock to them."

Curran.

Erra's eyes narrowed. "You like him."

I arched my eyebrows.

"You like the lion."

"I can't stand him. He's an arrogant ass."

"Your bed is rumpled and there are claw marks on your windowsill and the inside door frame. Are you rutting with him?"

I leaned back and crossed my arms. "What's it to you?"

"Are you a slut?"

I stared at her.

"Not a slut, then. Good." Erra nodded. "Our blood's too precious to rut with every pretty man you see. Besides, that's just asking for heartbreak. You have to guard yourself or you will never survive your first century. The pain other people cause you will tear you apart."

"Thanks for the lecture."

"About your half-breed. They are great fun in bed, little squirrel, but they always want children and family. Family is not for you."

I arched my eyebrows. Decided for me, did she? "How do you know what's for me?"

She laughed. "You know what you are? You're a pale imitation of me. Weaker, slower, smaller. You dress like me, you talk like me, and you think like me. I saw you fight. You love to kill. Just like me. You attack when you're scared, and right now you wonder if you could've shattered the ward on your door the way I did. I know you, because I know myself. And I am a terrible mother."

I petted Slayer on my lap. "I'm not you."

"Yes. And that will be your undoing. The key to survival is moderation. You haven't learned that and now you never will."

Getting a lecture on restraint from the woman who threw a hissy fit and blew up Babylon. That's rich. "Speaking of moderation, the Casino belongs to the People. Does my father know you attacked one of his bases?"

Erra shrugged. "Im would approve. It's so . . ." She frowned, obviously searching for a word. "Gaudy. It's everything I dislike about this age: too loud, too bright, too flashy. Nobody even notices the beauty of the building behind all the colored light and banners. The music sounds like there is a band of monkeys inside beating on cooking pots."

"They reported it to the authorities."

Erra's eyes widened. "They did? Pussies."

Ghastek didn't know what she was but Nataraja might have been close enough to Roland to have met her and know she was erratic enough to reduce the Casino to dust on a whim. He didn't want to take any chances.

Erra erratic. God, maybe the word was invented to describe my aunt. That would be crazy. "What did the Guild do to offend you?"

Erra rolled her eyes. "Is this my day to give lessons?"

"How often do you get to teach?"

She chuckled again. "Very well. When you want to take over an army, you walk up to them and say, 'Send your strongest man.' They do, and you kill him while they watch. You make it fast and brutal, preferably by hand. And while they're reeling from it, you shoot the small guy with a big mouth who heckled you when you first approached. That shows that you could've shot the big man, but you chose not to."

I nodded. Sounded reasonable.

"When you want to take over a city, you have to destroy the illusion of safety it provides. You have to hit the large well-protected establishments, find the powerful people who run them and are viewed as invincible, and kill them. You want to destroy the morale first. Once the people's resolve is gone and everyone is scared for their own skin, the city is yours. The Guild is full of little people who think they're strong. I could've killed their leader in his rooms, but instead I dragged him down and murdered him before their eyes. Not only will they not oppose me now, but they'll spread panic every time they open their mouths. And then, of course, the First wandered into the place as I was pulling my boys out. It was too tempting not to take a shot."

So Solomon's shapeshifter status was a coincidence. She'd targeted him because he was the head of the Guild, not because he turned furry. "But then you made Tremor look like Solomon. Why?"

Erra rolled her eyes. "Your father makes weapons and armor. I can do that as well, but mostly I make flesh golems. But a golem must be infused with blood fuel before it can move. When blood is introduced to the body, it takes on the visage of the blood donor. The stronger the magic, the better the golem moves and the more it resembles the donor. The first seven I'd made lasted for a couple of centuries, because I'd used my children. Now I have to rely on found talent, and pickings have been slim."

I choked a bit on my tea. "Let me see if I have it straight: you killed your children and piloted their undead bodies."

"Yes. Does that shock you?"

"No. You're a psychopath."

"What does that mean?"

I got up and brought her a dictionary. She read the definition. "That sums it up well, yes. The idea of social rules is false at the core. There is only one rule in this world: if you're strong enough to do it, you have the right to do it. Everything else is an artificial defense the majority of the weak set up to shield themselves from the strong. I understand their fear, but it leaves me cold."

She was what Voron wanted me to be. No regret, no hesitation, no attachments.

I smiled at her. She smiled back. "Why the big grin?"

"I'm happy I'm not you."

"Your mother was very powerful, from what I've heard." Erra added more honey to her cup. "But her spirit was weak. What sort of woman gets herself killed and leaves her child to fend for itself?"

Nice. "Testing me for sore spots?"

"Must be hard to grow up without a mother."

"It helps to know your father killed her." I drank my cold tea. "Keeps you motivated."

Erra peered at me from above the rim of her cup. "I kept fish as a child. They were these bright beautiful fish with vivid fins delivered especially for me from far away. I loved them. My first one was blue. He only lived two years. When he died, I cried for days. Then I got another one. Yellow, I think. My memory is fuzzy. He also died a few months later. Then I got another one. In the end, when my fish died, it became routine. I'd feel a pang of sadness, burn their little bodies with incense, and get a new one when I felt like it."

"Is there a point to this sob story?"

Erra leaned forward. "People are fish to us, child. Your mother's death hurts, because she was your mother and Im robbed your childhood of security and happiness. You're justified in your revenge. But to him, she was only a fish. We live a long time and they don't. Don't make his crime bigger than it is."

"I will kill him."

Erra's eyebrows rose. "You'd have to go through me first."

I shrugged. "I have to do something for a warm-up."

She laughed softly. "That's the spirit. I do think you might be my favorite niece."

"It warms my heart."

"Enjoy the feeling while you still have one. I'm going to enjoy your books after you die. You bred true by pure chance, and no matter what you do, you're weaker than me. If you see your mother on the other side, slap her for me for thinking she could bear a child to our family."

That's just about enough of that. I stared right into her eyes. "You'll lose."

"What makes you so sure?"

"You have no discipline. All you do is tear shit down. My father is a bastard, but at least he builds things. You turn cities into smoking ruins and blunder about like some hyper child, smashing anything you see. And then you sit here and wonder, 'Why did all of my children turn out to be violent idiots? It's a mystery of nature.'"

We rose at the same time, swords in hand. Grendel rammed the bathroom door, barking in a hysterical frenzy.

Power swirled around Erra, like a cloak of magic. "Alright. Let's see what you have."

I pointed to the door. "Age before beauty."

"Pearls before swine." She strode out and I followed her. Pearls before swine. Blah-blah-blah.

We headed out of the apartment and down the stairs. My side hurt like hell.

We strode out into the snow-strewn parking lot. I swung my sword, warming up.

"How's your wound?" she asked. "Does it hurt?"

I stretched my neck left, then right, popping it. "Every time I cut Solomon, he grunted in your voice like a stuck pig. It hurts you when the seven are wounded, doesn't it? Oh, yes, I do apologize. Not seven. Five."

"Make your peace." She waved me on.

"Are we going to do this, or will you keep talking?"

My aunt came across the snow, sword raised. Fast. Too fast. A woman that large should've been slower.

Her blade thrust. Quick. I dodged and struck at her side. She parried. Our swords connected. Shock punched my arm. And strong like a bull.

Erra sliced at my shoulder, I blocked, letting her blade slide off my saber, spun, and kicked at her. She leaped back. We broke apart.

My aunt tossed her leather jacket into the snow and motioned to me with her fingers.

"I'm sorry, am I supposed to bring it?"

"What?"

I charged and thrust. She parried, twisting. I hooked her leg with mine and sank the knuckles of my left hand into her ribs. Bone crunched. She rammed her elbow, aiming for my ribs. I turned with the blow and the jab barely grazed me. Pain ripped through my insides. We broke off again.

Liquid heat drenched my side. She tore the wound open. Great.

I saw the muscles on her legs tense and met her halfway. We clashed. Strike, strike, parry, strike, left, right, left, up. I danced across the snow, matching my movements to her rhythm and going faster, forcing her to follow mine. My side burned. Every small movement stabbed a white-hot needle into my liver. I clenched my teeth and fought through it. She was strong and inhumanly fast, but I was a hair faster.

We dashed back and forth. She struck again and again. I dodged what I could and parried the rest. Blocking her was like trying to hold back a bear. She nicked my shoulder. I ducked under her reach, slashed her thigh, and withdrew.

Erra raised her blade straight up. A drop of red slid down the blade. She touched it. "You know a lot of tricks."

"You don't." She was skilled, but all her attacks were straightforward. Then again, she didn't have to rely on tricks. Not when she hit like a sledgehammer. "You learned to fight when magic was a certainty, so you rely on it to help you in a fight. I learned to fight when technology still had the upper hand and I rely on speed and technique. Without your spells and magic, you can't beat me."

*You aren't better than me, nyah-nyah-nyah. Take the bait,
Erra. Take the bait.*

"Clever, clever little squirrel. Fine. I'll cut you to pieces by
hand, without using my power. After all, you are family and
one must make allowances for blood relatives."

We clashed again. Snow flew, steel flashed. I cut and diced,
putting everything I had into my speed. She defended too well
for a good body wound, so I went for her arms. If she couldn't
hold a sword, she couldn't fight.

Her knee caught me. The blow knocked me back. Pretty
stars blocked my vision. I flew and hit the snow. *Get up, get
up, get up.* I clawed on to consciousness and rolled to my feet,
just in time to block her blade.

Erra bled from a half-dozen cuts. Her sleeve dripped red
into the snow. She pushed me back, grinding her blade against
Slayer. My feet slid.

"Where is your blood armor, little mongrel child? Where
is your blood sword? I keep waiting for your power to show
up, but it never does."

"I don't need my blood to kill you."

"You're bleeding." She nodded at my side. My shirt stuck
to my body, soaked with quickly cooling heat. I'd left a trail of
red across the snow. "We both know how this will end. You're
better skilled, but you're wounded. I'll beat on you until the
bleeding slows you down and then kill you."

Good plan. Right now it seemed very plausible.

Erra nodded at the blood trail. "Use your blood while you
still can so at least I'll know you were worth something."

"I don't need it."

"You can't do it, can you? You don't know how to work
the blood. You foolish, foolish child. And you think you can
beat me?"

I dropped my guard and twisted to the side. She took a tiny
step forward, off balance, and I knocked her left arm up and
thrust. Erra jerked back. Slayer slid into her left armpit, quick
as the kiss of a snake, and withdrew. She screamed. Blood
streamed, but not fast. Not deep enough. Damn. I backed
away.

She laughed, baring her teeth, her hair falling about her
face. Her lips moved, whispering. A healing chant. Fine, two

could play that game. I murmured the incantation under my breath, chanting my side into regeneration.

"I like you. You're dumb but brave. If you run now, I'll give you a head start," she said. "Two days. Maybe three."

"You'd use the time to murder everyone I ever knew and then rub it in my face."

"Ha! You must be my child."

I bared my teeth. "If I was your child, I would've strangled myself in the womb with the cord."

She laughed. "I'll kill your pretty lion and wear his skull as a hat when I return to your father."

"Don't bring the lion into this. It's about you and me."

She attacked. I parried, and she drove me back across the snow.

Hit.

Hit.

Hit.

My arm was going numb.

She backhanded me. The apartment building jerked, dancing around me. The force of the blow spun me about. I staggered back, tasting blood in my mouth, and spat red into the snow.

Erra growled. Her left arm hung limp. Finally bled out enough to cause some damage.

"Pain is a bitch, huh?" I laughed. "That's the trouble with being on top too long—you lose your tolerance." The world teetered around me. My head rang. I couldn't take much more. She was wearing me down and I bled like there was no tomorrow.

Might as well use it. I swayed and let Slayer slip a bit in my fingers. Given that a pint of my blood decorated the snow in a pretty red pattern, swaying didn't prove hard.

Erra raised her sword. "Shake it off and take your last look around."

Anyone can kill anyone, as long as you don't care if you live or die. Erra cared very much if she lived. I did, too, but pain didn't scare me the way it scared her. I was better. If I timed it right, I might even live through it. I just needed to get a good strike and conserve my strength enough to deliver it. Let her do most of the work.

"Talk, talk, talk. You prattle on and on, like a senile old woman. Are you slipping into your dotage?"

She charged me. I saw her crystal clear, running through the snow, eyes wild, sword raised for the kill. Drop down, thrust up under the ribs. The way to a woman's heart is through her stomach. If I sliced through her heart, she wouldn't shake it off. She might be my aunt, but she was mortal, damn it.

The world shrank to my aunt and the point of my sword.

Curran, I wish we had more time.

Julie, I love you.

She came at me. The sword arm was too high. If I lunged under that first strike, she was mine.

Something hit me from the left. Breath left my lungs in a single painful burst. I gasped, trying to inhale, and saw the ground vanish down below. Something clamped me in a steel grip and dragged me up the building.

A bellow of pure rage chased us. "Come back here!"

I managed to suck some air in my lungs.

The arm that clenched me had scales on it.

I twisted my neck. Red eyes stared at me with slit pupils. Below the eyes enormous jaws protruded, long and studded with triangular teeth. Olive scales fractured the skin. A shapeshifter? Shapeshifters didn't change into reptiles. My arms were clamped. I couldn't even cough.

"What the hell are you doing? I had her!"

The jaws gaped open. A deep female voice growled at me. "No. You can't fight her."

"Drop me!"

"No."

"Who are you?"

The roof rushed at us. The edge loomed, and then we were airborne. We hit the next roof and she dashed across it.

"Put me down."

"Soon enough."

The creature leaped again. The ruined city streamed by.

"Why are you doing this?"

"It's my job. He tasked me to protect you."

"Who? Who told you to protect me?"

A familiar building swung into my view—Jim's safe house.

Jim had put a babysitter on me. I would kill him.

We landed on a roof with a thud. A man lunged at us. She rammed him, knocking him off the roof, and drove her clawed hand into the shingles. Wood screeched. She tossed a piece of the roof aside and dropped into the hole. We fell and landed on the dining table, knocking the dishes aside. Faces stared at me: Jim, Dali, other people I didn't know . . .

The creature let go of me. A deep roar rolled from her mouth. "Take care of her."

She whipped about. A heavy tail swung over me, and she leaped, vanishing through the hole in the roof.

CHAPTER 22

———•———

JIM STARED AT ME. "WHAT THE FUCK WAS THAT?"

"You tell me." I rolled off the table, shook the stars out of my head, and staggered toward the doorway, where a hallway promised access to the door. I had to get out of there.

"She's bleeding," someone barked.

Green rolled over Jim's eyes. "Dali, get Doolittle."

Dali dashed out.

Jim clamped his hand on my shoulder. "Who was she?"

The building swayed around me. "I don't know."

Jim pointed past me. "You, you, and you—quarter-mile perimeter. You don't know them, they don't get in. You—roof, find Carlos. Brenna, Kate doesn't leave. Sit on her if you have to. If I'm not back in half an hour, evacuate to the Southeast office."

He tensed and leaped up and to the right, bounced off the wall through the hole onto the roof. A blink and he was gone.

A woman gripped me in a bear hug. I peered at her face, trying to bring it into focus. Short hair cut in a bob, reddish brown hair, green eyes, freckles . . . Brenna. One of the wolves working for Jim as a tracker. Last time we met, I'd put a silver

needle into her throat and she bit my leg. She held my right
arm and some blond woman I didn't know held my left.

I fixed my stare on Brenna. Her face was smudged.
"Let go."

"I can't do that." She shook her head.

"Brenna, take your hands off me or I'll hurt you." If only
the room stopped spinning, I'd be all set.

"That's fine, Kate. I think I can take it."

Everybody was a smart-ass.

Dali ran into the room. A black man in his fifties followed,
wiping his hands with a towel. Doolittle.

"And what have you done to yourself now?"

His face crawled sideways. My stomach clenched into a
tight ball and I vomited on the floor.

"Let her go," Doolittle snarled.

The wolves released me. That's right. Never piss off a
werebadger.

Doolittle leaned over me. "Dizzy?"

I nodded. Pain rolled inside my head like a lead ball.

He touched my face and I jerked back.

"Easy, easy now." Doolittle's fingers pressed on my skin,
holding my left eye open. "Uneven dilation. Blurred vision?"

I knew the signs. I had a concussion, but it didn't seem
important. Slowly it sank in: Erra was gone. I'd lost my shot at
her. "I almost had her. I could've taken her."

"Lay her down on her back, gently. Gently now."

Hands clamped me and lowered me to the floor.

"I almost had her," I told Doolittle.

"I know you did, child. I know."

I wanted to get up, but I wasn't sure which way up was
and something told me I wouldn't figure it out anytime soon
either. "I have a concussion."

"Yes, you do." Doolittle cut through my sweatshirt. "Brenna,
put your hands on her head and keep her from moving."

"I almost had her. I could've taken her."

Someone, probably Brenna, pressed her hands on the sides
of my face. "Why does she keep saying that?"

"That's just a little perseveration. People with head injuries
do that. Nothing to worry about." Doolittle peeled my T-shirt
from my body. Draft chilled my skin.

"That's your reassuring voice," I told him. "That means I'm seriously fucked up."

"No foul language now. Who patched you up?"

"A rabbi at the Temple."

"He did a good job."

"I almost had her. Did I tell you that?"

"Yes, you did. Hush now." Doolittle began to chant. Magic stirred in me, slow and thick. He kept whispering, pouring power into the words. Slowly, like melting wax, magic grew liquid and warm and spread through me, flowing out from my chest all the way into my skull and toes.

"That's nice," I said.

"He said to hush." Brenna's hand brushed my lips.

"I almost—"

"—had her, we know," Brenna murmured. "You have to be quiet, Kate. Shhhh."

I closed my eyes. It felt like floating in a warm sea. Tiny hot needles stabbed my wound and danced inside my scalp. My side itched.

"I need to talk to her," Jim's voice said through Doolittle's chant.

A sharp screech, halfway between roar and chatter, cut him off. It sounded either like a giant pissed-off squirrel or a small but equally pissed-off bear. The hair on the back of my arms rose. There was a word for that . . .

"Bloodcurdling." I heard my own voice. It sounded slurred.

"If something is coming for her, I need to know what it is," Jim said.

"Make it quick," Doolittle said.

Jim leaned over me, his face a fuzzy smudge. That's right, get closer so I can give you a piece of my mind.

"Who brought you here?" Jim asked.

"I almost had her."

"Here we go again," Brenna muttered.

I grabbed his shirt and pulled myself up.

"Shit!" Brenna clamped her fingers on my cheeks.

"I almost had her," I squeezed out through my teeth. "I was a second from a strike and your babysitter grabbed me and dragged me up a building. You cost me my kill. Now all of you are fucked."

"Damn it, Jim." Doolittle grabbed my shoulders, pushing me down. "Keep her head stabilized."

Jim's fingers clenched my fist. "She wasn't mine."

"Bullshit. She was a shapeshifter and she brought me to your safe house."

"Did you tell her where the house was?"

Jim squeezed my hand, but I was too pissed off.

"I told her to drop me. She said it was her job to protect me. Who else would order a shapeshifter to guard me? How would she find your place? Did you put a sign above the door— SECRET PACK HOUSE HERE, STRANGE SHAPESHIFTERS BRING A HUMAN SNACK?"

Doolittle pressed a point just below my wrist, cutting off the circulation to my hand. My fingers went numb.

Jim pulled free. "We're clearing out."

Doolittle pushed me back down. "She can't be moved."

"An unknown shapeshifter punched a hole through the roof and took off before I could catch her. The house is compromised. How much time do you need to stabilize her?"

"Ten minutes."

"You have them, then we move."

Doolittle bent over me and began to chant.

Ten minutes later Doolittle clamped my neck into a brace and Brenna picked me up. She carried me down the stairs like I was a child. The stairs were impossibly high and swirling, like a spiral. I squirmed, trying to get away, but Brenna only gripped me tighter. "Don't worry, Kate. I won't drop you."

She loaded me into a small sled. People from Jim's crew moved around us. Doolittle strapped me to the sled, Brenna took the reins, and we were off.

I LAY IN THE BED, STRIPPED DOWN TO MY BRA and underwear, and watched the bag of O-negative empty into my veins. My attempt to explain that my head had cleared and I didn't need extra attention, and definitely not the extra blood, bounced from Doolittle like dried peas from the wall.

He pointed out that he had pulled me from the brink of certain death three times, and he apparently had given me blood transfusions before and he might be just an ignorant doctor, but as far as he could tell, I was still breathing and it would make his day if we could save some time and assume that he knew what he was doing. His life would be much easier if suicidal hardcases would take that into account, thank you very much.

My ribs still hurt, but instead of sharp stabbing jolts that made me growl, the pain fused into a solid heavy pressure.

Doolittle walked around my bed. "You will be the death of me."

"I'm pretty sure I'll die before you do, Doc."

"That I don't doubt."

He picked up a mirror from the table and held it up to me. I looked.

Most of me was pale and a bit green looking. A dark purple patina covered the corner of my jaw, promising to develop into a spectacular bruise. The second stain covered my midsection, where my aunt had kicked me. I'd flexed my stomach, so my innards didn't turn into mush, and the abdominal muscles took the brunt of the punishment.

"Green and purple, a stunning combination."

Doolittle shook his head, unplugged me from the empty blood bag, and handed me a glass filled with brown liquid, resembling iced tea. "You look like you've had an unfortunate encounter with one of the gangs from the Warren."

"You should see the other"—guy, no, wait, girl, woman—"person." Somehow that didn't quite deliver the snappy impact I had originally planned.

Doolittle fixed me with a stare. "Bed rest for the next twenty-four hours."

"I can't do that, Doc." Knowing him, he'd try to sedate me. So far he hadn't—I had watched my IV like a hawk. If I had things my way, I'd be up and running. Right now Erra was injured and at her weakest. It was a good time to hit her, but the chances of finding her, even armed with shapeshifters, were nil. My aunt was psychotic but not stupid.

Doolittle sighed. "Drink your tea."

I looked at my glass. I'd had Doolittle's iced tea before,

and exercising extreme caution was in order. I sipped a tiny bit. Sugar overload. I waited to see if my teeth instantly disintegrated from shock. Nothing. My mouth was stronger than I gave it credit for.

Doolittle sat down in a chair and looked at me, and for once his eyes were empty of their usual humor. His voice was soft. "You can't keep doing this, Kate. You think you're going to live forever. But sooner or later we all have to pay the piper. One day you'll laugh and joke and roll out of your bed, and you'll fall. And then it won't be three days of bed rest. It will be three months."

I reached over and touched his hand. "Thank you for fixing me up. I don't mean to cause you grief."

He grimaced. "Drink. You need fluids."

Someone knocked.

"It's me," Jim's voice said.

Doolittle offered me a sweatshirt. I pulled it on and he let Jim in. Jim looked like he'd chewed bricks and spat out gravel.

He grabbed a chair, set it by my bed, sat down, and looked at me.

I looked back at him. "Sorry I put my hands on you. Won't happen again."

"It's cool. You weren't yourself. You better now?"

"Yeah."

"Let's try this again, then. Tell me about the fight."

"Did Dali tell you about Erra?"

"She did."

I sketched the fight for him, leaving our family connection out of it, and described my rescue.

"Scales," Jim said.

"Yep."

I knew what he was thinking—shapeshifters resulting from infection by Lyc-V were mammals. There were several cases of humans turning into reptiles or birds, but all of those happened because of outside magical factors, not Lyc-V infection, and none of those transformations had an in-between stage. The shapeshifter who grabbed me was in a warrior form. Half-human, half–something scaled.

"What sort of eyes did she have?" Doolittle asked.

"Olive iris, slit pupil. Reddish glow."

"Glow isn't a good indicator," Doolittle said. "Hyena eyes reflect light in any number of colors, yet bouda eyes always glow red. But the slit pupil is interesting." He glanced at Jim.

"There was a man on the roof," I said. "She knocked him off. Is he okay?"

Jim nodded. "He says the same thing: scales, red eyes, tail. I've smelled a similar scent before."

"What was it?"

Jim grimaced. "A croc."

Shapeshifter crocodiles. What was the world coming to?

"Stranger things have happened." Doolittle pointed at my glass. "Drink."

I showed the glass to Jim. "The good doctor put a spoon of tea into my honey."

"You're drinking tea a honey badger made," Jim said. "What did you expect?"

Doolittle snorted and began packing gauze and instruments into his medical bag.

"If you didn't put her on me, then who did?"

"I don't know," Jim said.

It wasn't Curran. Security was Jim's territory; if Curran felt I needed a bodyguard, he would have asked Jim to take care of it.

Curran. Oy.

"Where are we?" I asked.

"One of the Clan Wolf's satellite houses," Jim said. "The Wolf Clan House is outside the city, but they have a few rallying points in Atlanta's limits. This was the closest."

"And Curran?"

"At the Keep."

"Did you tell him about this?"

"Not yet. Is there anything more you have to tell me?"

"No."

He showed no signs of moving. "Is there anything you want to tell me?"

Cat and spy master, lethal combination. "No. What makes you think that?"

Jim leaned back. "You're a lousy liar."

"That's true." Doolittle rolled up his stethoscope. "I've

played poker with you, young lady, and the whole table knew every time you got a good card."

"Deception makes you uncomfortable," Jim said. "It works for you on the street, because when you promise to hurt someone, there is no doubt in anyone's mind that you mean it. But if you came to me for an assignment, I'd fire you after the first minute."

"Fine. I'm a bad liar." I looked at Jim from above the rim of my glass. "That doesn't mean I'm hiding something. Maybe there is nothing more to that story."

"You've put the glass between yourself and me and you're keeping it pressed against your mouth so the words don't get out," Jim said.

I put the glass down.

"Is it an Order thing?" Jim asked.

"No, it's my thing. It has no relevance to the Pack."

"Okay," Jim said. "If things change and you want to tell me or if you need help, you know how to find me."

He got up and walked out.

I looked at Doolittle. "Why the sudden goodwill?"

"Who knows why cats do things. My guess is you taking a blade for him may have something to do with it . . ." Doolittle raised his head and grimaced. "They just can't leave well enough alone."

A knock sounded through the basement.

"Who is it?" Doolittle called.

"I've come to see the patient!" a woman's voice called.

"Is she naked?" another female voice asked. "I always wanted to see her naked."

"Shush. George, will you keep me standing here all day?"

I looked at Doolittle. "Is that who I think it is?"

He bristled and headed to the door.

Besides Curran, two shapeshifters in the Pack gave me pause: Mahon, the Bear of Atlanta and the Pack's executioner, and Aunt B, alpha of the boudas and Raphael's mother. The rest were dangerous, but those two made me take a moment or two and think things through before I blundered on. I'd seen Aunt B in action with her human skin off. Blowing her off wasn't in my best interests no matter how pissed off or weak I was.

"You're looking very fine, George," Aunt B said. Craning my head to see the two of them would destroy what little semblance of dignity I had left, so I stayed put.

"What do you want?" Despite Doolittle's Coastal Georgia Southern accent, the good doctor's voice lost all of its charm.

"Why, to see Kate, of course."

"The girl has a concussion. Your scheming can wait until her mind is clear."

"I'm not here to take advantage of her, George. My goodness."

I craned my neck. Doolittle barred the doorway, his finger pointing to the first floor above us. "Up there you are the alpha of the boudas. Down here is *my* territory."

"Why don't you ask the girl if she wants to see me? If she is too weak or uneasy, I will come back another time."

And she just outmaneuvered us both. If I refused to see her now, I might just as well stand on my bed with a giant neon sign: I'M AFRAID OF AUNT B.

Doolittle came up to my bed. "The boudas wish to speak to you. You don't have to say yes."

Yes, I do, and we both know it. "That's okay, I'll see her."

Doolittle looked up. "Thirty minutes, Beatrice."

Aunt B swept in. Behind her a young female bouda carried a platter. The aroma of spices and cooked meat swirled around me, instantly filling my mouth with drool. Hunger was good. It meant Doolittle's spells were working and my body was burning through nutrients at an accelerated rate.

The young bouda set the platter on my bed, stuck her tongue out at me, and departed.

Aunt B glanced at Doolittle. "Would you mind giving us a bit of privacy?"

He growled under his breath and stalked out.

Aunt B pulled up a chair and sat by my bed. In her late forties or early fifties, she looked like a typical young grandmother: a bit plump, with an easy smile and kind eyes that would convince a child in trouble to pick her out of a crowd of strangers. She wore a bulky gray sweater. Her brown hair sat in a bun atop her head. If she added a platter of cookies, she'd be all set.

She greeted me with a warm smile. You'd never know that

behind that smile waited a seven-foot-tall monster with claws the size of cake forks.

"You seem on edge, dear," she said. "How badly were you injured?"

Hi, Grandma, what big teeth you have . . . "Nothing major."

"Ah. Good then." She nodded at the platter. Beef, pita bread, and Tzatziki sauce. "Help yourself. Lunch is on me."

Not to take a bite would be an insult. To take a bite might obligate me to something and I'd rather be in debt to the devil than to Aunt B. I settled for sipping my tea. "You aren't propositioning me, are you?"

"Funny you should say that."

I paused with a glass in my hand. Just what I need.

"It won't be that kind of proposition." Aunt B gave me a bright smile.

I squished a shudder.

"I'll come straight to the point to make things easier on both of us." Aunt B pushed the plate to me. "Curran didn't return to the Keep last night. I'm neither blind nor stupid and I've spent more years sorting out shapeshifter lies than you've been alive. Please keep that in mind before you answer. Did he spend the night?"

Putting claws to my throat was never a good idea. I smiled. "None of your business."

"So he did. Did he use the word 'mate'?"

"What happened between me and Curran is our own affair."

Aunt B raised her eyebrows. "Congratulations. Then you are, indeed, the mate."

Why me? "That would be news to me."

"I wouldn't be surprised if you were the last to know. I've known he'd fall for you since he fed you that soup. It was tons of fun watching the two of you take so long to figure it out."

"I live to provide entertainment."

"There is no need to be so hostile." Aunt B pinched off a small chunk of her pita. "I've called to the Keep. There are no rooms ready for you. Has the Bear approached you?"

"Mahon? No."

"He's getting slow in his old age." She chuckled, baring

her teeth. A predatory light flared in her eyes. The effect was chilling.

"What do rooms have to do with anything?" I asked.

"Curran intends for you to share his quarters."

"Do I get turn-down service and a mint on my pillow?"

"You get to be the female alpha of the Pack," Aunt B said.

I choked on empty air.

"Here, drink your tea, dear. Honestly, what did you think that meant?" she asked.

I drank my water. Somehow when Curran said "mate," my mind didn't translate it as "the Pack's Beast Lady."

"I'm not equipped to be an alpha."

Aunt B smiled. "So you don't want the power?"

"I don't." I didn't want the responsibility either.

"What is it you do want?" she asked me.

"I want to kill the crazy bitch who is running around Atlanta murdering shapeshifters."

"Besides that?"

"I want him."

"Without the Pack?"

"Yes." I had no idea why I kept answering her questions. There was something in her eyes that made me want to tell her everything I knew so she would pat me on the head and tell me, "Good girl," at the end. Adolescence in the bouda clan would be hell with Aunt B around.

"You can't have just him." Aunt B's eyes were merciless. "Curran belongs to the Pack and we won't let you take him away from us. You need him to be happy, but we require him to survive. If he were to leave the Pack, the alphas would fight for power. No one among the alphas now could take his place and hold it. It would be chaos and blood. Eventually the strongest would win, but the strongest isn't always the best person for the job."

She leaned back. "We lucked out with Curran, and we all know that our chances of getting another Beast Lord like him are slim. I like you, but if you tried to lure him away, I'd be the first in line to kill you."

Today was the wrong day to threaten me. "Think you can?"

"You have a lot of power, but we have the numbers, so yes,

we can. I'm not telling you this to get your hackles up. You need to understand the situation clearly. Curran belongs to the Pack. Stand between him and his people and the Pack will tear you to pieces. Your meat is getting cold. Eat."

She was right. I knew she was right. They wouldn't let Curran go. And even if they did, he'd never leave them. He was a shapeshifter and they were his people. I had to find a way around it. "Why can't I be with him, but not be the alpha?"

"You want to have your cake and eat it, too. It simply doesn't work that way. You can't marry the king and not become the queen. You'll be the one he'll growl sweet nothings to in bed, and you'll be the one he'll ask for advice. You'll have unprecedented influence over his decisions, but you want none of the responsibility that comes with it. That's cowardly and that's not you. It's all or nothing, Kate. That's the deal and it's not negotiable."

"So I have no say in this?"

Aunt B frowned. "Of course you do. You don't have to mate with him. You can always reject him. But if you do mate with him, the burden of the alpha comes with it. Ask yourself, would you really settle for a fling? Or do you want him to yourself for always?"

I made a valiant effort not to ask myself that question. I was pretty sure I knew the answer. That way lay total surrender of all common sense. "I'm not a shapeshifter."

"True. Can you become one?"

I shook my head. "It's not physically possible. I'm immune to Lyc-V."

"Excellent."

She lost me.

"Were you to become a shapeshifter, you'd have to pick the species of your beast. You'd have to choose a clan and someone to donate Lyc-V, which means six clans would feel slighted and that one clan would expect preferential treatment. It's a can of worms nobody wants to open. This is one of those rare cases when being impartial is actually advantageous."

"You've given this a great deal of thought," I murmured. The sixty-four-thousand-dollar question was why.

"Look at it from our point of view. We want him to mate. As his mate, you have the right to question his decisions, something we can't do. If Pack members have an issue with him, they could come to you and plead for assistance. If you issue an order, technically he can overrule you, but he would be reluctant to do so. The Pack has been denied this avenue of appeal for too long."

She waved her pita around. "Curran is a fair alpha, one of the best. But he has his bad moments and right now nobody dares to contradict him during those. Sure, some people won't accept you, but that's normal. Anytime there is a power shift, people rumble. After you kill the first couple of challengers, you'll be fine."

She was definitely after something . . .

"Nobody questions your power, dear. The alphas have seen you fight and you're a good asset. Anyone able to snap the legs off two hundred demons with one word isn't to be taken lightly."

She bit into her bread. "Besides, if Curran didn't think you're fit, he wouldn't have made the offer. Yes, he's obsessed with you, but he's shrewd enough to take your ability into consideration. Alphas are typically attracted to other alphas. I wouldn't mate with a weakling, and neither would he."

"It's not that simple," I growled.

She laughed softly. "We know you have a history, dear. That much power doesn't come without baggage and Curran isn't an idiot. If he proposed to you, he must view your past as an acceptable risk."

Had an answer for everything, did she? "Why do you care so much whether I become his mate? You didn't come here out of the goodness of your heart."

She paused. Her face turned mournful. "Raphael is my third child. The first two went loup at puberty. After him, I said I wouldn't have any more. I couldn't keep killing my babies. My boy is everything to me. I'd rip the world apart for him. You and I both know the name of his happiness."

"Andrea."

She nodded. The pain in her eyes melted into pride. "My Raphael could have any woman he wanted. If he wanted you, you wouldn't be able to resist."

"I don't know about that . . ."

"Trust me. I've been courted by his father. Raphael had his

pick, but he chose the girl who is beastkin. Because my life wasn't complicated enough."

"Andrea loves him. She's smart, trained, and—"

She raised her hand. "You don't have to sing her praises. I know more about her than you do. But the fact remains, she's beastkin and she's my son's mate. She's dominant, strong, and cunning. I have no doubt she can fight off any challengers, which means that when I step down, the reins of the bouda clan will pass to a child of an animal. The boudas will accept her. But the Pack may not."

"Curran promised me she wouldn't be persecuted."

She pursed her lips. "It's one thing to ignore the presence of a beastkin in the ranks. It's another to have it rubbed in the alphas' faces. Other clans don't like us; they don't like our unpredictability and they fear our rages. As the bouda alpha couple, Andrea and Raphael will sit on the Pack's Council. That won't go over well with some people. The wolves and Clan Heavy, in particular, will find her presence tough to swallow. There are four hundred wolves and only thirty-two of us. But the Bear is by far the biggest threat. He's old-fashioned and he holds on to his prejudices. He practically raised Curran and he has a lot of influence with him. If I have any hope of safeguarding my son's future, I have to counteract Mahon."

Finally. It all became clear. "And you think that if I became Curran's mate, I'd intercede on Andrea's behalf?"

"Not only on her behalf, but on behalf of all boudas. There are six children in the clan now, four of whom are teenagers, all past puberty with no traces of loupism. If you think ordinary adolescents are wild, you're in for a shock. The last time we had that many young ones, Curran was hammering the Pack together and he himself was rather young. He chose to be lenient when my kids stepped out of line. He's secure in his power now and may not be as indulgent."

Lenient Beast Lord. That would be the day.

Aunt B leaned in and fixed me with a stare. "Suppose you become the alpha. What is the minimum acceptable distance between a female shapeshifter and Curran?"

"I don't know."

"Three feet, unless it's a battle. Any closer and she's

challenging you. You walk into a room at a formal gathering, do shapeshifters rise or stay down?"

"I don't know."

"The alphas rise to demonstrate that you acknowledge their power, the rest stay down, showing submission. If a shapeshifter shows you his teeth, is he smiling in greeting or is he trying to intimidate you?"

"I don't know." Broken record, that's me.

"If his head is bowed, he's smiling. If he's holding himself erect, you need to be snarling."

I'd had just about enough. "What is the point of all of this?"

"I have no doubt that you'll become Curran's mate. You love him, you nearly died for him, and you won't be able to let him go. When that happens, you'll be in over your head, dear. You must play by our rules and you don't know them." She smiled triumphantly. "Here is my offer to you: I'll give you two of my kids. They're very good, steady, and skilled. They won't go crazy unless you give them permission. Their loyalty is to you alone and they'll have your best interests at heart. They'll keep you from making any big mistakes. You'll still make small ones, but that can't be helped. In return, you promise to hold the bouda clan in special regard. I won't ask you to break the rules, but I may ask you to stretch them once in a while. It's a very good offer, Kate."

I met her gaze. "You don't have to bribe me. I wouldn't let anyone touch Andrea anyway."

"You may think so now, but friendships end and wither, while business arrangements persist. I'm an old-fashioned alpha as well, and I'd prefer to make the bargain."

Was there a downside to this? She was right, I knew nothing of the customs. If I chose to accept Curran's offer . . . What the hell was I thinking?

"If I do end up being his mate, we have a deal," I said. "That's one colossal 'if.' "

Aunt B's eyes lit up. "Excellent, dear. Excellent."

"I'll tell him about this."

"I expect you to."

"You do realize that he could change his mind? We didn't part on good terms."

She pursed her lips. "Mating is a volatile time for our kind. Newly mated shapeshifters are jealous, possessive, and prone to violence. Their instincts are in overdrive. You want to hole up with your mate somewhere safe, and if anyone looks at him for longer than two seconds, you have to fight with yourself not to sink your claws into her throat. It's not the most rational time in one's life, which is why the Pack Law makes provisions for the mating frenzy."

She reached into her bag and pulled out a small leather book with a clasp. She unlocked the clasp, revealing pages protected by clear plastic. A tiny photo album.

"These are all of my hooligans." Aunt B flipped through the pages and held the album out to me. A young man smiled back at me from the photograph. Thin to the point of skinny, he had glossy dark hair and a kid's grin: wide and happy.

"Alejandro," she said. "We call him Mouse, because he was always so quiet, you wouldn't know he is in the room. Five three, a hundred and twenty pounds wet. Arms like matches. Eats like a horse but nothing sticks to him. He's a shy sweet kid. Look at that grin." She smiled. "Not a mean bone in the boy. He got married last year to a very nice rat girl. Girls joked a bit: mouse got married to a rat. At his wedding, Curran remarked that his wife was very pretty. Alejandro jumped on the table and tried to cut Curran's throat with his dinner knife."

I blinked. "What happened?"

"Well, what do you think happened? Curran grabbed him by the neck and we had to go and get a loup cage to put the groom in until he calmed down. That's how he spent his reception, in the loup cage in the other room, screaming curses. His bride sat by the cage until he cooled off enough to be reasoned with and then got in there with him. He didn't scream after that." Aunt B rubbed the photo with her thumb. Her eyes were warm. "He's very embarrassed by it all now."

I didn't know the Pack law well, but I knew enough to recognize a challenge. "Curran could've killed him."

"Oh, yes. Would've been well within his rights, too. The Pack law is very careful. It doesn't say you can't punish a shapeshifter during the mating frenzy. It just says that you don't have to punish him. If you want to overlook his infraction, it won't be seen as a sign of weakness on your part. Mind you, Curran wasn't trying to rile Mouse up. He has to come to every wedding, because they always invite him, and he hates it. He's usually very careful with what he says, but he was tired that day and he said the first polite congratulatory thing that popped into his head. 'You have a beautiful wife, Alejandro.'"

"That was it?"

She nodded. "Yes, that's all that was said. This is the kind of insanity you're dealing with, dear. Except for you, it's much worse. Curran has a harder time controlling the possessive urges than most. He is . . . damaged."

"What do you mean?"

She grimaced. "It's not my place to explain this to you. What you need to know is that his protective drive is very strong. I'm amazed he hasn't rolled you in a blanket and dragged you off into the Keep. He's been insufferable since you had your falling-out. He loves you, Kate, and that's why he's waiting patiently for you to make up your mind."

"I know it may come as a shock, but it's sort of considered polite to wait for the consent of the woman. In fact, I'm pretty sure that if you don't wait, you may have to deal with pesky criminal charges like kidnapping and rape."

Aunt B rolled her eyes. "The boy isn't a maniac—no is no and he'll understand that. To force you would be going against everything he stands for and you know it as well as I do. For everything, there is a price in this world. His price is us. Ask yourself, is he worth becoming an alpha to the Pack? Do you love him enough? And take it from someone who buried two of her mates: you might want to decide fast. We live in a dangerous world. If you see a chance to be happy, you have to fight for it, so later you have no regrets."

CHAPTER 23

———◆———

AUNT B LEFT. I WAITED A FEW BREATHS, FOUND my shoes, and climbed up the stairs. And ran into Jennifer on the landing. Jennifer looked like she devoted her life to the god of running: long legs, long body, long face. Long teeth. Especially in the beast form.

Jennifer and her husband, Daniel, ran Clan Wolf. From what I'd heard, of the two, Jennifer was more aggressive and more likely to twist the head off your shoulders. Daniel could be reasoned with, but if you pissed off Jennifer, it was all over.

"Going somewhere?" The wolf alpha crossed her lean arms.

"Out."

"I can't let you do that."

I looked into her blue eyes. "You might want to rephrase that."

Jim wandered out of the kitchen and leaned against the door frame.

Jennifer raised her head. She had a couple of inches of height on me and she milked them for all she had. "You are the Beast Lord's mate and under my protection."

"Where did you hear that?"

"The wolf clan has its sources."

Well, wasn't that special. "Then the wolf clan also knows that my mate status is still in question. I haven't said yes."

Her eyes narrowed. "You dumped catnip on his bed and welded his weight bench together."

Jennifer two, Kate zero. "That's a private matter between me and His Furriness. Even if we were mated, I have my own name and I made my own rep. I don't think the term 'mate' should trump everything I've done. I've earned more than that."

Jim chuckled softly.

Jennifer took a step back and sized me up. "Point taken," she said finally. "But if you walk out of that door, I'll have to explain to Curran that I had you secured and let you go. I have enough to worry about as it is."

She had a point. "I have work to do. The magic is down, so it's unlikely Erra is still running around. She doesn't like technology much, and the last time I saw her, she was trying to redecorate the snowdrifts around my place in a lovely shade of red."

"No."

I looked at Jim. "I'm a bit fuzzy on my status within the Pack."

"Technically, you have none," he said. "Sleeping with a shapeshifter doesn't grant you Pack privileges."

I smiled at Jennifer. "Since I have no official Pack status, you have no power to detain me. I'm a lawful agent of the Order and I need you to step aside."

She looked at Jim. "Would you like to weigh in on this at any point?"

Jim shrugged. "If you get yourself fucked up and it gets out that Jennifer had you here and let you get hurt, it won't look good for the wolves. And you have a record of getting yourself seriously fucked up."

Thank you, Mr. Helpful. "Look, I appreciate the difficulty of your position, but I'm not going to sit here all cozy while my dog freezes to death." And as of now, I was my aunt's primary target. The more space I put between me and the shape-shifters, the safer they would be.

"Take an escort," Jim said.

"Are you offering to babysit me, Ms. Poppins?"

"Nope. I'll give you a vehicle and you can take Jennifer's wolves with you."

Brilliant. If I was attacked, I'd have some homicidal were-wolves to protect.

Jennifer looked at Jim. "Why, thank you for volunteering my people, cat. Any other orders for me?"

Jim gave her his hard stare. Jennifer's upper lip rose, showing a glimpse of her teeth.

I stepped back. "Please feel free to settle your differences." And while you're doing that, I'll quietly go on my way . . .

Jennifer paused her glaring for a second. "The cat is right. Take my wolves."

"I don't know your wolves." I looked at Jim. "Why can't you go if you're so concerned?"

He sighed. "Because certain people aren't altogether rational at the moment. If I came with you, I'd have to answer uncomfortable questions. I ask questions, I don't answer them."

"What kind of questions?"

"Why were you in a vehicle with Kate, alone? What were you wearing? What was she wearing? How long were you there? Did you do something or did you talk? What was the nature of your discussion? Could this trip have been avoided?"

I rubbed my face. "So basically you're scared that His Lordship might get his panties in a bunch?"

"That's one way to put it. The other way would be that I'm dedicated to observing the Pack's social protocol. If you were 'officially' mated and installed in his rooms in the Keep, it would be less of an issue. However, technically you're still available, since you have yet to commit."

I made an effort to enunciate my reply very carefully. "Available?"

"Up for grabs. On the market. Ready for action. Putting out the vibe."

He was just jerking my chain now. Two could play that game. "Fine, I don't care, give me an escort, send me in a car or a cart or whatever. Just don't send your girlfriend as a chauffeur."

A stunned silence issued. Jim's eyebrows came together. Judging by his expression, if Jim had been in cat form, every hair on his back would've stood up. "My girlfriend?"

Jennifer kept a perfectly straight face.

In for a penny, in for a pound. "You know, short, glasses, Indonesian, drives like a demon from the lowest bowels of hell?"

"She isn't my girlfriend."

"Oh, so she's still up for grabs? Fair game?"

"Putting out the vibe?" Jennifer added.

Jim turned and walked away without a word.

Holy crap, I'd struck a nerve. I had no idea that there was anything there. It was a total shot in the dark.

Jennifer looked at me. "I'll give you three wolves."

"Why three?"

"If there is trouble, one will take custody of you and execute a retreat, while the other two will run interference."

My jaw tried very hard to hit the floor. If it was physically possible, I'd be picking up my teeth from the carpet. "We've met before, right?"

"I do believe so, yes."

"Then you do know that if your wolf tries to carry me from a battle, I'll cut her arms off?"

"What are we chatting about?" Aunt B came out of the kitchen. "I just saw Jim and he had a peculiar look on his face."

"Jennifer wants to saddle me up with an escort. They're supposed to grab me and run like a bat out of hell if someone sneezes in my direction."

Aunt B raised her eyebrows. "There is no need. The boudas will provide the escort."

Jennifer's eyes turned flat like two chunks of ice. "Are you implying there is something wrong with my people?"

Now I knew why Curran was crazy.

"Of course not, dear." Aunt B's smile was so sweet, you could spread her on toast. "But Clan Bouda and Kate have a special bond."

Jennifer's voice turned equally sweet. "Clan Wolf and Kate have a special bond as well."

Steel slipped into Aunt B's smile. Her voice remained sugary sweet. "You should let me take the escort."

Jennifer's eyes flared with yellow. She gave Aunt B a big happy smile. "Take care, Beatrice. You're in my house."

"Why, goodness me, is that a threat?"

If you couldn't hear what they were saying, you'd think they were two Southern women catching up on local gossip at a church picnic.

Jennifer rocked forward. "I'm tired of you coming around here and poking your nose into everything."

A ruby glow sheathed Aunt B's irises. "You're young and you want to assert yourself. But don't think for a moment you will do it by taking me down. On your best day, you're only as good as I am on my worst with one arm tied behind my back."

"Is that so? Maybe we should test that theory."

I took three steps back and slipped into the hallway. Behind me a vicious growl announced someone going furry. I jogged to the end of the hallway. Two shapeshifters stood guard by the door.

"Aunt B and Jennifer are about to have a showdown," I told them.

They took off. I waited a couple of seconds for them to reach the stairs, opened the door, and walked out into the snow. If they wanted to fight, that was fine. I had a poodle to rescue. Jim's safe house was only thirty minutes from my place. Even with the snowdrifts, I'd make it in forty-five. Hold on, Grendel. I'm coming.

I TRUDGED UP THE STAIRS TO MY APARTMENT. My feet refused to move, as if filled with lead. My back hurt. I was so tired. In the last twenty-four hours, I've fought for my life twice and been healed with magic both times. Medmages accomplished miracles, but they used the body's own resources to heal, and whatever Doolittle did had drained me down to nothing. I was spent.

My eyes kept wanting to close and a couple of times I almost pitched over into the snow, because it looked soft and inviting. If it weren't for a Biohazard van I flagged down, I might have taken a nap along the road and frozen my ass off. As it was, the Biohazard medtechs gave me a ride, cutting my travel time down to a third. I'd scored fifteen minutes of half-sleep in the van on the way, safe and warm. My luck had to be turning for the better. One flight of stairs and I'd be home.

The splinters of my front door littered the landing in front of it. Fatigue vanished, burned in a rush of adrenaline. I stepped through the gaping doorway and stopped breathing.

Chunks of furniture and fabric lay scattered across my floor. Wooden shards protruded from the wall, marked with gashes and holes. The door to the library had vanished. The bookshelves inside had been pulverized. Four dozen glass bottles lay smashed, their contents staining the floor, mixing with torn pages of rare books and Greg's prized artifacts, now crushed and shattered. Herb dust swirled in the draft from busted windows.

My house wasn't just trashed. It was obliterated, as if a tornado had swept through it.

The bathroom door had been torn off its hinges. Deep gouges scoured it, too big for Grendel. Erra must've brought the Beast in. I checked the bathroom. No Grendel. No blood either. If she'd killed him, she would've left the body on display for me.

In the kitchen, holes gaped in the plaster where she'd ripped the cabinets from the wall. The wood was broken, not cut. She'd kicked them to pieces.

I stepped back into the living room, walking over the floor filled with mutilated books. One of Greg's dirks protruded from the wall, piercing Julie's pictures. Cuts sliced the photographs—Erra had stabbed Julie's eyes and face, again and again. Ice climbed down my spine. If she could've found Julie, I would be cradling my kid's corpse with her eyes sliced out.

I had to do the world a favor and kill the bitch.

When Greg died, he'd left the apartment and everything he owned to me. The books, the artifacts, the weapons. I couldn't let it go. I'd moved here, to Atlanta, to keep his memory alive. He was my last link to anything resembling a family. I assumed his place at the Order, and made his apartment into a home. This was my space. My corner of the world where

I felt safe and secure. A shelter for me and Julie. And Erra had violated it. She'd torn it apart.

There was no coming back from this. It was all gone. No matter what I did now, I couldn't restore the library or the apartment to its previous state. She had destroyed it so completely, it would never be the same.

It felt a little like dying. I've stared at death often enough to recognize being in a tomb. I should've felt something more, a deeper sadness, a sense of loss, but I just stood there, numb.

She'd made her hit. It was my time to hit back.

A small noise floated from the stairs. Grendel dashed into the apartment and hit me, pawing at me.

"Hey, you idiot."

I grabbed him and hugged his smelly neck, running my hands along his sides. No blood. His sweatshirt hung in shreds, but he seemed no worse for wear.

"Let's get out of here."

I walked out the door, the dog in tow, and didn't look back.

Twenty minutes later we made it to Andrea's, where I used my mad detective skills to deduce that she wasn't home. Her door was locked, and she didn't answer when I knocked. She was probably at Raphael's. That left me with one option: the Order. The Order had the added benefit of military-grade wards. It would take a small army of mages to break through them. Or my aunt. What a pleasant thought.

I dragged myself to the Order. Sleep still clung to me and fatigue made me slow and stupid. It took me over a minute to get the foldaway cot from the armory. I set it up in my office, and collapsed on it. Grendel flopped next to me and we passed out.

I HAD EXCELLENT REACTION TIME. THAT'S WHY I didn't run Andrea through with my saber when she barged into my office. Instead I dropped Slayer a fraction of a second after I'd grasped it and sat up slowly. Best friend, no kill.

Andrea glared at me. "You're here!"

"Where else would I be?"

She shut the door. "You have no idea."

"My apartment is in shambles. I stopped by your place, but you were gone, so I came here. It's safe and warm and there is coffee."

"You were at Jim's last night."

"Yes. Jennifer and Aunt B were about to have a fight and I made my escape. Normally I would've paid money to see something like that, but I had to go and get my dog. Where is my spawn of hell, by the way?"

"He was scratching by the door, and I let him out. That's how I knew you were here." Andrea shook her head. "After you left, Doolittle broke up the fight. Eventually everyone calmed down enough to realize you'd taken off. Doolittle wigged out because he'd loaded your tea with sedative and he thought you would pass out somewhere in the snow. Both the wolves and the boudas have been combing the snowdrifts for hours looking for you."

I picked up a book and bumped my forehead on it a few times. Why me? Why?

"And nobody thought to call here and check?"

"Jim called, but Maxine told him that you weren't here and she would give you the message when your shift started."

Of course. Standard policy of the Order meant that when a knight was off, she was off, unless it was an emergency. Otherwise knights tended to work themselves into complete exhaustion.

I concentrated. "Maxine?"

"She is out. Ted dragged her off to some meeting. There is nobody here but you, me, and Mauro."

"What meeting?"

"I have no idea." Andrea waved her arms. "Kate!"

"What?"

"Focus. Jennifer, Aunt B, and Doolittle are going to tell Curran this morning."

Hi, Your Majesty, we drugged your love muffin and then let her walk out into the dark, in the snow. Her apartment is destroyed and we're not sure where she is . . . "He'll need a lot of metal plates."

"What?"

"Never mind. It's not my job to comply with Aunt B's body guarding. I didn't agree to it."

Andrea leaned toward me and spoke very slowly and clearly. "You need to call the Beast Lord. Before he skins my boyfriend's mother, if at all possible."

I dragged myself to the desk and picked up the phone. Call the Beast Lord. Right.

Trouble was, I wasn't sure the Beast Lord and I were okay.

I dialed the Keep.

"Kate Da—"

The line clicked, and Curran's voice filled the phone. "Yes?"

Here we go. "Hey. It's me."

"I've been waiting for you to call."

Is that waiting good or waiting bad? "How's it going?" That's me, chipper.

"It's been better." He didn't sound like he was in the middle of skinning anyone. Although knowing Curran, calm voice didn't indicate much. I'd seen him calmly jump on a silver golem's back and be completely rational about it afterward despite the excruciating pain.

Andrea paced the floor like a caged tiger.

"Me, too. I'm at the Order. Been here since last night."

"That's not what I heard."

So they told him already. "Did you rip anyone to pieces?"

"Not yet. I'm thinking about it."

I leaned back. "Andrea is wearing a hole in my carpet, because she's worried you might be upset with her future mother-in-law. She is a little emotional about this issue."

Andrea paused her pacing and gave me her thousand-yard stare. I'd seen this precise look on her face when she peered through the scope of a sniper rifle sighting a target.

I rubbed the bridge of my nose. "Can I tell her to stop pacing?"

"Is that what you would like?"

"Yes. As a favor to me."

"As you wish."

I couldn't figure out who was the bigger idiot, him for saying it to me, or me for wanting to drop everything and go straight to him because he said it. This insanity had to stop. "Thank you."

"You're welcome. A favor," Curran said. "Would you let me pick you up at the Order today?"

He didn't finish but I knew what he left unsaid: *Let me pick you up and take you home, to the Keep.*

"My shift started"—I glanced at the clock—"twelve minutes ago. It ends at six. If it's at all up to me, I will be here waiting for you. I promise."

"Thank you. I'm sorry about your place."

"Me, too."

I hung up. That was the second civil conversation we'd had since we'd known each other. Too bad there was no champagne handy to celebrate the occasion.

"He's let it go. Satisfied?"

Andrea frowned. "The Beast Lord just asked you for a favor?"

"Yes, he did."

"Were Aunt B and Jennifer there?"

"I don't know, I didn't think to ask."

"I bet they were there." Andrea squinted at me. "Curran doesn't ask for favors. He doesn't bother. And he just let this whole thing go without an argument. That kind of influence is something only a mate would have . . . You slept together."

I gave her a blank look.

"You slept with Curran and you didn't tell me? I'm your best friend."

"It didn't come up."

"How disappointing for you."

Ha-ha. "That's not what I meant."

She pulled up a client chair and sat down on it. "Details. Now."

"We had a fight, screamed at each other for a while, I kicked him in the head, and then he stayed the night."

"That's it? That's all?"

"That's it."

She waved her arms in the air. "How was it?"

Like fireworks, only better. "It was good."

"Getting information out of you is like pulling teeth. Does Aunt B know?"

I nodded.

"That explains their collective panic attack. So did the two of you trash your apartment?"

"No."

"What happened?"

That wasn't a question I could answer with Mauro down the hall. I took a piece of paper from the drawer, wrote "My Aunt Erra" on it, and showed it to her.

Andrea paled.

I tore the paper to pieces and threw into the trash can. "The good news is I know who the Steel Mary is. Her name is Erra. The bad news is I know what she can do."

I gave her the rundown on Erra, her history, and her powers, keeping our family connection out of it in case anyone was listening. "She's completely amoral. She has absolutely no connection to any other human being except Roland. For Erra, the world breaks down into family and not-family. Not-family is fair game. And just because you were born to the family doesn't keep you safe. If she decides that you're not up to snuff, she'll fix the mistake of your existence. Her words, not mine."

"She has a high opinion of herself," Andrea said.

"Oh yes. When she gets into a car, her ego has to ride shotgun."

She tapped her fingers on my desk. "Are you thinking direct challenge?"

"Exactly. Issue a challenge, throw a couple of insults, use me as bait, since she hates me, and she won't be able to resist. If we do this somewhere outside of town, where she can't screw with the crowd, and throw every female knight the Order can scrape together at her, we may have a chance."

"I've asked Ted to let me assist you with this twice," Andrea said. "The second time in writing. It was denied."

"Ted went behind my back," I said.

"What do you mean?"

I sketched it out for her. Midway through it, she got up and started pacing across my floor again. Faint outlines of spots ghosted under her skin.

When I was done, she unclenched her teeth. "What he did was against the code of knighthood. But you have no recourse.

There is nothing in the Charter that protects your rights. You aren't a knight."

"I don't want recourse."

She spun to me. "Are you leaving the Order?"

Magic flooded the world. My heart skipped a beat. I chose my words carefully. "I have a problem with dedicating myself to an organization who considers my friends nonhuman."

"Ted Moynohan isn't the entirety of the Order."

"You've gone through the Academy. You know he isn't the only one." I leaned forward. "It's a deeply ingrained organization-wide prejudice. I understand why it's there, but I don't agree with it. Nonhumanity is a dangerous label. If someone is nonhuman, they have no rights, Andrea. No protection."

She stopped pacing and looked at me. "That's why you have to stay and fight. If people like you leave, the Order will never change. The change has to come from within to be effective."

I sighed. "It's not my fight, Andrea. Nor am I in a position to change anything. You said it yourself, I'm not a knight. I'm not part of the fraternity. I'm a barely tolerated outsider and I can be fired at any time. My voice doesn't matter and it won't be heard no matter how loud I scream."

"So you're just going to quit?"

"Probably. I can't compromise on this and I can't fight the entire Order. It's a losing battle. Some losing battles are worth fighting anyway, but this isn't one of them. Beating my head against this wall is a waste of time and effort. I can't alter the Order, but I can make sure it no longer benefits from my services."

Grendel dashed into the room, hurled himself past me and into the corner. A ragged snarl ripped from his mouth. He bit the air, barked once, and froze on rigid feet.

Something was scaring him half to death. I grabbed Slayer. Both of Andrea's hands had SIG-Sauers in them.

A loud boom rang through the building, resonating through my head. Someone had just tested the strength of the Order's ward.

"What the hell?" Andrea sprinted into the hallway.

I cleared the distance to the window in a single breath.

The ward blanketed the building like an outer invisible

shell. The Order's protective spell was strong enough to hold off an entire squad of MSDU mages, but whatever hit it had left a dent.

A solid wall of fire surged up over my window. Pale blue flashed as the invisible barrier of the protective spell strained under the press of the flames.

The fire died. A female voice rolled through the building. "Where are you, miserable rodent? I've come to burn down your tree!"

My aunt had arrived.

BOOM! THE WARD TOOK ANOTHER HIT.

The building blocked my view. I needed a better angle.

I sprinted into the hallway, turned left, and ran to Maxine's desk. Grendel followed me, snarling. Maxine's office was shallow, but long, and her window was the farthest I could get from the entrance short of breaking into Ted's lair.

I swung the window open and leaned out.

Below me and to the left a man in a tattered cloak punched the ward, trying to batter his way through the spell to the front door.

Boom!

Boom!

His bare arms glowed with dark red.

Torch. Power of fire. My aunt decided not to show up in person. I'd hoped I'd hurt her enough for her to lay low for a day. No such luck.

Andrea popped into Maxine's office with a huge crossbow in her hands. The crossbow sprouted metal gun-looking parts in odd places as if half a dozen assorted rifles had thrown up on it. Mauro followed her.

"The guy below is Torch," I told her for Mauro's benefit. "He's an undead mage with power over fire. Erra's riding his mind the way navigators ride the vampires."

"We can't take it outside." Mauro leaned to the side, getting a better look, and nodded at the new office buildings across the street. "If we fight him down there, he'll burn everything. Those buildings across the street are all wood. They'll go up like straw."

"Better to keep him contained." Andrea took my spot by the window, sighted Torch, and dropped her aim. "No good. Keep him engaged."

She moved into the hallway, jumped up, and pulled down the access door leading to the attic.

Boom!

Keep him engaged. No sweat.

I slid the window up, letting the icy air in, and sat on the windowsill. "Break it already, you're giving me a headache."

Torch looked up. About my age, solid black hair, American Indian features. Looked like a Cherokee to me, but I wasn't sure. "There you are!" he said in Erra's voice.

"What's the matter? Too scared to come out and fight me yourself?"

"Pace yourself, coward. I'm coming."

Boom! The building shuddered. The ward wouldn't hold him for long.

Mauro ducked into my office. "Andy says bring him closer to you, so she can get a shot. Here." He tossed me a jar. "Fire protection."

I dug in my pocket and pulled out a five-dollar bill. "Hey, Erra?"

Torch glanced in my direction.

I dangled five bucks at him and let it flutter down in the six-inch space between the ward and the building. "For you!"

Torch strode over and stared at the fiver. "What's this?"

"Some change for you. Buy your flunkies some decent clothes." I dipped my fingers into the jar and smeared thick fragrant paste on my face.

Torch frowned, mirroring the expression on my aunt's face. "Change?"

Oh, for crying out loud. "It's money. We don't use coins as currency now, we use paper money."

He stared at me.

"I'm insulting you! I'm saying you're poor, like a beggar, because your undead are in rags. I'm offering to clothe your servants for you, because you can't provide for them. Come on, how thick do you have to be?"

He jerked his hand up. A jet of flame erupted from his

fingers, sliding against the ward. I jerked back from the window on instinct. The fire died. I leaned forward. "Do you understand now?"

More fire.

"What's the matter? Was that not enough money?"

Flames hit the window. Hairline veins of blue appeared in the ward. Not good. Why the hell wasn't Andrea shooting him?

I waited until the fire vanished and popped my head back out. Torch stood with both arms raised, and his cloak hung open in the middle, presenting me with entirely too much of his full frontal view.

"Oh no, is it naked time?"

He opened his mouth to answer. A sharp twang sliced the air. A crossbow bolt sprouted from his open mouth, its point protruding from the back of his neck shining like a green star. The air hissed. The second bolt punched through his chest. The third took him in the stomach, just under the breastbone.

Green light pulsed once, like an emerald catching the sunlight.

The bolts exploded.

A torrent of green erupted into the sky. I ducked away from the window. "What the hell did she shoot him with?"

"Galahad Five warheads. Something the Welsh came up with to use against the giants. Packs a good punch." Mauro blinked against the light. "She demanded we get some after that whole Cerberus episode."

The flare finally faded. Erra's jeering voice called out from the street, "Is that all you've got?"

Couldn't be. I leaned to the window, Mauro next to me. On the street, Torch pulled the shreds of his cloak off his shoulders. The fabric broke to green-glowing ash under his touch.

He squared his naked shoulders and opened his mouth.

A blast of magic hit me, ripping through the protective spell like a thunderclap. Window glass exploded. The world went white in agony. The building quaked and bucked under my feet, shuddering from the aftershock of the ward's collapse. I clenched my teeth and clawed through the pain. My vision cleared. In front of me Mauro slumped on his knees among shards of the shattered window. Blood dripped from his nose.

He sucked it in and staggered to his feet, his face caught in a grimace. "A power word."

"Yes." Probably something along the lines of Open or Break. I glanced at the window. A translucent wall of blue blocked the view. Hairline cracks fractured the dead ward. The wall held together for another second and broke apart, melting into the wind.

So that was what a power word spoken by a six-thousand-year-old woman felt like.

Erra's voice rolled through the building in a cheerful song. "One little step! Two little steps! Three little steps! I'm coming up the stairs, little squirrel. Prepare yourself."

I pulled Slayer free of its sheath and strode into the hall-way. Behind me Andrea dropped through the access panel, landing in an easy crouch on the floor.

The door to the hallway flew open, ripped off its hinges, revealing Torch on the landing. His nude body glowed with an angry deep ruby light. A wide metal collar clasped his neck. *There goes my decapitation trick.*

He was undead, made with my family's blood. It gave me a chance, a small insignificant chance, but beggars couldn't be choosers. I pulled the magic to me.

Torch raised his left foot, stepping inside. Tiny sparks broke across his toes. His foot touched the floor and the sparks erupted into flames, spiraling up his limbs in a quick cascade.

Mauro braced himself.

The flames licked Torch's bare chest. Fifty feet of the hall-way lay between us, four offices on each side. I kept pulling, winding the magic around me. *That's right, bring him closer, Aunt dear.* The shorter the range, the greater the impact.

The crossbow string twanged. Twin bolts pierced Torch's chest. He ripped them out with an impatient jerk of the flame-sheathed hand. Andrea swore.

"Cute," Erra barked. "My turn."

The fire swirled around Torch like a mantle of heat and light. He raised his arms. Flames danced about his fingertips.

A huge hand pushed me back. Mauro thrust himself

in front of me. His shirt was gone. A dense wall of tattoos covered his back and chest. They glowed with tiny lines of bright red that shifted and flowed, as if inside Mauro's skin his flesh had turned to lava. He stomped, first left foot, then right, planting himself in the hallway, feet spread wide, arms raised at his sides.

"Get out of the way!" I snarled.

Mauro took a deep breath.

A fireball burst from Torch's arms, roaring down the hallway.

Mauro bellowed a single word. *"Mahui-ki!"*

The tattoos flashed with bright red. The wall of flame broke into twin jets five feet before the Samoan, shooting through Mauro's office on the left and Gene's on the right. Mauro stood untouched.

The fire died. The Torch cocked his head to the side like a dog. "What's this?"

Mauro grunted and stomped, one foot, then the other. The red lines on his skin flared.

Another wall of fire hit Mauro and twisted, deflected into the offices. Mauro packed a hell of a power. But now three hundred pounds of him stood between me and Torch and those three hundred pounds showed no signs of moving. The hallway was too narrow. I was stuck.

"Mauro, get out of the way."

"Hit me!" Mauro roared at the Torch.

Right. No intelligent life there.

"Brace yourself." Torch swung his arms, building up spirals of fire around his arms.

If I couldn't go through Mauro, I had to go around him. I ducked into the break room and kicked the wall. The old wooden boards splintered under my kick. The building was solid brick, but the inner walls that cleaved the inside space into offices were single board thin. I kicked again. The wood gave with a snap and I broke through into Mauro's office.

In the hallway Mauro roared, a raw bellow full of strain.

I hit the next wall with my shoulder.

Mauro's body flew past me. A thud shook the building— Mauro's back punching Ted's office door. A wall of fire followed, blasting me with heat. Andrea screamed.

I tore at the wall in front of me and squeezed through the narrow opening.

"Where are you, whelp? Did you run away again, maggot?"

The boards creaked. She was moving Torch in my direction. A wound to the stomach would do nothing to him and the collar kept me from slicing his neck. Not a lot of choices. If this failed, he'd burn us alive.

Torch passed by the door.

Now.

I lunged out of the room and clamped my left arm across his throat, pulling his back snug against me. Fire shot along his skin. I slid Slayer between his ribs into his heart and whispered a word into his ear.

"Hessad." Mine.

The world shook, as all of the magic I'd gathered tore from me at once. Pain streamed through my body, wringing tears from my eyes. Torch's mind opened before me, hot like boiling metal. I clamped it, dousing the flames, and smashed against the solid wall of Erra's presence. Her mind punched me and I reeled.

The immense force of her mind towered over me. Nobody was that powerful. Nobody.

Was that what looking into my father's mind would be like? If so, I didn't have a fucking prayer.

I pushed back, a gnat against colossus. An immense pressure grinding against me, sparking pain. I hung on, clenching my hand on Slayer's hilt. If I held it in his heart long enough, the blade would turn the undead tissue to pus. I just had to last.

Torch spun, lifting me off my feet. Fire licked my chest. "You shame the family. Weakling. Coward, who runs from the fight like a mangy dog."

I gritted my teeth against the pain and pushed back with my mind, extinguishing the flames. "It wasn't my idea. I had you and I would've killed you."

Hard fingers gripped my left wrist and pulled, slowly moving my arm from his throat. I strained. The moment he got free, he'd pull Slayer out and then we'd be done for.

"You dare to wrestle with my mind? I'm the Plaguebringer. Gods flee when they hear me coming."

"If my hands weren't busy, I'd clap for you."

Slayer gave under my hand, slightly loose in the rapidly liquefying undead tissue, and I jabbed it deeper into the wound. Erra grunted, a harsh sound of pain.

"Did that hurt? How about this?" I twisted the blade.

A fiery hammer hit my mind, tearing a groan from me. Heat shot from Torch. The air around me boiled. Fire spiraled up his legs.

"Did that hurt, whelp? I'll cook you alive. You'll beg me to kill you when your eyes pop from the heat."

Torch threw himself back, smashing me against the wall. I hung on to him like a pit bull. A few more moments. It didn't hurt that much. I just had to hold on for a few moments.

Erra slammed into the other wall. Something crunched in my back.

A dark shape sprang from Ted's office and sprinted to us. Erra saw it. Flames filled the hallway. I couldn't see. I couldn't breathe.

An enormous black dog shot through the fire. I saw eyes glowing with blue fire and ivory fangs. The creature smashed into Torch.

My mental defenses shuddered. I was done.

The giant dog clamped his teeth on Torch's arm and hung on. Torch shook him like a terrier shakes a rat, but the dog clung to him, dragging him down.

A second shape burst through the fire, this one pale and spotted. Deranged blue eyes glared at me from a face that was neither hyena nor human, but a seamless fluid blend of the two. Andrea buried her claws in Torch's gut. We crashed on the floor, Torch on the bottom, me on top.

The world drowned in pain, melting into hoarse snarls.

The flesh under Slayer's blade gave. I strained, forcing the saber through the soggy undead heart. The blade ground against ribs and burst out in a spray of dark fluid. The undead blood splashed on my lips and its sting tasted like heaven.

"I'll kill you," Erra gurgled. "I'll hunt you to the ends of the earth—"

I smashed my foot into Torch's neck, crushing the wind-pipe.

The awful pressure on my mind vanished.

I closed my eyes and floated in a long moment. Absence of pain was bliss.

And then an ache gnawed at my arms. My eyes snapped open.

A sleek creature rose from the Torch's stomach. Petite, proportionate, with elegant long limbs and well-shaped head, she was a perfect meld of human and hyena. Dark blood drenched her hands armed with long claws, staining her spotted forearms all the way to the elbow. Furious red eyes gazed at me from a human face seamlessly flowing into a dark muzzle.

She'd changed to save me.

Andrea's dark lips trembled, showing the sharp cones of her teeth. "God damn it."

She kicked Torch's corpse, knocking it off me, and kicked it again, sending it flying into the wall. "You bitch! Motherfucking whore."

I sat up and watched her punt and throw his body, spouting profanities. Being part bouda, she fought driven by rage. The quicker she let it out, the quicker she would be able to calm down enough to change back.

The enormous black creature lay down next to me and licked my foot.

"Grendel?" I asked softly.

The hell-dog whined softly in a distinctly Grendel-like fashion.

My attack poodle turned into a huge black hound with glowing eyes and shaggy fur. Figures.

The light dawned. The Black Dog. Of course. It was an old legend from so many cultures nobody knew exactly where it came from. Stories of giant Black Dogs with shiny eyes haunting the night have been passed around for years, especially in the United Kingdom and northern Europe. Nobody quite knew what they were, but when captured, they scanned as "fera," animal magic. Animal magic registered as a very pale yellow. When the medtechs scanned, their scanner must've failed to pick it up.

Andrea growled a few feet away. Grendel whined again and tried to stick his baseball-sized nose into my hand. Around us the office smoldered.

We'd beaten her again. Three undead down. Four to go.

CHAPTER 24

TO CALL HURRICANE SAVANNAH, WHICH FLAT-tened half of the East Coast some years back, "a gentle breeze" would be an understatement. To say that Ted Moyno-han was pissed off would be an understatement of criminal proportions.

He stood in the middle of the hallway, surveying the smok-ing soggy ruin that was the Order's office and radiating anger with dangerous intensity. After Andrea's rage died down, she changed back. Shifting back and forth pretty much wiped her out. We dumped snow and water on the fire, and the result wasn't pretty. Every window had been busted when the ward collapsed and icy wind howled through the building, juggling loose papers.

I'd laid out Erra's identity in broad strokes and made my report—lucky for me I had a lot of practice lying through my teeth. Mauro had been knocked out solid for most of the fight. He now sat in the middle of the hallway, pressing a rag filled with snow to a bump on his head. He didn't seem in a hurry to volunteer any information.

Ted said nothing. A dead silence claimed the office, the

kind of silence that usually only struck at 2 a.m., when the city sank into deep sleep and even the monsters rested.

Flame-retardant carpet and metal furniture had done its job. The building had survived and the damage to the office was mostly cosmetic. The damage to the Order, however, was enormous. The knights were untouchable. You injure one and the rest would show up on your doorstep, throwing enough magic and steel to make you think the world had ended. Erra had come into the Chapter, into the Order's house, and wrecked it. Ted had to hit back, fast and hard.

"The problem is, we don't know where Erra will attack next," I said. "We need to take the choice away from her. We killed three of her undead. She views it as an insult and she's arrogant as hell. She will respond to a direct challenge. We pick a spot outside the city, nice and private."

It was a simple plan, but simple plans sometimes worked best.

Behind us something thumped. A section of the wall crashed to the ground. Ted glared at it.

The phone rang in my office. I picked it up.

"Kate—"

"Help," Brenna's hoarse voice gasped. "Help us . . ."

A distant scream echoed through the phone, followed by a grunt. The disconnect signal wailed in my ear.

Oh no.

I dropped the phone and started to the door.

"Daniels!" Ted's voice cracked like a whip.

"One of the Pack's offices is under attack. I have to go."

"No."

I halted.

Ted gazed at me with glazed-over eyes. "You belong here. If you leave, then you don't."

"People are dying. They called me for help."

"We're people. They aren't. I'm giving you a direct order to stay here."

I looked at Andrea behind him. She stood still like a statue. Her face was bloodless.

Brenna's hoarse voice echoed through my memory.

Everything I had worked for, everything I'd done and

accomplished to keep Greg's legacy alive—but none of it was worth a single life.

"Daniels, if you do this, we're done. No second chances, no forgiveness. Done."

My fingers found the cord around my neck. I tore it off with a brutal jerk, dropped my ID on the floor, and walked out.

THE SNOW-STREWN CITY FLEW BY ME. I'D GRABBED the first rider I saw, jerked him from his saddle, and stole his horse, telling him to bill the Order for it so I wouldn't get shot in the back as we galloped away.

We rounded the corner at breakneck speed. The Wolf House swung into view. Dali's Prowler waited in the middle of the street. She stood next to it, staring at the building, her small body rigid.

She heard me and turned to look at me. Her mouth opened.

A body burst through the second-floor window in a cascade of glass shards. It plummeted through the air, a grotesque shape, neither human nor animal, huge claws poised to rend. The shape landed on top of the car and smashed into Dali, knocking her off her feet with a guttural snarl.

I tore at the reins, trying to slow down my horse. The horse screamed.

Warped, twisted, covered with random patches of fur and exposed muscle, the beast pinned Dali to the ground, clawing at her with black talons. Dali threw her arms up, trying to shield her throat.

I jumped off my horse and hit the ground running.

Blood sprayed the snow, shockingly red against the white. Dali's high voice screamed in a hysteric frenzy. "Stop, it's me, it's me!"

I snapped a side kick, putting everything I had into it. My foot smashed into the beast's side, knocking it back. The creature rolled and sprung to all fours.

If it was a shapeshifter in a warrior form, it was the worst one I had ever seen. Its left arm was too short, its pelvis tilted too far forward, its bottom jaw jutted to the side, overflowing with fangs. Above that awful jaw, its face was almost human.

Green eyes glared at me. Every hair on my neck stood up. I'd seen that face yesterday, smiling at me.

"Brenna?"

A vicious growl spilled from Brenna's deformed mouth. She shook. Gashes crisscrossed her body, oozing black pus and blood, as if her skin had randomly burst in places.

Dali scrambled back on her butt, leaving bloody tracks in the snow, until she bumped into the car with her head. "Brenna, it's me! It's me. We're friends. Please don't."

Brenna snarled again.

"Brenna, don't do this." I stepped toward her.

Brenna's eyes fixed on Dali with the unwavering focus of a predator about to charge.

"Please, please don't." Dali pressed tighter against the car. "Please!"

Brenna lunged.

Her mangled body flew above the snow, as if she had wings.

Brenna or Dali. No time to think.

I lunged forward and sliced at her back. Slayer cut through flesh, aborting Brenna's charge in midleap. She twisted in the air and hit me. Huge jaws fastened on my leg, searing my thigh with pain.

"No!" Dali screamed.

I cut again, cleaving through her spine.

Brenna's fangs let go. She crashed into the snow, jerking like a marionette on the strings of a mad puppeteer. Blood and spit flew from her terrible mouth. She growled and bit the air again and again, rending invisible enemies with her teeth. Behind me Dali sobbed uncontrollably.

I raised Slayer and brought it down. The saber pierced Brenna's chest. I twisted the blade, ripping her heart to pieces. In my head, Brenna's voice said, "Don't worry, Kate, I won't drop you."

Brenna stopped thrashing. The glow in her eyes dimmed.

Dali whimpered small incoherent noises.

A tortured snarl echoed through the street. I jerked Slayer free and whirled to the building. A clawed arm scratched at the first-floor window next to the door. Thick fingers slid on the glass, leaving bloody streaks.

Bloody hell.

I grabbed Dali and pulled her to her feet. "Dali! Look at me."

She stared, wild-eyed. "I knew, I knew something was wrong, I drove up, and it didn't smell right—"

"Get into the car. Drive down two blocks, go into the bakery, and call the Keep. No matter what happens, don't leave the store. Do you understand?"

"Don't go in there!"

"I have to go. If they get out, they might kill somebody."

"Then I'll come with you." She wiped at her face with the back of her hand. "I'm a fucking tiger."

A vegetarian, cross-eyed, half-blind tiger who got sick at the sight of blood. "No. I need you to get into the car and go call Curran. Please."

She nodded.

I released her. "Go."

A moment later the Prowler rolled down the street. I stepped over its tracks. The door of the house gaped open, like a black mouth.

I pushed the door open with my fingertips.

A body sprawled across the rug ten feet away. It lay in a tangle of shredded clothes, stained with black pus. A bitter odor filled the hallway, like the scent of chicken meat gone to rot.

I'd seen shapeshifters bleed gray before, when struck with silver. Silver killed Lyc-V, and the dead virus turned gray. To bleed black, Lyc-V had to be present in record numbers in the body. Only loups carried that much virus in them.

I stepped inside. The carpet muffled my footsteps. Above something thudded.

Slow and easy.

I reached the body. He lay on his stomach. Dark lesions striped his back, filled with viscous ichor, so dark it resembled tar. The odor of rot choked the air. I gagged and nudged the body with my foot. The head lolled. Unseeing milky eyes looked up at me from an unfamiliar face. Dead.

I kept moving through the long corridor.

Right room, clear.

Left, clear.

Right, clear.

Kitchen.

A pot boiled over on the stove. Two shapeshifters lay unmoving. One sprawled on top of the table, midway through the change, his body a mess of fur and skin. His deformed limbs clutched at the table, bones exposed, torn muscle oozing pus onto the green tablecloth. A chef's knife protruded from his neck, pinning him to the table.

The other body lay under the table, on the floor littered with chunks of peeled potatoes. A huge gash split open his chest, long ragged tears—a claw strike. The same black pus spilled from his lips, staining his chin. Nausea squirmed through me.

The scene played in my head: the shapeshifter on the right lunging over the table, striking at the guy chopping potatoes. His target taking a hit to the chest, thrusting the knife into his attacker's neck and falling . . .

I moved on to the stairwell. Upstairs or downstairs, to the basement?

I leaned to the side. Blood stained the green wallpaper on the landing above. Up.

The old stairs creaked under my feet. I ran up and pressed against the wall. Short hoarse grunts broke the silence in a steady rhythm, each grunt followed by the screeching of nails on glass. I checked the hallway.

Something crouched in the gloom, far to the right, on the clump of mangled bodies, digging in the flesh with bloody claws. The creature struck a corpse and wiped its deformed hand on the window. Claws scratched the glass. *Screeech.*

I stepped into the hallway.

Screech.

Screech.

The beast looked up at me. A girl. Barely older than Julie. She looked at me with pale dark eyes, the blood and black tarry pus falling from her mouth.

Her face was almost perfectly human. The rest of her was not. Her limbs protruded too far, ending in oversized hands. A hump bent her spine, sheathed in gray wolf fur. Her chest was concave and her ribs were piercing her skin.

"It hurts," she said.

I kept walking.

"It hurts." She dipped her hand into the blood pooling in the stomach of a woman next to her and wiped it on the glass. *Screech.*

"What happened?" I asked.

She leaped at me with a guttural snarl. I dodged left, and sliced across her side. She bounced off the wall, twisting, and lunged at me. I flipped the blade and sliced up through her stomach into the heart. Human teeth snapped an inch from my mouth. Her claws gripped my shoulder and she sagged on my blade, her life bleeding out.

I pushed the child off my saber gently and kept going.

Bodies lay strewn across the hallway, one after another, all facing to the end of the hallway, where the solid door to Jim's office stood half-ajar. They must've run here and didn't make it. I checked the faces as I walked, afraid I'd see someone I knew.

Whatever it was came through the front door. The first shapeshifter collapsed where he stood. The attacker hit the kitchen and headed upstairs. The shapeshifters on the first floor and in the basement must've heard the noise and chased after the intruder. Nine people dead, including Brenna and the child I'd murdered. Jim must've reinforced their numbers, expecting trouble. All of them went after the intruder. Nobody tried to get out until it was too late.

A muffled thud came from behind the door.

I pushed it open.

A naked man sat among the shambles of broken furniture and clumps of papers. A metal manacle clamped his ankle, attached to a spike in the floor by a chain as thick as my wrist. The loup chain—every Pack house had one.

A twisted mess of limbs and wounds lay in front of him. To the left a female shapeshifter hung on the wall, nailed by a sword to the boards.

The naked man looked up at me. An oily sheen slicked his skin, stretched tight over the lean body. His eyes were the dim yellow of old urine. The stench of rotting chicken swirled about him.

"My favorite niece," Erra's voice said. "Only you could make this better. Welcome to Venom's party."

The body in front of Venom moved.

"You again." The undead stabbed the shapeshifter with a wooden shard and jerked it out for the second blow.

I grabbed the body by the legs and pulled it to me, out of his reach.

"Too late." Erra snorted.

The shapeshifter's body shuddered in my hands. Black ichor oozed. I knelt and saw bright red hair. Dingo, one of Jim's men. Oh no.

A bloody hole gaped where Dingo's left eye used to be. His right looked at me, stark against the mangled mess of his face. "Got him with the chain," he whispered.

"You did," I told him.

His voice was a hoarse, pain-laced groan. "Dying. Kill me."

I raised my saber, brought it down, and then he hurt no more.

"Disgusting," Erra said through Venom's mouth.

Neither of us was laughing anymore. "These people were my friends. You made me kill them. You made me kill a child." I could still hear Brenna's voice in my head.

"Quit your sniveling. I have no patience for cowards."

I got up and slid the cabinet door open. With tech and magic dancing back and forth, most people stuck to things that always worked for backup.

Papers, boxes, nothing of interest. I moved on to the smaller cabinet to the right. "I figured out why you don't target women."

"Women are the future. One man can sire a nation, but kill the women and you kill a people."

"Nope, that's not it. You were trained to demolish armies. Not many ancient armies were made of women."

"You'd be surprised," Erra said.

A glass gallon jug of kerosene, still three quarters full, sat in the corner. I pulled it out and twisted off the cap.

"Why don't you gnaw off your leg and escape?" I asked.

"And miss out on your misery?"

"Oh, I'm pretty sure you'd be glad to miss it. If you lose your undead toy, you'll have to look for another body to drain of blood. You didn't escape, because making him chew off his foot would hurt you. And you don't like pain."

I strode to the undead.

Venom lunged at me. I sidestepped, catching his throat in my hand. My fingers touched his skin. I had already touched Erra's mind once. It took me a fraction of a second to find it again. I grabbed it and dumped the kerosene over Venom's head. Venom twisted, aiming a kick at my stomach. I let go and backed away, out of his reach, clinging to my aunt's mind, chaining her to Venom's body.

"Got a question for you."

"And?" Erra snorted.

An awful pressure ground on my mind. I unclenched my teeth. "Can you outlast me?"

I pulled a lighter from my pocket, clicked it on, and threw it at Venom. Flames surged, licking his skin.

Erra screamed. Her mind grabbed mine and shook, the way a dog shakes a rat when it wants to kill it. I hung on with everything I had. Every ounce of fury I had to crush to get through this house. Every drop of guilt at watching Brenna's blood splash the snow. I sank all of it into Erra's mind, fastening her to Venom.

Burn, bitch. Burn.

The air stank of burning hair and charred fat. Venom flailed on his chain like a rabid dog.

"I'll tear you limb from limb!"

"Does it hurt? Tell me it hurts."

Heat and pain wound about my mind in white-hot ribbons, and squeezed. Tears swelled in my eyes. Venom burned like a human candle, and I clung to Erra's mind.

The ribbons turned into blades and sliced into me, pulling me apart. I felt myself unraveling, as if my mind were disappearing thread by thread. An absurd vision of my veins being pulled from my body thrust itself before me. It hurt. Dear God, it hurt so much.

But the fire hurt her more.

Erra howled like a dog. "I'll rip you apart and suck the marrow out of your bones. I'll hunt you to the ends of the earth. You can't hide your blood, I'll know it anywhere. I'll track you down. I'll murder everyone who knows you and make you watch them die. You'll pay for this. You'll pay!"

The pressure ground my mind into nothing. "Quit your sniveling."

Venom crashed to the floor. A light exploded in my mind, like a razor-sharp star. I tasted my blood—my nose was bleeding.

Pushing the words out of my mouth took a long time and they came out slurred. "Death shock. That's what happens to a Master of the Dead when a vampire she navigates dies before she can let go of its mind. Since you keep your undead so close to your heart that it hurts you when they're battered . . ."

"Let me go!" my aunt screamed.

"This is how you die," I told her. "Chained to this undead piece of meat."

"You'll die with me," she snarled.

Pain crushed my skull. I slumped against the wall. Fragments of my thoughts dashed back and forth like frightened rabbits. ". . . worth it . . ."

A short shape dashed into the room. I focused. Dark clothes. Indigo veil. The old woman I'd saved from some low-lives on the way to the Order. What the hell?

She leapt over the bodies and landed by me.

Erra screamed in agony.

The old woman jerked her hand up. A short spear glinted with the light of the flames. Her black eyes glared at me. "I end this. Let go now."

I had no strength to fight her. I'd sunk all of myself into keeping Erra put. "Don't."

The spear spun in the woman's hand. She flipped it and rammed the butt into my solar plexus. Pain exploded under my diaphragm, dropping me to my knees. I clawed on to the mind link but it slipped from me. The pressure vanished. My aunt broke free.

Venom jerked one last time and died.

Not again.

I surged to my feet and lunged at her. She made no move to counter. I slammed her into the wall. "Why?"

A red sheen rolled over her eyes. Diamond-shaped pupils stared back me. "I must protect you. It's my job."

The wall exploded. A seven-foot monster broke into the room, her fur dark, eyes glowing with green from a nightmarish meld of human face and wolf muzzle. Smaller shapes streamed into the room.

"Protect the mate!" the werewolf snarled in Jennifer's voice. "Secure the room!"

Claws clamped me and threw me out of the room into the waiting hands of another shapeshifter.

I SAT ON THE STEPS AND WATCHED THE SHAPE-shifters carry bodies out of the house. Jennifer sat next to me.

I felt hollow and tired. If it wasn't for the wall propping me up, I'd collapse. If I concentrated hard enough, I could wiggle my fingers. Concentrating hurt.

Kate Daniels, deadly swordmaster. Fear my twitching pinkie.

A young female shapeshifter carried a misshapen body out of the house. She looked a little like Brenna with lighter hair, except she was alive and Brenna was dead, because I killed her.

"I killed a little girl," I said.

The werewolf-Jennifer stirred next to me. "She was my sister."

I was so numb, her words took a minute to register.

"I wouldn't let them leave." Jennifer's voice unnaturally calm. "I delayed evacuation. Because it was our house. We're the wolves. We can't be run out of our own den. Now Naomi is dead."

I didn't know what to say.

Jennifer turned to me. "Did she hurt when you burned him?"

"Yes."

"It's not enough." Jennifer looked at the bodies laid out on the snow.

"No. I wanted to kill her, but she stopped me."

We both looked at the woman. She sat cross-legged in the snow, her spear on her lap. Four werewolves watched her.

"Naomi was twelve," Jennifer said.

A year younger than Julie.

The alpha female turned to me. Her eyes were wet. "I hate you for killing her."

Welcome to the club.

A caravan of Pack Jeeps entered the parking lot.

"It hurts and you want to hurt someone, and you don't care who," I said. "Because hurting will make you feel better."

"Yes."

"It won't. I killed dozens of fomorians after Bran died. It didn't help."

"I'm not you," she said.

"We're all human," I told her.

An arm wrapped around me. My heart tried to leap out of my chest. Curran pulled me to him and kissed my forehead.

"I'm going to put a bell on you," I told him. "That way I'll have some warning."

He peered at my face. "Are you okay?"

"I killed Brenna and Jennifer's little sister. And the Dingo. Other than that, I'm great. Everything is lovely."

"Right." He looked at Jennifer.

She sat frozen.

"The cars are here. Load your people up. Daniel is waiting for you at the Keep." He turned to me. "Can you walk or should I carry you?"

I'd be damned if I let him carry me anywhere. I pushed to my feet. My legs wobbled a bit but held. We walked side by side to the Pack Jeep. He opened the passenger door and I got in. He gave some final instructions and we were off.

THE KEEP WAS MADE OF STAIRS. AND MORE STAIRS. And then more stairs. *Just keep climbing. One foot after the other.* Brenna's bite on my thigh burned. My lungs had shriveled up to the size of golf balls.

I would not collapse on the damn stairs. The higher we climbed, the more people stopped and looked at us, and I would not faint while half of the damn Keep watched.

"One more floor," Curran murmured.

I clenched my teeth.

Step, and step, and step. The landing before his private hallway. Made it.

The door barring access to Curran's quarters swung open. Derek held it ajar from the inside.

Curran turned to the small group of shapeshifters that had trailed us. "Leave."

I blinked and the stairs were deserted. Our escort had vanished at a record speed.

Curran picked me up.

"What do you think you're doing?"

"Nobody is going to see you. Your reputation is intact. It's just you and me."

I looked at Derek.

"He didn't see anything," Curran said, carrying me through the door.

"I saw nothing," Derek confirmed and bolted the door shut.

I put my arms around Curran's neck and let him carry me past his gym and bimbo room up another staircase all the way to his rooms.

"Where to?" he asked.

On the left a living room waited with a large gray sectional sofa. Up ahead was the door to the bedroom. On the right was another door.

"Bathroom," I said.

He carried me through the door on the right. An enormous bathtub took up most of the room.

Hot water. Heaven.

"Do you mind if I take a bath?"

He lowered me to the floor gently. "Can I get you anything?"

I shook my head and began to strip. He waited to make sure I made it into the tub and left.

I sat and ran the water so hot it was near boiling. Even with the water up to my collarbone, the tub still had a foot and a half of space left.

Sometime later Curran walked in, carrying a glass of water with ice. He sat by the bathtub and put his hand on my forehead.

"You have a fever."

I shook my head. "Brenna bit me."

Venom's poison must've been very potent. The Lyc-V virus would've multiplied in record numbers trying to counteract it, making the shapeshifters go from zero to complete loup.

Loups were contagious as hell and I'd got a walloping dose of Lyc-V from Brenna's saliva.

"It's nothing major. My body will burn through it in an hour or two."

Curran nodded.

I probably shouldn't have said that.

I took the water and sipped. "Why is everything so large?"

"The tub is sized for my beast form."

I smiled. "Do you take baths as a lion?"

"Sometimes. The wolves found one of their own in the basement of the Wolf House. He attacked them on sight. Did Jennifer tell you that?"

He was trying to help me with my guilt. "She was a bit busy. I'd killed her little sister and she was trying to hold it together."

I did what I had to do. I had no choice. We both knew it. Even Jennifer knew it. But knowing that didn't make any of us feel better.

"Do you need to be somewhere?" I asked.

He shook his head.

I scooted over to the side. He stripped his clothes off and slid into the tub with me. I leaned against his chest, with his arm around me, and we sank into the hot water.

"Where is the old lady?" I asked.

"In a loup cage downstairs. Any idea who she is?"

"Nope."

I closed my eyes. I'd dumped some foaming stuff into the tub from one of the bottles I found sitting on the edge and now it smelled clean and soapy, like Irish Spring. For all I knew, he used this stuff for his mane and I had just exhausted a month's worth of his shampoo.

Of course, with my luck, we were sitting in a tub full of his flea dip.

Curran's skin was warm under my cheek. I could sit like that forever.

"It won't last." The words escaped before I had a chance to think about it.

"What won't last?"

"You and me. Us. Even if we win this time, something else

will come along and ruin our lives. Eventually I'll lose a fight or you will, and it will be over."

He pulled me closer to him. "Something else will come along. When it does, we'll kill it. Later, something else will show up. We'll kill it, too, and then we'll go home."

I grimaced. "And climb a million stairs trying not to collapse."

"I don't do collapsing."

"Of course not. What was I thinking . . ."

His voice was rock-steady. "We don't live in a safe world. I can't give you the white picket fence, and if I did, you'd set it on fire."

True. "Only if I ran out of kindling."

"Or needed some hardened wooden shards to drive into someone's eye."

I stretched my legs. "You don't actually burn wood to harden it. You turn it over the fire, so it soaks up the heat but doesn't char."

He growled low in his throat. "Thank you for that little nugget of wisdom."

"You're welcome."

His arm stroked my back. "There are only two things that can screw this up for us: you and me."

"Then we're doomed for sure."

I had to tell him about my aunt. I just couldn't get myself together to do it.

"My father was the best fighter I ever knew," Curran said. "Even now, I'm not sure I could take him."

"We have that in common," I murmured.

"We lived on the edge of the Smoky National Park, in the mountains. I don't know if it was North Carolina or Tennessee. Just mountains and the four of us. My dad, my mom, my younger sister, and me. My parents didn't want to deal with any shapeshifter politics. We're older than most shapeshifters. Different."

Worry crawled up my spine. *The First were there first,* Erra said in my head. "What happened?"

"Loups," Curran said. His voice was devoid of any emotion. "Eight of them. They caught my sister first. She was seven and she liked to climb trees. One day she was late for lunch. I went looking for her. Found her up in a maple about a mile from the house. I thought she fell asleep and called out. She didn't answer, so I climbed up, right into their trap. They strung a silver wire and it caught my throat, like a noose."

He leaned back, exposing his neck, and I saw a pale hair-thin line across his throat.

"As I flailed, trying to keep from suffocating, they wrapped me in silver mesh. I remember hanging off the tree, burning up from silver poisoning my skin, and I could finally see Alice. They had eaten her stomach and her eyes and her face, all the soft parts, and leaned what was left on the branch to snare us."

Oh, God. "How old were you?"

"Twelve. My dad was next. He'd tracked me down by scent and he came into the clearing roaring."

The loups were stronger and faster than People of the Code. Eight against one, even Curran would have no chance.

"My father killed three," he said. "I watched the rest tear him apart. I learned then that you can't survive on your own. You need numbers. After they ate, they went after my mother. The wire on which I hung cut through the branch and I fell. By the time I got free, she'd stopped screaming."

I shifted closer to him. "And then?"

"I ran. They chased me, but I knew the mountains and they didn't. I lost them. They set up camp at our house. For about four months I lived on my own in the woods, trying to get stronger, while they tried to catch me. I'd come up the crags to watch their camp, waiting for an opportunity to pick them off one by one. Never got it. They were always together.

"In the fall, Mahon found me. His cousin made money guiding hunting parties into the mountains. The loups found one. Left nobody alive. Mahon took it personally and brought twenty shapeshifters with him, most family, some from other clans who owed him a favor. I watched them comb the woods for four days before I let them see me. Mahon offered me a deal. If he gave me a shot at the loups, I'd come with him out of the woods. I agreed."

"Did you get your shot?" I asked.

He nodded. "I got one of them. Bit his neck in half. It was my first battle kill."

Mine was at ten. Voron had paid a street tough half a grand to kill me. I killed him instead and I was sick after, and then he brought out the second guy.

Curran's eyes looked into the distance. "People think I built the Pack, because I'm the guy who has the welfare of all shapeshifters in mind. They're wrong. Everything I built, I did so that when I mate and have children, nobody can touch my family."

"That's why you stabilized the clans. No infighting."

He nodded. "That why I built the damn castle. I fight for them, I deal with their petty politics, I make them play nice with the Order and PAD and every other asshole with a badge. I do it all so my children won't have to see their sister's half-eaten corpse."

My heart squeezed itself into a tiny painful ball. "And here I thought you were only pretending to be insane."

Curran shook his head. "No, I'm the real thing. Paranoid, violent, not happy unless things are my way. Right now I'm back in that damn tree watching loups feed on my father. I promised myself I'd never feel it again, but there it is, right there. I built all this so I can protect you. I need to know that you want it. I need to know if you will stay."

I sat up straighter. "There are some papers in the pocket of my jeans."

He reached for the jeans and fished out several torn book pages, folded into a small square. I'd ripped them from a ruined book after Erra trashed my place.

Curran unfolded the pages.

The first showed a tall man in a cloak marching down the road to the city. Tendrils of smoke, made with short ink strokes, stretched from the man outward, like a foul miasma. Before him animals galloped through the fields, cattle, sheep, oxen, horses, dogs, all caught in a terrifying stampede. The caption below it said, *Erra the Plaguebringer.*

Curran looked at it for a long breath, wet stains spreading through the paper from his fingers, and dropped it on the floor of the bathroom.

Second page. The same cloaked figure walking through the street as people fell before it, their faces disfigured by boils. He discarded it, too.

The same figure with seven others crouching in the fog before him.

The fourth page, Erra again, depicted as a man, laughing, his arms held wide, as a temple burned behind him.

"Erra," I said. "Drawn as a man, but really a woman. Over six thousand years old. Roland's older sister."

Curran was looking at me.

I swallowed. Breaking twenty-five years of conditioning was a lot harder than I thought.

I pointed to the page. "What do you see?"

"An enemy."

Thank you for making it that much harder, Your Majesty.

I had to say it. He put his cards on the table and he had a right to know what he was getting into. *You can't smelt happiness out of a lie. The world doesn't work that way.*

I unclenched my teeth. "I see my aunt."

It took him a moment. Understanding flared in his gray eyes. Yep, he got it.

"She won't stop until she or I are dead," I said. "There is no place I can hide, and even if there was, I'm not running. You saw what she does. If I don't fight, she'll go after everyone I've ever known. She's my family and my responsibility. It's to the death now."

My throat was so dry, my tongue turned into a dry leaf in my mouth.

"If I lose, I die. If I win, Roland will want to know who nuked his sister. Either way I'm screwed. There are consequences to being with me. This is one of them. By my presence, I'll endanger you and your people. I know I said things before about wanting warmth and a family, but the truth is that I'm alone for a reason. Once we're together, you and everyone you know will become a target."

I couldn't read his face. I wished I knew what he was thinking.

"I'll never sit demurely by your side. I'll tell you exactly what I think and you won't always like it. I won't be your princess all snug and safe in the tower you built. That's just not me. And even if it was, no army in this world could make me safe. If I choose to have children, they may never be safe. That's the kind of mate I'd make."

He said nothing. I was rambling. This was important and I was mangling it all to hell.

My fingers had gone cold. All this hot water and I was freezing. My voice came out flat. "Being without you makes me very unhappy. I don't have enough willpower to walk away. I've tried. So, if you want to break it off, I need you to use whatever it is that made you Beast Lord and leave. Don't tell me what you think I want to hear, unless you really mean it. No hard feelings. Climb out of this tub, get Derek to find me a separate room, and I'll never bring it up again."

I looked at Curran. He still wore his Beast Lord face: flat and about as expressive as a stone statue. I was a hair from punching him in the jaw just to see some emotion. Any reaction would do at this point.

"Anything else?" he asked.

"No."

Curran shrugged and pulled me back to him. "You don't pick the family you're born into. You pick the one you make. I already chose my mate and glued her ass to the chair to make sure she knew it."

He didn't care. The stupid, stupid idiot.

"This gluing thing won't keep me put," I said.

"Maybe I'll chain you to it next time."

"Is that werelion humor?"

"Something like that."

I kissed him. He tasted like Curran and it made me absurdly happy. Everything took a step back: Erra, the dead, the guilt, the fear, the pain. I shoved it all aside. If one of us died tomorrow, at least we would have these few hours. We would make the best of them, and no force on earth, not even my bitch of an aunt, would interfere.

I brushed my hand through his blond hair. "You're a fool, Your Furriness."

Tiny gold sparks flared in his irises. "You're in my rooms in my bathtub naked and you're still mouthing off."

Did he expect something different? "Hey, I didn't kick you or punch you in the throat. I consider this progress. And you haven't choked me again, which is some sort of record for you . . ."

He grabbed me with a growl. "That's it. You're in for it."

"Very scary. I'm shaking in my—"

He locked his mouth on mine and I decided it was a good incentive to shut up.

CHAPTER 25

———◆———

I AWOKE BECAUSE CURRAN SLIPPED OUT OF BED. HE did it in complete silence, like a ghost, which was impressive considering the bed was four feet tall.

He strode out of the bedroom. A door swung open with a soft whisper. A barely audible voice murmured something. I couldn't make out the words but I recognized the rasp—Derek.

A moment later the door swung shut. Curran entered the bedroom and stopped when he saw me looking at him.

He looked . . . at home. His hair stuck out at a weird angle, probably dried odd, since we went from the tub straight to bed. His face was peaceful. I've never seen him so relaxed. It was as if someone had lifted a huge weight off those muscled shoulders.

And dumped all of it on me.

"What time is it?" I asked.

"A little past five." He paused in midstride and leaped on the bed.

I rubbed my face. I dimly recalled getting out of the bathtub, wrapped in a criminally soft towel, and letting him convince me that we needed to lie down and rest for half an hour. We slept for a solid ten hours at least. "I meant to go and talk with the old woman and to call Andrea. Instead I passed out here with you."

"It was worth it."

It was totally worth it.

"No more tubs for me." I jumped off the bed and pulled on a pair of Pack sweats. "They make me lose all sense."

Curran sprawled on the bed with a big self-satisfied smile. "Want to know a secret?"

"Sure."

"It's not the bathtub, baby."

Well, aren't we smug. I picked up the corner of the lowest mattress and made a show of looking under it.

"What are you looking for?"

"A pea, Your Majesty."

"What?"

"You heard me."

I jumped back as he lunged and his fingers missed me by an inch.

"Getting slow in your old age."

"I thought you liked slow."

A flashback to last night mugged me and my mind executed a full stop.

He laughed. "Ran out of snappy comebacks?"

"Hush. I'm trying to think of one."

As long as we kept sparring, I could pretend that surviving today would be a breeze.

Curran slid off the bed, presenting me with a view of the world's best chest up close. "While you're thinking, Raphael and Andrea are waiting for us downstairs. Nash doesn't matter, but if I keep the scion of Clan Bouda waiting for too long, I'll have to smooth his feathers, and I don't feel like it."

"Feathers?"

"Yes." Curran snagged a white T-shirt from the drawer. "B's precious peacock. Strutting around and making sure all the ladies faint in his wake."

I arched my eyebrow at him.

"He's not a bad guy." Curran shrugged. "Spoiled, arrogant.

Good in a fight, but thinks with his dick. When things don't go his way, he throws a tantrum. Andrea is perfect for him—unlike his mother, she doesn't buy any of his bullshit."

"So if I invite him over for tea and cookies . . . ?"

"As long as it's in public, it wouldn't be an issue. Just don't expect me to show up. I'll be indisposed. If you invite him into our rooms, I'll rip his head off."

"Is it because you're jealous or because it would be a breach of Pack protocol?"

"Both." The muscles along Curran's jaw tightened. "He handed you a fan so you could fan yourself while watching him. If he steps a hair out of line, he won't live to regret it and he knows it."

I slid Slayer's leather sheath on my back. "Now is probably a good time to mention that I made a deal with his mother."

Curran stopped. "What sort of deal and when?"

I sketched it out for him while putting on my boots.

Curran grimaced. "Typical. She picked a moment when you were at your weakest."

I shrugged. "It's a good deal for me."

"It is. But then she tried to feed you. That's my privilege." Curran held the door open. "B will always push you to see how far she can make you bend. I won't interfere with the way you handle her, but if it was me, I'd call her to a meeting once this is over. Somewhere public where the two of you would be on display. Make her wait. Half an hour ought to do it."

"Are you actually holding the door for me?"

"Get used to it," he growled.

I bit my lip so I wouldn't laugh, stepped through the door, and Mr. Romance and I went down the stairs to the conference room.

RAPHAEL PACED ALONG THE WALL, FLIPPING A knife. Andrea leaned against the table. Her face was grim.

Raphael nodded as Curran and I walked through the door. "M'lord. M'lady."

Andrea blinked, her eyes opened wide. "Kate? What are you doing here?"

"She's his mate. Where else would she be?" Raphael's voice dripped bitterness. Something had happened between them and it wasn't good.

"It's not the same for her," Andrea said without turning around.

"No, it's not. She actually came through when our people were dying."

"She had a choice. I didn't."

Raphael's eyes shone with red. "She had the exact same options you did."

"Enough," Curran said.

Raphael turned around, spinning his knife, and resumed his pacing.

Curran glanced at me. "You quit the Order."

"Ted made it a choice between Brenna's SOS phone call and keeping my ID on my neck."

"So you picked the shapeshifters over the knights," Raphael put in.

Andrea shot him a look of pure fury.

"No," I said. "I picked people in danger over a direct order to ignore them."

Now things were clear. I went to help the shapeshifters and Andrea stayed, and now Raphael wanted to bite her head off for it.

"I have your dog," Andrea said.

Thank you, Universe. "Has he barfed anywhere?"

"He ate my bathroom rug, but other than that he's okay."

"I owe you a rug, then."

She nodded.

I perched on the table. "What's the Order's plan for dealing with Erra?"

Andrea grimaced. "Ted's brought in some female knights from Raleigh and they're setting a trap for her at the Mole Hole. Tamara Wilson is here. Master-at-arms, blade. She's supposed to be out of this world good and immune to fire. Ted's going along with your plan to directly challenge Erra. They've put her name on a flag and are flying it over the Mole Hole."

The Mole Hole used to be Molen Enterprises

exploded. The slender glass tower once belonged to the Molen Corporation, owned by one of the richest families in Atlanta. Rumor said the Molens had gotten a hold of a phoenix egg. The plan was to hatch the egg, so the young phoenix would imprint on them, giving them a superweapon. The phoenix did hatch, but instead of going "Mommy!" it went boom. Took out the Molen tower and the three city blocks around it. Phoenix didn't squat once they hatched. They rose, like ancient rockets, straight into the sky.

Eventually the dust cleared, revealing a perfectly round crater. About a hundred and forty yards across, it gaped almost fifty feet deep and full of molten glass and steel. When the crater cooled two weeks later, a foot-thick layer of glass sheathed its bottom. Enterprising citizens cut steps in the crater's earthen wall, turning it into a makeshift amphitheater. All sorts of legal and illegal events took place in the Mole Hole, from skateboarding competitions and street hockey to dog fights.

"The Mole Hole is in the middle of the city." I frowned.

"Fifteen minutes from the People's Casino, twenty from the Witch Oracle in Centennial Park, twenty-five from the Water and Sewer Authority," Andrea said.

"How badly was the Order trashed?" Curran asked.

"It was still smoking when I left at the end of the day," Andrea told him.

"Then Moynohan needs to administer severe and very public punishment," Curran said. "The Order must save face."

"He'll get plenty of spectators at the Mole Hole," Raphael said. "The last time I was there, the buildings on the edge of it were packed full. At least three thousand people, maybe more."

I felt an urge to hit my head against a wall. "You were there when I told him that Erra loves to panic crowds, right?"

"I was there," Andrea confirmed. "I refreshed his memory. He told me to shove it."

"And that's the person for whom you will put yourself in harm's way." Raphael shook his head. "But you won't do the same for our people."

"He's one of many knights," Andrea said. "He's not the Order. His views are outdated and don't reflect the attitudes of the majority of the Order's members. I didn't swear allegiance to him. I gave my loyalty to the mission."

"And that mission is to clean you and me off the face of this planet!" Raphael growled.

"The mission is to ensure the survival of humankind."

"Yes, and Moynohan doesn't think we fit the description."

"I don't care what he thinks," Andrea snarled. "I'm there because I dedicated my life to it. It gives me a purpose. Something to believe in. Unlike you, I actually did something with my life instead of wasting my time rutting with anything I could hold still for thirty seconds."

"A lot of good it did you—you sit on your ass in the Order all day long, polishing your weapons, and the one time you could have made a difference, you chose to do nothing."

Andrea slammed her hands on the table. "I chose to obey an order from my commanding officer. Discipline, look it up."

"They were dying! They called you for help and you did nothing!"

"Yes, because Kate went there."

Derision twisted Raphael's face. "So you let her take the fall for you?"

"I'm not her!" Andrea pointed at me. "I can't just dramatically rip my ID off and walk away."

I glanced at Curran in case he decided to wade in. He sat next to me, his jaw resting on his fist, watching them the way one would watch a fascinating play.

Andrea kept going. "The Order was there for me when nothing else was. Where was your precious Pack and these fabled shapeshifters when I was sixteen with a sick mother on my hands and no way to feed myself? Where were you? I won't be a flaky slut bouda. When I give my loyalty, I mean it."

"You're giving it to the wrong people, can't you see that?"

Andrea's eyes blazed. "If I leave, Ted wins. I won't let that fucker force me out, do you hear me?"

"Do what you want." Raphael shook his head. "I'm done."

Oh, boy.

"There are only two streets leading from the Mole Hole, so if Erra panics the crowd, she'll run them either toward the Casino or toward the Water and Sewer Authority," I said. "Erra gets off on watching people run. The street leading to

Water and Sewer is dark, but the street to the Casino is well lit."

"The Casino is more likely," Andrea said. "Not only can she pick off the stragglers, but scared people naturally tend to run toward the light. It gives them an illusion of safety."

And the light will be full of vampires. "Erra might be reluctant to destroy vampires, which could limit casualties."

"The People won't enter the fight," Curran said. "They have nothing to gain."

"Nataraja may or may not know the connection between Roland and Erra, but Ghastek doesn't know," I said. "He realizes that something odd is going on and he wants a piece of it. He went through a giant guilt rant when I wouldn't let him have Deluge's head. He won't jump into the fight if you or I ask them, but if a knight of the Order calls them . . ."

"Ted would never approve vampire deployment. He wants this to be solely the Order's affair." Andrea crossed her arms.

"You're wasting your time," Raphael said. "She won't do anything to help you. It would endanger her career too much."

"You're an ass," Andrea snarled.

Raphael executed a perfect bow. "Does the Beast Lord require my presence any longer?"

"No," Curran said.

Raphael walked out.

Curran gave me a beautiful version of an "I told you so" look.

I turned to Andrea. "If you call Ghastek and tell him that Ted's planning a showdown with the navigator of undead mages less than two miles from the Casino and doesn't want the People involved, Ghastek will foam at the mouth."

"Thanks for the tip." Andrea grimaced. "Would've never thought of it on my own, being as I sit on my ass all day polishing my weapons."

Curran rose. "The Pack thanks the Order for its continued cooperation and goodwill. We look forward to successful relationships in the future."

That's it, you're done, go away now.

Andrea drew herself upright.

"I'm not done," I said quietly.

Curran ignored me. "You and I have an understanding, Andrea. Don't abuse it by insulting your friend and my mate."

Andrea walked out.

I sighed. "You don't get to decide when I'm finished talking to my friend."

Curran perched on the edge of the table. "The conversation was going nowhere. They're both hurt and neither of them was in the mood to listen."

That didn't change anything. "I thought this was a joint venture. Am I wrong?"

Curran fell silent for a long moment, obviously picking the right words. "Yes, it is. I know it goes against the grain, but please don't contradict me again in public. You can scream and kick me in private, but in public we must present a united front. Always. Anything we do outside of those rooms upstairs will be scrutinized and people like B will exploit every rift to their advantage. When a decision is made, I need to know that you will support it."

I tapped my fingernails on the table. "Even if the decision was made without my input?"

He exhaled slowly. "I'm not used to sharing. I've never had to do it before. If you cut me some slack, I promise I'll do the same for you. I will attempt to always include you, but it won't always be possible. You have to trust me."

"Trust goes both ways."

Curran leaned closer. "If she were one of mine, I would've had my claws on her throat. I permit her to insult you, because she is your friend and you don't play by the same rules. I want some credit for that."

This was going to be an uphill battle. I could see it in his eyes. "You permitted her to insult me because she is a knight of the Order and even you can't murder them with impunity."

"That, too."

"As long as you're aware that I will make my own decisions

and I will fight you if you attempt to interfere. I will make an effort to always include you, Your Majesty, but it won't be always possible."

Gold sparked in his eyes and vanished.

"I deserved that," he said. "We're even now. Peace?"

He watched me carefully. It was important to him. What I said would matter.

Curran was used to unquestioned obedience and I rejected all authority. He'd never shared his power before and I never had any. Both of us had to give and neither wanted to.

"Peace," I said. "This is going to be really difficult for us."

"Yes. But we'll work it out, with enough time."

If it got to be too much, there was always the gym.

We sat in silence for a long minute.

"What are you thinking?" I asked finally.

"Erra's down to three undead: wind, animal, and the third one."

"Gale, Beast, and Darkness. And nobody knows what Darkness does."

Curran nodded. "Assuming that whatever trap the Order sets for her fails—"

"Which it will," I added.

"—she'll chase the crowd toward the Casino."

"We have to keep her away from the crowd." I pulled Slayer from the back sheath and put it on my lap. "There is no telling how many she will kill, if they panic."

"Not that many," Curran said. "Most of the deaths will be from people trampling each other."

Thanks, Your Fuzziness, that makes me feel loads better. "Ted doesn't care about the loss of life. He deals in large numbers: the welfare of many outweighs the lives of the few. I can't do that."

"I know." Curran leaned back. "We'll take a squad from each clan, female fighters only."

I raised my eyebrows. "How many per squad?"

"Between five and ten. We position them along the roofs. You'll wait on the street by the Casino. She'll chase you. If you back away far enough, my . . . *our* people will swarm her undead helpers. You and I will key on her."

As plans went, it was painfully simple, but anything else depended too much on Erra's actions and she was unpredictable.

"It makes sense." I played with my sword, running my hands along the blade. "You shouldn't go to this fight. You're male and a shapeshifter; that makes you twice as vulnerable to Erra."

"I have to go. It's in the job description."

"It's not a fight that you can win, Curran."

"I don't get to cherry-pick the battles I know I'll win."

A narrow smile curved his lips. He looked wicked and almost boyish at the same time. Something jabbed me right under the heart, where I stored my fears, and they surged through me all at once.

He was mine. He cared for me, he made me lose all sense, he didn't give a damn about my father. He was what I wanted, because he made me happy. I wanted him like I'd never wanted anyone in my life.

I knew how this dance went—I'd gone through its paces before. As soon as I started to care about someone, death would snatch him from me.

Curran was going to die.

There was nothing I could do to prevent it. He would die, because that was what always happened.

My throat constricted. "Let me take care of it."

"No. You aren't strong enough on your own. You've fought her twice to a draw."

"I almost had her."

Curran nodded. "I heard. And you could've taken her, too."

My voice came out flat. "Rub it in, why don't you."

He grinned. "No time for that now. Maybe later."

I closed my eyes. There wouldn't be any later.

"Are you imagining me rubbing it in?" he asked.

"I'm counting to ten in my head."

"Is it helping?"

"No."

"It doesn't help me with you either. I used to lift weights to alleviate frustration, but someone blowtorched my weight bench. How did you do it, by the way?"

"I could tell you but then I'd have to kill you."

I felt like I was trying to hold back a giant rock as it rolled down the mountain. No matter what I did, it just kept rolling, grinding at me with its weight.

He was going to die.

"There is another reason," Curran said. "You're my mate. I installed you in my rooms. You aren't yet alpha. To get you confirmed as alpha, I'd have to bring you in front of the Council and they will bitch, and moan, and drag it out, and our time is short. Besides, the true alpha authority comes once you've proven yourself. That takes weeks, months sometimes, and several kills. Because you're my mate, the shapeshifters will treat you with courtesy, but in the field, when they're between life and death, they won't listen to you. Seven squads means seven female alphas. You've seen how well they get along on their own."

It was hard to argue with him, because he stubbornly insisted on making sense. "Put one of the alphas in charge, then."

Curran's blond eyebrows crept together. "And raise one clan above all others, while undermining your future authority? They'd never let you forget it."

I held his gaze. "I know Erra. I know what she is capable of. You don't. Do you at least respect me enough to let me take the lead on this?"

He didn't pause. "Yes. But I'm still coming with you. I need to be there."

The frustration burst from me. "Argh." I pushed to my feet. "I fucking hate her for putting me through this. When I get my hands on her, I'll rip her legs out and feed them to her, boots first."

THE SHAPESHIFTERS DIDN'T BELIEVE IN JAILS. TYPI-cal punishments were death or labor. In the rare cases when they did sentence someone to isolation, they exiled them to a remote area.

The Keep did have several holding cells, large, empty rooms equipped with loup cages. One of them held my "bodyguard." Curran insisted on walking with me to the door. Somehow, despite the early hour, the hallways of the Keep were full of shapeshifters, who made valiant efforts not to stare at me.

"For nocturnal people, you're terribly active in daylight," I murmured.

"The curiosity is killing them. They'd mob you if they could get away with it."

"That would go very badly for everyone involved. I don't like crowds."

Curran pondered that for a moment. "I have some final arrangements to make and then I'm free. Would you have a nice dinner with me?"

"I'll cook," I told him.

"You sure? I can have it made."

"I'd prefer to cook." It might be our last dinner.

"I'll help you, then."

He stopped by a door. "She is in there. Can you find your way back by yourself?"

"I have an uncanny sense of direction."

He presented me with his Beast Lord face. "Right. I'll have a compass, chalk, a ball of string, and rations for five days brought to you."

Ha-ha. "If I get in trouble, I'll ask that nice blond girl you designated as my babysitter."

Curran glanced at the young blond shapeshifter who'd discreetly followed us from his quarters. "You've been made. You can come wait by the door."

She walked over and stood by the door.

Curran took my hand and squeezed my fingers.

The shapeshifters froze.

"Later," he said.

"Later." I may have had a hell of a lot of baggage, but he was no prize either. Living with him meant living in a glass box.

Curran released my fingers, glanced at the hallway, and raised his voice. "Carry on."

Suddenly everybody had someplace to be and they really needed to get there.

I opened the door and walked into the cell.

A large rectangular room stretched before me, completely empty except for a loup cage, eight feet tall, with the bars the size of my wrist. The magic was down, or the bars would fluoresce with enchanted silver. Eight support beams extended from the cage's ceiling and floor, anchoring it to the Keep itself.

The woman sat within the cage, in the same cross-legged pose as the last time I'd seen her. Her spear leaned against the wall, well out of her reach.

I approached the cage and sat cross-legged on the floor. I could've covered the floor of the room with all the questions I wanted to ask her. The sixty-four-thousand-dollar question was, would she answer?

The woman opened her eyes. Completely black and impenetrable, like two chunks of coal.

We looked each other over. She had the face of a woman who spent a lot of time outside and laughed often—her pale brown skin was weather-beaten, crow's feet fanned from her eyes, and her mouth seemed perpetually hiding a sardonic laugh, as if she was convinced she was the only able mind in a world of fools.

"He's very strong." An odd accent tinted her voice. "Stubborn and proud, but very strong. He's a good choice."

She meant Curran. "What's your name?"

"Naeemah."

"Do you really shift into a crocodile?"

She inclined her head—a nod in slow motion.

"Crocodiles are cold-blooded."

"That is a truth."

"Most shapeshifters are mammals."

"That is a truth also."

"So how does it work?"

Naeemah gave me a wide smile without showing any teeth. "I'm not most shapeshifters."

Touché.

"Why do you protect me?"

"I've told you already: it's my job. Pay attention."

"Who hired you?"

Red sparked in Naeemah's eyes and melted into her anthracite irises. "Let me out of the cage and I will tell you."

I raised my eyebrows. "How do I know you won't stab someone in the back?"

Naeemah gave me a patronizing look. "Bring the spear."

I rose and got the spear. It was about five feet long, with a plain metal head, about nine inches long and close to three inches wide at the base. A tightly wrapped leather cord reinforced the socket, binding it to the shaft so well, the spear head seemed to sprout from the wood.

I raised the spear on the palms of my hands, bringing it to eye level. Bent. Almost as if it had been a branch at some point instead of a wooden pole cut perfectly straight from a larger piece of wood. Heavier than expected and very hard. The texture was odd, too, smooth, polished, and pale, like driftwood. Small black marks peppered the wood, etched into it with heated wire. Birds, lions, wavy lines, geometric figures . . . Hieroglyphs, written sideways on the shaft. Each set of characters was segregated by a horizontal line. Small vertical strokes ran in a ring just before the line, in some places only a few, in others so many they circled the shaft.

The burned marks ended a couple of feet from the spearhead. Interesting.

"Look there." Naeemah pointed to the last set of hieroglyphs. Her face took on a regal air. She seemed ancient and unapproachable, like a mysterious statue from a longforgotten age. "That is my name. Next to it is the name of my father. Following it is the name of his mother and then her older brother, and then their father, and their father's father before him."

"And these?" I drew my fingers across the short marks.

"Those are the assassins we have taken." Naeemah sneered. "We don't kill for profit. Any jackal can do that. We are the hunters of killers. That is what we do."

I checked the last name. At least three dozen marks, maybe more.

"How old are you?"

"My sons had children before you were born. No more answers. Decide."

I went to the door and stuck my head out. The blond shapeshifter waited for me in the precise spot Curran told her to stand.

"Do you have a key to the loup cage?"

"Yes, mate." She pulled the key out and handed it to me.

"Thank you. And don't call me 'mate,' please."

"Yes, Alpha."

Right.

Naeemah chuckled from her cage. I sighed and went inside.

I unlocked the door and handed her the spear. "It's not as funny when you're on the receiving end of it."

Naeemah took two steps out of the cage and sat back down. I joined her.

"I let you out, and I'm due some answers. Who hired you?"

"Hugh d'Ambray."

Knock me over with a feather.

It made sense in a twisted way. Hugh had seen me shatter the sword. He was either actively gathering information about me or planning to gather it, and he put a bodyguard in place to make sure nothing happened to me meanwhile. With my history, he ran the risk of standing on Roland's carpet explaining that he had found his long-lost daughter, but she got herself killed before he could gather enough evidence to prove her identity. That would fly.

She'd pronounced Hugh's name with distaste. I wondered why. "What's your relationship to Hugh?"

"Some years ago, when my children were young, he killed a man one of my sons protected and captured my son. We bargained for my son's life and I traded one favor of Hugh's choosing."

No love lost. Good for me, bad for Hugh. "Where is Hugh now?"

Naeemah's smile turned predatory. "I don't know. I'm not his keeper."

I tried a different plan of attack. "What are the precise terms of your arrangement with Hugh?"

Naeemah chuckled again. "He ordered me to watch you and keep you safe from those who are a danger to you. I wasn't to interfere or reveal myself unless your life was in grave peril."

Curiouser and curiouser. "For how long?"

"He didn't specify."

I had a hunch I'd just found a loophole big enough to drive a cart through. "Is Hugh excluded from those who are a danger to me?"

Naeemah's smile grew wider. "He didn't specify."

"Hugh isn't as clever as he thinks he is."

"That is a truth."

"What if I told you that Hugh is the second biggest threat to me, second only to Erra?"

"I would say I already know this."

"How?"

Naeemah leaned forward. The gaze of her black eyes fastened on me. "You shouldn't have conversations by the window, when the wall of your house is easy to climb."

She'd heard me and Andrea talking about Hugh. Probably every word.

"What will you do if Hugh attacks me?"

"I will protect you. My debt must be repaid."

Score. "And how long will you continue to guard me?"

"That would depend on you."

She had me there.

Naeemah drew herself straight. "I've protected people of power and people of wealth. Many, many people. I've judged you worthy. Don't disappoint me."

That was all I needed. Apparently, the Universe had decided that my life would be that much richer with a judgmental crocodile bodyguard in it. "I'll keep it in mind. I'm going to fight Erra tonight. If you attempt to 'rescue' me again, I will kill you."

"I'll keep it in mind."

I rose and Naeemah stood up with me. I had to do something with her and I had a feeling that getting her to work with the rest of the guards wouldn't go over so well. She'd need her own space. "Come with me, please. We need to get you a room."

She followed me out. The blond shapeshifter gaped at her, as if Naeemah were a cobra with her hood spread. Naeemah ignored her.

I headed back to Curran's quarters, my two babysitters in tow.

Jim would just love this. If I wasn't careful, I'd give him an aneurysm before my first month here was up.

CHAPTER 26

———◆———

SUNSET BLED ON THE SKY, SMOLDERING IN ITS final death throes. The encroaching twilight tinted the buildings black, turning the blanket of snow indigo.

I sat on top of the building, watching bonfires illuminate the rim of the Mole Hole through binoculars. Curran sat next to me. He wore his warrior form: a seven-and-a-half-feet-tall gray creature stuck on the crossroads between man and beast.

After Curran's guard suffered a collective apoplexy over Naeemah, I'd managed to install her into her own set of rooms and went to cook our dinner. The Beast Lord joined me a few minutes later. We made venison steak, french fries smothered in cheese, and a quick pumpkin pie. We ate, then we made love and slept, curled up together in his ridiculous bed, and then Curran changed into his warrior form and I spent two hours drawing the poem of Erra on Curran's skin with a little tube of henna. When I got tired, I made him call Dali and she took over. Her handwriting was better anyway. I had no idea if it would offer him any protection, but at this point I would try anything.

Behind us, female shapeshifters waited, positioned in

individual squads along the street leading to the Casino. The wolves were right behind us, the boudas lay in wait across the street, then the rats and Clan Heavy, jackals, cats, and finally almost three blocks out, Clan Nimble. The squad from Clan Nimble consisted of an older Japanese woman, who was apparently the alpha, and four slender women who looked like they were fifteen tops. Curran told me they were foxes. They held themselves with stern elegance and I bit my tongue and hoped they knew what they were doing.

Somewhere in the darkness Naeemah hid. She picked her own spot and I didn't argue. Her scent made the shapeshifters uneasy.

I looked back to the Mole Hole. A bonfire burned in the center of the crater, flanked by clusters of metal drums. To the left a row of Biohazard vans waited. People crowded the lip of the crater, medtechs, PAD, bowmen. Most were male. Despite my reports, Ted chose to put men at the crater, probably because he couldn't raise enough female fighters in time. I'd cursed when I first saw them. Curran shrugged and said, "Bullet meat."

Beyond the bonfires, a crowd had gathered in the remnants of office buildings. They sat on the makeshift wooden scaffolds, in the darkness of broken windows, on the roofs, on the mountains of rubble. Damn near half of Atlanta must've seen the flag and turned out to watch the Order slug it out with the Plaguebringer. Every single one of them could die tonight and there wasn't a damn thing I could do about it.

My binoculars found Ted standing next to a large, fit woman with short red hair. Hard pale eyes. Black pants, black leather jacket, a sheath at her waist with a blade in it. A boar's head on the pommel of her sword—Sounder's Armory. They made falchions, single-edged swords of medium length shaped like the bastard children of a longsword and a scimitar. Great-quality swords, but expensive as hell. Judging by the sword and the getup, I was looking at Tamara Wilson.

Ted had imported Order knights from out of the city. He'd planned this—it would've taken him at least two days to pull personnel from North Carolina. Whether I walked off or not, this wouldn't have been my petition anyway.

The magic rolled over us in an invisible wave. Showtime.

Tamara started down a staircase cut into the side of the
Mole Hole. She crossed the floor of the crater to the center,
where a huge bonfire burned on the glass. Positioning herself
before the bonfire, she held up a long pole with the Order's
standard—a lance and a sword crossed over a shield. The
light of the bonfire clutched at her black armor. She pulled a
watch cap onto her head, hiding her hair.

A lean creature climbed over the roof. Long, hunched over,
covered with clumps of gray fur, it moved with fluid quickness. Its feet and hands were disproportionately large, and
short black claws tipped its fingers. A conical muzzle flowed
into an almost humanoid face, framed by round pink ears.

A wererat. Stealthy, fast, deadly. They didn't make good
warriors but they made excellent scouts. And assassins.

She scuttled over to us and sat on her haunches, her arms
folded to her chest. Her muzzle opened, displaying oversized
incisors.

"The barrels are filled with napalm." Her misshapen
mouth slurred the words, but they came out clear enough.
"They have archers hidden along the edge, some with incendiary arrows."

Made sense: Erra walks into the Mole Hole, heads for the
standard, because it's a challenge. The archers hit the barrels
with incendiary arrows. Erra drowns in a sea of fiery napalm.
Tamara magically escapes. Good plan. Except for the part
that it won't work.

"Everybody is going to die," I said.

The wererat's dark eyes fixed on me for a second and flickered to Curran. "Also, the People have got themselves a bloodsucker party. They're camped about two miles behind us."

"Good," Curran said.

Andrea had come through. I never doubted she would.

A high-pitched scream erupted from the darkness of the
street to the left. It tore through the encroaching night, a long,
piercing shriek suffused with sheer terror. The shapeshifters
tensed.

A man emerged from the gloom. Of average height,
wrapped in a long cloak that flared with his every step, he
strode through the snow, and as he walked, snowflakes rose in

the air, swirling in glittering clouds. Gale. Erra's undead with the power of air.

Another man leaped into view and crouched on the rim of the Mole Hole. Nude, covered in dense dark hair, he was slabbed with thick muscle like a weightlifter on a life-long steroid binge. Huge and hairy. Right. *Here comes the Beast.*

Erra had brought at least two. No matter how strong her powers were, controlling two at once had to be hard. It was likely they would mirror each other's movements, acting in groups.

A third figure followed, a naked man so thin, his skin clung to his bones, outlining his ribs and pitiful chest. He turned his head, scanning the crater, and I saw his eyes, yellow, like egg yolks. Darkness.

The three undead froze, still as statues. Milking the entrance for every drop of the drama.

A long moment passed.

Another.

"Get on with it," I growled.

Another. This was getting ridiculous.

The mist parted. Erra strode into view, head and shoulders above her undead. The light of the fires washed over her. A white fur cape streamed from her shoulders, the waterfall of her hair a dark stain on the pale collar.

A hush fell over the Mole Hole.

Erra's gaze swept the crowd, taking in the archers, the Biohazard, the vans, the equipment, the audience up in the ruins nearby . . . She raised her arms to the sides. The cape slipped off her.

Glossy red fabric hugged her body. It clung to her like a second skin of pure scarlet. My aunt apparently had developed a fetish for spandex. Who knew?

Gale thrust his hand through his cloak. His fist gripped a large axe. The orange light of the flames shimmered along the ten-inch blade attached to a four-foot handle. The axe probably pushed six pounds in weight. A normal swordsman would be slower than molasses, but with her strength, it wouldn't matter. She could swing it all day and then arm-wrestle a bear.

Gale turned on his heel, walked five steps to Erra, and

knelt before her, offering the axe on the raised palms of his hands.

"We should clap or something," Curran said. "She's trying so hard."

"Maybe we could scrounge up some panties to throw." I adjusted the binoculars to focus on her face.

Erra raised her head. Power brimmed in her eyes. She looked regal, like some arrogant goddess poised above the chasm. I had to give it to her—my aunt knew how to put on a show. Would've been more dramatic if she had seven undead instead of three, but hey, at least she had some flunkies to bring.

Erra reached for the axe. Her fingers closed on the handle. She thrust it at the sky. With a hoarse scream, power pulsed from her like a shockwave, shaking the foundation of the ruins. It slammed into me, setting my blood on fire. Curran snarled. By the Mole Hole, people cringed.

Needles burst from Erra's red suit. Veins of dark crimson spiraled up her legs. The fabric flowed, thickened, snapping into recognizable shapes: fitted curaise, spiked pauldrons, gauntlets . . .

It wasn't spandex. Shit.

I leaned to Curran. "She's wearing blood armor. It's impenetrable to normal weapons, claws, and teeth."

His eyes darkened. "If I hit her hard enough, she'll still feel it."

I nodded. "My sword will eventually soften the armor, but it will take time. She doesn't know you're here. If you wait, you could get in a good shot."

My personal monster leaned closer. "Still trying to keep me from the fight?"

I slid my fingers along his furry cheek. "Trying to win. She made no helmet—she's too vain."

Ancient or not, she was still a human and he was a werelion. If he timed it right, he could crack her skull like an eggshell with a single blow.

"One shot," he said.

"I'll keep her busy. Just don't bite her. Broken teeth aren't sexy."

He grinned, presenting me with a mouth full of finger-sized fangs. I rolled my eyes.

Erra took a step forward. For a moment she towered above the drop, light dancing over her scarlet armor, and then she plunged into the Mole Hole. Gale chased her, a soundless shadow gliding across the glassy floor. Darkness and Beast remained behind.

Twenty yards to the center and the bonfire.

Fifteen.

Ten.

Tamara unsheathed her sword. Fiery sparks flared at the edge of the crater. PAD archers lighting their arrows.

Eight.

The archers fired.

The barrels exploded, punching my eardrums with an air fist. An inferno drowned the Mole Hole, emanating heat. Within its depths I glimpsed Tamara, unscathed, the fire sliding along her body but never touching her.

The spectators cheered at the human barbeque.

The roar of the flames gained a new note, a deep whistling tune. It grew louder and louder. The flames turned, twisting faster and faster, rising in a spiral, like a tornado of fire. The cone of flame parted, revealing Gale floating in the heart of the tornado, his hair streaming from his head, his arms crossed on his chest. His body leaned back, completely relaxed. His eyes were closed.

So much for napalm.

Below him Erra stood. A red helmet hid her face and hair. The blood armor encased every inch of her. Oh, good. Because it wasn't hard enough before. She had to go and put a helmet on.

The fiery tornado shifted out of her way. The helmet crumbled, revealing her face. Her mane of hair spilled over her back. Score. No helmet was good for us.

With a grimace, Erra swung her axe and charged.

Tamara struck, her sword preternaturally fast. Erra batted it aside like a toothpick and swung in a crushing reverse blow. The axe bit deep into Tamara's shoulder, cutting through the collarbone all the way into her ribs.

Tamara screamed, a desperate sound of pain and fear.

Curran clamped his oversized hand on my shoulder. "You can't help her. We wait."

Erra caught Tamara by her throat and lifted her off her feet. Her roar smothered Tamara's screaming. "Is this all you offer me? Is this it?"

She shook Tamara once, as if flinging water from her hand. The noise of the fire drowned out the telltale crunch of bones, but her head flopped to the side, loose on a broken neck.

"Where are you, child?"

I rocked forward.

"Not yet." Curran pushed me down.

"She'll kill them."

"You go in there now, we'll all die. We stick to the plan."

In the air, Gale opened his eyes.

"There is no escape. I'll find you," Erra promised.

The cone of fire unfurled like a flower and splashed against the rim of the Mole Hole, torching the archers. Tortured screams ripped the night apart, followed by the sickening stench of charred human flesh. Gale turned, and the inferno followed, roaring like a hungry animal. He cooked the survivors alive as they fled.

All around the Mole Hole, people in PAD and Biohazard suits ran aimlessly, their weapons abandoned. The idiot spectators still packed the building. Erra's magic didn't reach them.

"Here I come!" Erra thundered.

Charred, smoking corpses littered the opposite side of the crater. A thin female voice cried somewhere close, sobbing hysterically, a high-pitched note against the guttural screaming. At the far right, Darkness and Beast perched on the edge of the Mole Hole, untouched by flames. They must've circled around while we watched the human barbeque. "Wait," Curran said.

I clenched my teeth.

A gust of air erupted from the bottom of the Mole Hole, lifting Erra to the edge. A moment later her three undead joined her.

"Go." Curran released me.

I ran across the roof, grabbed the rope attached to the fire escape, and slid into the street.

•   •   •

SNOW CRUNCHED UNDER MY FEET. BEHIND ME THE Casino floated in a cloud of ethereal light streaming from the powerful feylanterns.

I had a simple mission. Get Erra's attention. Draw her down the street, away from the crowd, so the shapeshifters could get behind her.

Yeah. Piece of cake.

I braced myself. "Strawberry Shortcake called, she wants her outfit back."

Erra turned to me.

I waved my fingers at her. "Hey, Twinkle Toes."

A gust of air shot from Gale. I ducked, but not low enough. Wind slammed into me. The ground vanished and I flew a few feet and slammed against a parked truck with a thud. My back crunched.

"We don't run from a fight and we don't hide behind lesser men." Erra started toward me. "You're young and weak, but have no fear. I'll help you. I won't let you flee and shame the family twice."

I rolled to my feet and swung my sword, warming up my wrist. "Shaming the family is your job. Nothing I've done could ever compare."

"You flatter me so."

She started toward me, bringing her goons in a triangular formation: Beast on the left, Gale on the right, and Darkness in the center. Keep coming, Auntie dear. Keep coming.

"I'm just giving you your due. Every war your brother started, you managed to screw up. You have a record of failure thousands of years long." I spread my arms. "How could I compete?"

"Before you die, I'll set you on fire," she promised. "I will burn you slowly for hours."

"Promises, promises." I began backing up again. She followed. *Come with me, away from people. Come with me, Erra. Let's dance.*

Darkness raised his arms. Magic pulsed from him like a blast wave after an explosion. The world went white in a haze of panic. I couldn't breathe. My thoughts fractured and scurried off, leaving me lost and unbalanced. A luminescent haze floated before me, like a thundercloud backlit by splashes of lightning, and beyond it I sensed a gaping void. Nothing but calm empty darkness.

So that was what Darkness meant. Fear. All-consuming, overwhelming fear, so powerful that it tore you from your life and threw you into the void, alone and blind.

Rage reared inside me. I grabbed it like a crutch and pulled myself up, back to reality. My vision returned. I shook myself like a wet dog.

"Is that all? I thought it would be something powerful."

She raised her arm, showing off the segmented gauntlet. "Where is your blood armor, whelp? Why don't you cut your wrist and grow a blade? What's the matter? You can't do it, can you? You don't know the secret of molding the blood. I do. All you do is talk and run."

My family was full of overpowered assholes. I kept walking. We were four blocks from the Mole Hole now. I had no idea what her range was. "No matter what you do or how hard you try, you will never surpass your brother. Always the bridesmaid, never the bride."

Magic splayed from Darkness in dark translucent streams, bending back, flooding the Mole Hole behind him and stretching farther and farther, to the decrepit buildings, to the hundreds of people packed like sardines into the concrete shells of the ruins. The enormity of his power shook me.

"Watch," Erra called out.

The Darkness brought his arms together. No, God damn it, no . . .

A wild howl pierced the night. Another voice joined, another, more . . .

A torrent of people burst from the ruins behind Erra.

Fucking shit.

People streamed toward me, eyes mad, mouths gaping open, running like crazed cattle. I ducked behind a car. The human stampede thundered past me. Bodies thudded into the metal, making it shudder. Screams filled the air and above it all Erra's laughter floated, like the toll of a funeral bell.

A blast of magic ripped from Darkness. Reality fractured and I floated among the pieces, unsure who I was or where I came from. Thoughts and words swirled around me, round and round, in a glowing cascade. Darkness beckoned just beyond the chaos. I reached into the cloud and pulled a word out.

"Dair." Release.

Magic bit at me with needle jaws. I shuddered, shaking, the shock of the pain tearing the haze.

A body landed next to me, shaggy with fur. Mad eyes glared from a face that was neither beast nor human. A female shapeshifter. Her body snapped, twisted, jerked, and a coyote stood before me. She leapt up and dashed down the street, galloping after the herd of terrified people.

He didn't send them after the undead? Not yet. We'd agreed. I jerked upright and saw Erra in the middle of the street, the undead behind her, no shapeshifters in sight. The lone shapeshifter must've been hit with a stray blast of power.

Every inch of me hurt from magic spent too quickly.

You're the distraction. Get up and do the distracting.

I got up and walked into the open, Slayer bare.

She started toward me, and I backed away. Half a block to go. Close enough to the Casino, far enough from the Mole Hole, the perfect distance for the shapeshifters to strike.

"Again you run."

"Not my fault you walk too slowly to catch me." Up close her armor resembled scale mail: bloodred scales, some large, some small, overlapping over her frame. Now why couldn't I do that? What was I missing?

I crossed over the manhole cover. The last of the stragglers dashed by. The street was empty except for me and her, and her three corpses.

She charged. The world ground to a screeching halt. I heard myself breathe, my chest rising slowly, as if underwater.

In the three seconds it took her to cover the distance between us, I heard Voron's voice from my memories. It said, "If it bleeds, you can kill it."

She bled—her armor testified to it—and I was better.

Erra smashed into me. I leaned back, letting her axe swing past me, ducked, thrust, and sliced under her arm. Slayer glanced off. She whipped around, but I danced away. She lunged, I ducked and jumped clear.

"You can't win," Erra snarled.

Behind her, dark shadows lined the roof. Of the fifty Curran had brought, only half were left. Here's hoping it would be enough.

"I'm not trying to win," I told her.

"What are you trying to do?"

Keep you occupied.

The shapeshifters dropped off the roof like clawed ghosts.

A seven-foot-tall scaled monster hit Beast. They clashed in a mess of fur and claws. The primeval deep roar of an enraged crocodile rolled through the street.

I launched a whirlwind of strikes. My sword became a whip, cutting, slashing, dicing, left, right, left. Focus on me. Focus on me, damn you. As long as I kept her busy, she would have trouble coordinating the movements of all three undead at once and keeping me at bay.

Over Erra's shoulder, Gale rose into the air, clutching Darkness in his arms.

The shapeshifters had missed them. Damn it.

Erra's axe ground against Slayer. She drove me back.

Gale soared above the street twenty feet in the air, wrapped in a cone of wind. Foul magic pulsed from Darkness.

A chorus of enraged snarls and howls answered, punctuated by an eerie slice of hyena laughter.

Erra kept pushing me back. I veered from the wall and danced back, toward Gale. I ducked and dodged, trying to turn her, but she barreled at me like a freight train.

To the left of me an enormous werewolf crouched on the pavement. She hooked the manhole cover with her clawed fingers, did a 360, and hurled it at Gale. The metal disk cut like a knife through the whirlwind surrounding Gale and smashed into Darkness.

A deep female voice yelled, *"Noboru! Sekasu kodomot-achi! Noboru! Noboru!"*

Red-furred shapeshifters surged up the walls of the buildings—the foxes of Clan Nimble.

Erra elbowed me. I flew back and rolled into a crouch, just in time to swipe her legs from under her. She fell. I struck her twice on the way down and withdrew.

Dark slashes scored her armor, like the strikes of a whip—places where Slayer connected. None looked deep enough to do any damage. Voron had promised me that the saber would slice through blood armor, given enough time, but so far Slayer wasn't cutting it. If she'd been wearing regular armor, she would have been bleeding like a stuck pig. If wishes were money, the world would have no beggars.

Still something looked different about her. Something . . .

The spikes on her armor were gone.

I backed away. Where the hell did the spikes go?

Erra hefted her axe, her face demonic in its fury. Her chest heaved. My arms ached like they were about to fall off. A slow pain gnawed on my back, and when I turned the wrong way, something stabbed my left side with a hot spike. Probably a broken rib. That was okay. I was still on my feet.

The werefoxes launched themselves at Gale from the roof. They clung to him, biting and clawing. The fox on the left ripped out an arm.

Erra snarled. Gale dropped Darkness, shuddered, and plummeted to the ground, banging into the buildings as he fell, the foxes still clinging to him. Gale bounced once off the pavement and the rest of shapeshifters swarmed him.

Erra looked no worse for wear.

When out of options, mouth off. I nodded at Darkness, lying only twenty feet away. "Whoopsie. Did that hurt? Now there is only one."

"One will be enough." Erra grinned.

A small chunk of her armor broke from her shoulder and fell to the asphalt, turning liquid. I watched it sink into the snow. A tiny streak of vapor escaped and then it vanished into the white.

A crumb of her armor. Her blood. A drop of her blood.

Behind us, the snow churned by our feet marked our trail—we'd drawn a circle in the street and all the while we beat on each other, she'd been dripping blood from her armor.

A dark shadow loomed on the roof behind Erra. Curran.

"No!" I lunged at her, but it was too late.

He dived off the roof. Erra dodged at the last moment, but

Curran's paw connected to her skull. The blow took her off her feet. She flew, nearly plowing into me.

"Run!" I lunged at her prone body and stabbed with all my strength, again and again. "Run, Curran!"

Erra roared. Slayer's blade kept glancing off.

A wall of red flames surged up from the snow, sealing the four of us from the shapeshifters. She'd locked us in a blood ward.

Erra rolled, knocking my legs from under me. I stumbled back and she jumped to her feet. Blood dripped from her cheekbone and poured from her mouth. The left side of her head was caved in, dented by Curran's blow.

I lunged at her and ran right into the spike topping her axe. It took me in the stomach, just below my ribs. Pain exploded. I jerked free and she kicked me, driving me back into the snow. The axe jabbed through my left side. I screamed. She'd pinned me to the ground.

Erra spat blood and teeth and swung, as if throwing a baseball. Spikes shot from her armor, falling in a ragged line between Curran and me. The blood ward snapped up just as he charged and he crashed into it at full speed.

She'd halved the circle: her and me on one side, Darkness and Curran on the other.

"You want to rut with a half-breed," she snarled. "Watch. I'll show you exactly what he is."

Curran spun toward the undead.

A torrent of magic burst from Darkness, tearing at Curran. The blood ward cut us off and I felt nothing—Curran got the full dose. He stumbled, shook once, as if flinging water from himself. His body shifted, growing leaner, slicker. Fur sprouted along his back.

This was it, the Darkness's power. It would make Curran go wild.

I writhed under the axe, trying to break free. The Beast Lord took a step forward.

Erra's hand clawed the air. Darkness vomited another torrent of crippling fear. Curran shuddered. His hands thickened, growing longer claws.

Another blast of magic. He kept walking.

Another blast.

"Look!" Erra leaned into the axe, grinding it into me.

Curran crouched in the middle of the street. Dense fur sheathed him, flaring into an enormous mane on his back and disproportionately huge head. No trace of a human or lion remained—his body was seamless and whole, a nightmarish mutated blend that was neither. Long limbs supported a broad, muscled body, striped with dark gray. His eyes glowed yellow, so bright and pale, almost white. I looked into their depths and saw no rational thought. No intelligence or comprehension.

He raised his head, unhinging his enormous jaws, and roared, shaking the street, all teeth and fur.

Curran had gone mad.

I wouldn't lose him. I would not lose him on this dark, cold street. It wouldn't happen.

The beast that used to be Curran leapt at the undead. Huge hands grasped Darkness, pulling him up. Muscles bulged and Curran tore him to pieces, dismembering his body as if it were a rag doll. Blood gushed from the savaged body, drenching the snow.

Erra's hands shook on her axe, but her weight kept me down.

Curran smashed into the blood ward. Magic boomed. He hit again, the impact of his body shaking the red wall and the street beneath. His eyes blazed white. The fur on his arms smoked from the contact with Erra's blood ward.

Again.

Again.

Again.

Cracks formed in the blood ward.

Erra stared, her face slapped with shock.

Curran rammed the ward.

The red wall cracked and fell apart. He burst through it, roaring, his fur on fire, and crashed into the snow. Magic tore at me, like a typhoon wild in it fury. I screamed and Erra echoed me, doubling over in pain over me, her hair falling like a dark curtain.

I grabbed her hair and jerked her down with all my strength straight onto my sword.

Slayer slid into her eye. I felt it pierce the bone and drove it in all the way.

Erra vomited blood. It drenched me like fire, my magic mixing with my aunt's lifeblood leaking from her body. I felt the magic in it, the way I'd felt it in the rakshasas' golden cage.

I smeared our mixed blood onto her face, pushed, and saw a forest of needles burst through her skin.

She screamed and laid on the axe, and I screamed as the spike ripped my innards. The needles crumbled and melted into her skin.

"You will not take me down," Erra ground out. "You will not . . ."

Her legs failed and she crashed to her knees.

"It's over," I whispered to her with bloody lips.

Desperation claimed her broken face. She clawed at the spear, trying to pull herself upright. Our blood painted the snow a bright rich scarlet.

"Die," I told her.

She fell on all fours next to me. Her one good eye stared into mine. "Live . . . long, child," she whispered. "Live long enough to see everyone you love die. Suffer . . . like me."

Her words clamped on to me like a curse. She collapsed in the snow. Her chest rose for the last time. A single breath escaped with a soft whisper and the life faded from her eye.

I looked at her and saw myself, dead in the snow.

The smoking ruin that was Curran raised his bloody head.

"Curran," I whispered. "Look at me."

The burns blotching his monstrous face melted. Fur sprouted, running along his frame, hiding the wounds. His eyes were still pure white.

He strode to me, swiped at the axe, and plucked it out of me like a toothpick. Clawed hands picked me up.

"Talk to me." I peered into his eyes and saw nothing. "Talk to me, Curran."

A low growl reverberated in his throat.

No. No, no, no.

Emaciated twisted shapes dashed by the ward—the first vampiric scouts. They'd watched the battle until they figured out the winner. Curran saw the vampires. A horrible sound broke from his mouth, halfway between a roar and a scream.

He lunged at the ward. In the split second before we hit the scarlet flames, I thrust my bloody hand into Erra's defensive spell. Magic shot from me. The red collapsed, and everything went black.

CHAPTER 27

———◆———

EVERYTHING HURT.

"Don't move." Urgency filled Jim's quiet voice.

I lay absolutely still, my eyes closed. The magic was down. The air smelled of blood.

Something fanned my face. I opened my eyes just enough to glimpse a clawed foot passing out of my field of vision.

"You're on the floor," Jim said. "I'm at the door directly in front of you. When I say, run to me."

My eyes snapped open.

Jim crouched in the doorway, Doolittle next to him. Derek stood to the left, his face white. Beyond them I saw Mahon looming like a mountain.

Jim's eyes shone with green.

"She doesn't understand," Doolittle murmured.

Jim leaned an inch forward. "You're in the Keep. Curran brought you here three hours ago. He's pacing back and forth around you. He attacks anyone who tries to enter. He isn't talking. He doesn't recognize me or anyone else." He paused, waiting for it sink in. "Kate, he may have gone loup. You must get out of here, before he kills you. If you run, we'll shut the door as soon as you make it out. We've got enough people to hold it."

Three hours. *He hasn't spoken in three hours.*

I sat up. A dark bloody stain slicked the floor under me. I must've bled. I turned and saw a furry gray back at the far wall and above it a tangled, bloodstained mane. Curran.

"Kate!" Jim hissed.

The beast that used to be Curran whipped around. White eyes glared at me.

I stood up.

He leaped across the room, covering the distance between us in a single bound. His hands clamped my ribs. He jerked me up to a mouth full of teeth.

"Hey, baby," I said into his maw, breathing out to let him inhale my scent.

White eyes peered into mine. A deep growl rolled from him.

"Very scary," I told him softly. "I'm terribly impressed."

He snarled. Teeth clicked a hair from my throat.

"Curran," I whispered. "Remember me."

He inhaled my scent. His ears twitched. He was listening to the shapeshifters at the door.

"Close the door, Jim."

Jim hesitated.

"I'm his mate. *Close the door.*"

A moment later the door clicked shut.

I put my arms around his neck. "You're mine. You can't let her win. She can't have you."

He was listening but not hearing.

"I love you," I told him. "You said you would always come for me. I need you now. Come back to me. Please, come back to me."

I put my head against Curran's mane.

"Come back to me. I know you're in there. You brought me here. You didn't kill me. You must know who I am."

Fur slid under my fingers. He stood rigid.

"If you come back to me, I'll never leave you," I whispered into the furry ear. "I'll make you all the pies you could ever eat."

All of the magic I had, all of the power of my blood, all

of it was useless with the magic down. He was slipping away, farther and farther, with each passing second. "Come back to me. Please. Remember you wanted me to say please. I'm saying it now. Please come back to me."

Nothing.

"Who'll protect me from myself if you're gone? Who'll fight with me? I will be all by myself. You can't abandon me, Curran. You can't orphan the Pack. You just can't."

He clenched me to him. Pain exploded and I cried out.

Curran snarled and gripped me tighter.

He didn't remember me. Curran was lost. She took him from me. She ripped him right out of my life with her dying breath. The world broke to pieces and caved in on me. I couldn't even breathe.

My eyes grew hot. Something inside me broke and I cried. I hugged his thick neck and cried and cried, because he was dying second by second and I could do nothing.

"Come back to me. Don't leave me all alone. Don't die on me, you stupid sonovabitch. You goddamn fucking idiot. I told you to stay out of the damn fight! Why the hell don't you ever listen? I fucking hate you. I hate you, you hear me? Don't you dare die on me, because I need to kill you with my bare hands."

The fur boiled under my hands and my fingers grazed human skin. Curran's gray eyes looked at me from a human face.

"Talk to me, baby," I whispered. "Please talk to me."

His lips moved. He struggled for a long moment and forced it out.

"Not dead yet."

His eyes rolled back in his head. He swayed and we crashed to the floor.

DOOLITTLE WIPED HIS HANDS WITH A TOWEL. "HE'S comatose. His body is human, but whether his mind returns is the question. However, he spoke. We heard him through the door and it was clear and coherent. That gives us hope."

"When will he wake up?"

Doolittle looked at me, his eyes troubled. "I don't know."

"Can you do anything? Can't you fix him?"

He shook his head again and pulled back from me. "I'm out of cures. It's up to his body and time now."

Jim thrust himself into my view. "You need to let him fix you."

I stared at him.

"Let the doctor fix you," Jim said, as if to a small child. "You're hurt. It's not good for you to be hurt."

I wanted them to leave me the hell alone. "Since when did you turn into my nursemaid?"

Jim crouched by me. "By now the whole Keep knows the Beast Lord is in a coma. They're scared and pissed off and they want blood. What they need right now is the Beast Lord's mate standing on her own two feet. You need to be up and running, so I can walk you through the Keep to keep people from panicking."

"I'm not going anywhere while he's like this."

Jim shook his head. "You're going to pick yourself up and take up right where he left off. That's your job now."

"Leave me the hell alone, or I'll hurt you," I growled at him.

"That's real nice," Jim said. "But first we'll need to fix you."

Doolittle put his finger on my jeans a couple of inches above the knee. "Cut from here to the ankle."

Jim flashed a knife, slicing my jeans along my right leg. Doolittle pointed down. "Look here."

My knee had developed a large bump on the left side. The muscle around it had swelled, disfiguring the leg.

"You know what this is," Doolittle said.

"Dislocated kneecap."

"Good girl. You have two broken ribs, severe bruising, a wound in the stomach, and at least four deep cuts that I can see, and all of them are filthy. Your wound did seal itself, but if we don't take care of it now, you won't be here if he wakes up."

He said "if," not "when." If he wakes up.

Doolittle grasped my ankle. "Hold under her knee."

Jim caught the underside of my knee in his hand.

Doolittle's eyes found mine. "You know how this goes."

I clenched the armrests of the chair. "Do it."

He twisted my leg. A red-hot shaft of pain shot through me, tearing a scream.

Doolittle peered into my eyes. "That ought to bring you back to earth. Are you with us now?"

I squeezed my eyes shut against the pain.

"Good," Doolittle said. "Now let's see to those ribs."

DEREK KNOCKED ON THE DOOR. I KNEW IT WAS him, because he always knocked twice.

I closed the book I was reading out loud. "Yes?"

Derek stepped in. The boy wonder looked me over with a worried look on his face. "How are you feeling?"

"Same."

It had been three days since Curran collapsed. He showed no signs of waking up. I had him moved to the couch, because the bed was too high, and I'd made a bed for myself on the floor next to him. I hadn't left his side longer than the few minutes I needed to go to the bathroom. The boy wonder had the devil of a time getting me to eat.

"Julie called me," he said. "She says the school won't let her contact you."

"It was a precaution against Erra. I didn't want her to find out Julie was alive. Is she angry with me?"

"She's hurt," he said. "I'll talk to her."

I could tell there was more. "Give, Derek. What else?"

"The Pack Council is going to convene in four hours. They are going to debate what to do if Curran doesn't come around."

"And?"

"There is some talk of expelling you from Curran's quarters, since you're not officially an alpha."

My laughter rang through the room, sounding cold and brittle.

Derek took a step back. His face softened, his voice gaining an almost pleading quality. "Kate? Bring the creepy down a notch. Please."

"Don't worry about it," I told him. The magic had hit for a few hours yesterday and Doolittle spent most of the wave putting me back together, since he could do nothing for Curran. I wouldn't be able to fight Erra again right this second, but I had enough left in me for one good show.

"Any calls from Andrea?"

"No."

The shapeshifters had reported that Andrea had survived the fire at the Mole Hole, but she'd made no attempts to contact me. My best friend had abandoned me and I missed her. But then I probably wasn't good company right this second. Maybe it was for the best.

"Still no word on Naeemah?" I asked.

He shook his head. "But there are two people from Clan Bouda here. They say you have some sort of arrangement with Aunt B."

I pushed myself off the chair and handed him the book. "Page 238. Read to him while I talk to them. Please."

Derek licked his lips. "I'm not sure he can hear us."

"When I was out after the rakshasas nearly killed me, I heard voices. I heard Curran, Julie, you, Andrea. I didn't know what was being said, but I recognized the voices. That's how I knew I was safe. I want you to read to him, so he knows he's not dead and he isn't alone."

Derek sat in my chair and opened the book.

I went through the door into the meeting room.

A man and a woman rose at my approach. The man was of average height and built like a young lightweight boxer: ridiculously toned but without any bulk. Those guys were wicked fast. You'd think you could take one out, and then you'd be waking up on the nice cold floor. His face was sharp-featured and his hair blazed bright red. It was a wonder he didn't set the room on fire.

The woman was black, six inches taller, twenty pounds heavier—all of it muscle—and she was trying very hard not to scowl. She failed miserably.

They bowed their heads. Both looked to be in their mid-twenties.

"Aunt B sends her regards," the man said. "I'm Barabas. This is Jezebel."

I arched my eyebrow at him. "Ambitious names."

"Bouda mothers have high hopes for their children," Barabas explained. "Our alpha tells us we're yours. If you find us suitable, we'll serve you from this point on. If not, she will send replacements."

I sat into the chair. "What made you a candidate for shit duty, Barabas?"

He blinked.

"I don't see Aunt B passing an opportunity to kill two birds with one stone. So what did you do to make her want to eject you from everyday bouda dealings?"

"My mother is a bouda," he said. "My father is from Clan Nimble. I drew Nimble from the genetic lottery."

When two shapeshifters from different clans mated, which happened more frequently with boudas, since there were only thirty or so of them, the children had an equal chance for either parent's brand of Lyc-V. "What do you turn into?"

"Mongoose. There are dominance issues in the clan," he said.

"He won't play by the rules," Jezebel said.

Barabas sighed. "I'm gay. They view me as competition and treat me as they would treat a bouda female, which means a strict pecking order. I don't fit in well and I have no wish to slaughter a load of my cousins so I can be a proper bouda female."

I looked at Jezebel. "And you?"

Jezebel thrust her chin at me. "I challenged my sister for her place in the clan."

"How did it go?"

"I lost."

I sat up straighter. Duels for dominance between the shapeshifters were to the death. Always. "Why are you still breathing?"

"She stabbed me in the heart with her claws. I went into cardiac arrest and was clinically dead for eight minutes. When I came to, my sister couldn't bring herself to kill me the second time. It reflects badly on her and on me. I'm a walking dead, and as long as I'm around, I'm the proof that she was weak."

Great. You really had to admire Aunt B. If either of them left the clan on their own, it could have been taken as a sign of cowardice on their part. As it was, their honor was intact.

"Are you any good at Pack politics?"

"He's very good," Jezebel said. "I'm better with force, but I know the rules. I know what people can and can't do. I'm not stupid and I can be useful to you."

I sighed. "You're both hired. I have a Council meeting in four hours. They're going to try to remove me. Find out what I should expect."

I got up and went back to Curran. I was two thirds of the way through *The Princess Bride* and he would want to know what happened next.

When I walked in, Derek rose from the chair. "About Julie . . ."

"Yes?"

He straightened, his new face looking too tight on his bones. "I lied. She didn't call me."

I fought an urge to slump over. Now he was lying to me. "Is she okay?"

"I'm okay," a thin voice said from the middle of the room.

I turned. Julie sat on the floor with her feet under her. She wore a black sweater and her face seemed very pale against the dark wool, almost transparent. Huge dark eyes looked at me.

She got up. "I ran away."

I crossed the floor and hugged her. Derek backed out of the room.

"I went home," Julie said softly. "I was worried. There is no home left. All of our stuff is gone. What happened?"

"It's a long story." At least I kept her safe.

"Am I in trouble?"

"No, kiddo." I squeezed her to me and kissed her blond hair. "You're alive. Everything else we can fix."

FOUR HOURS LATER I SAT IN CURRAN'S PRIVATE meeting room. Barabas sat across from me. Jezebel perched on the table and Derek leaned against the door. Julie had volunteered to read to Curran.

"You are not universally loved," Barabas said.

Tell me something I don't know.

"There are seven clans," he continued. "Of the seven, you can count on the support of Clan Cat, and unless my Great Aunt B is doing a complete turnabout, the boudas are on your side as well. The wolves are fanatically loyal to Curran. Normally they would be behind you all the way, but you killed Jennifer's little sister."

The twisted body of the little werewolf flashed before me. "It couldn't be helped."

"Nobody is disputing the kill," Barabas said. "It was a justifiable death, and given time, Jennifer will see that. But right now, she is in mourning. She has to blame someone, because she can't blame herself any more than she does already. All of that puts Daniel in a difficult position. He won't oppose you. That would be disloyal to Curran. But he can't support you either, because he has to be loyal to his mate. The proper course of action in cases like this is to abstain, and Wolves always do the proper thing. So he won't hurt you, but he won't help you either."

"That's three," I said.

Barabas nodded. "Next we have Clan Heavy, the large predators who don't fit into the other packs. Wereboars, werebison, werewolverines, even a werebaboon, but most of them are bears and bears hate to be surprised. They like the status quo and Mahon is a typical bear. He will probably oppose you. It's nothing personal. You just don't fit into his picture of the way it ought to be." Barabas leaned forward and framed an imaginary square box with his hands, palms facing each other. "At eighteen, people like me have a choice: we can stay with the clan of our parents or we can go to the clan of our beast. I chose to stay with the boudas. All my friends were there and my family, and I didn't know anybody in Clan Nimble. Mahon sat me down shortly after and wanted to know why."

"He had no right to ask," Jezebel growled.

"We just had a conversation." Barabas glanced at her. "I explained my reasons, but he couldn't wrap his head around it. To him, I was a mongoose and my place was with Clan Nimble, because that's the way it ought to be. You're a human who is the Beast Lord's mate and who now nominally occupies the place of Pack Alpha. That doesn't compute in his brain and he will dig his heels in."

"He also raised Curran," Jezebel said. "He's a strong supporter of the Beast Lord, and the Beast Lord chose you."

Barabas nodded. "She's right. When Mahon looks at Curran and you, he sees little babies, which to him means dynasty and stability. If he thinks there is a chance that Curran will pull through, he may decide not to make waves."

"So he could go either way?"

"Yes," Barabas said. "Clan Nimble is being secretive as usual, so we couldn't find out anything. Clan Rat is problematic."

Derek stirred. "You know the Lonescos."

A predatory light flashed in Barabas's eyes. "Why, because all gay men know each other?"

"You ran patrols of the north side with the rats for two years," Derek said.

Jezebel snorted at Barabas. "Dumbass."

Barabas grimaced. "Fine, I walked into that one. The rats are neophobic. They hate new, they don't attack unless they know they can win, and they trust nobody. The Lonescos don't know you. They won't help you."

So far, this was shaping decidedly not in my favor.

"Your biggest problem is the jackals," Barabas said. "They're a new couple. They came from the West about two years ago, waited for the required time in the Pack, and challenged the old alphas. Took them right out. They're nasty in a fight and ambitious. They see you as an easy mark and they're itching for a chance to snarl and show everybody their big teeth. They'll kill you and won't think twice about it."

"Can the Council remove me?"

Barabas grimaced again. "It's a touchy situation. Technically, yes. You're mated to Curran, nobody questions that. But you have yet to prove yourself as an alpha. Until the mate of an alpha proves herself, she is treated as a rank-and-file member and is subject to the authority of the Council. This almost never happens. I could only find one case in the last twenty years, where the alpha of the Clan Wolf died before his mate could prove himself."

"What happened?"

"The mate stepped down."

I looked at them. "I won't be stepping down. I'm not leaving Curran alone."

Derek left the room and stepped back in. "The Council will be ready for you in ten minutes."

I rose. "We go now. Derek, stay here and double the guard while we're gone."

We left Curran's quarters and headed down the stairs, Barabas on my right and Jezebel on my left.

"Don't provoke the alphas," Barabas said. "An alpha can't challenge those below him. The challenge has to come from a lower pack member to the higher. Since you technically have no status, as long as you don't openly challenge them, if they attack, it's an assault, and we can help you."

"You can't bring a sword or any weapons to the challenge, other than a six-inch knife." Jezebel pulled out a sturdy double-edged knife and passed it to me. "In case. If you do fight, fight to the death. Don't leave them alive."

The Council had scheduled the meeting while the tech was up. Trying to put me at a disadvantage.

As we turned into a hallway, I could hear Doolittle's voice. ". . . spoke. The words were clear, not slurred. That indicates a return of cognitive ability—"

"There is no guarantee that the Beast Lord will wake up," a male voice interrupted. "Surely we would all love for him to rise like Phoenix from the ashes, but we have to face a hard fact: he may not. His so-called mate is not a shapeshifter. She has no place in the Beast Lord's quarters. When the same situation occurred within the wolf clan, the mate stepped down."

"The wolf clan is not ready to voice an opinion," Daniel's even voice said.

"Now is the time for leadership," the unfamiliar male jumped in. "She must be removed to make room for a new alpha."

"And who would that be, Sontag?" Aunt B inquired. "Would that be you?"

We reached the door.

"If you challenge someone, we can't interfere," Barabas murmured. "Remember, don't provoke them."

I kicked the door open and walked in. Fourteen pairs of
eyes glared at me from around the table. Beyond the alpha,
fourteen other shapeshifters waited—the betas of each clan,
invited as a courtesy.

I looked from face to face.

"What the fuck do you think you're doing?" the male voice
said.

Third man on the left. Tall, wiry. Sontag.

I looked at him. "Ready to put your claws where your
mouth is, or are you going to cringe behind the big boys and
yip all day?"

His eyes flared with yellow. "Is that a challenge?"

"Yes, it is."

He burst from the chair, turning furry in midflight. I sidestepped and slashed with my knife across his neck. Blood
spurted from the severed carotid like a jet from a water pistol,
spraying the table. He swiped at me. I kicked him in the knee.
Bone crunched. He went down. I grabbed his hair, cut hard
across his neck, and kicked his head. His neck crunched, and
Sontag's skull rolled across the table.

His mate lunged at me. I stabbed her in the heart. She
clamped her teeth on my right arm and I jabbed my fingers
into her eye sockets. She howled. I jerked the knife out and
stabbed her until she stopped moving.

The whole thing took about half a minute. Eternity in a
fight.

I turned to the Council. Their eyes glowed. Their nostrils
flared at the scent of blood. They said nothing.

An older couple rose from among the betas and walked
over to the table. The woman kicked the dead body of the
female alpha out of the way and the two of them sat down in
bloodstained chairs.

"Clan Jackal has no objection to the mate's presence in the
Beast Lord's quarters," the new alpha of the Jackals said.

An older Japanese couple at the far end stirred. "Clan
Nimble has no objection to the mate," the man said.

"We remember Myong," his mate said in a heavily accented
voice. "We do not forget."

I surveyed the rest of the Council and looked directly at

Mahon. "Some of you know me. Some of you have seen me fight and some of you are my friends. Have your vote. But know this: if you come to remove me, come in force, because if you try to separate me from him, I will kill every single one of you. My hand won't shake. My aim won't falter. My face will be the last thing you'll see before you die."

I jammed the knife into the table and walked out.

I got to the stairs before my vision swam and my legs turned to rubber.

A firm hand gripped my elbow. Jezebel hefted me upright, bearing all of my weight, and we kept walking.

"Way to play it cool there," Barabas ground through his teeth. "Every idiot who wants to make a name for himself will be gunning for you now. Jezebel, let go of her. She will be seen. She must walk."

"She's bleeding. She'll fall."

"It's better that she falls. She has to walk on her own."

"I've got it," I growled and made myself walk up the stairs. Every step jabbed a knife into my knee. Fucking stairs. When he woke up, I'd make him install a damn elevator.

"Only four flights to go," Jezebel told me. "Is Doolittle behind us?"

Barabas glanced back. "Yes."

"Good."

A year later Derek shut the door behind us and I collapsed on the carpet in the hallway. Moments later Doolittle stepped through the door. "Pick her up, quickly, quickly."

Jezebel swiped me off the floor and jogged with me to Curran's rooms. "What's wrong with her?"

"Her knee cap was shattered and the tendons in her left arm are torn. It took hours to get her walking properly. And she reopened her wounds. Foolish, Kate. You're a God-damned fool, that's what you are."

By the time they got me to the room, the adrenaline had worn off and I was screaming. As Doolittle jabbed the needle in my arm, emptying a syringe full of painkillers into my vein, I saw Julie's face. "It's taken care of," I told her. "I got it done. Did he wake up?"

She just stared at me.

"Did he wake up?"

"No."

I closed my eyes and let the medicine take me under.

THE COUNCIL DECIDED IN MY FAVOR. THE WOLVES and Clan Heavy abstained; the rats voted against me; the cats, boudas, Clan Nimble, and Clan Jackal voted for me.

Three days later Mahon came to see me. I was being bandaged at the time—the shapeshifters had declared open season. This was the fifth attack since I'd killed the alpha jackals. I was still winning but barely.

I'd kept Mahon waiting for about five minutes. When I finally walked out of our rooms, Mahon looked as if a storm had ridden in on his thick dark eyebrows. Derek was impassive and my two boudas obviously were wordlessly conspiring to murder Mahon if he took a step out of line.

"I want to see him," Mahon said.

I stepped aside.

"You as well. I have some things I wish to say to both of you."

I led him inside.

He stared at Curran. I looked, too. I kept thinking he'd wake up any minute, and I watched for the tiniest hint of movement, until I started seeing things that weren't there.

"You aren't fit," Mahon said. "You aren't a shapeshifter. You don't understand us and you probably never will. This"—he spread his massive arms, indicating the bedroom, me, and Curran—"was against my better judgment. I told him so before. He has had many women. I thought it would pass."

I watched him. If he attacked me here, I'd lose. I couldn't take Mahon at my best, and right this minute it was a fight to remain standing.

"As I said, this is unwise. But he chose you. I respect the man he has become and I respect what he has done for us. And I respect you for standing by him." Mahon met my gaze. "You may never be my alpha. You will have to live with that. But he will always be my liege."

I felt like some pretender to the throne in a medieval drama.

Mahon leaned over Curran and touched his shoulder. "Sleep well. I won't challenge her and neither will my people. We will talk more when you wake."

He walked out.

I WALKED INTO THE ROOM, CARRYING A CUP OF tea and leaning on my cane. Derek rose from the chair, nodded at me, and left without a word. I sat on the edge of the couch and sipped my tea.

Curran lay immobile, an IV dangling from his arm. He'd lost weight. Thirty pounds, at least. His skin was pale. It hurt to look at him.

I forced dread aside. "I didn't have to kill anybody today. Remember, the first couple of days they were coming three a day, then two, then one. Today nobody challenged me. It's late now, so if somebody does show up, your castle guard will tell them to come back in the morning. Maybe it's slacking off."

I pulled my boots off, wincing at the stab of pain. "Julie has appropriated your bimbo room. I made them throw away the sheets—who knows what sort of crazy crap is on there—and she has a new set. Black. She painted the walls black. The curtains are black lace. I tried to convince her to keep the furniture white, but I saw her carry a paint can in there, so I think it will be black by morning. It's like a freaking dungeon in there."

I pulled off my sweatshirt and slid next to him. My voice was soft. "That's the good news. The bad news is that it's been eleven days since you fell asleep and I'm beginning to get scared you won't wake up."

I held my breath, but he lay still.

"Let's see . . . What else? I'm sick of killing. Doolittle says there might be permanent damage to my left leg. It will heal eventually, even if he doesn't think so, but meanwhile it hurts like hell. He wants me to stop putting pressure on it, so he gave me this lovely cane. I can only use it up here so the rest of the Keep won't see me as weak."

I just wanted him to wake up. Of course, he didn't, so I kept talking, trying to keep the panic at bay.

"Still no calls from Andrea. Jim is keeping his distance, which I can understand. Derek says he's helping from behind the scenes, whatever that means. The wolves keep finding ways to screw with me. They've made me mediate a divorce. Well, they requested I do it, and according to Barabas, I can't say no. It's a Japanese couple. They were members of a small pack and married very young and had two boys. The husband was expelled from the pack under suspicion of stealing. The wife remained behind, because the grandparents had the kids."

He lay next to me, warm and alive, and if I didn't look at him, I could almost imagine that he was listening. I shut my eyes. My body ached. Doolittle wanted me on bed rest, but the boudas wanted me out and about, demonstrating that I was fit as a fiddle and ready to take on everyone and anyone.

"Apparently the husband had made his way over here and you took him in about eight years ago. I had Derek pull his record and it's clean, so if he's stealing, he's brilliant at hiding it. I've met him. He seems like a decent guy. This September, the small local pack asked to join your Pack, and of course, you took them in again. Now they are stuck. The husband has someone else, the wife also has someone else, but by wolf law they're mated for life and the grandparents on both sides are horrified. It doesn't help that all of them are Japanese. I put them in the same room—nobody talks. Everybody is embarrassed and they keep apologizing to me nonstop. I don't know what to do."

"Have you tried the Second Chance Law?" Curran said.

I shut my eyes tighter. I was losing my mind. Now I imagined him talking in my head.

Even an imaginary conversation was better than nothing. "No, what's that?"

"It's the law that says any shapeshifter joining the Pack has a one-time right to a new identity. If the husband didn't use it when he joined, declare him officially dead and let him rejoin under a new name. His former wife will officially be a widow."

A warm arm hugged me. My eyes snapped open.

He was looking at me. He was pale, his eyes were sunken, but he was looking at me.

"You stayed with me," Curran said.

"Always."

He smiled and fell asleep.

Curran stirred again, an hour later. I raced into the kitchen, and by the time I returned with a steaming bowl, he was sitting up and pulling the IV out of his arm. "What is this shit?"

"It kept you alive for eleven days."

"Well, I don't like it."

I handed him a bowl of soup. He put it aside, reached for me, and clenched me to him. I buried my face in his neck. My eyes grew hot and I cried.

His hand stroked my hair. "You stayed with me."

"Of course I stayed with you. Did you think I would abandon you?"

"I heard you reading. And talking."

I kissed him and tasted my tears. "Through your sleep?"

"Yes. I tried to wake up, but I couldn't."

I just held on to him. "Let's not do this again. Ever."

"That sounds good." He kissed me.

"You need to eat."

"In a minute." He clamped me tighter. We sat together for a few blissful minutes.

Two sharp knocks echoed through the door. Derek. He always knocked twice.

"Kate?"

"Come in," I told him.

Derek walked in. "I have a wolf out here who wants to see you. He says it's an emergency. Probably another challenge. What do you want me to . . . ?" His mouth hung open.

Curran looked at him. "Bring him in. Don't tell him that I'm awake."

Derek closed his mouth with a click and went out.

"Help me up?"

I grabbed his hand and pulled him off the bed. He blinked at the windup clock on the wall. "Is today Wednesday?"

"Yes."

He picked up the bowl of soup and drank from it.

The door swung open. A large Hispanic man stepped through. He saw Curran and froze.

Curran finished draining the bowl and looked at him. "Yes?"

The wolf dropped down into a crouch and stayed there, his head bowed, his gaze on the floor.

"Nothing to say?"

The wolf shook his head.

"The Council is due for a meeting in three minutes. Go down there and tell them to wait for me, and I might forget you were ever here."

The wolf turned, rising, and left without a word. The door shut behind him.

Curran swayed. I caught him. My leg gave and we crashed down onto the couch.

"Ow."

Curran shook his head.

"Are you sure you're ready for a Council meeting?"

He turned to me. Gold rolled over his eyes, cold and lethal. "I'm sure. They better be ready for me."

He pushed himself up and headed to the bathroom. I followed him in case he tipped over. He did, on the way back, and caught himself on the wall.

I slid my arm around his waist.

"The soup will kick in in a minute," he said.

"Sure. Lean on me." He did and we slowly made our way to the door. "Some tough pair we are."

"Tough enough," he growled.

Five minutes later he walked to the Council room on his own power. The shapeshifters saw him and stepped aside, silent. We reached the room. I could hear people mumbling inside. Curran took a deep breath, thrust the door open, and roared.

The sound of leonine rage burst like thunder, shaking the windows. People in the hallway cringed. When it died, you could hear a pin drop.

Curran held the door open for me. He walked to his seat at the head of the table, got another chair, put it next to his, and looked at me. I came and sat. He lowered himself into his seat.

The alphas stared at the table. Not a single pair of eyes looked up.

Curran leaned forward, his eyes drenched in furious gold. "Explain yourselves."

EPILOGUE

———◆———

THE BUILDING WAS SOLID BRICK, CONSTRUCTED according to the new fashion, rather than the old—only two stories in height, squat, thick metal grates on the windows, and a very sturdy-looking door. It sat on a quiet street just past the northwestern industrial district, which was now an old ruin. Aside from being sturdy and in good shape, I couldn't see anything special about it.

"What is this?"

Curran smiled next to me. "An early Christmas present."

I looked at the house again. After the last three weeks, a Christmas present was the last thing I'd expected.

Curran felt betrayed by his Pack. From his point of view, he'd worked years for the benefit of his people, and their loyalty had lasted less than forty-eight hours. In return for his service, they'd tried to expel his mate, and when she wouldn't leave him, they'd tried to kill her. Curran took the marathon of my fights to the death very personally.

Each year the Pack celebrated the traditional Thanksgiving feast, which consisted of a dinner of epic proportions. Curran usually spent hours there, talking to everyone. This time he walked in, growled, "You have my permission to eat," and walked out. We had a private dinner in our rooms and he gorged himself on pie. Aside from that, he refused to leave our quarters. For fresh air, we went out on the roof, where he had a giant patio, complete with a fire pit and a grill. I built a snowman, and Julie practiced shooting it with a crossbow. We visited his private gym. That was it. So when he asked me to come to the city with him, I decided it was a good sign. It took us less than an hour to get here and I enjoyed the drive.

I cocked my head and looked at the house from a different angle. No special insights or revelations presented themselves.

Maybe he bought me a new place to live. "Is this your convoluted way of inviting me to move out?"

"You're never moving out, as long as you want."

Curran strode to the door through the snow and opened it.

I walked in. From the inside the house looked just as sturdy. The windows were small and barred, but numerous enough to let in plenty of light. The front room took up most of the floor. Two desks waited in opposite corners. Filing cabinets guarded the walls. I strode through to the doorway on the left. A narrow, long room full of shelves, half empty, half filled with jars and boxes of various herbs. Looked like someone did a decent job stocking up on alchemical supplies.

"There is more upstairs."

A cursory inspection of the second floor showed a basic armory and a room with some diagnostic equipment, magic and otherwise. It wasn't out of this world, but it was enough to get by.

I came back downstairs and sat on the staircase. "What is this?"

He gave me his Beast Lord look. "It's yours."

"I'm sorry?"

"The house and the contents. It's yours if you want it. The Pack is backing you up as a business: it purchased the supplies and is fronting your salary and a modest operating budget for a year, after which it will have a twenty percent claim on your profits. It will drop to ten when your loan is paid off. I had Raphael draw up the paperwork." He crossed to the desk and lifted a manila folder. "All you need is to fill in the name, and it's off to the Secretary of State."

I looked at him.

"Your own Order. Or your own Guild. Whichever way you choose to go."

"Why?"

He crossed his arms on his chest. "The Pack cost you your job."

"I cost myself that job, and it was rotten anyway."

He shook his head. "You came to help. It's the Pack's chance to help back. Everybody has something, that one thing they must do to feel happy. I think this is yours, and I want you to be happy. You don't have to do it, but it's here if you choose to come back to it."

"Is there a catch?"

"A couple. Standard Pack clauses: Pack requests take precedence, always. The safety of the Pack's members overrides everything else, and the Pack's interests must be protected at all costs. In a case where a Pack member may be suspected of criminal activity outside the Pack, you must inform the Pack lawyers, so the suspect can be provided council."

I smiled at him. "Do you have any requests as well?"

He locked his jaw.

I laughed. "Out with it. I know if you had your way, I'd be locked up in your rooms, all safe, barefoot, and pregnant."

"I'm not that crazy."

I raised my hand, with my index finger and my thumb a small space apart. "A little. I know it's killing you to do this, so what would help you breathe easier?"

He blew air out like a whale. "Come home. Every night. Have dinner with me. If you go out of the office for longer than a few hours, I'd appreciate a call so I know you're safe. If you're in trouble, you tell me. No lies, no evasions, no secrets. And if you need muscle, for any reason, you use the Pack. You don't run in there all alone to get killed."

My personal psycho in all of his glory, trying his best to be reasonable. "Anything else?"

"No business on Wednesday afternoon, if you can help it. Wednesdays we hear petitions and disputes."

I grimaced. "I hate petitions."

"I do, too, so I shouldn't suffer through them alone. Also, I'd like it if you made time to attend the formal functions with me if they're scheduled during the week, so I don't die of boredom. That's it."

We looked at each other.

"So do you like it?" he asked.

"I love it." I got up and swiped the folder off the table. "Thank you." We kissed and headed out.

As we walked away from my new office, he asked, "So what are you going to call it?"

I smiled at him. "I'll have to think of something witty. Something that makes reference to my ability to solve cases in a blaze of intellectual glory."

"Your ability to chop at everything in your way with your sword, more like it."

"Whatever, Your Furriness."

New Atlanta Journal-Constitution:

Notice is given that articles of incorporation that will incorporate Cutting Edge Investigations, Inc., have been delivered to the Secretary of State for filing in accordance with Georgia Business Corporation Code . . .

READ ON FOR
AN EXCITING EXCERPT FROM

BAYOU MOON

THE NEW EDGE NOVEL BY
ILONA ANDREWS
COMING OCTOBER 2010
FROM ACE BOOKS

WILLIAM SIPPED SOME BEER FROM THE BOTTLE OF
Modelo Especial and gave the Green Arrow his hard stare.
The Green Arrow, being a chunk of painted plastic, didn't
rise to the challenge. The action figure remained impassive,
exactly where he'd put it, leaning against the porch post of
William's house. Technically it was a shack rather than a
house, William reflected, but it was a roof over his head and
he wasn't one to complain.

From that vantage point, the Green Arrow had an excellent
view of William's action figure army laid out on the porch, and
if he were inclined to offer any opinions, he would've been in
a great position to do so. William shrugged. Part of him realized that talking to an action figure was bordering on insane,
but he had nobody else to converse with at the moment and he
needed to talk this out. The whole situation was crazy.

"The boys sent a letter," William said.

The Green Arrow said nothing.

William looked past him to where the Wood rustled just
beyond his lawn. Two miles down the road, the Wood would
become simply woods, regular Georgia pine and oak. But
here, in the Edge, the trees grew vast, fed by magic, and the

forest was old. The day had rolled into a lazy, long spring evening, and small nameless critters, found only in the Edge, chased each other through the limbs of the ancient trees before the darkness coaxed predators from their lairs.

The Edge was an odd place, stuck between two worlds. On one side lay the Broken, with no magic but plenty of technology to compensate. And rules. And laws. And paperwork. The damn place ran on paperwork. The Broken was where he made his money nowadays, working construction.

On the other side lay the Weird, a mirror to the Broken, where magic ruled and old blueblood families held power. He was born in that world. In the Weird, he'd been an outcast, a soldier, a convict, and even a noble for a few brief weeks, but the Weird kept kicking him in the teeth the entire time until he finally turned his back on it and left.

The Edge belonged to neither world. A perfect place for the man who fit in nowhere. That was how he first met the boys, George and Jack. They lived in the Edge, with their sister, Rose. Rose was sweet and pretty and he'd liked her. He'd liked what they had, she and the kids, a warm little family. When he watched them together, a part of him hurt deep inside. He now realized why: he'd known even then that a family like that was forever out of his reach.

Still, he'd tried with Rose. Might have had a chance, too, but then Declan showed up. Declan, a blueblood and a soldier, with his flawless manners and handsome face. "We used to be friends, before we screwed it up," William told the Green Arrow. "I did beat the shit out of him before he left."

The joke was on him, because Declan left with Rose and took the boys with him. William let them go. Jack required a lot of careful care and Declan would raise him well. And Rose needed someone like Declan. Someone who had his shit together. She had enough trouble with the boys as it was. She sure as hell didn't need another charity project and he didn't want to be one.

It had been almost two years since they'd left. William lived in the Edge, where the trickle of magic kept the wild within him alive. He worked his job in the Broken, watched TV on weekends, drank lots of beer, collected action figures, and generally pretended that the previous twenty-six years of his life did not exist. The Edgers, the few families who lived between the worlds like he did, kept to themselves and left him alone.

Most people from either the Broken or the Weird had no idea the other dimension existed, but occasionally traders passed through the Edge, traveling between worlds. Three months ago, Nick, one of the traveling traders, mentioned he was heading into the Weird, to the Southern Provinces. William put together a small box of toys on a whim and paid the man to deliver it. He didn't expect an answer. He didn't expect anything at all. The boys had Declan. They would have no interest in him.

Nick came by last night. The boys had written back.

William picked up the letter and looked at it. It was short. George's writing was perfect, with letters neatly placed. Jack's looked like a chicken had scratched it in the dirt. They said thank you for the action figures. George liked the Weird. He was given plenty of corpses to practice necromancy on and he was taking rapier lessons. Jack complained that there were too many rules and that they weren't letting him hunt enough.

"That's a mistake," William told Green Arrow. "They need to let him vent. Half of their problems would be solved if they let him have a violent outlet." He raised the letter. "Apparently he decided to prove to them that he was good enough. The kid went and killed himself a deer and left the bloody thing on the dining room table, because he's a cat and he thinks they're lousy hunters. According to him, it didn't go over well. He's trying to feed them and they don't get it."

What Jack needed was some direction to channel all that energy. But William wasn't about to travel to the Weird and show up on Declan's doorstep. Hi, remember me? We were best friends once, and then I was condemned to death and your uncle adopted me, so I would kill you? You stole Rose from me? Yeah, right. All he could do was write back and send more action figures.

William pulled the box to him. He'd put in Deathstroke for George—the figure looked a bit like a pirate and George liked pirates, because his grandfather had been one. He also stuck King Grayskull in for Declan. Not that Declan played with action figures—he'd had his childhood, while William spent his in Hawk's Academy, which was little more than a prison. Still, William liked to thumb his nose at him, and King Grayskull with his long blond hair looked a lot like Declan.

"So the real question here is, do we send the purple Wildcat to Jack or the black one?"

The Green Arrow expressed no opinion.

A musky scent drifted down to William. He turned around. Two small glowing eyes stared at him from under the bush on the edge of his lawn.

"You again."

The raccoon bared his small sharp teeth.

"I've warned you, stay out of my trash or I will eat you."

The little beast opened his mouth and hissed like a pissed-off cat.

"That does it."

William shrugged off his T-shirt. His jeans and underwear followed. "We're going to settle this."

The raccoon hissed again, puffing out his fur, trying to look bigger. His eyes glowed like two small coals.

William reached deep inside himself and let the wild off the chain. Pain rocked him, jerking him to and fro, the way a dog shook a rat. His bones softened and bent, his ligaments snapped, his flesh flowed like molten wax. Dense black fur sheathed him. The agony ended and William rolled to his feet.

The raccoon froze.

For a second, William saw his reflection in the little beast's eyes—a hulking dark shape on all fours—and then the interloper whirled about and fled.

William howled, singing a long sad song about the hunt and the thrill of the chase, and the promise of hot blood pulsing between his teeth. The small critters hid high up in the branches, recognizing a predator in their midst.

The last echoes of the song scurried into the Wood. William bit the air with sharp white fangs and gave chase.

WILLIAM TROTTED THROUGH THE WOOD. THE raccoon had turned out to be female and in possession of six kits. How the hell he missed the female scent, he would never know. Getting rusty in the Edge. His senses weren't quite as sharp here.

He had to let them be. You didn't hunt a female with a litter—that was how species went extinct. He'd caught a nice juicy rabbit instead. William licked his lips. Mmm, good. He would just have to figure out how to weigh down the lid on the trash can, so she couldn't get into his garbage again. Maybe one of his dumbbells would do the job . . .

He caught a glimpse of his house through the trees. A scent floated to him: spicy, reminiscent of cinnamon mixed with a dash of cumin and ginger.

His hackles rose. William went to ground.

This scent didn't belong in this world outside of a bakery. It was the scent of a human from beyond the Edge's boundary, with shreds of the Weird's magic still clinging to them.

Trouble.

He lay in the gloom between the roots and listened. Insects chirping. Squirrels in the tree to the left settling down for the night. A woodpecker, hammering in the distance to get the last grub of the day.

Nothing but ordinary Wood noises.

From his hiding spot, he could see the entire porch. Nothing stirred.

The rays of the setting sun slid across the boards. A tiny star winked at him.

Careful. Careful.

William edged forward, a dark soft-pawed ghost in the evening twilight. One yard. Two. Three.

The star winked again. A rectangular wooden box sat on the porch steps, secured with a simple metal latch. The latch shone with reflected sunlight. Someone had left him a present.

William circled the house twice, straining to sample the scents, listening to small noises. He found the intruder's trail leading into the woods. Whoever delivered the box had come and gone.

He approached the house and looked at the box. Eighteen inches long, a foot wide, three inches tall. Simple unmarked wood. Looked like pine. Smelled like it, too. Nothing ticked inside.

His action figures were as he'd left them. His letter, pinned down by the heavy Hulk, remained undisturbed. The spicy scent didn't reach it—it was untouched.

William pulled the door open with his paw and slipped inside. He would need fingers for this.

The pain screamed through him, shooting through the marrow in his bones. He growled low, shook, convulsing, and shed his fur. Twenty seconds of agony and William crouched on human legs in the living room. Ten more seconds and he stepped out on the porch, fully dressed and armed with a long knife. Just because it didn't tick didn't mean it wouldn't blow up when he opened it. He'd seen bombs that were the size of a drink coaster. They made no noise, gave off no scent, and took your leg off if you stepped on them.

He used the knife to pry the latch open and flip the lid off the box. A stack of paper. Hmm.

William plucked the first sheet off the top of the stack, flipped it over, and froze.

A small mangled body lay in the green grass. The boy was barely ten years old, his skin stark white against the smudges of crimson that spread from a gaping wound in his stomach. Someone had disemboweled him with a single vicious thrust and the kid had bled out. So much blood. It was everywhere, on his skinny stomach, on his hands, on the yellow dandelions around him . . . Bright, shockingly red, so vivid, it didn't seem real. The boy's narrow face stared at the sky with milky dead eyes, his mouth opened in a horrified O, short reddish hair sticking up . . .

It's Jack. The thought punched William in the stomach. His heart hammered. He peered closely at the face. No, not Jack. A cat like Jack—slit pupils—but Jack had brown hair. The boy was the right age, the right build, but he *was not* Jack.

William exhaled slowly, trying to get a handle on his rage. He knew this. He'd seen this boy's corpse before, but not in a picture. He'd seen the body in the flesh, smelled the blood and the raw, unforgettable stench of the gut wound. His memory conjured it for him now, and he almost choked on the bitter phantom patina coating his tongue.

The next picture showed a little girl, tiny, ten at most. Her hair was a mess of blood and brains—her skull had been crushed.

More pictures came, eight in all. Eight murdered children lay on his porch. Eight changeling children, taken out of the prison known as Hawk's Academy for an outdoor exercise. Fifteen years ago, he was just like them, locked in the sterile rooms of Hawk's, the place where the country of Adrianglia exiled its changelings to turn them into "productive members of society." The studies were taxing, the exercise exhausting, the rules rigid, and freedom was in short supply. Only outdoors, the children truly lived. These eight must've been giddy to be let out into the sunshine and grass.

They had been led to the border between Adrianglia and the Dukedom of Louisiana, its chief rival. The border was always hot, with Louisianans and Adrianglians crossing back and forth. The instructors allowed the kids to track a group of border jumpers from Louisiana as a routine exercise. He had done it before a few times, when he was small.

William stared at the pictures. It should have been an easy track-and-find. But this time, the Louisianans turned out to be no ordinary border jumpers. They were agents of Louisiana's Hand: spies, twisted by magic and powerful enough to take out a squad of trained soldiers. They led the children on a merry chase, toying with them for a few miles, and then they let themselves be caught.

When the kids failed to report in, a unit of Legionnaires was dispatched to find them. William was the tracker for that squad. He was the one who found the children dead in the meadow. It was a massacre, brutal and cold. The kids hadn't gone quickly. They'd hurt before they died.

The last piece of paper waited in the box. William picked it up. He knew what it would say. The words were burned into his memory.

He read it all the same.

Dumb animals offer little sport. Louisiana kills changelings at birth—it's far more efficient than wasting time and resources to try to turn them into people. I recommend you look into this practice, because next

*time I'll expect proper compensation for getting rid of
your little freaks.*

Sincerely yours,
Spider

Mindless hot fury flooded William, sweeping away all reason and restraint. He raised his head to the sky and snarled, giving voice to his rage before it tore him apart.

For years he'd tracked Spider as much as the Legion would permit him. He'd found him twice. The first time he'd ripped apart Spider's stomach—and Spider broke William's legs. The second time, William had shattered the Louisianan's ribs, while Spider nearly drowned him. Both times, the Hand's spy had slipped through his fingers.

Nobody cared for the changelings. They grew up exiled from society, raised to obey and kill on command for the good of Adrianglia. They were fodder, but to him they were children, just like he once had been a child. Just like Jack.

He had to find Spider. He had to kill him this time. The child murderer had to be punished.

A man stepped out of the Wood. William leapt off the porch. In a breath he pinned the man to the trunk of the nearest tree and snarled, his teeth clicking a hair from the man's carotid.

The man made no move to resist. "Do you want to kill me or Spider?"

"Who are you?"

"The name is Erwin." The man nodded at his raised hands. A large ring clamped his middle finger—a plain silver band with a small polished mirror in it. The sign of the Adrianglian Secret Service, the Hand's greatest enemy.

"The Mirror would like a word, Lord Sandine," the man said softly. "Would you be kind enough to favor us with an audience?"

CERISE LEANED OVER THE TEA-COLORED WATERS of Horseshoe Pond. Around her, massive cypresses stood like ancient soldiers at attention, the knobby knees of their roots straddling the water. The Mire was never silent, but nothing out of the ordinary interrupted the familiar chorus of small noises: a toad belching somewhere to the left, the faint scuttling of Edge squirrels in the canopy above her, the persistent warbling of the bluebill . . .

She rolled up her jeans and crouched, calling in a practiced singsong, "Where is Nellie? Where is that good girl? Nellie is the best rolpie ever. Here, Nellie, Nellie, Nellie."

The surface of the pond lay completely placid. Not a splash.

The rolpie was in there. Cerise was absolutely sure of it. She'd tracked the stubborn animal since three past midnight when Arthur heard Nellie break out of the rolpie enclosure. Cerise had been going from stream to stream for the last four hours. The trail—a long smudge in the mud, flanked by swipes from the paws—ended five feet to the left of her.

"Here, Nellie! Here, girl. Who is a good girl? Nellie is. Oh, Nellie is so pretty. Oh, Nellie is so fat. She is the fattest cutest stupidest rolpie ever. Yes, she is."

No response.

Cerise looked up. Far above, a small chunk of blue sky winked at her through the braid of cypress branches and Mire vines. "Why do you do this to me?"

The sky refused to answer. It usually did, but that didn't stop her from talking to it.

A chirp echoed overhead and a white globe of bird poop plummeted from the branches. Cerise dodged and growled at the sky. "Not cool. Not cool at all."

It was time for emergency measures. Cerise leaned her sword against a cypress knee, anchoring the scabbard in the muck, shifted her weight, pulling the backpack off her shoulders, and dug in the bag. She fished out a length of rope with a headcollar, designed to fit on the rolpie's muzzle and loop behind her ears, and arranged it on the mud for easy access. The can opener was followed by a small can.

She held the can out and knocked on it with the can opener. The sound of metal on metal rolled above the pound. Nothing.

"Oh, what do I have? I have *tuna!*"

A small ripple wrinkled the surface about thirty feet out. Gotcha.

"Mmmm, yummy, yummy tuna. I'll eat it all by myself." She arranged the can opener on the can and squeezed, breaking the seal.

A brindled head popped out of the water. The rolpie sampled the air with a black nose framed with long dark whiskers. Large black eyes fixed on the can with maniacal glee.

Cerise squeezed the top of the can, letting some of the fish juice drip into the pond.

The rolpie sped through the water and launched herself out onto the shore. From the bottom up to the neck, she resembled a lean seal armed with a long tail and four wide half-legs framed with flat flippers. At the shoulders, the seal body stretched into a graceful long neck, tipped with an otter head. When she was a little girl, Grandpa once told her that rolpies were reptiles and their fur was actually modified feathers, but looking at one, you wouldn't think it.

Cerise shook the can. "Head."

Nellie licked her black lips and tried her best to look adorable.

"Head, Nellie."

The rolpie lowered her head. Cerise slipped the collar over her wet muzzle and tightened it. "You'll pay for this, you know."

The black nose nudged her shoulder. Cerise plucked a chunk of tuna from the can and tossed it at the rolpie. Razor-sharp teeth rent the air, snapping up the treat. Cerise swiped her sword off the ground and tugged on the leash. The rolpie lumbered next to her, wiggling and pushing herself across the swamp mud.

"What the hell was that? Breaking out in the middle of the night and taking off for a stroll, are we? Did you get tired of pulling the boats and decided to take your chances with Mire crocs?"

The rolpie squirmed along, watching the can of tuna like it was some holy relic.

"They can bite bone sharks in half. They'll look at you and see a plump little snack. Brunch, that's what you'd be."

Nellie licked her lips.

"Do you think tuna grows in the mud?" Cerise plucked another chunk of fish out of the can and tossed it at Nellie. "In case you didn't know, we live in the Edge, between two worlds. We have to get our tuna from the Broken. The Broken has no magic. But you know what the Broken does have? Cops. Lots and lots of cops. And alarm systems. Do you have any idea how hard it is to steal tuna from the Broken, Nellie?"

Nellie emitted a small squeal of despair.

"I don't feel sorry for you. It takes four days to get to the boundary that separates the Edge from the Broken, because it's three miles off-shore, and crossing the boundary hurts like hell. And we can't afford to get arrested in the Broken. They don't know the Edge or the Weird exist. Most of them don't have enough magic to see the damn boundary, let alone cross it. Can you imagine how hard it is to explain why you have no ID to a Broken cop? If you think that you'll get tuna treats every time you decide to take a stroll in the moonlight, you have another think coming, missy. Besides, I work hard and I have better things to do than drag my butt out of my very comfortable bed and chase you all around the damn Mire."

The vegetation parted, revealing the dark water of Priest's Tongue stream. A green Mire viper lay in the mud. It hissed as they approached. Cerise hooked the snake with her sword and tossed it aside.

"Come on." She threw another bite of tuna to the rolpie and led her into the stream. Cerise wrapped the leash loop tighter around her wrist and slid her arms around Nellie's narrow neck. "You get the rest when we get home. And no dives into the peat at the bottom either." Cerise clicked her tongue and the rolpie took off down the stream.

TWENTY MINUTES LATER CERISE SHUT THE GATE on the rolpie enclosure. Someone, probably the younger boys, had made a reasonable attempt to repair the chain-link fence, but it wouldn't hold if Nellie decided to ram it. In the twisted creeks and rivers of the swamp, rolpies were vital. In some places, the water was completely stagnant and the swamp vegetation blocked the wind. The rolpies pulled the light swamp boats all over the Mire to help save gasoline.

As long as a human was present, Nellie was an excellent rolpie: obedient, sweet, powerful. The moment you took the person out of the equation, the silly beast freaked out and tried to take off.

Maybe she had separation anxiety, Cerise reflected, starting up the hill toward the Rathole. Segregating Nellie in a smaller enclosure would only lead to disaster. Knowing her, she would bray night and day, because she was alone. And reinforcing the fence was too much labor just to secure a single rolpie.

Cerise chugged up the hill to the Mar family house. Water dripped from her clothes and squished between her toes inside her boots. She wanted a hot shower and a nice meal, preferably with some meat in it. Things being what they were, she'd settle for fish or bacon. She'd have to oil her sword, too, but that was part of living in the swamp. Water and steel didn't mix very well.

The Rathole sat on top of a low hill, a sprawling two-story monster of a house. Fifty yards of cleared ground separated the house from the nearest vegetation. The kill zone. Fifty yards was a lot of ground for enemies to cover, when they had rifles and crossbones trained on them.

The ground floor had no entrance or windows. The only way in lay up the stairway to the second-floor verandah. As she approached the stairs, a small shape slipped from behind the verandah's colonnades and sat on the stairs. Sophie. Lark, Cerise corrected herself. She wanted to be called Lark now.

Her sister gave her a weary look from under dark tousled hair. Her skinny legs stuck out of her capris like matchsticks. Mud smudged her calves. Scratches and bruises covered her arms. She hid her hands, but Cerise was willing to bet that her nails were dirty or bitten off, probably both. Lark used to be a bit of a neat freak, as much as an eleven-year-old girl brought up in the swamp could be. All gone now.

Worry pinched at Cerise. She kept her face calm. Show nothing. Don't make Lark self-conscious.

She came up the stairs, sat next to Lark, and pulled off her left boot, emptying the water out.

"Adrian and Derril are riding the Doom Buggy through the Snake Tracks," Lark murmured.

The dune buggy was a hell mobile made of pure fun. In fact, Cerise had snuck away with it before and had so much fun, she'd flipped it over. But touching the dune buggy without adult supervision was strictly forbidden. Stealing it and wasting expensive gasoline were punishable by three weeks of extra chores.

Of course, both fifteen-year-old Adrian and his fourteen-year-old sidekick, Derril, knew this and could handle the consequences. The most pressing issue was that Lark had just tattled. Lark never tattled.

Cerise forced herself to calmly pull the other boot off. The very core of her sister's personality was changing and she could only watch, helpless.

"The boys didn't take you with them?"

The answer was so quiet, she barely heard it. "No."

Six months ago, they would have. Both of them knew it. The urge to reach out and hug Lark's bony shoulders gripped Cerise, but she kept still. She'd tried that before. Her sister would stiffen, slide away, and take off into the woods.

At least Lark was talking to her. That was a rare thing. Normally, Mom was the only person who could get through to her and even she had a hard time drawing Lark out lately. The kid was slipping away into her own world and nobody knew how to pull her out.

"Did you tell Mom?" Cerise asked.

"Mom isn't here."

Odd. "Dad?"

"They left. Together."

Cerise frowned. The family had been feuding with another clan for the last eighty years. Sometimes the hostility between them burned bright and sometimes, like right now, it smoldered, but the feud could burst into warfare at any moment. The last time the feud had flared, she lost two uncles, an aunt, and a cousin. The standing rule was: you go out, you let someone know where you're going and when you're planning on coming back. Even Father, who was the head of the family, never strayed from this rule. "When and why did they leave?"

"At sunrise, and they left because Cobbler got his butt bit."

Cobbler, an old wino, bummed about the swamp doing odd jobs in exchange for moonshine. Cerise never cared for

the man. He was mean to kids when he thought their parents
weren't looking and he'd stab anyone in the back just out of
spite. "Go on . . ."

"He came over and told Dad wild dogs got into Grandpa's
house. They chased him and one bit him on the butt. His pants
had holes."

The Sene Manor had been boarded up for years, ever since
their grandparents had died there of red fever twelve years
ago. Cerise remembered it as a sunny house, painted bright
yellow, a spot of color in the swamp. It was an abandoned
wreck now. Nobody went near it. Cobbler had no business
going there either. Probably was looking for something to
steal.

"What happened next?"

Lark shrugged. "Cobbler kept talking until Dad gave him
some wine and then he went away. And then Dad said he had
to go and take care of Grandpa's house, because it was still
our land. Mom said she would go with him. They rode out."

Getting to Sene Manor by truck was impossible. They
would've gone on horseback.

"And you haven't seen them since?"

"No."

Sene Manor was half an hour away by horse. They
should've been back by now.

"Do you think Mom and Dad are dead?" Lark asked in a
flat voice.

Oh, Gods. "No. Dad's death with a sword and Mom can
shoot a Mire croc in the eye from a hundred feet. Something
must've held them up."

A muted roar rolled through the trees—the dune buggy's
engine getting a workout. Dimwits. Didn't even have the
patience to turn the engine off and roll the buggy back up to
the house. Cerise rose.

"Let me deal with this, and if Mom and Dad aren't back by
the end of the hour, I'll go and check it out."

An old dune buggy burst out from between the pines,
splashing through the mud on its way to the house. Cerise
raised her hand. Two mud-splattered faces stared at her from
the front seat with abject horror.

Cerise drew in a deep breath and barked. "Cramp!"

Magic pulsed from her hand. The curse clutched at the two boys, twisting the muscles in their arms. Adrian doubled over, the wheel spun left, the dune buggy careened, and the whole thing toppled onto its side in a huge splash, sliding through the sludge. The hell mobile turned, vomiting the two daredevils into the mud, spun for the last time, and stopped.

"Feel free to go over there and kick them while they're down. When you're done, tell them to clean everything up and head straight to the stables. Aunt Karen will be overjoyed to have two slaves for the next three weeks."

Cerise took her boots and headed into the house. She'd have to take at least two people with her. Someone steady and good in a fight. Someone who wouldn't fly off the handle.

This wasn't going to end well—she just knew it.

Penguin Group (USA) Inc.
is proud to present

GREAT READS—GUARANTEED

We are so confident you will love
this book that we are offering a
100% money-back guarantee!

If you are not 100% satisfied with
this publication, Penguin Group (USA) Inc.
will refund your money!
Simply return the book before
August 1, 2010 for a full refund.

M662G0310

DON'T MISS THE NEW SERIES FROM
NEW YORK TIMES BESTSELLING AUTHOR

ILONA ANDREWS

ON THE
EDGE

Rose Drayton lives on the Edge, between two worlds: on
one side lies the Broken, a place where people shop at
Wal-Mart and magic is nothing more than a fairy tale; on
the other is the Weird, a realm where blueblood aristocrats
rule and the strength of your magic can change your
destiny. Only Edgers like Rose can easily travel between
the worlds—but they never truly belong in either.

M634T0110

FROM *NEW YORK TIMES*
BESTSELLING AUTHOR

ILONA ANDREWS

When magic strikes and Atlanta goes to
pieces, it's a job for Kate Daniels...

MAGIC BITES
MAGIC BURNS
MAGIC STRIKES
MAGIC BLEEDS

PRAISE FOR THE KATE DANIELS NOVELS:

"Kate is a great kick-ass heroine, a tough
girl with a heart, and her adventures...
are definitely worth checking out."

—*Locus*

"Fast-paced, action-packed urban fantasy
full of magic, vampires, werebeasties, and things
that go bump in the night."

—*Monsters and Critics*

"Fans of urban fantasy will delight in Ilona
Andrews's alternate-universe Atlanta."

—*Fresh Fiction*

penguin.com